# Wanderer: Origin of the Nature Walker

Nancy E. Dunne

Cover Design and Format by

Nancy E. Dunne and Brian Collins



ISBN: 1484150937
ISBN-13: 978-1484150931

# DEDICATION

To Mama Gin's Boys.
You know who you are.
Check your bind points.

# CONTENTS

# ACKNOWLEDGMENTS

So many thanks are due to my gaming "family" who breathed life into the inspiration for this tale, and especially to my family and my husband for having my back and being my biggest fans.

Special thanks to Mike for trusting me with *Sathlir;* and to Sean and Brian for keeping me honest in my writing, grammar, and storytelling. Much love to you all.

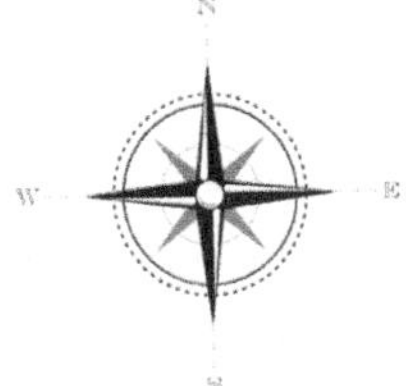

# PROLOGUE

It has been nearly 200 years since the Forest War divided the races of Orana. For the humans, that meant multiple generations had come and gone, half as many for the Qatu, and only a handful for the longer-lived races - the elves, dwarves, and the gnomes. It was a long while before the races began to intermingle, as had been their way before the War, and the conflict had taken its toll on that interaction as well. Relationships outside of one's own kind did not happen, save those friendships between the wood elves and the high elves. Intimate relations that lead to offspring such as the dragonkind were not tolerated, and any that survived their childhood ended up living in the south with the humans who did not seem to mind one way or the other. The world had grown smaller during the War, and grew smaller still after the Peace Accord.

In Aynamaede, the tree city, the wood elves whispered that the current *Nature Walker,* druid master and leader of the wood elf council, was not trustworthy, for he and his wife were always away on missions for a strange and secret organization. In Alynatalos, the High King of the elves spent his time alone, mourning the loss of his parents in the War and never mingling with his subjects the way his father had. Life in the forest was unsettled, and only made worse by the rumor that a rogue Qatu, known as the Bane of the Forest, was attacking elves under the cover of darkness. Only the return of a true *Nature Walker* could bring balance back to the Great Forest and its inhabitants.

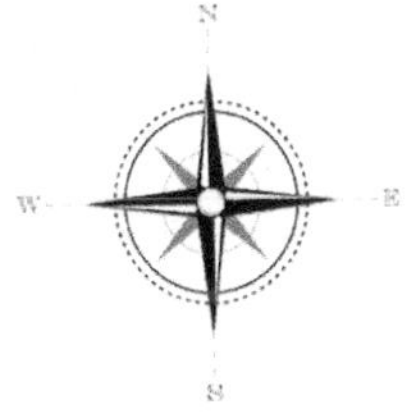

# ONE

The mist hung heavy over the hilly landscape, as it did every evening, making the journey from the citadel back to Aynamaede tricky at best. Allynna quickened her pace a bit, her keen vision scanning each tree she passed. In addition to the undead and the orcs that made their nightly rounds of the forest, there were rumors spreading that a monster was loose and no one of her kind was safe. She dug into the ground with her staff as she went, her bow slung over one shoulder and secured with a leather strap to her quiver. Instead of the school's backpack, she carried her essentials in two packs tied onto her belt. Allynna's blond hair was pulled back in a ponytail that bobbed as she walked ever faster yet resisted the urge to break into a telltale run for her treetop home. The voice of her guild master rang in her ears, repeating over and over the lesson about when to stay and fight and when to run. "Remember, if you run, it's a sure sign of weakness and your enemy will pursue as you open up your vulnerable backside to attacks." She had to return, drop off her things, and then she could be off to meet her new protégé at the stone circle.

Allynna took a deep breath as she focused on steadying her steps. Suddenly she felt her tunic snag on something, most likely a low branch, and she turned, swearing under her breath, to free herself.

"Evening, ma'am," came a deep, resonant voice that seemed to surround her. She looked around wildly for the source of the voice but saw no one. "Down here," said the voice, and she felt another tug at her tunic. She looked down and gasped as she spotted the teal feline eyes gazing back up at her.

The scream rising in her throat never made it to open air. A large clawed hand wrapped around her neck like a vice, and she felt herself lifted off the ground.

"Mm yummy," said the voice, pulling her into the shadows. Before her was a Qatu, an Oranian race of cats that walked upright like humans. Allynna kicked and squirmed, but the giant cat just laughed. He tightened his grip with one hand as he ran the tips of his massive claws on the other down the sides of her face and chin. She grimaced as his fingers slowly circled her cheek. Suddenly, his teal eyes locked onto hers. Allynna could not speak. She merely stared back into those beautiful and terrible eyes as they glowed in the moonlight like precious stones, and she trembled from head to toe.

"Sad," the Qatu said, smirking at her. "I would have liked to have heard your voice before you died." Her eyes widened as he tightened his grip, and then the light within them seemed to snuff out, like a torch extinguished. Her head lolled over as her broken neck could no longer support its weight. The Qatu pressed her body against his face and inhaled deeply before he dropped her to the ground. A quick search earned him several gold and silver coins, two belt packs of food, a bow of turned dark wood, and a quiver full of brand new arrows.

"Ranger, eh?" he said as he made a final sweep of her pockets for money. Finding none, he turned her lifeless body over on her back. The moonlight caught something shiny around her neck and he leaned in to investigate. It was a silver necklace with a single ornament: a round piece of silver with something engraved in the language of the Elves. After giving her a few more shoves to make sure she was dead, the Qatu stole off into the night to investigate his treasures.

Ginolwenye, a young wood elf, sat studying at the kitchen table, spell book open, as she anxiously awaited her mentor's return from the citadel. Allynna, who was several seasons her senior and her schoolteacher, had agreed to take her on as an apprentice, teaching her the skills needed to hunt with a bow and fight. She could hardly wait.

The sound of shouts outside caught her attention. She closed the spell book, which belonged to her mother, checked in to make sure that her younger sister Lairceach was soundly asleep, and then crossed the room to the small round window that looked out into the forest. The warriors were swarming down out of the treetop city and forming ranks by the lift on the hill north of her section of town. Gin, as she was known by most, scurried out of her tiny home that she shared with her parents and siblings, and ran to the edge of the platform to get a better look. A hand catching her arm and yanking her back from the edge startled her.

"You'd better go back inside, Gin," said Garrik, her childhood friend and class mate, now a handsome young man who would soon be training to be a bard. His nimble fingers lingered on her arm a moment, and then released her. She smiled at him, hoping that he would not take this opportunity to tease her as he usually did.

"What's going on? Why have the warriors been called in?" she asked.

"Another killing." Garrik's face fell. "Someone we knew this time, Gin. Oi'deh Allynna was found not long ago in the Forest, her neck broken. I suppose that our time in school is done, no?" Oi'deh was the Elvish word for teacher, and at the news, Gin felt as though she had been punched in the gut.

"No..." she whispered. "NO!" Her eyes blazed, remarkably void of tears. "Who? Who did this?"

"They're not sure," the young bard said in hushed tones, "but the gossip is that it was the Qatu again." He took Gin's hand and stroked the back of it. "I'm sorry, Gin, I know she was important to you. She was an incredible teacher, to be sure. You've come so far in your schooling and you will excel in training to be a druid."

"I suppose I have no choice now," she said, hanging her head. She sighed loudly, then her eyes widened. "What if it was the Qatu, Garrik?" she said, her voice trembling a bit. "I didn't think he was real, but there have been so many deaths..."

"Aye, it is intriguing," Garrik said, his eyes twinkling. "Perhaps one day I will compose an epic poem about the mighty druid Gin taming the Qatu Bane of the Forest?" Gin smiled and Garrik grinned in response. "Ah, there we are, much better." She hugged him, and then took a step toward her house.

"Inside with the doors locked for me then?" she said. "Cursik is out and my parents are away, so it's just me and Lairky in tonight."

"Aye Gin, for your own safety. I'll be round to let you

know when I find something out," Garrik said. He suddenly grabbed her arm, pulled her to him, and kissed her on the cheek. "It will be all right, Gin," he whispered, and then seemed to disappear off the side of the platform.

"Show off," she said, grinning as she shut and locked her door behind her.

The necklace twinkled in the candlelight as it hung over the Cat's giant claw. "Very pretty, this will sell well," he said, a purr behind his words. He thought briefly of the neck that used to wear the bauble, but quickly pushed that thought from his mind. He instead focused his attention on carefully placing the necklace into one of the belt pouches he'd looted from the dead ranger, and then settled back into the soft grass of the forest with some food he'd found in the pouches. He soon dozed off, his stomach full and his work for the night done.

After a few hours, Gin's tears gave way to exhaustion and she fell asleep while still sitting at the table, waking from troubled dreams with a start to her brother shaking her. "Ginny!" he hissed as he shook her arm. "Wake up!"

"What? Dear spirits, Cursik, what is it?" She sat up on her elbow and rubbed her eyes. His emerald gaze was wild and full of worry.

"It's the Qatu again, Ginny!"

"Oh, yes, I know," she said sadly. Gin pushed herself up to a sitting position, pushing her brother back a bit. He sat down across the table from her and took her hands in his. "Are you all right? Did the warriors call you and your guild out to help search for him?"

"Aye, and I couldn't get back home to make sure you and Lairky were all right," he replied, his eyes still wide with concern.

"She's fine," Gin replied. "She's been asleep for hours. Our Lairceach is an inquisitive one, but she wears herself out exploring." She squeezed her brother's hands and then got up from the bed, pulling her cloak around her. "Garrik came by to check on us."

"He's a good boy," Cursik said. Gin scowled at him, making him grin. "Sorry, young man. I'm sorry; you will always be children to me, just like our Lairky will always be a baby." Gin beamed a smile at him as they both wandered into the larger room. Cursik stoked the fire as Gin settled in on a cushion. "I have something for you, little sister," he said as he pulled a small bag from his backpack.

"What is it?" she asked, holding out her hand. Cursik carefully placed the bag in her hands. Gin immediately recognized it as Allynna's and her eyes filled with tears. "Oh, thank you, does this mean that…did you see…what happened to her?"

Cursik clenched his jaw. "I did. Are you sure that you want to know?" Gin nodded. "Her neck was broken. The…Ginny? You've gone pale…" Gin waved her hand for him to continue. He took her other hand in his, kneeling in front of her. "There was a handprint of bruises around her neck, meaning that this creature is enormous if he can lift her with one hand. Most of her belongings had been taken, but this pouch was tucked into the inner pocket of her tunic so the Qatu didn't find it."

"They're calling him the Bane of the Forest, Cursik," Gin whispered. Her brother nodded. "How are we to make sure we are safe? If he truly is Qatu he can climb trees, can't he?"

"Filthy beast," Cursik said, spitting at the fire. "You don't have to worry, Ginny. I will not let anything happen to you, and once Mama and Papa are back with the rest of the druids, we can join with them to make sure that he never hurts any of our kind again. I promise."

He took Gin in his arms and hugged her and she stayed for a few long moments, happy to have someone there to take care of her and protect her. Nevertheless, Allynna's face filled her mind suddenly. No one had been there to take care of her. "I want to help, Cursik," she said, pushing away from his embrace.

"Don't be silly, Ginny," he replied. "Perhaps Mama and Papa will have something for you to do when they return, but for now your place is here with our sister. Lairky needs you." Gin frowned but she knew her brother well enough to know not to argue.

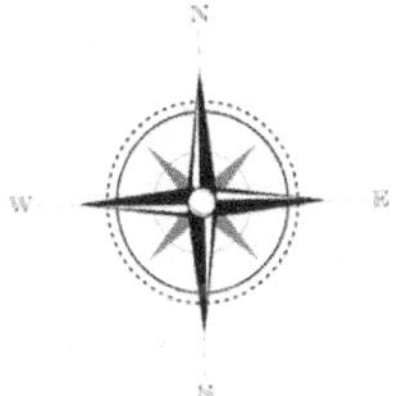

# TWO

*Many seasons later…*

Gin gathered her strength and focused on the wolf on the hill in front of her. She had properly recited all of the spells that she had to memorize, so Aiudin had sent her out into the forest once more to work on some new spells. A wolf looked over its mighty shoulder at her as she began the recitation, and then suddenly turned and came charging down the slope toward her. Gin closed her eyes and continued the spell work, though admittedly at a more frenzied pace. She braced herself for the impact of the wolf's body against hers as she heard it draw closer to her, its razor-like claws tearing into the soft moss of the forest floor. Closer and closer, it came, until she could almost feel its breath on her face…and then there was nothing. Gin slowly opened one eye and peered about. The wolf was sitting in front of her; just as docile and calm as the domesticated dogs she had seen following the high elves of the citadel. Carefully and slowly, she extended a hand to touch the wolf's head, and as she did so, the wolf licked her palm. She nearly fainted with relief until the words of her guild master, Aiudin, came racing back into her mind: *The charm works a short time, and it will be even shorter for you as you have only just begun practicing.* Sure enough, as she gazed into the eyes of the wild beast she could see the clouds caused by her spell falling away and clarity returning. Gin took a step back from the wolf just as it sprang for her neck. She darted away, quickly reciting the words for a spell that grants camouflage as she did. As she felt herself fading from vision, the sharp crack of something heavy against the wolf's skull caught her attention. Had the poor creature hit a tree?

Gin looked out from behind her veil of camouflage to see the largest man she had ever seen kneeling next to the body of the wolf. She ran at him in a moment of rage and grief for the wolf. "What have you done?" she cried out, her well used and cracked wooden staff raised to the level of her eyes…which was the level of his elbow as he stood to face his accuser. His eyes searched the darkness straight out in front of him, unable to locate the source of the voice.

"I've stopped the wolf that was about to maul an elf, is what I did…" His voice sounded puzzled. "But where she went I cannot say, and where are you that address me in such a manner?" He removed his helm and gazed in vain into the darkness of the trees. "Show yourself!"

Gin sighed loudly and undid her camouflage spell. "Look down, you oaf," she said, gasping slightly when his eyes met hers. His eyes seemed to burn into her, and they appeared as red as her blood. Dark magic, clearly. He was twice her height, with chain mail and plate armor covering almost every inch of his body. The horned brass helm that had obscured his features earlier had made her think that he might be a troll or an ogre.

"Look at you!" he said, amusement rampant in his raspy, deep voice. She took an involuntary step backward, thinking suddenly of childhood tales in which evil humans took elves for pets...or worse. "Dorlagar of the Dawnshadows, at your service, my lady elf." He cocked his head to one side, grinning. "Why, I could put you in my pocket, little one!" he mused as he knelt before Gin.

"I wouldn't try it," she said, silently reciting ancient words that would draw the strength of the ground beneath her into her body just in case he tried anything. "What brings a human to the forest anyway?" she demanded, her hands on her hips.

"What causes an elf to ask so many questions?" the human sneered back at her. Gin felt an uneasiness creep up through her bones as he stared down at her. "What business is it of yours, little one?"

Carefully and clandestinely, Gin fingered the staff that she had strapped to her side moments before. "As a servant of Sephine, the All-Mother, and protector of these lands, I make it my business," she said, almost surprised by her words. "Now, I'll ask again what you're doing in the forest."

Dorlagar looked down his nose at the tiny wood elf. He was impressed by her bravado, but did not have time for this nonsense. He had been told all of his life to avoid the forest ...why in all of Orana had he ever gone to this awful place in the first place, so far from his home in the south. Why had he let his childish pride and arrogance lead him here, to this verdant land of drakes and giant wasps and wolves...and of impudent elves like the one in front of him now? "None of your business, wood elf," he huffed and pushed past her, headed for the tree city. Gin staggered but did not lose her footing. She watched him go, knowing that humans are like scourge in the forest, and that this one would likely find no rest there tonight. She smiled and then continued her work.

Dorlagar stood for a long time looking up into the trees at the home of the wood elves. The wooden platforms, ornate dwellings, and suspension bridges connecting them all seemed to fade in and out of the mist. He finally approached the lift, which seemed to go up and down with only the power of magic, and waited until others had boarded it to join them as it started its ascent. His human awkwardness in comparison to the catlike grace of the elves belied him as the lift silently began its journey upward: he nearly fell off the side, to the giggling amusement of some neophyte rangers standing on the other side of the platform. As the platform slowed to a stop, Dorlagar bowed deeply before the gaggle of elves, as a seasoned performer would before an applauding audience. Under his helm his eyes turned as red as blood, and he memorized the faces of each of the rangers, then imagined them all dead at his feet.

As he stepped off the platform into Aynamaede, he was struck by its ingenuity and beauty. The dwellings were so very tiny, and they seemed to fade into the vegetation. There was a merchant set up just to the left of the platform, and Dorlagar hurried to ask her directions to the cleric's guild.

The female's eyes narrowed as Dorlagar stopped in front of her wares. "Be gone, human," she said, her tone sinister and low.

"I seek only information, kind lady," Dorlagar said, trying to pull an ounce or two of charm from deep within him. "I have come seeking the cleric's guild, do you know..."

The wood elf cut him off. "I said, be gone!" she roared. Dorlagar quickly headed for another merchant, fearing she had attracted the attention of the guards by the lift. His quest to find out what had happened to his sister, Raedea, would not be an easy one if no one in Aynamaede would speak with him.

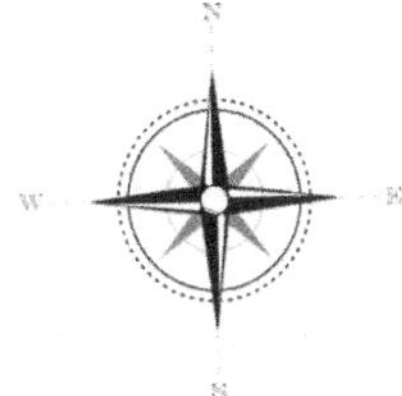


# THREE

Nelenie stretched and stood, her movements unusually catlike, even for a high elf. Her meditating had gone quite well that afternoon, and she felt strong enough to cast any of the spells she had learned that day. Unfortunately, her guild master would not meet her to test her until the moon shone full again in the night sky, so she would just have to wait…or would she? A smile crept across her chiseled face. Nelenie quickly bound her long golden hair up in a ponytail on top of her head, pulled on her traveling coat and breeches, and then slid her feet into her dwarven-made boots that had been a gift from her master upon completing an important part of her training as a knight. She stopped to admire herself in the large mirror on the outer wall of her home in the high elf citadel.

Her traveling coat had been given to her by her parents the day that she finished her guild training. It was made of soft black wolf hide, and had an intricate pattern woven with bleached spider silks all the way around the edges and cuffs of the sleeves.

The spider silks looked like normal white thread during the daytime, but under the full moon, they shined like polished silver. Nelenie could put this coat on and nearly disappear into the darkness while traveling through the forest at night. She tiptoed out of her family dwelling and began running for the northern end of the walled citadel, and the entrance to the forest.

Her eyes adjusted automatically to the dark as she ran past the guards, and she began to follow the path that would lead her north to the tree city of her wood elf cousins. Nelenie wrinkled her nose at the thought of the wood elves living in trees, foraging for food… In her estimation, there was no need to live that way when one could live in the magnificent splendor of the citadel, like the civilized folk. The legends told that the wood elves were merely high elves that had gotten lost in the forest and remained there, seeking shelter in the trees from the orc threat on the ground. It was because of their need to camouflage themselves that each successive generation was born smaller in stature that the previous, and why the wood elves that Nelenie now knew were as tall as her shoulder.

Grunting noises to her left stopped Nelenie in her tracks. Without moving a muscle, she shifted her eyes to the left until she spotted an orc youngling hiding behind a tree, clearly watching her run past. Nelenie quickly closed her eyes and called on the spells she had memorized already, but when she opened her eyes, she nearly gasped aloud at what she saw.

Just as the orc stepped out from behind the tree to attack, the tree began to shimmer and shake with light. Nelenie found herself frozen with fear and curiosity. A blast of orange light streamed from the tree into the orc, igniting the orc's skin. The orc turned his horrific face toward the tree in astonishment as more sparks flew from the sides of the tree in his direction.

He turned to run as Nelenie scanned the area for the magic user that had scared him away, but saw no one. "Show yourself," she said in the common tongue, language of the humans and the most common language spoken on Orana, and as she did, she gathered up all of the authority of a much more seasoned warrior into her haughty high elf composure. "Are you behind that tree?"

Tinkling laughter filled the leaves of the trees above her, as though being carried along on the slight breeze that lifted tendrils of her golden hair. "Not so much behind the tree," said a voice that sounded at the same time feminine and masculine, both whispering and booming, "as much as IN the tree!" Nelenie blinked, and before her stood her distant cousin and childhood playmate, Gin. "Glad to know that tree-form spell works," the wood elf giggled.

"Don't you spend enough time in those trees as it is?" Nelenie teased her, switching to back to the common language of the elves, just in case there were more orcs about. As soon as the girls were old enough to begin their guild training, they rarely saw each other anymore. Nelenie was often lonesome for her friend and cousin, as her natural abilities made her training easy and left her with a lot of free time.

"Orana's bounty is all around us, Nel," the wood elf said, her voice softening with obvious respect and awe. "The breeze that caresses our cheek is Her hand. The soft moss that we sit on to rest and mediate is Her lap. The trees that you so malign," said Gin, grinning at her cousin in jest, "are but Orana's fingers, holding us skyward and keeping us safe." Gin looked closely at Nelenie, her features turning sad for a moment upon noticing Nelenie's slightly wrinkled nose and disdainful expression. "You've started to become like the rest of them, haven't you?" she asked sadly.

"What do you mean? What, 'rest of them'?" Nelenie muttered something in the elder Elvish language, and Gin pointed her finger at the other girl's ivory nose.

"That, Nelenie! Speaking the language of the elder Elvish races in front of me, speaking of my religion with condescension in your voice…" The smaller elf's eyes rimmed with tears. She sniffed a bit, wiping her nose on the sleeve of her rawhide tunic. "You think of us wood elves as your chambermaids and servants. I had just hoped that you and I would always be friends, but I suppose that's not to be."

Nelenie's eyes were also brimming with tears. "You're no better," she said, changing back to Elvish. "You expect me to be haughty and self-important because I'm a high elf." Nelenie sniffed loudly and then continued, regaining her composure. "You're the ones that think ill of us, wood elf, and not the other way around." She folded her arms over her chest and glared down at Gin, who was reciting a spell. "What are you doing?"

Slowly and carefully, Gin's feet left the ground as a pocket of air coagulated beneath them. She rose from the ground until she was looking Nelenie squarely in the eyes.

"Say that again, high elf, but look me in the eye and smile this time," she hissed, trying to keep her giggles at bay and maintain a stern expression. Nelenie smiled at her, also fighting off a fit of laughter as Gin bobbed in front of her. "Oh, and by the way," she added, grinning from ear to ear, "tag, you're it!" Rapping Nelenie soundly on the top of her blonde head, Gin dashed off into the trees. Nelenie charged after her, laughing as she had not since the two were tiny girls, zooming in and out of the trees. She ran right up to Gin immediately, using the additional length of her legs to her advantage. Just as she would have rapped Gin on the head, the wood elf disappeared into the canopy, using magic to make herself invisible.

"Drat!" Nelenie exclaimed, still grinning. "Rule number one: never play tag with a druid. They CHEAT!" She could hear Gin's tinkling laughter in the leaves as she continued down the path alone.

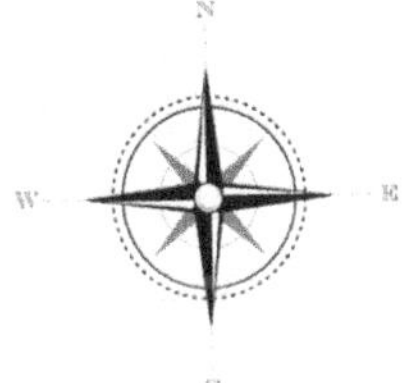

# FOUR

"Just one more step back, Shadow Knight," the merchant said. "If you just back up a bit, so that no one thinks I'm selling to the likes of you, I'll consider your trade." Dorlagar looked over his shoulder, but the now swirling mists obscured his view of his surroundings. "Go on, if you want the information you seek, step back!" The tiny wood elf could barely contain her excitement. One more step and the human would topple over the edge of the platform, smashing his disgusting skull on the ground below.

"One more step and I'll fall," Dorlagar said, his voice sounding low and ragged as he struggled to keep his anger in check. Dark magic using warriors were magically able to draw in the aggression and hatred of their opponents in battle, and Dorlagar felt the familiar rush of emotion coming from the wood elf merchant. He had hoped to trade some of his looted weapons for information on the cleric's guild in Aynamaede, but now he was not even sure there was such a place.

"Now I couldn't take your trade if you fell, could I human?" the female taunted him. "I've spent too long arguing with you as it is, either you step back or we have no deal." She folded her slender arms across her chest and glared up at Dorlagar, who took a deep breath and prepared himself for what would likely be a nasty fall, and then stepped backward.

Gin felt herself reappearing at the lift to Aynamaede. She quickly scampered up a nearby hill and began reciting the words that would make her levitate. Aiudin had told her that she needed to learn how to get into the tree city without using the lift, and so far, she had managed to get high enough to jump on the lift after it began its ascent. She felt her feet leave the ground, and ran straight out into the air, headed for the platform.

Dorlagar was not sure if it was the rush of air or the turning of his stomach that let him know he was falling. Knowing that there was nothing to grab onto between the platform and the ground because the elves made sure their city was impenetrable, he merely closed his eyes and tried to call up a spell to heal himself…if he should survive the fall at all. When his body did collide with something from below, he was surprised to find that it was not the forest floor…it seemed that he had landed on a body! Dorlagar rolled to his side, and off whomever he had hit, as stabbing pain shot through his upper body. Gradually, his wounds began to heal from the spell cast in mid-air, and he could hear the wood elf merchant shrieking with pain from above him. A satisfied smile spread over Dorlagar's face. His magic came from a very dark place indeed, and in order to heal his wounds, the magic would exact its price from the closest living thing. His face twisted with delight at the sounds of agony from above.

As soon as he could, Dorlagar pushed up on his elbow in an effort to see the damage his fall had done. There was a body there indeed, but it just looked to be another one of the wood elves that were now scurrying above him, trying to heal the human sized wounds still bombarding the merchant's tiny body. Dorlagar, pleased that the pain was not as great as he had assumed it would be, studied the limp form next to him. "One more dead wood elf," he murmured. "Oh well, there's plenty of them here, they won't miss this one." A chain mail armored arm covered the elf's face, but Dorlagar could clearly tell that his victim was female. "Wonder if she'd really miss that sword," he said in a whisper as he ogled the ebony blade in the elf's tiny fingers. "Not going to need it where she's going anyway," he chuckled to himself as he inched over to the body. He did not relish the idea of breaking the elf's slender fingers to get the blade from her, but a second glance at the jeweled hilt of the blade steeled his resolve. "That armor's probably worth good coin per piece at the market," he mumbled as he lifted the elf's arm.

He was amazed at how light her arm felt to him, even though it should have been weighted down with the armor that she wore all over her body. The metal was a deep azure in color, and reminded Dorlagar briefly of the night sky in his home city. Reminding himself to focus, he set to the task of uncurling her fingers from the hilt of the blade. He did not see her open her eyes ever so slightly, and did not hear her begin mouthing the words to a spell in Elvish. All Dorlagar saw or heard was a flash of light and the crackle of his skin igniting. He stumbled backward with a bellow and drew his blade, clouds of pitch coalescing around his fingers as they always did in combat.

Gin slowly got to her feet, her blade thrust forward at the human. She continued to recite magical words in her language, and once again, Dorlagar felt as though he was on fire from the inside out. "You kill my wolf, fall on me and then loot my body for armor and weapons before you're even sure if I'm dead? Typical of a human," she hissed at him, her tiny frame suddenly seeming large and more forceful than it had moments before. Dorlagar blinked, knowing her size now to be a spell or glamour, and tried to back away, but she was again reciting something in the Elvish language. Roots sprang from the ground under Dorlagar; they wound around his boots and up his legs, and held him fast. "I don't know if I should kill you or let the guards do it," Gin said, staring down the human. "All it would take is a word from me..."

"Where is the compassion you showed that wolf?" Dorlagar blurted out. He silently chided himself for showing fear, but as the sole and now-hated human in a glade of magic-using elves, he felt a bit outnumbered. "Can you not show me compassion, wood elf?"

Gin's gaze remained stalwart, but the roots weakened, so Dorlagar continued his plea. "I did not hurl myself from the platforms of your cursed city with the intention of squashing you like a beetle," he said, his voice regaining some cool steadiness. "Instead I was tricked into backing up and falling off the edge. I am in fact indebted to you, my fair elf," he said, purposefully trying to charm her into not zapping him again with that fire spell. "Had it not been for you, my dear, I would have been the squashed beetle."

He stood still, feeling the magical roots that held him fast to the ground fall away. Gin made no move to strike him, but he was not about to sheath his blade until he was sure he could either fight or get away. "In fact, my lovely little blueberry colored elf, I believe that I am indebted to you for my life." He inched closer to her, intent on relieving her of her weapon as an angry expression exploded onto her face.

"Your little blueberry...what?" she roared. As he lunged for her, she deftly jabbed at his armor with her sword, but her blow bounced off the now-dented metal that covered Dorlagar's chest. Following the momentum of the blow, she spun around and sunk her blade into his arm at the elbow, amazingly catching the few inches of skin exposed between pieces of armor. Dorlagar howled like a beast, and the black clouds began forming around his hands once more.

Drawing back as though cocking a bow with an arrow, Dorlagar thrust his hands forward toward Gin with a loud cry, dark magic pouring from his fingers toward her. She felt as though she was turned inside out. All of the hatred and anger that she had felt for Dorlagar came surging like a tidal wave into his body. Eyes glowing blood red, he ran at her and dealt her a blow to her cheek with his own blade that sent her reeling to the ground. The sound of the melee alerted the guards, who came running. Gin felt moisture on her face, and touched the spot. It was blood. The human's blade had sliced open her cheek!

"This will teach you to enter the forest, human!" yelled one of the guards as he brought his sword down onto Dorlagar's chipped helm. Gin scrambled to her feet and grabbed the guard's elbow, shrieking at him that Dorlagar was her kill, but the guard merely tossed her aside like a rag doll. The elven guard and Dorlagar exchanged blows as Gin stood to the side watching. She focused her energy on Dorlagar, ready to delve into his mind and to try to calm his anger, but the image that she saw in his mind nearly knocked her off her feet. In a flash of pictures and feelings, she suddenly knew why he was in the forest. She saw him with his sister, Raedea, felt his love for his twin, and nearly wept at the pain of their parting.

"Stop!" she called out to the guard. "Let him go, he's no threat to us here." The guard ignored her and continued to match Dorlagar's assault, blow for blow. Gin ran in between them and threw her arms up in the air, releasing her blade and calling on her magic to soothe them and to reduce the aggression in both of them. By dropping her weapon, she gave Dorlagar the perfect out that he needed, and he took it. Grabbing her around the throat with one of his now bloody arms as he scooped up her weapon in the other hand, he tightened his grip until she was gasping for air, which completely interrupted her spell casting.

"Let me leave or I'll kill her," he hissed at the guard. He pressed the tip of the ebony blade into the soft flesh just under her chin, but Gin did not seem to notice. Gin kicked at his legs and wriggled about trying to free herself from his grasp, but found that she could not. The human was simply too tall, and her feet were dangling in mid-air. She silently reprimanded herself for dropping her blade when she raised her hands to cast that spell. Pleading with her eyes, Gin locked her gaze on the guard. The guard looked from her to Dorlagar and then backed up three paces.

"Leave this glen," the Guard barked. "Do not return. By order of the Soldiers of the Forest Guard, you are now Kill-On-Sight in the whole of the forest. Gin, daughter of the forest, Druid of Sephine, your certain death will be avenged," he said before turning back to his post at the lift. Dorlagar did not wait for the guard to make good on the oath and ran toward the stone circle with a struggling Gin still caught firmly in the crook of his elbow.

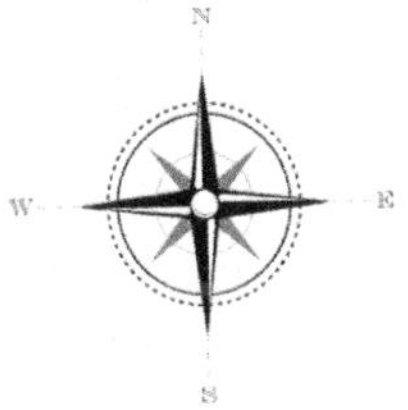


# FIVE

Nelenie crept through the forest, on the move and on the hunt. Though it was generally her way to stride boldly into conflict and combat, daring anyone to engage her, she decided that a slightly subtler approach might be interesting to try. Her backpack was nearly dragging the ground with the treasures she had looted so far. The orc younglings were the best to engage, she thought. They often yielded up cash in addition to bracers and weapons.

Suddenly her skin was alive and tingling, as if someone using magic on her. She spun around, looking to either thank or punch her invisible benefactor for startling her, but saw no one. "Gin?" she said, carefully inspected each tree near her to make sure there was not an elf hiding inside.

"Gin?" said a familiar male voice. "What's a Gin? Isn't

that the wood elf that used to follow you about?"

"Ben!" Nelenie exclaimed, leaping into the air with delight. Taeben had long been a friend and schoolmate of Nelenie's. They were the same age, and Ben often joined in the games that Nelenie and Gin would play in the forest. Nelenie had just begun her studies to become a holy knight, the defenders of Alynatalos and the elven races who were able to use healing spells and some defensive magic, as Ben had left the citadel to apprentice as a magic user. The two had not seen each other for a very long time. Ben's departure had left a huge hole in Nelenie's heart, and seeing him now overwhelmed her somewhat. She ran to her friend, and Ben swept her up in his sinewy arms and spun them both around in circles. They fell to the grass, laughing and dizzy. "What are you doing back, Ben?" Nelenie asked, nearly breathless from laughter.

"My apprenticeship is done," Ben said. Nelenie noticed, with some pleasure, that when he spoke his now deepened voice seemed to resonate throughout her body. She looked up at him and felt as though he was looking straight down to her soul. His hair was a deeper red than she remembered, probably due to more time indoors studying and less time out in the sunshine. He had grown into a handsome young male and was just a tad bit taller than Nelenie herself.

"Hello? Nel? You in there?" Ben was waving a hand in front of her eyes when she returned from her memories.

"Yes, sorry, what did you say?"

"If you'd stop checking me out and pay attention you'd know what I said, ya dumb blonde," Ben said, playfully punching her in the arm. Nelenie's jaw dropped in mock indignation, and she punched him squarely in the chest. Ben doubled over, the air knocked out of his lungs. "Where…did you…learn that?" he wheezed.

"I'm a knight now, remember?" Nelenie said, grinning. "I could take a little wizard like you with **no** problems." She hopped to her feet, fists balled. "Come on!" she taunted him, using just a little of the magical skill she had learned to pull her opponents to her. Ben rose to his feet slowly, much like the adversaries she had taunted in the past, and came toward her, his hands out in front of him.

"You think so?" he said, and a blueish-purple light shot from his hands, blinding Nelenie for the moment. She felt like she could not move but did not really want to move anyway. Everything was peaceful and calm and she even contemplated taking a nap.

Just then, Ben burst through the purple-blue haze and grabbed Nelenie by the throat. As quickly as the happy and contented feelings had come on, they dissipated, and Nelenie was left with the cold reality of Ben's lithe fingers pressing into her windpipe. She felt as though she was rudely awakened from a deep sleep.

He pulled her very close to his face and whispered, "Don't ever underestimate me, my sweet Nelenie." Before she could utter a word or writhe in protest, Ben brought her face to his and kissed her roughly. Nelenie fought him a moment, but then gave in and let herself go limp against him, eyes closed. He released her slowly and carefully, and when she opened her eyes, he was looking at her as though amused.

"Still my beautiful girl, are you?" he asked, eyes twinkling.

"Always, Ben," she said. "But I'll get you back for that cheap shot, though. I can fight as well as any boy, my trainer said so," she said, pouting slightly. Ben smiled and smoothed a hair away from her face.

"Aye, you can. That was quite a punch you dealt me, Nel." The young elf rubbed his chest. "Quite a punch. You with a weapon and that strength…the mind reels."

"Reels? Bah! It should quake in fear!" Nelenie said, rising to her full height and placing her hands on her hips. She pouted slightly as Ben broke into laughter, but soon joined him in a giggle.

"Someday soon you and I will go out hunting, my beautiful Nel," Ben said, taking Nelenie's hand and beginning to stroll through the forest. "How is that younger sister of yours, by the way?"

"Tairneanach is the same spoiled child she's always been, only taller," Nelenie said with a scowl. "Her latest trick is to use one of her spells to reappear as a human or a half-elf, of all things! She always does that when I'm mad at her."

"Ah, yes," Ben said, a hint of malevolence creeping into his eyes. "A good spell indeed, but she must be careful with that one. She might reappear in a more dangerous situation than the one she'd have just left." His eyes quickly shifted back to their regular shade of silvery gray. I'd love to see her," Ben said, absently stroking the back of Nelenie's hand with his thumb as they walked along, fingers entwined. "Where is she, do you think?"

Nelenie's face fell. "I don't know," she said, "and further, I don't care."

Ben bit his lip and then smiled halfheartedly at her. He was clearly irritated with her lack of knowledge but tried to hide it. "Come sit here, Nel," he said, sitting on a downed tree and motioning for her to join him. "I am just curious to know if your sister is following the same training I did," he said gently. Nelenie nodded. "I'm curious about her transport magic."

"What do you mean transport? Stop talking to me like I'm a child." she said, eyebrows knotted in confusion.

"I mean it's like a magical doorway. You know how you never play tag with a Druid because they cheat?"

"Yes."

"Same thing. Druids can jump from one place to another. That is how they cheat. We all can do it; wizards have the same magic ability druids have whereas others simply have to find the portal. For you, it is like finding the doorway to the hall that will take you somewhere else. Druids and wizards like me and our Ginny can just cast a spell and poof!" Ben smiled a genuine smile at Nelenie's confusion. "Perhaps I should show you?" Nelenie nodded, always up for an adventure. "All right," he said, standing and taking her hand in his, "Come with me. We're going to take a little trip." Ben spoke ancient words as Nelenie held onto his arm tightly, making him smirk. She gasped as a column of fire formed around them and let out a shriek that was cut short as they winked out of existence in the forest, leaving a rustle of leaves in the trees in their wake.

For a moment, everything was dark and Nelenie, who had closed her eyes tightly, had trouble taking a breath, but then she felt the ground under her feet again. She opened her eyes and discovered that they were under the tree city, a good distance away from where they had started. She looked around and started to ask how it had happened. "Ssh, let's go back now, I just wanted to show you how it works," Ben whispered in her ear. Nelenie clung to Ben's neck, her entire body trembling, as he once again spoke the ancient words that brought up the column of fire around them. She closed her eyes, pressing her face into his cobalt robes and whimpering.

"Don't worry, love, you won't get singed," he whispered to her as the spell took hold. "There, see? Open your eyes; no worse than it was on the way there, was it?" Nelenie tentatively opened her eyes and looked up at Ben, then around behind them. They were back in the forest, in the middle of enormous marble spires, very close to where they had been before. She tried to step away from him but found her legs to be as uncooperative as a newborn foal's, and she stumbled. Ben caught her, pulling her back close to him. "How was that, then?" he asked, his silvery gaze traveling all over her face before settling on her eyes.

Nelenie coughed, managing a large gasp of air. "Ben, let go, you're hurting me," she said, pushing back on his chest with her hands. He released her, but locked her gaze with his.

"Just making sure you could stand on your own first, love," he said, his tone icy. "And yes, anyone can transport themselves about that way, really, even without magic. All you have to do is find the portals…go to the servants that wait here in the spires and ask to be transported to wherever you wish to go on Orana.

"There is a magical place between the continents where the servants are trained in secret and then sent to the four corners of our world to serve as living conduits for transportation." Ben pretended to examine his fingernails as he watched Nelenie digesting the information, gauging her reaction. Beautiful though she was, she might not have the mental stamina he needed in a mate.

"So they have different magic, then, similar to yours?" she asked tentatively. Ben smiled at her, trying to hide his annoyance.

"Yes, love, they do. Only the magic of transportation, nothing more. Mind numbing work, if you ask me, but useful," he replied. "Your sister, for example, would need the servants for most of her travel, as she only has one spell of transport that will return her home. Only those that follow the wizard and druid paths can fully access the magic that will permit travel."

Nelenie's face flushed red. "Why is it that Tairn gets that and I don't get anything?" she demanded. "Is it because she has no other defenses, really, and she's so weak?" She shrank back as

Ben's eyes narrowed.

"Your sister is anything but weak. While you and that wood elf friend of yours, Ginny, were playing with dolls and making crowns of flowers for your hair, your sister was out learning how to use a dagger," he hissed at her. "I taught her everything I knew to keep spell casters like us alive in a fight. I daresay she could match you blow for blow."

Nelenie stared at him for a moment, her eyes wide, and then burst out laughing. "You have got to be joking," she said, punching him playfully in the shoulder. Ben almost lost his balance, which spurred Nelenie to bend over double laughing. "See that? I barely touched you." She moved back close to him, sticking her index finger at his face and nearly brushing the tip of his nose as he glared down at her. "Warriors like me are what keeps you spell casters alive in a fight, Ben, and you'd do well to remember that." She grinned up at him, her grin slowly fading as anger crept into his eyes, turning their normal silver into a darkened gunmetal gray.

"You would do well not to underestimate me," he said, his voice low and tone laden with malice. "I am much too powerful for you to make an enemy of me, Nelenie." Nelenie took an involuntary step back, causing Ben's face to split into a malevolent grin.

"Nel!" The voice of a wood elf female seemed to break Ben's hold on Nelenie and he growled low. "I was coming to meet you but they said you weren't at home so I came out here!" Nelenie turned to the blonde female who stood as high as her shoulder.

"Elysiam," she said, her tone level but threatening. "You are early. I told you that you were to wait for me if I did not meet you at the appointed time." She took Elysiam's arm, pinching slightly, and turned her back toward the path that led to the

Citadel.

"Oh, we are finished here, love," Ben said, his eyes filled with amusement. "Do you and your…pet there have somewhere to be?"

"PET?" Elysiam thundered, yanking her arm away from Nelenie's grasp and turning back to face the wizard. "I am not her PET!" Ben's eyes narrowed as Nelenie again grabbed Elysiam's arm and swung her around. "Let me go! I can practice some of what you…" Nelenie's other hand cut off Elysiam's words as her slender fingers wrapped around the wood elf's face and pulled her backward.

"Ben, I will see you soon I hope?" she said, her face reddening as she dragged a kicking Elysiam back toward her home.

"Count on it," he called after her. Ben watched them go, blonde ponytails bobbing in the dappled sunlight that filtered through the forest canopy. "But in the meantime, what are you and a wood elf doing that no one needs to know about, I wonder?" He watched them until they were out of sight. "I think it may become my business to find out," he said, murmuring ancient words as he walked.

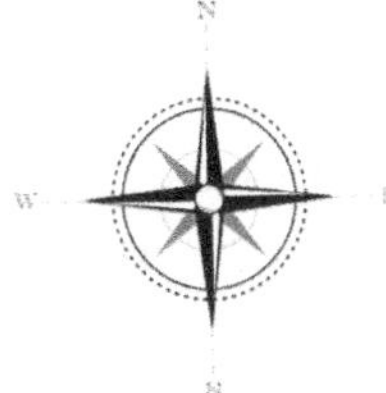

# SIX

Raedea Dawnshadow shivered and pulled the scratchy wool blanket tightly around her chin. Her pallet in the initiates' hall was thin and the cold crept up from the marble floor like a sickness worming its way into her bones. She rolled over onto her back and gazed out the solitary window in the room at the moon. "Hello, my friend," she said in hushed tones to the glowing globe hanging in the night sky. "You look the same to me here as you do at home, yet I feel a million miles away." Home seemed so far away now, though there was just an expanse of flat lands that separated her home in Ardend on the edge of the grasslands from her new home in Calder's Port. After quick and furtive glances to make sure that the matron was snoring away in her bed, Raedea slipped from her pallet and crept out the door.

She was fully dressed still, and had only to grab her cloak from the nail outside the sleeping quarters before beginning the arduous task of finding the exit. The Temple of Isona in Calder's Port contained a huge oval center, and there were passageways linked by staircases that wound around the center in a corkscrew. It was said that the design was inspired by Isona's own heart, with its many chambers that held love and mercy for all. For mere mortals, however, the problem lay in knowing where to get off the corkscrew to go out the front door rather than walk in on the elders during their rites…something that Raedea had done on many occasions following her arrival at the Temple.

Ten seasons earlier, she had knocked on the heavy front doors to the Temple, begging for entry even though she was not a citizen of Calder's Port. The intricately carved wooden doors had seemed heavy and imposing as she banged on them with all her might. As it often did in that season, it had begun to rain as Raedea stood at the Temple doors. Her ash brown hair was escaping its braid and had begun forming channels for the rain to run down her face and into her eyes. When she heard footsteps on the other side of the door, Raedea tried to smooth the hair back from her face and improve her appearance.

Sister Serena squinted out of the cracked door into the rainy night. "Who disturbs the Temple at this hour?" she called out, but there was no power behind her voice. Her eyes lit on the young girl standing there shivering, and she immediately opened the door. "Come in, you poor thing," she said, cooing in the way a mother would to a child. She quickly pulled an initiate robe from a nail near the door and wrapped it around Raedea's shoulders. "Why are you out on such a night, child?"

"I…wish to join the Temple," Raedea stammered, determined to regain control. "I wish to be a cleric in service to Isona, Goddess of Love and Mercy. There is too much anger and killing in our world." She looked up at Serena, meeting the older cleric's dark stare with her nearly ice blue eyes. "Please, ma'am, you just have to take me in…"

Sister Serena's eyes danced with amusement. "Young lady, we do not HAVE to do anything. I will bring you to our guild master, and she will see if you are fit to begin training in the ways of the cleric." She put an arm around Raedea and led her further inside.

Raedea thought back on that first night as she pulled the cloak tightly around her neck and shoulders. What she had hoped would be a new life filled with hope, love, and service had turned out to be near slavery, hatred, and lies. The local militia was a corrupt bunch that was not above taking the initiates of Isona out for "service work," only to become the recipients of the service. Raedea could still feel their dirty fingers ripping the robe from her back…she could still hear their whispered warnings about what would happen to her fellow initiates who told the guild master…she could still smell the stale honey mead on their breath and in her clothes and hair. How upset Sister Serena would have been had she known what "her girls" were being forced to do! Raedea grimaced as she imagined the sadness that would fill the eyes of the woman that had quickly become like a mother to her.

Walking quickly, she soon made her way out of Calder's Port and back to the city gate on the western side. As she passed the guards at the gate, she carefully hid her face with her hood. She had no idea which of the militia were on duty there or if they would recognize her. When she was far enough away from the gate not to alert the guards, she unsheathed her weapon and headed through the gates – hood up – and strode up to a merchant camped just inside the gates.

"Ah, an initiate of Isona I see," the merchant said, his booming ogre voice able to be heard for miles. He looked over the weapon she had brought to trade and eagerly began counting out the appropriate coins for an exchange.

"I am not sure how that is any of your business, good sir," Raedea said, having noticed that the guards nearby were paying close attention to the merchant and his mystery patron.

"By that answer I'd judge you really aren't an initiate in service to Isona and you've looted the cloak off the body of an initiate...but that's none of my business, you're right little one," the ogre said, handing over the coins.

"I thank you, good sir, for your service," she said, and then leaned in close to the ogre, "and your discretion." Raedea pressed a platinum coin into his monstrous hand. "You bought nothing from me. You did not see me," she said, silently reciting the spell to lull a beast and hoping that the ogre was beast enough for it to take hold.

"Nothing," he repeated with his booming voice now soft as a babe's. "I saw no one," he said, eyes drooping.

"Correct," Raedea said, slipping behind him and heading for the gates.

The common lands outside of the west gate were bustling with activity. New arrivals to the city were running errands for citizens, taking on quests, and getting used to the terrain. Raedea wandered along the wall, watching for signs that someone recognized her. One of the militiamen seemed to be following her, and when she heard him bark at another traveler, she recognized his voice. Sir Hanvers, one of the cruelest and most sadistic of the Calder's Port militia, was just a few feet from her. Sir Hanvers had taken her on outings alone a few times, and she had invariably returned with bruises and cuts that healed with spells before re-entering the Temple. One of his favorite games was to take Raedea to the river's edge and shove her off the bridge into the water. Raedea was not a good swimmer at first, and Hanvers would stand on the shore and laugh at her as she flailed about, trying to keep her head above water as well as avoid the biting fish and other creatures that swam freely through the city's waterways.

Finally, he would stride into the water and yank her up by her neck, dragging her to an out of sight area under the bridge. At first, she would try to get away from him, but finally she learned that the more she struggled the more she would have to heal before returning to her guild master.

As Hanvers grunted and strained on top of her, Raedea would let her mind wander to the cool nights of her youth back home, playing tag with her twin brother under the moon's watchful gaze. She squashed thoughts of slitting Hanvers's throat with his own blade and instead tried to remember the feel of the grass under her feet and the sound of her brother's laughter as they played.

Now, many seasons later, her throat still tightened and her stomach twisted at the sound of his voice. She pulled her cloak up tighter around her face and moved closer to the wall. Raedea inched along the wall, feeling her way with her hand as she kept her eyes on Hanvers.

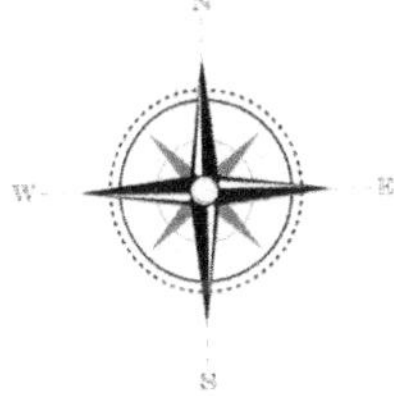


# SEVEN

"That was TOO close," Nelenie hissed in Elysiam's ear as she dragged the wood elf along toward the elven citadel. "Do you not realize the danger we are in, or that what we are doing is forbidden?" She spun the smaller female around to face her, the frightened look on the Elysiam's face giving her pause. "I'm sorry to snap at you, Elys, but this is not allowed. Wood elves do not become knights! Do you understand? We could both be banished if I was found teaching you what I know."

"Not good enough to be knights like you, are we?" Elys said, the bravado in her words belied by the tremble in her voice. "Ginny was right, you do all grow up to think you're better than we are." She tried to free her arm from Nelenie's grip, but the older and taller elf held Elysiam fast.

"It isn't that at all," Nelenie said, releasing the druid and sinking down to sit, her back against a tree just outside of the main gates. "There are rules, Elys, rules that the Gods have set down for us, which we have to follow. One of those rules is that the only elves to become knights are those of my race. Can you imagine if one of those horrible dark elves from the underground citadel of Kairen could learn my magic and possess my strength?" She shuddered. Elysiam studied her mentor, her blonde head cocked to one side.

"Rules, huh? Well, as a druid, I'm supposed to be a follower of Sephine, but I chose to follow Kildir. He came to me once when I was sleeping rough in the canyons near the common lands, and said I was to be one of his soldiers." Elysiam stared Nelenie in the eye as though daring her to comment on the vision. "I know to some that makes me crazy, but it is the truth. What else could that mean, soldier, other than a knight? But don't you see? This is the best of warrior and healer, Nel. This is why you have to teach me!" She bit her lip. Nelenie smiled down at her.

"And so, I will, Elys. We just have to be more careful, is all. I mean, I trust Ben, but it would just put him in an awkward position if we are found out and he is questioned. Does that make sense?" Nelenie smoothed an unruly piece of hair back behind Elysiam's ear. The smaller female was the little sister that Nelenie had wanted. She barely even saw Tairneanach anymore, and when she did, the exchanges were not pleasant. In contrast, Elysiam longed to be like her and soaked up everything that Nelenie could teach her. She smiled at her protégé. "You understand, don't you?"

"Don't patronize me," Elysiam said, pushing Nelenie's hand away. "Of course I understand. It's just not fair, is all." Nelenie smiled sadly at the younger female.

"No, it isn't. Why do some get to learn spells that will take them far away from the forest by just saying a few words, and I had to fight tooth and nail to get any magical training at all?"

Nelenie sighed. "It is just the cards we are dealt, Elys. Now, shall we get on with your training?"

"Yes, Nel," Elysiam said, grinning. From behind a nearby tree, Taeben was doing anything but grinning.

"Sharing our secrets, our training, and our skills with wood elves?" he hissed under his breath. Catching himself, he remembered that he was under an invisibility spell so he bit his lip to stay quiet. Nelenie had looked around when he spoke, and he feared that he had given himself away.

"What did you hear?" Elysiam asked, tugging on Nelenie's arm to get her attention.

"Nothing," Nelenie said, grinning. "Let's get going though, just in case." They got to their feet and headed down the path toward the high elf citadel's main gate. Taeben stayed as close as he dared. He knew that while most druids had magic that would allow them to see the invisible, he doubted that Elysiam would. She seemed far too bloodthirsty for mundane magic.

"A female after my own heart," he muttered, grinning to himself as his long strides easily brought him in step with Elysiam. Lovely to look at as well, he thought as he studied her. There was something about the other elves that was appealing, but he knew it had more to do with their subservience than their appearance. He kept his eyes on her as he dodged trees and tried not to run into the guards at the gate. Soon his prey was inside the main gate and headed for Nelenie's home in the barracks, so Taeben let them get a bit ahead of him lest they see him materialize. Once they were out of sight, he dropped his invisibility and sped toward the barracks. It would be fun to watch a bit of the training before he alerted her guild master. *Nel will not doubt my power now, and I will be all she has to lean on,* he thought, a malevolent smile crossing his features. *She will be a fine bodyguard.* Images of her upturned face, her petulant smile, and finally her complete submission spurred him on to find the knight's guild master. "Not long now, pet. I will have Tairn as my companion and you as our watchdog," he murmured as Nelenie's blonde ponytail came into view in the arena.

The two females began to spar, and Elysiam matched Nelenie blow for blow. "Very good!" Nelenie exclaimed. "You've been practicing!" Taeben watched, fascinated, for a moment before slipping away to find the guild master.

Elysiam beamed a wicked smile at her mentor. "Yes, yes I have," she said. The druid spoke ancient words that caused roots to grow inexplicably from the tile floor and wind around Nelenie's boots. A flick of her wrist and a swarm of stinging insects bore down on the other female's head. Nelenie swatted them away, cursing, as Elysiam sprang at her, raining blows on the knight's head, just as she had been taught.

"Enough!" At the shout from the knight's guild master, both of the women fell silent. The bees dissipated and Elysiam was left panting, having used up most of her energy in casting the magic. "What is your business here, wood elf?" he called out, looking down his nose at her.

"Master, she is a friend of mine, we were merely sparring," Nelenie said, stepping between Elysiam and the guild master.

"That, sadly, is not the tale I was told," the guild master replied. "Move aside, Nelenie. Now." She did as he asked and he snapped his fingers. Four large members of the citadel's guard entered the room and surrounded Elysiam.

"Master?" Nelenie said, the panic in her voice rising.

"Take the wood elf and remove her from the city. She is no longer welcome inside our walls for choosing to attack one of our own holy knights," the guild master said. The four guards picked Elysiam up and began carrying her out the door. She kicked and screamed in protest until one of them rapped her soundly on the head, knocking her unconscious.

"Stop! Stop!" Nelenie ran around in front of the guards. "She was not attacking me! We are friends and we were sparring… I told you!"

"No need to defend her now, Nelenie, my dear." The guild master took her by the elbow and pulled her out of the path of the soldiers. "She will answer for her treachery in her own city, with her own kind."

"But there was no…" Nelenie took a deep breath. "I was training her. I was teaching her the skills I have been taught."

"You WHAT?" The guild master's face went from alabaster to crimson. "You know the rules, Nelenie!" She hung her head. "You are lying."

"I am not," she said quietly, meeting his gaze as she shook her head. The guild master sucked in a sharp breath.

"GUARD!" he called out. Nelenie took a step back from him, and bumped into the guard that had come running into the room behind her. "Take her to the lockups. I will deal with her myself."

"No!" Nelenie screamed as the guard grabbed her by the arm. "I can explain, please!" Her guild master turned his back, his head in his hands in grief. That simple act was her undoing, and Nelenie was reduced to sobs. "NO….no no no…" Her voice echoed off the moss-covered walls as she was lead to the cells, and soon there was no sound, save the clanging of the metal door and the click of the lock.

"Elysiam, daughter of Elaith, your deeds have caused your mother such great pain that she has made a very difficult decision," said Captain Silverwind as he glared down at Elysiam through the slits in his shiny metal helm. "You, the progeny of one of the leaders of the druid guild, should sneak off to be in cohort with a rebel daughter of Alynatalos! What did you think she would really have planned for you, foolish young one? Were you going to be her equal? Surely you know the high elves and their feelings toward those of us in the trees better than that." Elysiam made no sound, but held his gaze with a ferocity that made him look away. "You are no longer a daughter of the druids, nor of Elaith. You are no longer a daughter of Sephine." At that, Elysiam sucked in a sharp breath, but still did not respond. She was kneeling on the floor in the main hall of the guild of druids, with her mother in front of her and her many sisters and brothers to either side of the guild master. Elaith made no sound, and did not even shed a tear as she glared down at Elysiam. "Have you any final words for this wretch?" he said, addressing Elaith.

"No." That one word from her mother nearly broke Elysiam. She swallowed hard and forced her gaze over to that of her mother, her eyes burning with a white-hot mixture of anger and betrayal. Her mother met her gaze with one of equal fury, but Elysiam did not look away.

"Have you any last words for this assembly?" Silverwind barked at Elysiam.

"Aye." She took a deep breath. "May Kildir's breath be always at your backs." Elysiam stood on shaky legs, her arms bound in front of her at the wrists. "You accuse our cousins in Alynatalos of looking down on us, thinking we are nothing but savages and simpletons. Yet what is this? What have you done to one of your own who wanted NOTHING more than to be able to better protect you?" Elysiam's voice quavered with mitigated rage as she fought against screaming at them. "You have proven them right. I can only hope that you will one day see that the elitism that glimmers off the shining walls of that citadel echoes in the tree branches of our own city. If this is service to Sephine, you can bloody well keep it!" Silverwind growled and took Elysiam by the arm, and then dragged her toward the door. "Goodbye, MOTHER!" Elysiam hissed as the guard pulled her along to the edge of the platform.

"If you tell anyone I did this I will deny it," Silverwind whispered in Elysiam's ear as he spun her around to face him and quickly took off her wrist shackles. He looked into her eyes for a moment. "I understand your motives, Elys. I understand you, better than you think." She stared at him, slack-jawed, as he pulled her close to him for a moment. "Cast healing magic on the way down and when you land, run south east. When you see the forest flatten into the grasslands, head straight for that and you will be free," he said, and then released her. "The Outpost will take you."

"But I don't…what? On the way down what?" Elysiam said, and then horror-struck, she realized what he was about to do. "Silver, don't, please…" She closed her eyes as he hauled her over the edge of the high platform and released her. Her stomach flipped up into her throat as she fell, and she barely remembered his instruction to cast a spell of healing before she crashed into the soft, mossy forest floor. She opened her eyes to see him, a tiny speck on the edge of the platform, salute her and then disappear. Elysiam wasted no time in getting to her feet, casting a bit more healing magic, and then beating feet southeast to find the grasslands and her new life.

Across the forest in Alynatalos, Nelenie was brought before a tribunal of her own kind. Ben was sitting outside of the gate room that lead to the great halls, watching the shimmering sunrise on the magical lake that surrounded it, when he heard the boots of several soldiers tromping toward him. He quickly cast an invisibility spell, and moved to the side of the great doors just before they opened and a quad of sentries led by the knight's guild master marched past him with a bound and chained Nelenie in the middle of them. Her head was high and even though she squinted into the sun that reflected off the golden walls of the city, her gaze was one of authority. Just like the holy knight she is, Ben thought. He quickly and imperceptibly fell into step behind the cadre of military personnel, curious as to the punishment they would deliver for Nelenie's crimes.

She did not say a word all the way to the great hall, nor did she make a sound when the soldiers forced her to her knees in the middle of the marble floor. The guild master stepped out of the mass of armor and weaponry and turned to face Nelenie. "Will you have anyone here to witness, Nelenie?" he asked, his voice tight. She had long been one of his best pupils and a favorite of the entire guild, and this turn of events was clearly wearing on him.

"No, sir," she said, her voice loud and clear and absent of any intimidation.

Ben dropped his invisibility. "In the place of her family, if it pleases you, General, I would witness for Nelenie? Perhaps this way it will save her family a bit of disgrace should the proceedings go in a way not befitting a long-standing family of such as hers?" Nelenie's brave exterior crumbled as she spun her head around to stare at Ben. He met her gaze, smiling at her, and she smiled back before mouthing a thank you to him.

"Taeben, were you not the informant in this matter?" the General replied coolly. "Do you have another agenda or do you truly wish to stand witness for this disgraced knight of Alynatalos?" Nelenie's gaze rocketed back and forth between the General and Ben, her eyes saucer-like, but she said nothing.

"I was merely concerned for the welfare of my fellow citizen," Ben said, his countenance utterly calm and projecting concern. "It was my fear that the wood elf had gained entry under false pretenses in order to cause chaos within our fair city's walls, and, worse even, to harm our Nelenie." He smiled at her again, ignoring the narrowing of her eyes in his direction.

"Of course, of course," the General replied, much to Ben's great relief. "We shall continue, then. Nelenie, daughter of Alynatalos and follower of the sacred path, you have been found to be teaching the ways of our people to outsiders, something you know to be forbidden." He walked over close to Nelenie and looked down at her. "You are one of our brightest and best, Nel," he said, his voice lowered. "Tell me that what you are accused of is not true. Please."

Nelenie sucked in a deep breath and held it for a moment before releasing it to speak. "It is with great regret that I must tell you it is true, General, sir," she said, not meeting his gaze but rather looking off to the side of him as she had been taught. "Though if I may be permitted, I did have the best of intentions and the security of all of the forest on my heart and mind when I made the decision to take Elysiam on in training."

"The best of…security of…" the General spluttered, his face rapidly growing crimson under his helm. "We, the high elves of the citadel, are the security and, in fact, the very support that keeps the forest safe from the dark forces that would overtake us. You have been trained in that way, Nelenie, and yet you somehow feel your training is lacking?"

"No, sir," she said quickly.

"Then why would you think it necessary to include the wood elf Elysiam in this training? Have you lost faith in your race?" he bellowed. Nelenie swallowed hard, trying not to let her emotions rise to the surface and overtake her.

"No, sir."

"You make no sense, child," the General said as he turned on his heel and returned to the front of the hall. "While I have it on good authority that the information you imparted illegally to the wood elf known as Elysiam will go no further than her ears, I feel that you must be made an example so that others with similar sympathies toward our wayward cousins will not repeat your mistakes." He turned to face Nelenie. "On your feet, soldier," he commanded, all traces of emotion gone from his voice. Nelenie obeyed, though still shackled she managed to rise gracefully to her full height. Ben's heart caught in his throat, awaiting the decree from the General.

"Yes, sir," Nelenie said, planting her feet and raising her eyes to stare into those of the General.

"You will leave Alynatalos," he said, his voice cool and even. "While you are not banished from our home here in the forest, you will make no residence within our walls. You are hereby relieved of your duties as knight in the service of Sephine, the All-Mother. You may earn your living as a mercenary, but you may not solicit work from anyone here in the citadel." Nelenie stared straight ahead, no emotion visible on her face. Ben gripped the wall he was standing next to for support to keep his anger in check. This was NOT the agreement he had made with the General! "Do you understand what I have told you, child?"

"Yes, sir," Nelenie said.

"And for you, Taeben, will you bear witness to this proceeding and inform Nelenie's family of the outcome?" Ben turned to stare at the General.

"If I may, sir, why can't she bear this news to her own family if she is not being banished?" he asked. "I am happy to vouch for this former soldier and take her under my wing that she may see the error of her ways and perhaps one day be permitted to return to..."

"Silence!" The General stared at Ben. "Will you carry the information, yes or no? The matter of her punishment is resolved."

"Yes." Ben fought back the urge to let loose a few well-placed lightning bolts on the head of the General as he stood up straight and turned to face Nelenie. "Your family will be told of your countenance and acceptance of your fate," he said, following the ritual of trials as held in Alynatalos. He turned on his heel to leave, still fuming.

"WAIT!" Nelenie cried out, stopping everyone in their tracks. "Will you take care of my sister?" she asked, her eyes filling with tears that she had held back since the quad came to fetch her from her cell earlier. "Please, Ben, look after Tairn? She is young and impressionable and…powerful." Her voice caught in her throat as the guards moved closer to her to keep her from running after him.

"Aye, Nel," he said without turning back to face her. She did not need to see the wickedness that crept into his gaze as he thought about her redheaded younger sister. "I will look after her. You can be certain of that." He would indeed look after Tairneanach, and all the beautiful redheaded children she would bear him. The power that the blending of their bloodlines would impart was staggering. Taeben barely managed to wait until he was out of the building before he grinned.

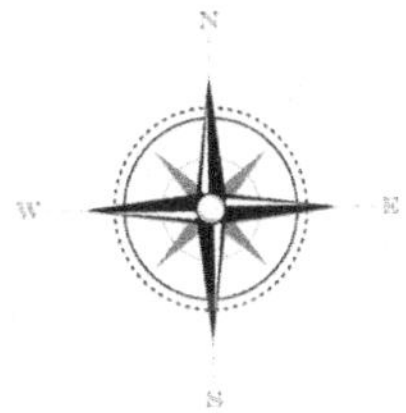

# EIGHT

As Dorlagar sped across the verdant expanse of the southern end of the forest, Gin kicked and scratched at him like an angry cat. Thankfully, he had thought to sheathe his blade before he picked her up at the lift by the Aynamaede, or he would not have had a free hand to cover her mouth and she would have been screaming as well. Finally, he decided that he was far enough away and it would be safe to put her down. For such a small thing, carrying her was starting to slow him down. He skidded to a stop but held onto Gin for a few minutes longer. "If I put you down, will you promise not to run?" She nodded. "If I take my hand away, will you scream?" She shook her head. He took his hand away and she remained silent, her eyes burning twin holes in his own. "Okay, I'm putting you down now, remember, you promised not to run."

Her boots made no sound as they hit the grass. She shook

herself, her indigo tinted armor making a soft tinkling sound as though it was made of bells. Dorlagar could see that she was tempted to run. Her emotions were clear in the scowl she wore as she stared up at him. He took a chance and bent forward to stretch out his back, groaning loudly as the knots under his shoulder blades loosened a bit. His neck muscles were still as tight as a bowstring so he could not see the wood elf from this position and he was certain that there would be a blow or some sort of defensive magic hurtling his way soon. "Stop staring at me, wood elf, it's unnerving."

"My name is Ginolwenye."

"Gin..ol…what?"

"Just call me Gin."

Dorlagar stood up and looked down at her, smirking as she took a step backward. "You look like a little blueberry in that armor. I heard the guard say something that sounded like that word, must have been your name." He made a show of dusting off his chest plate. "These tiny boot prints might not be noticeable."

"Was there something you wanted," Gin asked, her hands on her hips, "or are you just going to stand there and tell me how small and apparently blue I am?" Dorlagar studied her. There was fear behind her words and her eyes.

"No, just needed you to make sure those guards didn't just shoot me in the back as I ran. They did not and now I am no longer in need of you." He found that the shocked look on her face hurt him a bit, but he pushed that feeling into the back of his mind and concentrated again on the task at hand. "I have urgent business and the people in your cursed city were of no help so I must be on my way."

Again, the look on her face surprised him, as the fear and

anger melted into compassion. "Your…sister, yes?" she said.

"What did you say?"

"You are searching for your sister, are you not?"

Dorlagar grabbed Gin up by the shoulders and pulled her close to his face. "What do you know of my sister?" he demanded. Her eyes widened as she averted her gaze toward the ground, but she said nothing. He shook her slightly. "What do you know of Raedea?"

"Nothing, really," she said, her voice barely a whisper. "I only know what I saw in your mind as you were being attacked by our guard." The wood elf swallowed hard before continuing to speak, and Dorlagar put her down hurriedly. No need to terrify her if she was willing to speak. He marveled for a moment at this surge of compassion that he felt toward this strange female. It was a feeling buried long ago, not seen since… "I tried to stop them but they wouldn't listen because you are a human and…" She hung her head.

"I did not realize," he replied, chagrined. This was another strange emotion.

Gin stared up at him for a long moment. "Is there…oh, I can't believe what I'm about to ask you…can I help?" He stared back at her in disbelief, quickly followed by suspicion. "Her name is Raedea, yes?"

"Why are you offering to help me?" he asked, one eyebrow raised as he glared at her.

The wood elf looked genuinely dumbfounded by his question. "Because you need help," she said matter-of-factly. "Where was the last place you saw her?"

"I have not seen her since we were children," he replied flatly.

"Okay, that was not the right question to ask," Gin said. She thought for a moment before she spoke. "Where was she the last time you heard from her?" He noticed her shoulders sag with relief when he nodded.

"She told me that she was going to join the Order at the Temple of Isona, in a letter many seasons ago." Dorlagar bit the inside of his cheek as his fists clenched. "She had waited for me to return home for a long time, I think. Finally, she gave up and left to join the Order. I didn't get the letter right away, but several seasons after she wrote it, so I don't know if she is still there or…There was another letter, from the Sisters of the Order, that stated she was dead but I don't think that is true."

"If it is a lie, that is a very good place to start, at that temple," Gin said. "I am not familiar with this Isona, is she a human goddess?" Dorlagar sighed loudly. "I have never left the forest," she said, pride clear in her face and her voice. He tried not the laugh, but his amusement broke forth in a grin.

"She is a goddess, yes," he said. "Her main Temple is located at Calder's Port, on the Dark Sea. She is a light shining in the darkness, or some such." He shook his head. "Silly superstitions."

"So then we need to head to Calder's Port?"

"I am going to Calder's Port," he said, his smile fading. "You are free, my little blueberry, do as you wish." He turned on his heel and began walking in the direction that he thought would take him out of the forest and toward the Dark Sea to the west. Forgetting that her boots made little to no sound on the lush forest floor, he looked over his shoulder after a few minutes and was surprised to see her in step behind him. "What are you doing?"

"Helping," she said, her eyes on the ground. "It is what I feel I must do." Dorlagar smiled. At the very least, it would be nice not to be alone for the journey. At best, he thought as his eyes began to smolder a deep blood red, she would be good collateral for any humans with a taste for elven females that might have information for him. After many hours of the same trees and low hanging canopy and just general green color all around, the landscape began to change signaling their closeness to one of the human settlements near the Dark Sea.

Many weeks of walking almost silently followed for Gin as she kept pace as best she could with Dorlagar. She wasn't ever sure when she put her head down at night that he would still be there in the morning, and she tried to keep track of where they were in her journal in case he left her behind. Nevertheless, he did not, and even though their conversations were limited to directions and food choices for the most part, she felt safer, somehow, when she would open her eyes at first light and see him sitting with his back to her, scanning the expanse of the grasslands for danger.

"Will we be staying in Calder's Port long?" Gin asked on the third consecutive day of hiking through the tall fields of the Grasslands. She had noticed that the terrain had started to flatten a bit, so she thought they must be close.

"I will stay there as long as it takes to find my sister," came Dorlagar's curt reply, the same as ever. Gin sighed as she trudged along, making mental notes about their path that she would enter into the map she was keeping in her journal. "Why?"

Gin's head snapped up to look at him and she almost ran into him, as he had stopped in the path and turned to face her. "I...was just making conversation," she stammered. Dorlagar exhaled loudly and then turned back to the path, continuing in silence.

Calder's Port was a bustling city but was just as insulated as the tree city where Gin was born. She stared in amazement at the tall buildings made of a mixture of stone and wood and at the humans that seemed to all be in a hurry as they moved about the city's cobblestone streets. Dorlagar was not the first human she had ever seen, but there were so many of them! She was gawking at a couple that strolled arm in arm and did not notice that Dorlagar had stopped until she ran into his backside. "Oof!"

"Do you have magic that will make you invisible?" he asked.

"Um, yes, but I need to consult my spell book," she replied. "Why do you need it?"

"I don't, little one," he said, smirking at her. Gin's hair on the back of her neck stood on end when he made that face, her entire being sounding an alarm, but she tried to ignore it. "Your kind is not often seen here and I'd rather move quickly to the temple." They were just inside the main gate that lead to the inner parts of the city, so Gin took out her spell book and plopped down in the grass to look for the spell. "I suppose I could get us some food," Dorlagar said under his breath. "Don't move." Gin had not intended to move until he was back, and nodded at him as he stalked away. She had just found the right section in her spell book when a shadow fell over her from behind. She turned around to ask the creature casting the shadow to move so that she could read her spell book and laughed aloud at what she saw.

"You working on any spells other than the healing ones?" Nelenie said, grinning down at Gin who hopped to her feet and threw her arms around her oldest friend. "Hey! Watch it; you'll knock yourself out on my armor!"

"Oh, Nel," Gin said, big tears springing to her eyes. "When I heard what they did to you and Elys, it just wasn't fair, I..." Nelenie stopped her with a look, pushing Gin back to arm's length.

"I knew what I was getting into," she said darkly. "So did

Elys. I just wish I knew how they found out. They said it was Ben, but…" Her eyes narrowed. "He had better not cross my path again if I find that to be true."

"You mean Taeben? He would never do anything to hurt you, Nel," Gin said, her eyes wide as saucers. "Never."

"I don't know, Gin," Nelenie said, joining Gin on the grass as she resumed her seat and began packing away her spell book. "You haven't seen him in a long time. I thought that he was apprenticed to become a wizard, didn't you?"

"Yes."

"Well, he can use transport magic and cast spells like a wizard, but can use other, darker magic as well. I didn't know that was possible," Nelenie said, her expression grim. "I have been trying to find my sister since I was exiled, but my family…well…they will have no contact with me. I asked Ben to look after Tairn, but knowing what I know now…" She bit her lip.

"I'm sorry, Nel."

"No, don't be," the knight said, removing her helm and wiping a tear from her eye. "Now, what are you doing these days?"

"I am…on a quest," Gin said halfheartedly. What had seemed exciting and new moments before now seemed silly with Dorlagar not there. "There was…a human that I met in the forest and he needed my help and…well, here I am, still helping but I fear I cannot do much more than keep his cuts and scrapes healed." She studied a stray thread on her tunic. "I do not seem to have it in me to hurt another, even if that other is trying to hurt me."

Nelenie smiled at her. "Tis the hand of our Mother Sephine that has led me to you today, Gin," she said. "I know of a place where your talents will come in handy, and you will learn to use your other druid talents in battle." Gin cocked her head to one side, looking quizzically at her friend. "Before I left Alynatalos, I spent some time working as a mercenary in secret. I worked for anyone that had enough platinum pieces, and often found myself in well over my head." She looked off into the distance for a moment, clearly reliving some of those awful days, and shuddered. "But then I met Naevys and things changed. After my exile, she took me in and gave me shelter, food, and work. She is one of the most talented druids I have ever met in my life."

"Would she…teach me?" Gin asked tentatively. "I don't know if I can abandon the human I am sworn to help, do you think she would understand and perhaps lend aid?"

"I'm sure she would," Nelenie smiled. "She's a wood elf like you." Gin returned Nelenie's broad smile. "Now, how long will it take you to pack up your things?"

"I'm packed," Gin said, "but I don't know about Dorlagar, he's just gone off to get us some food." She paused, noticing Nelenie's slack-jawed expression. "What is wrong?"

"Did you say Dorlagar? Dorlagar of the Dawnshadows?" Nelenie asked, making a display of saying his full name that made Gin laugh at how much it looked like him.

"Aye. Do you know him?"

"I'd say she does," Dorlagar said from behind Gin. She cursed herself inwardly at the surprised squeak that escaped her lips. "And Nel, you know full well that Naevys won't help me in my quest to find my sister, I've already asked and that's why I'm out here alone." Gin cleared her throat loudly. "Well, I'm being followed by a blueberry but otherwise I'm on my own." He and Nelenie laughed and then Nelenie threw her arms around Dorlagar's neck, hugging him tightly.

"She sent me after you, idiot," Nelenie said as she cuffed Dorlagar on the ear. "She has changed her mind and has sent me to help you, and it seems the All-Mother and Kildir have sent us our Ginny to help as well. What?" she asked as Gin scowled at her.

"Don't call me that," Gin said. "It's just Gin now."

"Right, Just Gin," Dorlagar said with a grin, "Shall we go find my sister? Or do you need to go back home first?"

"I don't have a permanent home anymore. Let's go!" Gin said, matching his grin. Nelenie spoke some strange words and an icy cloud surrounded them for a moment, obscuring her view. She jumped at the sound of a loud whinny, moving quickly away from the white horse that appeared next to Nelenie, who swung up into the saddle on the back of the magical steed.

"Do you have a horse?" Nelenie asked as she pulled Dorlagar up onto the horse behind her. Gin shook her head, frowning. "You're in luck, then. Here." Nelenie dug around in one of her packs and produced a rope, which she tossed down to Gin. "Repeat what I just said while holding the bridle. Beau is one of the best magical horses in Naevys's stable." Gin did as she was told, and then gasped as a smaller black pony appeared next to Nelenie's massive white horse. The magical animal nuzzled Gin's shoulder until she turned around and stroked his nose.

"Hello, Beau," she said softly as the horse let out an equally soft whinny into her hand. "Oh, Nel, he is magnificent!" She swung up into the saddle as she had seen her friend do moments before, giggling like a young elf as she settled onto the back of the pony. "It's like he was made for me!"

"In a way, he was," Nelenie said. "It's part of their magic. Now, shall we?" She kicked her horse lightly in the ribs and it moved into a slow trot. Gin did the same and she and Nelenie's horses headed for the front gate leading away from Calder's Port.

"We are camping near the grasslands," Nelenie explained as Dorlagar protested the direction. "We need to check in with her and introduce her to Gin." She winked at Gin who smiled back at her childhood friend. "You're going to love Naevys, I just know it!"

Months went by, and Gin was accepted into the little "Family of Misfits" that the druid called Naevys had fashioned for herself. The hunt for Raedea had resumed immediately, but the trail grew more and more cold and soon Naevys again called it off. Dorlagar's disappointment and anger were palpable with every interaction with his sworn leader, but he always managed to stop himself just short of attacking verbally or physically.

Many nights that found Dorlagar sitting by the fire talking strategy with another member of the group, Lyrea, a half-elf, as Gin wrote hasty letters home to Cursik and Lairky. Gin had never met a half-elf before, though she had heard of their existence. Like most of her race, Lyrea had chosen to live with her human relatives rather than her Elvish ones, but she had returned to the forest to seek out her mother's people and met Naevys. The two became fast friends and started hunting together. They met Dorlagar along their travels and he fell in with them, hoping they could help him find answers about his sister's death. Finally, Nelenie had become a part of the family and with Gin, Naevys declared that they were complete and ready to take on all that adventuring through Orana had to offer.

They were sitting around the campfire one night, deep in the Grasslands, plotting an attack on the dark elves that had taken over a stronghold in the southeastern corner of the forest, when Naevys called Gin off to one side. "A word, my darling Gin?" the older druid said. Gin immediately got up and followed her new mentor. "I want to tell you that I am so proud of you for being such an efficient healer when we are engaged in battle, dearie,"

Naevys said. "Truly, you are amazing, and have saved all our lives many times over."

"But you want me to learn to use my other skills as a druid, I suppose?" Gin asked apprehensively. "The offensive magic?"

Naevys smiled at her, an almost sad expression on her face. "My dear, you are not fit for that."

Gin's mouth popped open in surprise, forming a perfect O. "Not…fit?" she stammered.

"No, pet, you aren't." Naevys smoothed a bit of hair that had escaped her ponytail behind one of Gin's ears, her actions resembling a mother interacting with a child. Her hawkish stare held Gin's gaze for a moment before she spoke. "You are not made of stern stuff like our Nel there. You are a healer and a caretaker, nothing more, nothing less."

"But…Nel said you could help me with the other parts of being a druid!" Gin said, almost stamping her tiny foot in annoyance. A raised eyebrow from Naevys silenced her. "Apologies," she muttered, casting her gaze down at the floor.

"None needed, dearie," Naevys said, still looking at her with a raised eyebrow and a suspicious gaze. "I just want to make sure that you know your place in our little family. I know it was you that threw out the magical stinging insects on our last opponent, and while it did help us beat back the foe it took your focus away from your role, which is keeping all of us bathed in healing magic."

"So…I don't need to learn all those spells?"

"No, I'm not saying that at all. There may be times when you are alone and need to defend yourself," Naevys said, a slight trace of annoyance creeping into her voice. If Gin noticed it, she paid it no mind. "I am saying that you need to know your place. That is all. Does that make sense, dearie?" Gin looked up into that face that so resembled her own, their racial features so similar, but saw in the elder druid's eyes a different spark than she knew looked out from her own icy blue eyes. Naevys's eyes shone with a lust for battle and carnage that should never have taken hold in a follower of the All-Mother.

"Aye," Gin said, resentment bubbling up within her. After all, both Naevys and Lyrea possessed skills in magic that could offer healing to the wounded. Why was she being singled out to sit back out of the fray, on her horse Beau? She had to know the truth. "May I ask, at least, is it that I am not good enough to fight?" Tears overflowed her lashes and coated her cheeks.

Naevys sighed loudly. "No, my dearie, you aren't. I'm sorry to say that, but it's the truth." Gin blinked a few times and then nodded her head, saying nothing. Naevys patted her on the shoulder and returned to the group, leaving Gin alone with her spell book. The younger druid stared down at the pages, wishing that she could erase all the words there that she would never say with the tears still falling onto the long ago dried ink. The damaging magic that she was supposed to know, she now would never use.

"Better to stay with what I know, I suppose," she murmured as she wiped her eyes. She replaced the spell book in her haversack and then joined the others at the fire.

"You all right, Blueberry?" Dorlagar asked her. He studied her face, as he did so often when he thought she was asleep around the fire and it was his turn for night watch. She was sure he had memorized every line and crease in her face and the soft waves of her hair.

Gin scowled at him. "Don't call me that," she said.

"What's wrong?" Nelenie scooted closer, in between Gin

and Dorlagar. "What did Naevys say to you?" Her eyes searched Gin's own. "You aren't…leaving us are you?"

"What? No!" Gin stared back at her old friend. "Never, Nel. Never. She just wanted to make sure I didn't have any questions about any of the spells I'm learning, is all," she lied. Nelenie's stare burned into Gin's eyes. "What? That's all it was, I promise." It was not exactly a lie.

"Okay, well, if you go I go," Nelenie said. "We're in this together, yeah?" She squeezed Gin's hand and then, making fleeting eye contact with Dorlagar, got up from the fireside and wandered out into the woods to collect more firewood.

"I'm, uh…glad you're not going," Dorlagar stammered. Gin's eyes met his and she thought for a moment that he had stopped breathing.

"Thanks." Gin looked down at the ground. "I'll try really hard not to get any of you killed." She stood up and wandered along behind where Nelenie had entered the forest, knowing that if she did not get away from all of them she would burst into tears. Once she was past the tree line, she spoke quick words and magically assumed the form of one of the nearby trees. Now I can think…and cry, she thought.

Dorlagar sprinted after her, stopping as he entered the trees and could no longer see her. "I'm glad you're not going because you're mine, Blueberry," he whispered, his voice low and menacing. He leaned against a tree for a moment, and then pulled his hand back in shock. It felt warm, not like a tree at all! Backing away, he said silent words of protection before sprinting back to the campfire. The tree he had touched shook slightly, and then shrank until it was again the form of a wood elf.

Gin wrapped her arms around her body to try to control her shaking. Everything was going wrong. Why was Nelenie mixed up with this lot? What had Dorlagar meant, she was his?

All she had ever wanted to do was help him find his sister, and that seemed to be a dead end. She had never given him reason to think of her that way…had she? "I have to get away from here and go back home," she whispered. "But how?" She sat down on the forest floor to think. A shout from their camp a few minutes later interrupted her thoughts. Gin hopped to her feet and ran back toward the campfire. Everyone gathered there, anxiously awaiting Naevys to speak. The white-haired wood elf was perched on top of her mount, watching them with her silvery gaze.

"My darlings, we have a rare privilege," she said, looking each of them in the eye. "Each of you, even our Gin who has not been with us long, has come so far in your training and I could not be more proud. Nevertheless, to be able to fight together, you must know and trust each other. You must be able to depend on each other's abilities as though they are your own, and you must recognize your own weaknesses as well as those of the others. In that, we will cease to be individuals and will function as one being against those that would challenge us." Her horse whinnied and she patted the magical animal on the neck, calming it.

"I think we know each other pretty well," Dorlagar said. His eyes skated over Gin and then wandered back to Nelenie, who grinned at him. Gin saw the interaction and frowned, but then let it go.

"Aye, you do, but the only real way to test your skills and that knowledge is with the event I have planned for us," Naevys said, positively vibrating with excitement. Gin's stomach clenched as Naevys walked around the group, handing each an envelope bearing her own seal. "This will tell you where to go and when to be there." Pulling her companion Lyrea to her side, Naevys spoke ancient Elvish words of transportation magic. The two winked out of existence, leaving Nelenie, Dorlagar, and Gin standing there staring at their envelopes. They opened them, staring at the contents a moment, then at each other.

"She can't be serious!" Gin exclaimed.

"This is fabulous!" Nelenie said happily. "Gin, you can take us there, right?"

"Yeah, let's get going. Hug the druid," Dorlagar said, moving a bit too close to Gin for her own comfort as she recited the spell. "Finally, a real chance to find my sister and punish those that took her from me." The familiar feeling overtook Gin, that of being pulled inside out, and she closed her eyes as the spell took hold. "Home," she said, the final word in the spell determining where they would land.

The familiar smell of the forest filled Gin's head and she opened her eyes to find herself on her backside on the lush grass. She paused a moment before getting to her feet to thank the All-Mother for safe travel and sink her fingers into the strong ground beneath her. "Sorry about the landing," she said as she stood up. Nelenie, still on the ground, laughed.

"Not the first time, and it won't be the last time," she said, winking at Gin as Dorlagar helped her up. He pulled a bit harder than she was expecting, and Nelenie fell into his arms, giggling. Gin turned her back to them and unrolled the map that Naevys had given them. Hopefully, this mission would see Dorlagar reunited with his sister and Gin back on her way home. She sighed as she began following Nelenie and Dorlagar away from the direction of the lift that would carry her up to her people, to her home in the trees. They headed south to Calder's Port.

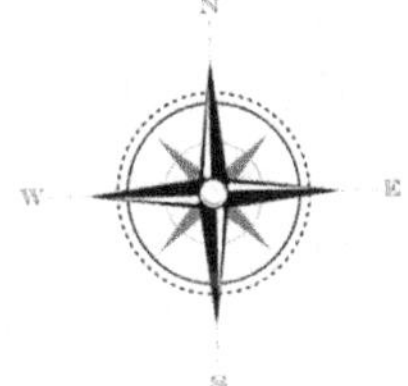

# NINE

Raedea nearly fell through the door of the pub, overcome with exhaustion. This was the last establishment before the landscape began to rise into small hills and the dark forest that was home to the elven races of Orana. She slung her bag into a chair and sat down next to it, happy to be off her weary feet.

"Room for the night, pet, or just a pint and a meal?" asked a woman that seemed to appear out of nowhere at the end of the table that Raedea was slumped across. She looked up to find warm, friendly blue eyes looking out at her from a halo of orange curls. She returned the woman's smile.

"All of the above, if you don't mind?" Raedea replied. "But...I don't have much..." She dug into her backpack while holding up a finger to the barmaid. She retrieved a small pouch from her bag and fumbled around inside. "One platinum piece," she said, face flushed with embarrassment. "Will that be enough for a night's rest? I don't really need any food, I suppose, if that will…"

"Shush you!" the woman replied, grinning from ear to ear. "That's plenty for supper and breakfast and a clean and comfortable bed for the night." She snatched the coin from Raedea and started for the kitchen, but then turned back and ran a hand over the top of Raedea's head, a familiar gesture from Raedea's childhood. It was then that Raedea looked past the hair and the dancing blue eyes and saw the wrinkles around the corners of the woman's eyes and across her from years of smiling. Tears sprang unbidden to Raedea's own eyes as she remembered her own mother.

"Thank you," she whispered and the barmaid nodded, a knowing smile on her face as she headed for the kitchen. Once again, Raedea nearly melted into the table, this time from a mix of fatigue and the overwhelming memories that flooded her mind and heart. She stayed in that position until she heard a commotion behind her and sat back up to see what was going on.

"Oh, no, not again," the same barmaid was saying as she pushed back against the tallest figure Raedea had ever seen. "You couldn't pay the last two times, Cat."

"Oh, Ivy, come on now," said a deep voice from under the hood that obscured the face of the tall figure. He was clearly male, but had the strangest undertone to his voice that Raedea had ever heard. It was almost like a purr, but was her mind imagining that because the barmaid, whose name was apparently Ivy, had called him "Cat"? Raedea had heard of a settlement on an island in the northwest, past the forest of the elves, where a race of felines lived who were as large as humans and walked upright. They were called the Qatu, but Raedea had never believed that they were real…until now.

"Nope, sorry Sath, not happening," Ivy said, but her eyes told another story. Raedea could hear the purring sound now and wondered if that was why Ivy seemed to soften a bit. "I can let you have a pint, I'm not a monster, but that's all, you hear me?"

"Course I do, darlin," he replied, still not removing his hood as he moved past her. "Hey, what's going on here?" he said as he stopped in front of Raedea. "Excuse me, little girl, you okay?" Raedea realized he was talking to her when he waved a hand in front of her face…but it was more like a paw, really, than a hand. His long fingers, covered with cream-colored fur tipped in black, ended in horrible sharp claws. She jumped back a bit and looked up into teal eyes that seemed to glow in the darkness of the hood. "Does she not talk, this one?" he asked over his shoulder toward Ivy who was pulling a pint for him behind the bar.

"Sit down, you big hairball," she said as she wiped the overflowing foam from the edge of the glass and brought it to table near where Raedea was sitting, transfixed. "Leave the other customers alone."

"Yes ma'am," he replied, knocking his hood back with one clawed finger. Raedea gasped in spite of herself. "Lemme guess, never seen a Qatu before, right?" His gaze held her fast as he took a deep swallow of his pint.

Raedea took a deep breath and managed to find her voice. "No, I haven't," she said. Glancing around toward the bar, she hoped to see Ivy coming with her food, but there was no one there. "I apologize for staring, good sir." She looked down at her hands, lacing her fingers together in front of her. After a moment or two, she could feel that he was still staring at her and she looked back.

"What's your name, ma'am?" he said as his gaze seemed to bore into her. "I'm Sath…"

"Yes, I heard Ivy call you that," Raedea replied. "Well, that and Cat." She grinned but the smile faded as she noticed that he was not smiling. "My name is…Rae."

"Nice to meet you, Rae," Sath replied, nodding toward her and finally cracking a smile. Raedea could see why he had not smiled before…his teeth were that of a large cat, and she found herself unable to breathe for a moment as her mind called up memories of the wild cats that she had faced in her journey through the grasslands. Some of those encounters had ended a little too close for comfort. She swallowed hard and looked away just as Ivy appeared with a steaming bowl of stew and a large loaf of bread on one tray and a pint on the other. Thankful for the distraction, Raedea smiled up at Ivy and then picked up a spoon to sample the food. She glanced back over at Sath and noticed that he was staring again, but this time at her food. She sighed and after a quick word of thanks to the Gods, she put down her spoon.

"When was the last time you ate?" she asked. The Qatu looked up at her and then quickly looked away. "Seriously. When?"

"Why?"

"Because I have well more than I need here and if you are hungry I would like very much for you to have some of this food, that's why," she replied as matter-of-factly as she could. The truth was that she saw the hunger in his eyes and she did not want to become his dinner once she was alone and unprotected in her room for the night. Better that he should have a full belly if she could make that so.

"Why?" he asked, cocking one furry eyebrow. "You afraid I'll eat you instead?" Again, his face split into a grin but this time he gave her a clear view of all of his teeth and she jumped involuntarily. His face fell. "That's what I thought," he said. "Thanks, but no thanks." He turned his attention back to his pint.

Raedea was horrified at her own reaction. What would her Goddess say to see her treating this creature with something less than mercy? She stood up from the table, gathered the bowl of stew and the bread and took it over to Sath's table. Without a word, she put the food in front of him and then turned back to the table to get her pint. When she turned back, he was staring up at her. "Let me get another spoon," she said, "and we can share it."

Several hours later, they were still at the table. Ivy had long since retired for the evening, having given the two of them two large casks of ale and several helpings of stew and bread before she left. "So, what did you say you did to that lowlife Havens?" Sath asked, his words slurring a bit. He had taken off his cloak and Raedea marveled at how human his appearance was, though covered head to clawed toes in fur. She also wondered at how she was no longer as afraid of him as she had been only a few short hours earlier.

"I didn't do anything," she said, cheeks flushing slightly with embarrassment. "I am only permitted to kill when it is in defense of my life and there is no other option available to me or in order to have food to eat. And with the latter, I eat mostly plants and other foods that I can obtain without killing."

"Like that stew we just polished off?" Sath said, leaning forward a bit and grinning. Rather than flinching like she would have before, Raedea leaned in and returned his grin.

"Touché, good sir," she said, chuckling. "I suppose I take some comfort in the fact that it was not I that dispatched the cow that provided the beef for the stew, but not much in truth." She ran a finger around the rim of the bowl, collecting any bit of stew that was left there, and then popped her finger into her mouth, sucking on it for a moment before she spoke. "But enough of me, what is your story, Sath?"

"Oh, not nearly as interesting as yours," he said, picking a bit of food out of his teeth with one of his claws. "I fear it would bore both of us to sleep.'

"Then tell me about your people," Raedea said, leaning on her elbows with her fingers steepled under her chin. "You know that I have never met anyone like you before. What is it your race is called again?"

"Qatu. I have always thought it was ridiculously obvious that we are called Cat-Too," Sath replied, chuckling. "I guess at some point it was thought we wouldn't be able to remember who we were otherwise."

"Well, didn't the god or goddess that created you give you that name?"

Sath raised an eyebrow at her. "No deity created the Qatu," he replied, clearly amused. "Do they not teach you the history of our world in your homeland?"

Raedea's brow wrinkled as she frowned at him. "Of course they do. However, forgive me, Sath, so little is known about your kind that we are only taught that you exist, but not much more. You are as exotic to us as the dragonkind."

It was Sath's turn to frown. "Bah, I have no need of the dragonkind, nor do they have need of us." His face darkened as he took a long drink from his glass before continuing to speak. "Our legends teach that we were once beasts, like those that you no doubt have encountered as you have moved farther and farther away from the settlement at Calder's Port." Raedea nodded, not daring to speak for fear that if she did, he would stop telling her the story of his kind. She found his voice, in combination with the ale that she had consumed, to be soothing to the point of making her a little sleepy, so she sat up straighter in her chair. "We were merely giant cats, roaming the Grasslands and living our lives as creatures with no real sentience. We were afraid of humans, but not of much else that we found in our world.

"Then one day, there was a great rumble throughout our world. It was as though Orana herself had shouted and broken her very crust. The dragonkind, who had been hibernating in her mountains, burst forth in the fiery lava that erupted from their peaks, and with them came the magic of Orana. That magic touched everything on her surface, from plants and trees to oceans to even the beings that lived in her care." He paused a moment to take a sip of his ale. "I am assuming that nothing I have told you so far is new, darlin?"

"No, you assume correctly. We learned about the birth of the dragons and the dragonkind," she said, still entranced by his story.

Sath smiled at her. "Well here is something you don't know. When that magic flowed out alongside the lava and dragons, it swept over the face of our world and filled Orana's creations. It created the druids and rangers from the wood elves, those already so in touch with our world that it was not a stretch for them to be able to control the natural world. It filled the high elves of Alynatalos and gave them the powers of healing and protection, as they were best suited to watch over their elven cousins."

"And it filled my kind with a mix of all of it," Raedea said, finding herself becoming a bit anxious to hear of the Qatu and uninterested in what she had already learned from school. "We are healers and druids, we are rangers and knights, and we have also some that learn the ways of the darker side of Orana's magic."

"Aye, the corrupted ways of those elves that choose to live underground and take from the source directly," Sath said, spitting and hissing a bit. "I underestimated your education, darlin. Then how is it that you do not know of the creation of the Qatu?"

Raedea shrugged her shoulders. "We truly did not learn anything about you, Sath. I do not know why, but I always assumed you were a sort of...byproduct, if you will, of the dragonkind." His face twisted into a snarl that told her he did not care for that analogy, but softened as he looked at her.

"We are a byproduct, of sorts," he said, resigned. "It was the magic of Orana that filled us, the highest order of beast that she had created, which caused some of us to begin to evolve. My ancestors were the beasts that had traveled the farthest away from the others of our kind, and we think that's why the change occurred only in us." He took another sip of his ale and, upon discovering that his glass was empty, frowned. "Several generations were required for us to become the modern Qatu. Our language evolved from the vocalizations our ancestors used to communicate very basic information, which is why I have been told that Qatunari sounds like growling and purring." He chuckled. "Have you ever heard it?"

"No! Would you teach me some?" Raedea asked eagerly.

"Ah, I would be honored," Sath said, "but not tonight. I think that coming to the end of my story and the ale at the same time are signs too obvious to be ignored." He stood and stretched, still a bit wobbly from the ale. "Perhaps I shall meet you here again another night and we can trade languages? Surely you know more than the common tongue, yes?"

Raedea smiled. "I know most of the languages, actually," she said, blushing again. "It was my favorite subject in my training at the Temple." She glowered a bit. "I will not be here after tonight, I fear. Where are you staying?"

Sath laughed sadly. "Wherever I can find a tree and some soft ground," he said.

Raedea smiled up at him and then shook her head. "No you aren't. You may stay in my room tonight; it is already paid for." Sath raised his eyebrows as his eyes widened in surprise. Raedea looked at him for a moment, puzzled, before his misunderstanding occurred to her. "OH! No, no I am not suggesting… I mean not that we… or that you and I…no, not at all." Her face flushed as red as her cloak that she quickly gathered up and fussed over until she got herself back together. "I meant…"

Sath put one clawed finger in front of her lips to stop her from talking. "No worries, *darlin,*" he said gently. "I understand what you meant. I have a bedroll and will happily take the spot in front of the fireplace in your room for the night." His gaze caught hers and held it, and she could see the depth of his sincerity. "I promise you, nothing will happen tonight except two friends getting a good night sleep. We are friends, aren't we?"

Raedea nodded and held out her hand to him. He took it, grasping her forearm as she did the same to his. "Aye we are. Raedea Dawnshadow at your service, sir," she said with a grin.

"Sathlir Clawsharp, at yours my lady," he replied as they both broke out into a fit of laughter. Raedea led him up the stairs to the tiny room she had rented, feeling happy and safe for the first time in many seasons. She saw him pause out of the corner of her eye as she put her bag down next to the bed, and then smiled as he came on inside and shut the door. "Shall I bolt it?" he asked tentatively.

"Yes, please," she said. He laid the bolt carefully in place and then crossed the room. Raedea was amazed at how silently he could move, being as big as he was. He rolled out his bedroll in front of the fireplace, taking care to be a safe distance in case there were sparks.

"Good night, my lady," he said. Raedea had turned around and was climbing into bed herself, but looked over her shoulder as he spoke. His teal eyes were warm as they met her gaze, but still guarded.

"Rae, please. Call me Rae," she said. "Sleep well, Sath."

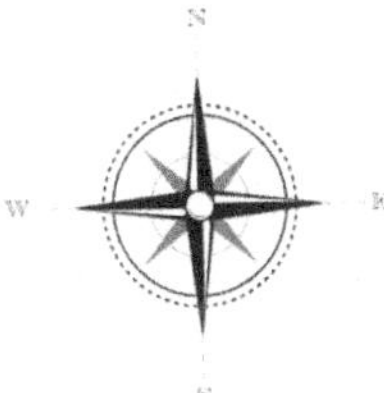


# TEN

The months wore on for Gin as she and the rest of her little tribe struck out following dead end after dead end in pursuit of Dorlagar's sister: it became one year, and then two since she had taken up with them. She watched, concerned, as the light seemed to drain out of his eyes like sand through an hourglass. He became calculated, cold, and heartless in his hunting and killing, and she no longer felt safe with him nearby. To make matters worse, Naevys had said to her on several occasions that she was sure that Dorlagar had some very strong feelings for her and that Gin was to make sure that he did not leave their little family, regardless of how she did it. And the more Gin pulled back from Dorlagar, the more Nelenie seemed to be drawn to him, a fact that worried Gin and often kept her up at night.

They had stopped for a time near Calder's Port to

replenish their stores of food and water, and Dorlagar spent a lot of that time in the local pub. They had looked for any signs of his sister in every pub in their path, and only found one barmaid that may have seen her. Ivy, as she was called, told them stories about a human woman matching her description who was traveling with a Qatu whose name she refused to give up. Dorlagar was convinced that was a dead end as well, because his sister would have no way to know any Qatu as none had been seen near human settlements for hundreds of years. The only Qatu that Gin knew anything about was the Bane of the Forest, but even then she didn't know his name.

Dorlagar was drunk most of the time that they were in Calder's Port, and as a result, he did not go out and hunt with them at all. When they returned, he would be waiting out in front of the pub, more often than not because he had been thrown out of it for causing a ruckus. On their last day there, Nelenie and Gin had gone out to hunt just the two of them, and as they headed back to the inn where their rooms were, he was again out front, red in the face and looking for a fight.

"Where have you two been, then?" he called out as they tried to walk past in a hurry.

Nelenie stopped and turned to face him. "Dor, babe, you need sleep. Come on, Gin and I will take you to your room so you can grab a nap before we eat." She reached out for one of his arms and he yanked it away, nearly backhanding Gin in the process. "Okay, you want it the hard way," she muttered. "Fine. Gin, grab his feet once he's off them, yeah?"

"NO!" he bellowed. Gin reached for his knees but did not expect Dorlagar to be moving as quickly as he was. He snatched her up, her head in the crook of his elbow and her feet off the ground. She kicked at him but he merely laughed. "I'll go when I'm ready!" he said, his chuckle turning dark as he spoke.

"Put her down, Dor," Nelenie said, her eyes narrowing as she glared at him. "You don't want to hurt Gin, do you?"

As though he had just figured out who she was, Dorlagar turned her around to face him and kissed her roughly on her cheek. "No, you're right, I don't," he said, flinging Gin to one side. "It's you I want to hurt." As he squared off against Nelenie, she turned back to Gin quickly.

"Go get Naevys," she hissed at Gin and then raised her broadsword to the level of her eyes. Gin scrambled away, jumping as she heard steel clash with steel behind her. They would be lucky if the local militia did not drag both of them to the stocks for fighting in the street. Soon she was running up the stairs to the suite of rooms they had rented and banging on the door with her tiny fists.

The door swung open and Lyrea's angry gaze met hers. "What do you want?" she barked. There was no love lost between them since Gin had asked too many questions about Lyrea's parents, and why she had not chosen to live in Aynamaede with her Elven father.

"It's Nel and Dor, they're fighting in the street," Gin said in a rush, nearly out of breath.

"And?"

"And Nel asked me to get Naevys," Gin snapped. Lyrea was a good foot or so taller than Gin and she moved very close to her, looking down at Gin with fire blazing in her almond-shaped dark brown eyes.

"And I'm telling you not now," the half-elf replied brusquely before slamming the door in Gin's face. Gin stood there a moment, pushing back the angry tears that pricked the backs of her eyelids. She took a breath and again knocked on the door.

There was no answer this time. Gin returned to the room she shared with Nelenie and Dorlagar and began packing her things. This had gone too far. There was nothing for her here, and it was time to try to get back home.

She was sitting on the bed when Nelenie burst through the door, dragging an unconscious Dorlagar along behind her by one of his boots. "What happened to you?" she snapped at Gin. "I sent you for help!"

"Lyrea wouldn't let me get to Naevys," Gin said quietly. "I tried."

With one last shove, Dorlagar was through the doorway and thrown into a heap at the end of one of the beds in the room. His armor was halfway unlaced and his helm was tucked in one of his backpacks under his arm. "You didn't try hard enough and you certainly didn't come back to tell me any of that or help me with him," Nelenie said with a grunt as she slammed their door. "Are you going to eat with them tonight?" Gin shook her head. "Fine, stay here and watch him then." Nelenie crossed the room and pulled off her own helm and then splashed some water on her face and redid her ponytail before storming out the door. Dorlagar stirred, moaned, and then lay down on his back. Gin went over to him and smoothed his hair back before turning him over on his side in case he was sick. She would not be there to help if he was.

Gin quickly replaced her armor, as it was not a good idea to travel through unknown lands unprotected. Once she had all of her armor secured, she slipped out the back door and summoned Beau. She lifted herself up into the saddle and took one long look toward their windows. She was sure that she had heard Dorlagar calling after her as she had scampered down the stairs, and as she rode away, she was certain she heard him calling after her, but she made no answer.

"Never again," she swore under her breath, and clung to Beau's neck as he flew out the front gates and across the countryside toward the forest. "I swear it. I am finished with Naevys and the lot of them." A twinge around her heart gave her pause as she thought of Nelenie, but she had to let that go. This was a new dawn and a new day for her, and thoughts of her old life with them would only hold her back. The minute she was far enough away, she released Beau to the four winds and cast a spell that would take her back home to the forest. Hopefully, the druid's guild would take her back in; as a nanny or servant, it hardly mattered, she would take whatever they offered. Gin lifted her chin as the spell took hold, striking a proud pose even though she was terrified on the inside. "Home," she said as she winked out of sight.

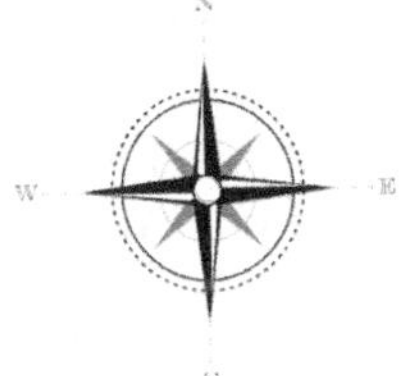

# ELEVEN

Gin was accepted back into the community of wood elves, but many of her former friends kept their distance except to offer pleasantries. The druid's guild took her in and set her to work training young druids, but she was monitored as she led the young ones through their lessons, just as her mentor had led her a few seasons prior. It frustrated her but she knew that Naevys had left no friends in Aynamaede and her association with the older druid had all but ruined Gin's name among her guild.

She was sitting in her classroom one day preparing the next day's lessons when she was interrupted by a loud argument just outside the door. She got up, chuckling as she recognized the voices as belonging to her younger sister, Lairceach, and their cousins Iseabel and Kaewenye.

"There is nothing wrong with being a ranger, Kae," Iseabel

was complaining. She and Gin's own sister had started with the ranger's guild at the same time, as they were the same age. Their strikingly similar appearance had caused quite a stir, and they were known for pulling pranks on their guild masters. Kae, as she was called, pushed a stray lock of jet-black hair behind her ear.

"How do you think rangers like you, who don't have any kind of transportation magic, can get in and out of tight spots? You can't without one of us to scout the way first!" she fired back. On the other side of the door, Gin smiled at the young girl's bravado. She had been that sure of herself once.

"I don't need a scout as long as I have my bow," Iseabel replied sourly. "I can take out enemies before you even reach them while tracking."

"Uh, we can use bows too you know," Lairky (as Gin called her) snapped at Kae. "We may not have the range but we don't need it. With my tracking ability, I can sneak up behind an orc and bury an arrow to the fletching in its grubby neck before it even knows I am there. Beat that!"

"Girls," Gin said, seeing that this argument was going nowhere and deciding to intervene before one of them got a demonstration of the other one's skill with a bow. She stuck her head out of the classroom and the three young wood elves fell silent, each blushing with mortification.

"You won't tell my guild master, will you Ginny?" Lairky said cautiously. Due to their age difference, Gin had been more mother than sister to the young girl; but in her absence Lairky had come to take care of herself. Their older brother, Cursik, spent more and more time away and hunting with the older rangers, and was barely here at all. Gin scowled at the use of the nickname but decided not to bring that up at the moment.

"No, of course not," she said. "But you girls must learn

that every skill is important, none more than any other," Gin said. "Every person has gifts, and as long as you are focused only on your own talents, you will not see those that others have to offer." She smoothed a piece of blonde hair out of Isaebel's face, causing the younger elf to pull back from her touch. Gin frowned. "I wanted to be a ranger like you when I was younger, Izzy," she said softly. Isaebel's eyes widened. "I was going to go against my nature, my family, and my upbringing and be taken into the ranger guild. But it was not to be." She paused a moment to wipe away a tear. "My mentor was killed by…well, she died, most unexpectedly, and I could not think of anything at the time but how that would affect me and my training. She was one of the most talented rangers ever to come from our tree city and I should have joined with the community to mourn her loss but instead I could only think of my own ambitions. It's why I didn't pay attention as I should in my own training, and why now I'm only fit to provide healing magic in battle."

"Well that's just stupid," Lairky said, causing the other two to gasp in surprise. "Seriously. I have seen you, Gin, you're just as good a druid as any other. You just let that traitorous Naevys tell you that you weren't."

"Lairky. That's enough," Gin said, her eyes blazing. "The All-Mother provided for me and made me into a druid as was Her will. If we all stop trying to take control and let Her in, she will provide." She looked from face to face, and then smiled. "What are you girls doing out at this hour anyway?"

"Lairky and I were working on our safe falling skill, Gin," Iseabel said, "when Kae turned up to brag." Iseabel poked her sister in the ribs causing Kae to spin around and draw her dagger.

"I'd like to see YOU jump off that platform and not die, my sister!" she exclaimed as she shoved Iseabel toward the edge.

"ENOUGH," Gin said, and immediately the girls separated. "Lairky, if you would, please take them back to ours and start supper preparations? I will be along soon." The three nodded and headed off toward the hut that Gin shared with her sister while her parents were away on a hunt with the rest of the elder druids. She watched them go for a moment, and then turned around to head back into her classroom.

Arms closed around her and pulled her backward against rough chain mail armor as a hand closed around her mouth. "Don't make a sound," a male voice rasped in her ear. Immediately Gin stilled, not making a peep, and then gasped as she stumbled free. She looked up at her attacker and grinned as she saw her brother Cursik staring down at her, frowning. "What was THAT? No reaction? Where is my feisty little sister?" he said, his hands on his hips.

"You'll find out if you don't help me up," Gin said, unable to contain her happiness. He held out his hand and she took it, flying up and into his arms in a hug. "You're here! You are home! I can't believe it!" She pulled away from him and studied his face. "You're thinner than you were."

"You are as bad as our mother…was," the older elf said, attempting a scowl but finally surrendering to the grin that split his face. "How are you, Ginny?"

"Oh shut it," Gin said happily, again pulling her brother to her in a hug. "I'm so glad you're here and you will not believe how grown up Lairky is. Have you been out adventuring, my brother? Is that why you are so thin?"

"That again!" Cursik laughed and Gin felt her heart simultaneously leap with joy and contract with sorrow at how much the sound reminded her of their father. "If you must know, yes, I have been farther away than ever before and I have learned so much about…" He stopped suddenly, lowering his voice. "I have been following the trail our parents left, Ginny," he said.

"You've been hunting with them? How are they? It has been so long since they have been home and we have not heard from them in ages," she replied, eyes wide with wonder as she gazed up at him. He released her and crossed the room to the desk where she had been preparing her lessons for the next day. "Well?"

"What is all this?" he asked, rifling through a stack of parchment. "My sister, one of the most gifted of all of us in terms of magic, is…a school teacher?"

"That is a long story, my brother," Gin said, her annoyance clear in her tone as she moved quickly to the desk and gathered up the parchment. "What is going on with Mama and Papa?"

Cursik sank down into the chair at the desk and Gin climbed nimbly up onto it, sitting cross-legged as she studied her brother. He finally looked up at her and the pained expression he wore lanced her heart. "It is far worse than I feared when I headed out to search for them, Ginny," he said quietly as he began spreading out a map on the desk. Gin sat silently, waiting for him to explain. "I have documents and letters as well as a map tracing their route." She picked up one of the letters, finding it written in a language she did not recognize, and wrinkled her eyebrows. "You look the spitting image of Mother when you make that face," Cursik said, brushing a stray hair off her face and holding her chin cupped in his hand for a moment.

"Aye, she used to look at you that way when you were once again up to something," Gin replied, smiling at him. He grinned back at her but the grin did not spread to his eyes. "Tell me what you have found, my brother? When are they coming home?"

"Before I do, this will not leave this room, do you understand me Gin?" he said, and she nodded, wincing at the use of her full name. He must be serious. "That letter that you can't read is written in Eldyr, the language of the original dragons," he said. Gin gasped.

"Eldyr…but that just isn't possible, Curs!" she exclaimed. "You're having a laugh at me. There is no such language. It died out with the dragons after the War!"

"That's part of the story, but not the worst part," he replied, frowning. "Ginny…they're gone. Mama and Papa are gone." Gin sat very still. All the air had left the room for her, and she was afraid to take a deep breath for fear that it would hurt too much or make what he said too real. "Did you hear me, Ginny?"

"Yes. What does this have to do with the dragons, Curs?" she asked, her voice soft and distant. Through her shock and disbelief, she tried to focus on **that** aspect of what Cursik had said in the hopes that she had misunderstood him about their parents being gone.

"Ginny, our parents are dead, we have to tell Lairky."

"She won't remember them." Gin was fighting a losing battle against the scream that was rising in her throat. She knew that if she let it out, she might not stop. "She was too young when they left…the last time. Now tell me what our parents have to do with the dragons and dragonkind."

"Our parents were…I think this word translates to *supporters of the dragons*. That's what this letter says…and that's why they were traveling through the mountains when they were ambushed and Father was killed."

Gin stared at her brother in utter disbelief. "Our parents…were involved… with…dragons?" she stuttered, unable to believe the words even as they were coming out of her own mouth. "Cursik, that just can't be true. It has been hundreds of years since the last dragon was seen on Orana."

"Shall I read the letter to you, my sister?" he asked, his countenance suddenly grim as he matched her stare, his eyes a mirror image of her own.

"Yes. In Elvish, please, as I'm sure you've surmised I don't speak…Eldyr or dragonese or whatever that language is." She scowled at her older brother.

"Eldyr, you were right," Cursik said, the corners of his lips lifting into a sad smile. "By the Gods it is good to see you again, little sister. No one out in those frozen mountains could make me smile as you can." Gin tried to fight the grin that was threatening and finally gave in. "There's my girl," he said, making her smile even wider.

"Well? Are you going to read the letter?" Gin asked her brother. She pushed a stray lock of hair behind one of her pointed ears as she studied him. "You really have lost a lot of weight, Cursik. I wish you'd tell me what has happened, to you I mean, not only with our parents."

"I've been traveling with…some other adventurers who are…different than we are, Ginny," he said. "Some of them were dark knights and…well; do you know how they practice magic?" Her frown deepened, telling him that she did, but she kept her mouth shut. It would do no good to call up memories of Dorlagar now. "It is hard to be in a group of them for someone like me," Cursik said, fiddling with the edge of the parchment as he spoke. "They have great and awful magic, Ginny, and at times I was the target of their spell work."

"WHAT?" Gin's mouth fell open, remembering the many times that Dorlagar could have used his life syphoning magic to regain his health by draining hers, but he had refused. "They life-tapped you?" Cursik's face darkened.

"Life-tapped? Ginny, how do you know so much about their spells that you even know their slang?" Cursik demanded, looking at her with an accusatory stare. He quickly rose to his feet and moved to where she was still sitting on the end of the desk, taking her face in his hands. "Tell me that you never…you haven't…"

"No! Of course not. I…did travel with a group for a time before returning home, Cursik, surely you have heard about that, and one of them was a dark knight. But he never used that power on me, only on our enemies in battle." Gin placed her oaken tinged hands over her brother's, which were still gripping the sides of her face. "I swear, Cursik. I have never let that happen to me, nor will I, voluntarily." Shame crept into his gaze as he released her face and turned away from her. "Oh, no, I didn't mean that…" She placed a hand on his back and he winced. "Cursik…"

He turned back to her, his face a mask of normality. "It's fine, Ginny, I knew what you meant," he said. "The one that I traveled with most of the time was a dark elf. Her name was Maelfie and she was…kind." His voice was so sad and wistful that Gin bit her tongue to keep from demanding to know what he had been thinking to trust a dark elf. "She was turned out by her family when she did not become a necromancer, but a dark knight instead. Her family was very traditional and didn't believe that females could be warriors."

"I believe I know something about that," Gin muttered. When Cursik's eyes met hers, her cheeks flushed with embarrassment. "I'm sorry. Go on."

"You would have liked her, Ginny," he said, smiling. "The

two of you were very similar. I kept thinking of those days when you were younger, proclaiming that you were going to be a fighter like me rather than just a druid as you were promised to be." Cursik chuckled. "JUST a druid. Ginny, you were never JUST anything." He ruffled her hair playfully and she swatted at him as she laughed.

"So you and this Maelfie were…together?" Gin asked, trying to hide the sudden revulsion she felt at the idea of her brother in love with a dark elf. She learned her entire life to fear and shun her underground-dwelling cousins. Cursik frowned.

"We were, aye. She was my mate, Ginny, and I lost her…in the mountains," he replied, blinking back the tears that pricked his eyes at her memory. "She was traveling with me in search of our parents, Ginny, helping me gain access to parts of our world where only those of her kind are welcome. We had crossed paths with another dark knight in the mountains that gave me this letter and…" Cursik rummaged around in a pack that he had slung to the floor earlier, finally producing a gold ring with a shimmering fire emerald in the middle of the band, a sigil carved in the stone. "Do you recognize it?" he asked, knowing the answer already as the color ran out of his sister's face.

"How did you…where did you…?" Tears flowed unhindered down Gin's cheeks. "This is Father's ring…yes?" Unable to tear her eyes from the ring, Gin's hands covered her mouth in an effort to hold back long repressed sobs that threatened to break free in the face of this undeniable proof that her parents were gone.

"It is, Sister," Cursik said, putting an arm around her and pulling her into the support of his shoulder. Gin cried for a moment, then wiped her eyes on the sleeve of her tunic and once again focused her attention on the ring. "Let me read you the letter, it will answer some questions." Gin nodded, extending her hand as if demanding the ring. Cursik put it carefully on her palm and then released her, returning to his seat at the desk. Gin stared at the ring on her open palm, tracing the flame sigil on the stone with her eyes, as she remained seated on the desk, still as statue.

He smoothed the parchment under his long fingers, and then began to read as he rested one hand on his sister's knee, just to his right. "To our Brothers and Sisters of Tooth and Scale, Greetings and Most Well Met. I write to you in the waning of this great conflict over the lands to our south to bring you hope to carry you through the oncoming darkness." Cursik stopped and looked at Gin whose face wore a completely blank expression. "Friends have come from the Forest to the south, friends that wish to end this conflict and unite our kind and theirs…Gin? Lost, are you?" She nodded. "Okay, I will sum this up for you, because this only marginally involves our parents. This was written, from what I can tell, from a time near the end of the Forest Wars," he continued, but then stopped, frowning as the blank look returned to her face. "Really? Did you even attend your history lessons? A legion of dark elves led the dragonkind into the Forest, close to our tree city, fighting broke out and we drove them back north? Mother Dragon flew away toward the Dark Sea, never to be seen again?" Gin nodded her head as her memory caught up with Cursik's tale.

"But what does this have to do with our parents?"

"That part I don't know exactly," Cursik said, his eyes darkening. "I never learned why those such as Mother and Father were chosen to assist the dragonkind after the War was over, but this letter names them as allies. Most mature dragons kill wood elves and high elves on sight, as do their minions, so it makes no sense.

"Mae and I thought that it might have something to do

with the work our mother had done as a diplomat with the Qatu, so we headed for their settlement off the coast of the Volcanic Mountains." He paused a moment before he spoke again. "We had gone to the Highlands, to the human outpost there and the dwarf settlement to try and trace our parents' footsteps. Ginny, you remember that their final journey landed them in that outpost, yes?" She nodded. "We met another dark knight there, one that was known to Mae and other dark knights as a renegade. He asked to travel with us and we allowed it - but with much trepidation. Mae had not heard anything from Dorlagar since he left his studies in the Outlands." Gin gasped at the familiar name, causing Cursik to pause for a moment and look over at her. "Are you all right, Sister? I know that I was more familiar with Mae than my family would have preferred, but..."

"No, it isn't that," she said. Her mind raced. Cursik and his mate, this Maelfie, knew Dorlagar. How had that happened? "Please, go on."

Cursik looked at her suspiciously, but continued his tale. "We traveled with him for a week or so, but one night as we were camped in the Outlands, he told us that he had received terrible news from home and had to leave us. He handed over a rucksack that he said had enough loot in it to keep us on our path, wished us well, and then was gone." His face darkened. "We investigated, and inside found the letter and the ring."

Gin felt like the world had dropped out from under her. "Does that mean that...he killed...Mother and Father?"

"Oh, it gets much worse than that, my Sister. I wanted to go after him and demand answers, but Mae was weak from our last encounter and I could not leave her without..." He looked away from Gin, his face filling with shame. "By the time she was well enough to travel, he was long gone. I hope that he has met the wrong side of a broad sword since leaving us." Cursik balled up his fists in anger. "We continued on to the settlement where we met a survivor of that expedition where our parents died: a woman who was one of the healers, and she was able to confirm for us by his description that it was Dorlagar who had killed them. With that knowledge, all that was left for us to do was find out why the dragonkind of Tooth and Scale selected our parents, and for that we ventured on to the Volcanic Mountains…where I lost her."

"You don't have to go on, Brother," Gin whispered. Her parents were dead, her family destroyed, and it was Dorlagar had killed her parents. Dorlagar, who had taken many wounds in her defense, who staunchly refused to use his dark magic on her to heal himself when she no longer had the power to heal him, who was her friend and companion… but was he? She remembered the uncomfortable glances, and him calling for her the night she left. "This must be put right," she muttered. Cursik looked up at her sharply. "I will put this right."

"You will do no such thing, little sister," he barked at her. "I have lost too much. To lose you along with Mother and Father and Mae…I forbid it!" Gin smiled at him as genuinely as she could, running her hand down the side of his face. As it had when they were children, her touch seemed to soothe him. They were two years apart in age, and had been inseparable as children.

"Of course not," she lied, amazed at her own ability to look her brother in the eye and not tell the truth. Something else she had learned from traveling with the dark knight, no doubt. "I merely meant that when you are ready, you must continue your search, even if it means going back to where you lost your…Maelfie." Cursik smiled at her through tears and Gin felt as though her heart would burst forth from her chest. "I do not think we should tell Lairky, Cursik," she said, relieved when he nodded in agreement. "She would take off after Dorlagar and we would lose her too. We must tell her that Mama and Papa are not coming back, but not that we know the identity of their killer."

"Aye, this will be our little secret," he said sadly. "I should find lodging, Ginny, I'm exhausted. We can talk more tomorrow, yes?"

"Of course, and you will stay with me and Lairky," she replied. "I will go out to hunt tonight and you can have my bed. I'm sure that Lairky will have thousands of questions about your victories in battle, so be warned." She hopped off the table as Cursik gathered up his things and then she headed for the door, to be stopped cold by his hand on her arm. "Don't worry; I will be back."

"I mean it, Ginny, you forget that name, Dorlagar, do you understand me?" he hissed as he glared down at her. A chill ran down her back as she nodded. Cursik now was the spitting image of their father when he had been angry with Gin for skipping her studies with the druid guild master. "We need you here. I need you," he said, his words lost in a sob as he grabbed her and held her fast against his chest. Gin bit her lip as she rubbed a hand absently on his back.

"Now then, do you really want Lairky to see you like this? Stay at home with me, have some warm stew and a bit of ale and you'll be back to yourself before you know it. I won't be gone long, I promise." Cursik smiled at her and she turned to open the door, a silent curse on her lips. She would make Dorlagar answer for this wrong, and soon.

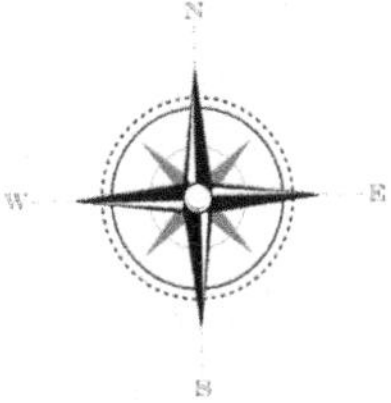

# TWELVE

An almost palpable silence hung in the air as Dorlagar entered the arena just outside of Calder's Port. Why had Gin asked him to meet her here? This was an area designated for the settlement of disputes and arguments by means of combat, often ending in death. The last time they had both been in the city it had ended so badly…he sighed as he remembered that day as the last time he had seen Gin.

He removed his helm, placed it on the ground with the rest of his traveling gear, and ran one tired hand through his gray hair. All that her message had said was to meet her here and to come alone, followed by her careful signature at the bottom. She would have no way to know that he had long since left Naevys and Nelenie's company, departing the day after Gin herself left, and had been traveling alone ever since. He was still no closer to finding his sister. Dorlagar scanned the arena as he paused in the doorway. The walls were stone and higher than any man's head. He walked over to one side and tentatively touched the wall. It was smoother than it looked, and he wondered if that smoothness was to prevent a combatant from scaling the walls to safety. Dorlagar moved toward the center of the arena.

As he approached the marble throne that was surrounded by a wooden structure, the place for whomever was to negotiate the dispute to sit, he thought he caught a glimmer of movement. "Who's there?" he called out, his hand instantly closing around the hilt of his sword. There was no answer, so he moved closer to the throne. It was made of shining white marble, a stark contrast to the dull gray stones of the walls. While bloodstains were visible everywhere else in this desolate place, the throne appeared pristine, as though it existed outside of the grim reality of the arena.

"Stop." Gin's voice seemed to resonate inside of Dorlagar's head, and for a moment, he thought he had imagined it. "Come no closer, Dorlagar."

"Gin? Where are you?" he said, eyes scanning the arena. Dorlagar quickly recited a spell that would magically improve his vision and his eyes began to tingle in the quickly growing darkness. "Why the formality?" He rubbed his right arm. The price of the increased vision.

"I know what you did, Dorlagar," Gin's voice said. Dorlagar still could not find her, and a prickly fear began crawling up the back of his neck. "I know what happened at the human outpost."

"What are you talking about?" Dorlagar demanded, blatant annoyance in his voice. "Come out here, Blueberry! Stop playing games."

Gin's normally tinkling laughter was maniacal and cold as it assaulted his ears. "Games? Hardly. We have moved beyond games, Dorlagar," she said. Dorlagar turned around to see the wood elf seated on her steed Beau, directly behind him.

"There you are," he said, taking a step toward her. The tip of her sword hovered just inches from his chin.

"Far enough," she said. "Recognize the sword? You gave it to me, if memory serves. Fitting that I should bring it here today."

"Gin, what is going on?" Dorlagar growled, his patience growing thin. "Why are we here? After all this time with no contact, why do you greet me this way? What happened at the outpost that upset you?" Risking the point of the sword piercing his throat, he moved as close to her as he could, and even placed a hand on Beau's neck. The horse whinnied a greeting but was silenced by a subtle jerk on his reins from his mistress.

"My parents were murdered there," Gin said through gritted teeth. "They were devoted servants of the All-Mother and Orana, good and decent people. They were druid healers, saving countless lives from the evil forces that mean to throw our world out of balance and into darkness."

Gin took a deep breath before she continued. "They were on a mission there, acting as healers for a group devoted to the right side of the Forest Wars, when their group was attacked by a throng of horrible creatures. There were too many of them to overtake, so the group began to run to safety. My father began preparations as they ran to teleport the group to safety, but a young knight blundered into his path."

Dorlagar's breath caught in his throat. A memory came rushing into his consciousness, a memory of a time many seasons ago when he had gone out hunting alone. He was traveling through the mountains, and had sought refuge at the human outpost, hiding from bandits and killing local beasts for food. He remembered in that moment the trials of finding shelter where none would take him in, living from meal to meal, not knowing which one would be his last. He remembered sitting by his small fire one particular night and thinking of his sister, Raedea.

When he was still a young man, a letter had arrived at his guild house. He could remember how he opened it with shaking hands after seeing the seal of the Temple of Isona on the front. He could remember the smell of the parchment and the faded brown color of the ink. One sentence graced the page, written in a swooping longhand script. "To inform Dorlagar, only living relative of our dear Sister Raedea Dawnshadow, of her untimely death, we hereby set our great seal of the servants of the Temple of Isona." That one sentence, however, had seared Dorlagar to his core and driven him to journey out alone, in search of the details of her death. He had sworn on his blood, drawn by his giant sword, that he would drive that sword through the heart of every servant of Isona he met until one could tell him the story of his sister's demise.

Now, standing in the arena and staring at Gin, Dorlagar felt an icy coldness grip his heart. Numbness spread throughout him, and when he raised his eyes to meet Gin's, an equally bitter gaze met his. "Tell me more, Druid," he said, his eyes narrowing as he took a step back from her sword. "Tell me how your dear parents met their end at the hands of one of my kind."

"Not one of your kind, Dorlagar," she said, spitting his name through her still clenched teeth. "You. My parents were running for their lives, still healing their group members as best they could with bandages and spells. My parents cast the transportation spell that would evacuate the group to safety, but just as their images began to blur my mother heard a cry for help from behind her." Again, Gin had to stop a moment and take a deep breath to keep her emotions from overwhelming her. "She stepped out of the magical circle that she had created to see my father bent over the form of a young man, dead from the look of him, with beasts advancing on them at top speed. My mother did what she could to fend off the creatures. However, she used all of her magical energy to perform the teleport spell. They took up weapons and fought off the beasts in an effort to preserve the poor soul's corpse and drag it to safety. They should have left it there to be eaten by the scavengers, so that I would not have to look upon it now."

Gin lowered her sword so that it took aim at Dorlagar's heart. "But you see, the young man wasn't really dead. Being a practitioner of dark magic, he could feign death so convincingly that he could ward off attackers." Dorlagar met her gaze, his own cold and steeled. "My father was torn in half by the beasts and my mother left bleeding to death. It was then that she saw, through the haze of near unconsciousness, the corpse of the young man spring to life, laughing at its good fortune to be alive. Only one member of that party survived, a kind woman who was too far away from the magical circle. She tried to save them, but they were too far-gone, beyond her healing abilities. All she could do was take shelter and flee once the beasts were satiated and left." Gin sheathed her sword a moment and removed one of her gloves. She held out the hand that bore the fire emerald ring that her elder brother Cursik had given her a few nights prior.

"Cursik!" Dorlagar hissed. He had given the ring to the ranger in exchange for food and a warm fire. Cursik had been an occasional companion of Dorlagar's during the past months, but he knew nothing much of the ranger and his dark elf mate. Dorlagar's eyes searched the ground suddenly, making a mental list of what he would do to the male if ever their paths crossed again. His eyes glowed red as he imagined Cursik's corpse at his feet. "Still, the ring proves nothing," he said, not raising his eyes.

"Cursik told me to whom this ring belonged, Dorlagar. He recognized it, as did I when I saw it, because it belonged to our father," Gin said. Dorlagar clenched his fists…Cursik was Gin's brother. Of **course** he was. "I should hardly have been surprised that you looted my parents' belongings before you even knew for sure that my mother was dead, for you did the same to me under the tree city." Dorlagar looked up at Gin. "You didn't even wait around to see, did you?"

"How…she was dead…if what you say is true there is no way your parents could have survived, so how can you be sure it was me?" he demanded, trying to recover his blunder of admission.

"The woman left behind saw you take my father's sword from his hands. She heard you claim it in your name," Gin said, her voice choking in her throat periodically as she spoke. "Members of her party came back when it was discovered she did not magically transport with them, but by then it was too late. They found the woman that had been left behind and she led them to my parents." Gin raised a tiny hand to her mouth a moment, and regained her composure. "Cursik told me your tale when he gave me Father's ring, the one YOU took from his dead hand."

Dorlagar stared at Gin, his mouth gaping. Before him was the woman who had found the soul he had buried deep within him. She had coaxed out of him the man he had once been, and she had taught him more about love and faithfulness than any companion he had ever known.

Memories flashed before his eyes of her charging into battle, her silvery eyes boiling with anger. Her screams of rage at enemies that had cut him down to near death rang in his ears. The remembrance of the feel of her tiny hands on his skin as they healed his wounds, once cool and soothing, now burned like white-hot coals. All along, he had marveled at her fierce devotion not only to her companions but also to him, a dark knight, a servant of the evil she was sworn as a druid to keep at bay.

Lost in his confusion, he did not see Gin slowly dismount from Beau's back. He did not notice the tenderness with which she stroked the pony's nose and paused a moment to breathe in the smell of his fur. The sound of the magical horse's whinny as it faded away brought Dorlagar back to reality, and he now gazed down at Gin as she stood before him, sword drawn. "Now, I will avenge my parents' death, Dorlagar, or I will die in the attempt," she said in a low voice. Her hands trembled slightly, causing the tip of the blade to quiver. "If my time with you has taught me nothing more than this, I have learned the sweet taste of revenge."

"This is a fight you cannot win, Druid," Dorlagar said as he shoved the last bits of his soul back down into the cold place where he had carefully buried it years before, the pain at seeing her like this taking up space next to his memories of his sister. "Surely you know that."

"I know only that my parents died at your hands, Dorlagar," she said, her voice steady and low. She raised her sword toward him, the customary way to begin a duel. "Now you will die at mine!" Gin charged at Dorlagar, throwing down her shield and using both hands to swing the ebon blade at his chest.

Her blow landed well, and Dorlagar stumbled back a few feet. Instinctively he began reciting his spells of magical combat, and Gin soon felt as though she was being turned inside out. She fell to her knees.

"Stop this, Gin," Dorlagar said in a commanding tone. "I have no wish to kill you, and it is not the way of the Druid to seek vengeance."

"No magic," she said in a choking voice. "I will kill you with my blade alone, no spells." She rose awkwardly to her feet and charged at him again. This time Dorlagar managed to raise his sword to the level of hers and dodge her blow. He stepped back from her, still not advancing with his weapon but also not assaulting her with magic. Gin stumbled but recovered, and landed a well-placed slice across Dorlagar's cheek.

The dark knight howled in pain, and then without consciously realizing he was speaking, cast a spell on Gin as she ran at him for a third time. She froze in her tracks, grasping at her chest. Her blood seemed to boil in her veins, and she collapsed into a heap at his feet. Dorlagar wiped the blood from his face as the spell's reverse effect filled him with renewed health and advanced on her, sword raised. Gin managed to thrust her blade upward as he drew close to her, sinking it into the flesh at his knee just where his greaves tied. Through the blinding pain in his leg, Dorlagar slammed the hilt of his sword into Gin's back, and in doing so ripped her hands from the hilt of her blade and pummeled her into the stone floor of the arena. She lay still for a moment, assessing damage and reciting a spell to regenerate her body and allow her to stand back up and continue to fight. Nevertheless, it was slow going, and Gin found that she was still in a great deal of pain.

Dorlagar quickly removed the blade from his leg, no longer feeling the pain as shock settled in on his body and mind. He tossed her blade to the side, finding himself smiling at her defeat. In other battles, Gin's healing magic would have been washing over him at this point, healing his wounds and restoring him to health. This time she could not even heal herself.

Gin raised herself up on one arm and then slowly dragged her knees up until she was on all fours. With aching slowness, she rose to her feet and faced Dorlagar. Her hands, first at her sides and then thrust out toward him, began to glow and sparkle, and then it seemed that electricity crackled between her fingertips. She recited loudly words in Elvish that he did not understand, and suddenly a bolt of lightning rose up from the ground to meet one rocketing down from the heavens, trapping Dorlagar in between them. He staggered but somehow managed to keep his feet as another bolt raced up his spine. The third bolt nearly drove him to his knees, but gave him just enough time to lunge at Gin, catching her tiny neck in his massive hands. He lifted her off the ground, his grip tightening on her windpipe, and felt the familiar rush of adrenaline as his prey's life drained through his fingers like sand.

Gin locked her eyes on his. She could not speak, and felt the suffocation of his fingers closing on her windpipe. His image swam before her, and her struggles soon slowed. Just before her eyes rolled back into her head in death, they widened with surprise as Dorlagar dropped her in a heap on the ground. He staggered away and collapsed as well. "I told you," he said, "I have no wish to kill you." Gin coughed and sputtered as her lungs filled with precious air.

"And I told you," she said through gasps, "that I know only to kill you… or to die trying." She pulled herself along the ground closer to him, managed to get herself into a kneeling position, and then stood shakily. Gin recited the words to heal herself, and felt the pain in her throat and lungs melt away. She looked up at Dorlagar, as he stood over her, his eyes blood red. "I suppose it is magic then, is it?"

Dorlagar smiled down at her. "There is still no way for you to win, Blueberry," he said, enjoying the pain in her face at the use of the old nickname.

"We…shall see," she said, slowly rising to her feet. She began chanting aloud, in Elvish, and Dorlagar felt roots rise from the stones and tangle around his legs. He remained, watching her in amusement. It would be the work of a moment to remove those roots, and she knew it as well as he did.

Gin took a few steps back, and cast her healing magic once again. The color returned to her cheeks as she met his gaze. Next, she spoke the words of a different spell in a loud voice, and a swarm of stinging insects formed in a dense cloud around Dorlagar's body. The dark knight roared in pain as the hundreds of insects stung him repeatedly. Through the haze of his pain, he saw Gin sitting in front of him, watching the bees sting him…and smiling. Her eyes were cold and distant…not unlike his own. The last fragments of his heart froze at that very moment, and he summoned up the deadliest spell he possessed.

"Die, wood elf!" he screamed as he channeled the magic directly at her. Gin leapt to her feet, but felt the magic pierce her armor and sear through her left shoulder. Her world seemed to spin and blur as she collapsed to the stone floor, grasping madly for the phantom weapon that had dealt incapacitating blow. The roots fell away from Dorlagar's feet and he ran to her, pleased with the damage he had inflicted.

Gin was still for a long time, but finally she was able to curl up into a ball on the ground. In a hollow voice she said, "You have bested me, Dorlagar." She swallowed painfully before she continued to speak, her voice barely a whisper. "I have not avenged you, Mother and Father, rather I have failed you." Slowly she lifted her head and looked up at Dorlagar. "Finish it," she said. "I have not the strength to fight you."

Dorlagar stared at her a moment as a switch seemed to flip deep in his heart, and then, on unsteady legs, he walked out of the arena without saying a word. He closed his eyes and winced as he heard Gin screaming at him to come back, calling him a coward and several other things in her language that he was sure were not flattering. The irony of this situation juxtaposed with him calling for her as she left Calder's Port was not lost on him, and he began to run across the landscape, heading far away from the sound of her voice.

Back at the arena, Gin beat the stone floor with her fists, screaming for the coward to return and finish what they had started. When she realized he was truly gone, she let loose sobs that had been stored carefully away since Cursik had told her of her parent's demise. She lay on the ground for a long time, even after her tears had dried, and again assessed damage. Her strength was returning, and she drew herself up until she was on all fours.

Finally, she found herself able to stand, and she tore at her armor until she stood in her tunic and short pants, the rest of her things flung about the arena floor. A blast of icy air enveloped her, and soon she felt Beau's soft nose nuzzling into the back of her head. Gin turned to face her beloved magical pony, and throwing her arms around his neck, she buried her face in his silky mane.

"I didn't think I'd see you again, boy," she whispered. Beau whinnied softly, and Gin smiled at him. "You're right, another day. We'll finish this another day." She gathered her things and stuffed them into her packs that Beau willingly carried strapped to the saddle. As she swung up into the saddle, she pulled the sword from the pack and lifted it above her head. A long ride back home might be what she needed to clear her head, but it would not clear her conscience.

"This is not over, Dorlagar. Only blood flowing will end it," she swore. Urging Beau to movement, he flew like the wind out of the arena, bearing her away from Calder's Port and the humans of the settlement, and toward her home in the forest. She had been right to leave the life she had led with Dorlagar behind, but it would not truly be over for her until one of them was dead.

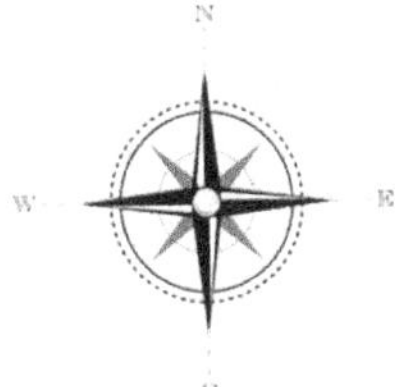

# THIRTEEN

The passageways leading through the lower mountains were long and dark. Gin's footsteps echoed off the walls and, every so often, they were followed by the scampering sounds of the creatures that made these caves their home dashing past her. She was thankful that they recognized her as a potential threat and left her alone. Her brow furrowed as she continued her trek to the great desert, her mind and heart heavy.

"I failed you, my parents," she murmured aloud, cringing slightly as her voice bounced about in the air. "I failed to kill the dark one that killed you, and I fear now that it is only a matter of time before he returns to kill me." Swinging her blade absently at her side and occasionally scratching it along the walls, she sighed loudly. "I will not fail to honor you in death, however," she said as she turned the corner toward the exit that lead to the desert. The passageways, built by the dwarves many centuries prior in an effort to avoid the creatures that dwelt on the surface while traveling, were just short cuts between the different topographical areas of the world. Gin stopped in the opening that led out of the tunnel and looked up at the night sky, again thinking of her parents. "I will not dishonor you again. That I swear."

"Are all you druids this melancholy and depressing?" said a growly voice to her right, coming from the darkness just inside the tunnel. Gin stopped in her tracks, straining to recognize the speaker because even with the improved vision of her kind, she could not see into the pitch dark. "If you're not yelling at me to stop killing bears, you're whining about your forlorn lives...it truly becomes old."

Gin closed her hand on the hilt of her sword. "Show yourself," she said, hissing the words. The hairs on the back of her neck stood on end as she took a step back from the dark corner.

"All right, if you're sure you've got a good grip on that blade," the voice said, chuckling. A tall Qatu male stepped out of the shadows to the right of her. Gin took a sharp breath in and raised her sword a bit.

"Leave me be," she said, squaring her shoulders and resuming her pace. The tip of one shiny metal claw pressed into her chin and she stopped. "I said leave me be!"

"I wish I could, truly, but you see I'm on a bit of a mission and... well... you're the mission at the moment," said the giant feline. "Druids like you tend to have lots of goodies stored away in all those backpacks, and I'm in need of some food and drink. Hand them over."

"This is not a wise decision, you… beast," Gin said, trying to sound braver than she was. "You will let me pass."

The Qatu laughed, and there was a purring growl audible in his voice. "Bah, some druid you are. I grow weary now, hand over the backpacks." Gin gaped at him for a few moments, making him laugh harder. "Do you think that I have never seen druid magic, up close and personal? I have had it directed at me more than I would care to admit. Now then, backpacks, if you don't mind?" Keeping the claw pressed against her jawbone, he waggled his other clawed fingers at her and she tried not to flinch.

"They are not yours to take," Gin said angrily and shoved her way past the giant cat. The tip of the claw that had been lightly grazing her skin drew a jagged gash up the side of her face and she gasped aloud in pain but kept moving.

"Can't anything be easy?" the Qatu exclaimed, clearly exasperated. He inhaled deeply, the smell of fear in her blood teasing the vicious beast inside him. "Do you want me to hurt you? Is that it?" He approached Gin rapidly and grabbed at one of her packs, knocking her to the ground as the shoulder strap broke. As she gathered herself back up, she saw the cat digging hungrily through her belongings.

"Give that back!" she shouted as she ran at the feline, her blade raised above her head to strike. From the shadows ahead bounded a large tiger that halted in front of her, blocking her access to the Qatu who was now hungrily devouring her food. "That's all the food I have!" She began reciting the words that brought fire down upon all living creatures in range, but the tiger continued to stare her down and she fell silent. She stared back at it with a mixture of curiosity and terror. It seemed to be guarding the larger cat as he ate.

"Well… it's more food than I've had in weeks, my lady," he mumbled, his mouth full of berries and marmalade sandwiches, "and you don't look like you need this much food anyway, tiny thing that you are." He stood and wiped his mouth on the back of his arm, then continued to look Gin over. "Aye, I think I could carry you around in my pocket...if I had pockets."

Gin winced...Dorlagar had said the same thing to her when

he first met her. She frowned, trying to push back against the tears that were coming. As her face contorted, the wound on her cheek stung and she felt salty tears well up in her eyes. They flowed down into the wound and Gin scowled…now there would be no healing it, at least not completely.

"Fine," she said. "Take the food; just give my packs and my money back. I have no wish to hurt you, good sir Qatu."

"Sathlir," he said just before swallowing another marmalade sandwich whole.

"I'm sorry, I don't speak Qatunari," she said.

"That's my name, ya silly elf," he said, clearly amused at her. "Sathlir Clawsharp, Bane of the Forest, at your service." He downed the last sandwich, missing the horrified look that crossed her face, and eyed her other backpacks that she was clutching to her chest. "Good food there, but it left me awfully thirsty," he said, moving toward her. Gin pitched one of the backpacks at him and ran back down the long passageway the way she had come. She had no desire to engage the Bane of the Forest this day or any day, if she was honest.

Sathlir watched her run, laughing as he sent his pet bounding after her. "So you've heard of me?" he called after her through chuckles. "That ought to give her a good run to the other side of the mountain if she doesn't watch for the turn," he chuckled. Retrieving the backpack she had thrown at him, he opened it and pulled out a flask of water. As he sipped from it, he rummaged further through her pack. It was not really stealing; she had technically given him the pack. A leather book caught his eye and he pulled it out of the pack. He sat down and opened the book.

"Oh, this looks like a journal," he chuckled. "This should be stunning..." He flipped through the pages, skimming them as he went. "Blah blah blah, foraging in the forest, spell casting...how boring it must be to be a druid," he said as he continued reading. A paragraph caught his eye, and he stopped to read it carefully.

"I have failed to avenge my father and mother, but how could I have ever succeeded?" Sath read aloud. "How can I kill Dorlagar when I barely have it in me to harm any living thing? Where do I go from here, other than a slow march to my own demise?" Sath looked up from the book a moment, furrowing his brow. "Well then," he said, "this will keep me occupied until Rae comes back with our money from the last job." Kicking his giant feet up on to the pile of now empty backpacks, he continued to read. His pet had returned, having given her a good scare, and settled at his feet.

Gin tried to count her steps as she ran, fearing that she had entirely missed the turn that would lead her out of the mountain on the same side and not cause her to have to start completely over again. Once she could no longer hear the giant tiger breathing as it bounded along behind her, she dared to slow down and look over her shoulder. It was gone and she was able to take a deep breath, so she slowed to a walk just as she came upon the turn. She ducked around the corner as if it was an alleyway and leaned against the wall, her breath coming in gulps.

She had lost everything to that Qatu. What else could go wrong? She had no food or water now, and all of her maps and belongings had been in those packs. She did not dare go back, however. He was the Bane of the Forest, and it had to be just dumb luck that he had been satisfied with just her backpacks and not taken her life as well. Gin started walking again, and before long allowed herself another moment to rest.

"Sath?" Raedea's voice rang off the walls of the tunnel as she walked along, the money she had gotten from trading the goods from their last hunt jingling in the pouch she had tied under her cloak. "I told him to meet me just here," she complained to herself as she arrived at the opening to the tunnel that led into the mountain. She paced back and forth, worried more than annoyed that he was not there to meet her as he had promised.

"Keep your hair on, Rae," Sath said from the shadows just inside the tunnel entrance. "I'm here, just keeping a low profile, you know?"

Raedea grinned at him. "I know, I was just worried, but LOOK!" She untied the strings of the pouch and handed it to him. "That last time out was very profitable. No more 'borrowing' things from druids or rangers for you…Sath?" She leaned in close to look at him and he jumped away, furiously wiping away the marmalade that he knew was on his face. "Is that jam?"

Sath blushed to the roots of his hair. "Yes…well, no, it's marmalade actually."

"And where did you…oh, Sath, you didn't!" Raedea's grin melted away as she stared up at him. "Was anyone… Did you…"

"No, I didn't kill the wood elf," he replied. Raedea opened her mouth to speak but Sath held up a clawed finger. "She left with all her limbs intact and I got a snack to tide me over until you got back. Everyone wins! I promised you that I would stop killing them, and I have."

"But that implied that you would also stop stealing from them, Sath." The disappointment was heavy in her voice and in her gaze. Sath hung his head. "Well? Is there anything left or did you eat it all?"

"I ate all that was food. There's a spell book in here and a journal and some other stuff but…yeah, I ate all the food." Raedea held out her hand and he hung the backpack on it. "What are you going to do with that?"

"Which way did she go?"

"Why?"

"Sath…"

"Fine." Sath ran a hand over the top of his head, clearly frustrated. "She headed back the way she'd come," he said, gesturing down the tunnel toward the center of the mountain, "but there's a turn down there that will bring her back out on this side if she didn't miss it from running."

"Why was she running? Oh, of course…" Raedea ran her hand across the tiger's head and it pressed up into her palm, purring loudly. "I don't know which is worse," she said sadly. "The hunting full stop or the enjoyment you derive from it."

"Aw, now darlin, I don't really, you know that." Sath sighed loudly. "When it comes down to me eating or them eating, I make a decision, that's all."

"Well, I'm making a decision this time, Cat," she replied, handing him the backpack. "Take this back to her."

"You're mad," Sath said, chuckling. "She will run if she sees me, you know that."

"You can run faster than she can," Raedea reminded him. "Just head out here and go to the opening of the other tunnel and leave it there, in the middle of the path so she can see it." Sath stared at her and then realizing that she was serious, sighed loudly and took off out the tunnel door. She sat down and began counting the money and dividing it up. About the time she was done, he appeared in the doorway. "Did you wait for her to pick it up?"

"Yes."

"Did she see you waiting?" Sath growled a little under his breath. "Fine, of course she didn't. Now then, here is your part of the money. Shall we go find a place to stay for the night?"

"After you, boss lady," Sath said, making a clumsy and exaggerated bow that made Raedea laugh as she headed further down into the tunnel. He paused a moment before following her to tuck the journal into his own backpack. "I'm not giving this up just yet," he whispered.

"Sath?"

"Coming!" He beat feet down the tunnel, catching up to Raedea and sweeping her up into his arms, making her laugh hysterically before putting her back on her feet. "It's not very far to the outpost just outside the tunnel on the other side. Race ya!"

"There's no way I can keep up with your long strides, cheater!" she called after him, chuckling as she watched him run on ahead.

After a very long time sitting pressed up against one of the walls, Gin finally plucked up the courage to leave the tunnel. Without her spell book, she found herself unsure of her magic, even the spells that she had long since memorized and used on a daily basis. However, she could not hide there in the safety of the tunnel forever, of this she was sure.

She stepped out of the tunnel and stared at the bag in the

middle of the path in front of her. It was her backpack, the one she had thrown at the Qatu. Gin stopped, still as a statue, and set her kind's ability to track her environment on high alert. A rustle in a nearby tree caught her attention but by the time she turned, there was nothing there. She took a few cautious steps toward the bag, certain that the Qatu would spring out and grab her as she touched it, and grabbed it as she ran in the direction that she hoped would lead her to the forest. She did not stop running until the tree line came into view, and even then she only slowed slightly. Aynamaede came into view and she slowed to a walk, gasping as she fought her aching lungs to breathe.

Finally, she felt safe enough to look behind her, though she knew that there was no one there. She stopped, overcome, and fell to her knees. "Mother," she said, her hands out in front of her in supplication. "As your child and a protector of Orana, I come before you now to thank you for your protection both in the arena and in the mountain tunnels. While I am not sure that I deserve to have survived either, I am humbled by your presence and will devote my life and my work to your will as you reveal it to me." She swallowed hard as memory of her failure left a bitter taste in her mouth. "I do not understand the path you set before my parents and their place in the aftermath of the Forest Wars, but I will do my best to learn. And Mother, thank you for your mercy in the form of the Qatu who not only did not end my life but also returned my things to me. I will do my best to show others the same mercy, including…" Gin paused a moment. She had almost said Dorlagar, but she did not believe that she could and knew that the All-Mother would not either. "Including the Bane of the Forest, may he be able to find the error in his path and correct it, as you will."

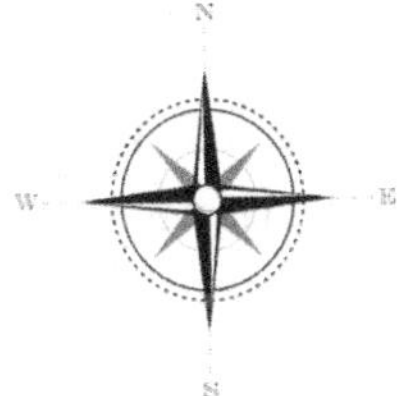

# FOURTEEN

"Two rooms, please?" Raedea said as she slid the coins across to the innkeeper. "Next to each other if possible." The innkeeper nodded as his grubby hand closed over the money. He produced two room keys and slid them across the desk back to her.

"Fourteen and fifteen," he said. "End of the hall." He leaned over and winked at Raedea and the smell of his breath nearly caused her to gag. "Adjoining."

"Thank you, sir," she replied and turned around to face Sath. A low, rumbly growl was coming out from under the hood that obscured his features from the patrons. They were as close to the homeland of the elves as he had been since his days as the Bane of the Forest, and they did not want to take any chances.

"Will you have food and ale brought up to us?" The innkeeper nodded, winking at her again and chuckling.

"How can you stand to let him think that of you?" Sath hissed in her ear as they climbed the stairs. "Where I come from, females are revered, almost worshipped. Not gawked at and preyed upon, as they seem to be among you humans."

"Because that wasn't at all what you were doing with the druids and rangers, right? I mean, they were all males, right?" she replied. Sath fell silent. "I'm sorry, Sath, I'm just tired."

"No, you're right. Once again, you are right, Rae," he replied, clearly chagrined. She handed him the key with the fob that had the number fifteen written on it and continued down the hall. "Rae, wait."

"What now?" she asked, rubbing the bridge of her nose as she turned around.

"Give me fourteen," he said. "That way you will be at the end of the hall and I will be between you and any males that saw you arrive."

"Sath, really, I don't see the…"

"Please, Rae."

Raedea sighed. "Fine. Will you come eat in my room then, before I kick you out to stand guard or preserve my honor or whatever it is you will be doing for the rest of the night?" Sath nodded, beaming a toothy grin at her that made her laugh.

Several hours later, Raedea found herself unable to sleep. She had dozed off a few times to fitful dreams of her brother and their childhood and finally had given up and gotten out of bed.

She wrapped her cloak around her and padded over to the door that joined her room to Sath's and knocked. "Sath?" she whispered. "You up?" There was no response. She pushed on the door and found it unlocked, so she stuck her head in the doorway. "Sath?" Calling up some of the simple magic she had learned at the Temple, Raedea pushed her own energy out through her fingertips toward the candelabra on Sath's dressing table and the candles lit. He was not in the room.

Raedea moved into the room, concerned. Surely he had not gone out. It was too risky, as the humans at this outpost traded with the wood elves of the forest and might recognize him. There were not that many Qatu in this part of the world. His cloak was gone, so that was good at least. Raedea had turned to go back to her room when she spotted a leather bound journal on his night table. She had never seen it before, and her curiosity got the better of her so she walked over and picked it up.

"This must be that druid's journal!" she exclaimed as she thumbed through the pages. "Oh, Sath, I thought you took this back…" Raedea's knees felt weak as she came across a familiar name in the journal. "Dorlagar…it can't be…" Leaning against one of the walls for support, she rifled through a few more pages looking for anything that would tell her if the Dorlagar in the journal was her brother, and soon found what she was looking for. "He only dreams of his sister, his twin, the other half of his soul, lost so many years ago." She dropped the journal and backed up, her hand covering her mouth as the color drained out of her face. When she ran into someone behind her, she screamed until a fur-covered hand covered her mouth, silencing her.

"Rae, it's me, shush now, what's wrong, *darlin*?" Sath whispered in her ear. The whispered Qatu word meaning *'darling'* or *'loved one,'* underscored with a purr that he knew Raedea found soothing helped her relax in his arms, so he released her and turned her to face him. "I'm sorry, Rae, I know that position is frightening for you but I couldn't let you keep screaming. It's me, Sath; not that guard from Calder's Port." He tipped her chin up with one of his fingers until she looked him in the eye.

"I know who you are, Sath, it's not that. What is this," she asked, picking up the journal. Sath looked at it and hung his head. "You did not return this with the druid's things. Why?"

He tried to snatch the journal from her hand but she was too quick and he caught a fistful of air. "It's not important," he said. "Why were you so afraid when I came up behind you?"

"Stop trying to change the subject."

"I answered your question. It is not important," he said, rising up to his full height and glaring down at her. She merely kept her eyes locked on his, with no hint of intimidation at his size or demeanor.

"Sath."

"I don't know why." Sath hung his head, resigned. "There is…something…I don't know what it is. I just wanted to keep it."

"So you've read it?"

"Yes. It's not the most compelling, but there is just something there."

"So you know who Dorlagar is?"

"Who?" Sath looked at her, puzzled. "That name is in there, yes, but I don't know who that is, no. Why?"

"Not important." Raedea took a deep breath and then put the journal under her arm. "Just curious. Shall we…"

"Oh no, no way you are going to get off that easily, having just held my claws to the fire like you did, lady," Sath said, grinning as he stepped in between her and the door between their rooms. "Who is this Dorlagar to you? CLEARLY you recognize the name."

"It is a name from a long time ago." She pushed past him but he grabbed her wrist. "Sath, let me go, it is no concern of yours."

"Well, see, I think it is," he said quietly. "Because the Dorlagar I read about in the druid's journal seemed to be an all right guy, if not a little bloodthirsty at times, but he turned into a murderer. Also, because I intend to continue traveling with you, I would like to know if we are likely to cross paths with this Dorlagar so that I will be ready for a fight." Raedea bit her lip.

"He is not a murderer," she muttered. "The chance that we will encounter him is slim unless you have changed your mind about the path we are traveling now." She pushed past him again and this time he let her leave the room through the adjoining hallway, following closely on her heels.

"But who is he to you, Rae?" She did not answer, but picked up her pace. "Please? Just tell me that and I will let it go."

"Will you agree to give the journal back to the druid?"

"Now how can I possibly do that?" he asked, becoming more frustrated with every step. "Rae!" he roared and she stopped so quickly that he nearly stumbled over on top of her.

"If I tell you, you will agree to take that journal to Aynamaede and return it to her. Look, it has her name in it, here." She pulled the journal out and opened it to the first page, pointing at the name scrawled in Elvish. "Gino…something, my Elvish is not that good."

"Mine either, I'm just lucky she wrote it in the common

language. When I see that word I just use the first bit, Gin, in my mind because I can't read the rest of it." Sath frowned. "I can't just waltz up to that tree city, calling for Gin to come get her journal back, now can I? They will kill me on sight."

"You will figure that part out, I'm sure. But for now, will you give me your word?" Raedea demanded, replacing the journal and then glaring at him, hands on hips. She blew a stray bit of her black hair out of her eyes, and Sath reached up to smooth it away. She flinched away from him. "Promise me," she said quietly.

"Aye, woman, I promise, how did I EVER end up with such a difficult human?"

"Well," Raedea said, her frown fading into a grin, "they do say that like attracts like…" Sath rolled his eyes and she laughed.

"So, who is Dorlagar?"

Her laughter ended abruptly. "He is my brother, my twin brother," she said quietly. Sath was gob smacked, standing with his mouth hanging open in surprise. "I have not seen him since we were much younger. He left for warrior training and I waited for him to return…but my talents for magic were starting to show, so I left home to join the Temple of Isona." She began walking again as she spoke and Sath followed her. "They have an extensive network of scribes throughout our world, and I often wrote to them, asking if there was any word of him. I followed his life, his work, but I was discovered using the Temple's resources for my own personal gain. Such a thing is not permitted."

"Not permitted? You are expected to give your life to this goddess of yours and she does not permit you to even keep up with the family you left behind?" Sath asked angrily.

"It isn't like that, Sath, keep your fur on," she snapped.

"We are willing to give up our familial ties in order to grow closer to Her, it is part of the process. That way we can focus more on our role in the world, bringing mercy and being a beacon of Her love." Her face darkened. "Well, that's the official line anyway. I was never able to completely give up on Dor though, it was like he was a part of me, of my body and my soul. I prayed and meditated on pushing him out of my mind, but he was always there. I thought that if I could just keep up with where he was, and know he was safe, then I could focus more on my training."

"Your training with the Calder's Port militia, you mean?" he sneered. "I'm sorry, Rae, but I can't see how any of this spreads love and mercy."

"The Sisters didn't know that was going on, Sath, and we loved them too much to tell them and risk the militia retaliating against the Temple," Raedea replied sadly. "Haven't you ever loved someone or something so much that you were willing to do whatever you had to in order to keep it safe?" Sath's eyes took on a faraway look for a moment, and then he nodded, sadly.

"Go on, please."

"My information stopped coming, and when I wrote to find out what had happened to my brother, I was taken to seclusion by the Sisters. It was then that I knew life at Temple was not for me and I needed to leave. I have been looking for him ever since."

"Wait, taken to seclusion? How did you escape that?" Sath looked down at her, eyes full of pity. "I too know what it is like to be incarcerated, and have…removed myself from that situation, shall we say."

"It wasn't incarceration, Sath. The Sisters have no means of such a thing." Raedea's eyes brimmed with tears as she remembered her encounter with one of the elder Sisters the night she left. "But once you join the temple, you see, you no longer exist as you were. I fear that Dorlagar thinks me dead." She pressed her fist into her mouth to hold back a sob.

An image of a journal page crossed Sath's mind. The druid had spoken of a letter that she had found in this Dorlagar's belongings, a letter from the Temple of Isona that he had only hinted at when telling her of his search for his sister. His face fell. "Rae, I fear that you are right," he said and gathered her into his arms, letting her give in to tears, purring as loudly as he could. "I swore to you, my friend that I would return the journal and I will…and then we will find this brother of yours."

"No." Raedea pushed away from Sath. "No, you have more to do on your path that I feel you must do alone, Cat," she said as she wiped her tears. "If the gods will that I see my brother again then no doubt our paths will cross. But I do not dare to second guess and try to achieve that on my own." Sath sighed loudly. "I know that your kind do not believe in the gods as I do, but please, allow me this. No more talk of finding Dor, please?" He nodded, resigned. "Now, we are headed to the forest but there's no reason we can't see a bit of the world on the way, is there? I'm in the mood for a new adventure, what do you say?"

"Whatever you need, Rae," he replied. "You have done so much for me; I can deny you nothing."

"Well, except for a bath, you seem extraordinarily good at denying me that!" she said, giggling. Sath beamed a toothy grin at her in return.

"Off we go then," he said, "avoiding as many lakes and streams as we can!"

# FIFTEEN

Sath and Raedea traveled for many miles, sleeping rough with only a campfire and their bedrolls to keep them warm at night. The money from their last mercenary work had been enough for her to purchase enough food and drink to keep them well fed as they went and allowed them to avoid the outposts, both human and otherwise, in the Grasslands and the Outlands that stretched out between them and the forest.

One particular night, as they were sitting up around a small campfire and sharing a meal, Sath's feline senses detected something off in the distance. This was not the first time in the past few days that he had the feeling that they were being followed, and this time whomever it was that had been tailing them was incredibly close.

"What is it, Sath?" Raedea asked, leaning forward, her forehead creased with worry. She had been unbraiding her long, black hair, and her pale fingers glowed against its inky depths as she froze in place.

"Maybe nothing," he said. "Stay here and I will check it out."

"I'm coming with..."

"RAE." She recognized the tone in his voice and remained where she was. There were times when discussion and debate were possible with this Qatu male, and other times that it was useless. A wall would spring up between them, and he would take on a haughty, almost regal bearing that at first had threatened to send her to her knees. After time with him, she found herself no longer threatened by the attitude, but she knew also that arguments would do no good. Sath crept off into the darkness and Raedea strained her eyes to watch him, but humans did not have the same abilities to see in the dark as the Qatu. He was soon out of her view.

Whomever it was that was following them was good, Sath would have to give credit where it was due. Almost at the skill level of a Qatu, but not quite. There was a rustling now and then and it would lead him off in a new direction. Every time he changed course, however, he made sure that he looked back over his shoulder to spot the campfire and Raedea's anxious form huddled next to it. The Outlands were expansive and it took a careful traveler not to lose one's course completely.

Back at the fire, Raedea had given up trying to follow Sath in the darkness and decided to pull out the journal and read a bit more. She had not had a moment to herself since they left the tavern, and she did not want to revisit the topic of her brother so she had not gotten the journal out again. As she thumbed through the pages, scanning the handwritten lines for her brother's name, she found herself longing to meet this one called "Gin," who had clearly become a big part of her brother's life...and whose parents her brother had inexplicably killed. "What is your story, Gin?" she whispered as she turned the page to keep reading.

"I don't know the answer to that," a male voice said from behind her, "but I'd certainly like to know yours." Raedea stilled, hoping against hope that she still had the dagger hidden in her boot that she had put there earlier. Footsteps behind her told her that the male was not alone.

"Nothing to tell, really," she said as she tucked the journal under her bedroll and rose to her feet. "May I offer you food and drink instead, sir?" She turned and met the gaze of Sir Havens of Calder's Port's militia. She gasped and stumbled backward right into the arms of another militiaman who held her fast.

"Dagger in the boot," Havens barked at his accomplice who had thought to put a gloved hand over Raedea's mouth. A third man grabbed her legs and pulled the boot off, flinging the dagger toward the campfire. "Now then, you thought you'd leave us, after all the fun we had?" he sneered at her as he drew very close. Raedea struggled against the man holding her, trying to remember the things that Sath had taught her since traveling with him about self-defense and fighting and protecting herself. However, the men were much bigger than she was and stronger, and her magical abilities were of no help if she could not speak to cast the spells. Havens grabbed her chin roughly and peeled his compatriot's hand away, then covered her mouth with his own. She bit down hard on his lip and he recoiled, but then grinned at her maliciously as he licked the blood away.

"My companion will be back any minute," she said angrily. "You do not want to provoke a Qatu, believe me."

"He will be kept busy long enough," Havens replied as he ran a grimy hand down her neck and into the front of her tunic. "How do you think we knew when to strike, you stupid girl? We drew your pussycat away to chase invisible mice so that you and I could reunite in peace." His long fingers brushed the side of her cheek as the other men each held her still, each with one hand on her arm and the other on her legs. Havens smiled as he slowly ripped open her clothes with his free hand. "If she wounds me, you both will die, understood?" he said to his men who responded affirmatively. "If she pleases me, you may have her before she dies." The men nodded and Raedea closed her eyes, praying to Isona to end her pain quickly and keep Sath far away and safe. Their grip on her tightened and her airway was constricted. Raedea's eyes popped back open in time to see darkness closing around the edge of her vision. "Thank you, Isona…Dor…" she whispered as her eyes rolled back in her head.

Sath had been tracking the intruder for long enough that he was ready to give up and just move their camp. Perhaps it had just been an animal after all. He looked back over his shoulder and was horrified to see how far away from the campsite he was – it was merely a speck on the horizon. He inhaled deeply to clear his head with the now cold night air and caught a new scent, one that he had missed before. Human blood. "Rae," he hissed as he headed for the campsite at a dead run. The closer he got, the stronger the coppery smell of blood burned in his nostrils. He finally skidded to a stop, unable to move any closer to the scene in front of him.

"Rae," he whispered. Her body, broken and stripped naked and bloody, lay on the ground next to the campfire. He could detect the scent of human males but it was faint, implying that they were long gone. Sath roared in frustration, clenching his fists until his claws pierced his own furry hide.

"Sath?" The sound of her voice stopped his roaring and brought him swiftly to his knees next to her. He grabbed a blanket from his bedroll to cover her with and lifted her head gently in his hands.

"Rae, I'm here, sssh," he said, trying to keep his purr from becoming another roar. "Who did this to you?" She blinked, her eyes rolling wildly as she gasped for air. Sath ran a hand down her side and found a dagger stuck just in between her ribs…her own dagger. "Sssh, lie still, the dagger has…"

"Havens." Her body convulsed and her fingers grasped at air, so Sath leaned down and she was able to wind them into the fur on his arms. "Havens. Sath. Forget Dor."

"Sssh, Rae, darlin, you're not making sense, just lie still and I will try to see if I have any healing potions in my pack, all right?" His eye passed yet again over that dagger in her side and he knew, without a proper healer skilled in magic, she was not going to live.

"Sath. Listen. Proud Cat. Forget Dor. Tell Gin. Parents avenged." She took a wet, rumbling gasp of air that Sath had heard many times in his enemies. "My blood. Clean slate. My life…for theirs."

"No!" Sath shouted, dropping his pack and cradling her in his arms. "Rae, don't worry about that, okay? Stay with me."

"Cat," she said, a sad fondness in her voice as it grew soft. "I'm cold. Is…the fire…out?" She wrenched her head to one side and tried to reach for the campfire with her free hand, but her arm would not move. "Dor, where is Dor?" Tears filled her eyes as she tried several times to take a breath but could not. "Sath, find Gin," she wheezed.

"Ssh, I will, Rae. I will. Rest now. Rest…Rae…Rae?" Her eyes stared, unseeing, just past him, up toward the stars. Her fingers fell away from his fur and he stared down at her. "Rae?"

He carefully closed her eyes and then settled her back down onto the ground, smoothing her dark hair away from her freckled face. "I swear to you," he said, "I will burn Calder's Port to the ground to avenge you, Raedea Dawnshadow, and to make sure Havens is dead for taking away my best friend."

As the sun began its ascent in the sky, Sath stood over the small grave where he buried Raedea's body. He did not know what human funeral rites were like. Qatu tradition required that the bodies of the fallen were burned before they were returned to the earth, but he did not think he could bring himself to do that for Raedea. It was hard enough to bury her. Sath had found garments in the bottom of Raedea's bag that resembled robes worn by priests in his homeland and he had dressed her in them, carefully and respectfully. He clumsily plaited her hair as he had seen her do so many times, picking some daisies that he found close to the campsite and placing them in the braid.

Now, as he looked down at the grave, he felt a sharp pain in his chest. Just as he had done when he left home and become the Bane of the Forest, Sath pressed a clawed hand into the middle of his breastplate and pushed, as though physically pushing the pain at losing Raedea away just as he mentally put that part of his life away. She would not have wanted him to make any sort of attack on Calder's Port in her name, despite his vow sworn to her just the night before.

"You saw the best in me," he said. "You wanted the best for me. How can I honor your memory, my kind friend, without continuing down the path you showed me?" He ran a clawed hand over his face, and then up onto his head. Find this Gin, she had said to him. *Tell her that the slate is clean*, she had ordered. Sath nodded his head slowly. "I will do as you ask, Rae. I swear."

He picked up his pack and then hers, and after a long glance in the direction of the forest, he headed toward an area just to the east of the Dark Sea that he knew to be a neutral space. He needed to find someone to serve as a go-between, or he knew he would not live long enough to deliver the journal back to the wood elf and pass on Raedea's message. After that? Sath shrugged to himself as he walked. The elves might still seek revenge. Nevertheless, if he managed to live past that encounter, it might just be time to head back to Qatu'anari. It had been far too long.

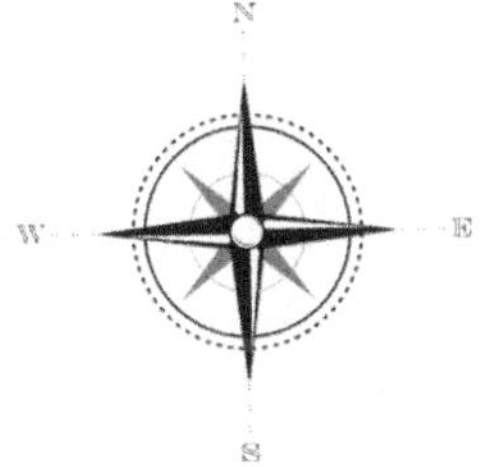


*Several years later…*

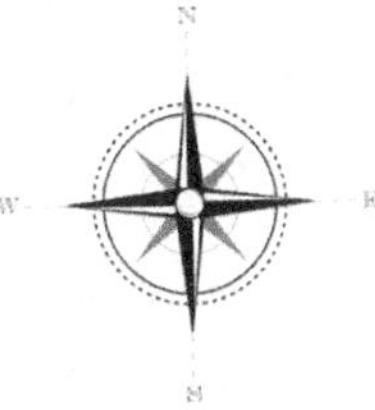

# SIXTEEN

"Ginolwenye!" called Ailreden, as he drummed impatient fingers on his desk. As leader of the Fabled Ones, he governed a guild of adventurers who had banded together to travel and explore Orana as well as perfect their individual skills and talents. Well known across the whole of Orana for their noble deeds, becoming a member was a badge of honor, not taken lightly. Gin was a probationary member, and she was not doing very well in the tasks required of her for full membership.

She frowned as she got up off the floor of the great hall and went up the stairs. The great hall consisted of a great room with a balcony that overlooked bankers and merchants as well as a space for gathering or sparring. She found Ailreden was sitting behind his desk under the giant stained glass window in the center of the balcony, and he did not look happy.

"Yes, sir?" she said, trying her best to seem upbeat and unaware that anything was wrong. "How may I serve?" The customary response to one's guild master seemed hollow today.

"I have concerns, my dear," he said, steepling his fingers and leaning on them with his chin. Ailreden's eyes were narrowed, although more likely in fatherly concern rather than anger. "I had expected so much more of you, knowing who your parents were." Gin hung her head as angry tears stung the back of her eyes. "Now, now," Ailreden said, rising from his desk and coming over to rest a hand on her shoulder. "I think that training you as a solitary druid is not the way for you. I do not think that you are meant to hunt on your own."

"I know, sir," she said, her voice soft. "I know that all I am fit for is healing those in my group when there is no one trained in the cleric way to be had."

Ailreden put his finger under her chin and raised it until her eyes met his. "Not at all, child," he said softly. "You are progressing quite well in the other magical talents afforded to druids, and I think that your skills will best serve a group of adventurers."

His hand left her chin and caressed the back of her hair, as a parent would. "I fear for your safety alone, child, not because you lack in skill, but because you have too much heart. Killing is not in your nature, and I fear that if you are on your own it will be you that will meet death and not your enemy."

"Am I being dismissed from the guild?" she asked slowly, her eyes wide with fear as she met his gaze.

"Oh, no child, not that. Never that." Ailreden returned to his desk and gestured toward a cushion on the floor nearby. She obeyed, sitting down on the cushion with her legs crossed under her. "In fact, because of your good heart and your need for justice in all things, I would that you succeed me in guild leadership if anything should happen to me," he said quietly.

Gin's eyes flew to his. "Sir?"

"Not now, Gin. Nevertheless, I will be honest with you; I am drawn to other shores and other adventures. I have been a guild leader for a long time, and I would like to escape it for some rest." The horrified look on Gin's face left him silent a moment. "That time is not now," he said solemnly, "and we shall not speak of it again until it is the right time, agreed?" She nodded, though her eyes were still wide. "For now, there is someone I want you to meet," he said, snapping his fingers and then making a beckoning gesture.

A tall male Qatu seemed to appear out of nowhere and cross the balcony from the corner, stopping at the guild leader's side. He sniffed the air, and then smiled down at Gin. It was the Bane of the Forest, who had stolen Gin's backpack and food. "Sathlir Clawsharp, at your service *darlin'*," he said, purring. His teal eyes seemed to twinkle with inner light as he bowed his head toward her. "You can call me Sath, if you like."

"What is HE doing here?" Gin scrambled to her feet, drawing her scimitar and holding it at the level of her eyes as she backed away from him, almost tumbling over the edge to the main floor below. Her hand involuntarily flew to the scar on the side of her face, and Sath sucked in a loud breath as he noticed it.

"Ah, you two have met, have you?" Ailreden said, chuckling. It was quite clear by the elder elf's demeanor that he already knew they had. "Gin, I want you to travel with Sathlir. I think that he can help you progress while giving you the protection and group hunting practice you need." Gin stared at Ailreden as though he had just told her to jump off the roof. "But of course, you're right; two does not make a group. I am also sending two of our guild's finest warriors, Hackort and Teeand, and to help you continue your studies, one of our most talented druids, Elysiam."

Gin's heart leaped at Elysiam's name. The two had grown up together and had been friends until Elysiam was banished from Aynamaede for training with Nelenie without permission. Gin had found the Fabled Ones through Elysiam, and it had been like finding a long lost family.

"He is…but sir, he…You are…" she stammered, staring at Sath.

"Does she always stutter like that?" Sath asked Ailreden, chuckling. "Ah well, I like a quiet group, and Elys already talks enough for two wood elves."

"I HEARD THAT!" rang out a female voice from downstairs.

"You…you kill druids," Gin said, her face pale and her scimitar still raised and her posture still stiff. "Sir, you cannot trust this…this…BEAST," she said.

Ailreden looked sadly at Gin. "He has come to us wanting to make amends for those early deeds, Gin," he said, placing a hand on Sath's forearm affectionately. "Believe me; Elysiam has already helped him atone for many of those sins." A malicious female laugh from downstairs caused a grin to spread across the guild leader's face. "It is your task as well, my girl, with your pure heart, to forgive Sathlir. Can you do that for me and for the guild?"

Remembering her oath to the All Mother years before, Gin nodded hesitantly. "For you, sir. But I will be watching you, Cat," she said, pointing one of her tiny fingers at the massive Qatu, hoping that he wouldn't see how much it trembled. "I may forgive but I can never forget."

"I hope so," he said quietly, beaming a smile at her and trying his best to hide his deadly teeth. "I do hope so." Gin winced and stuck her hands in the pockets of her tunic, scampering away and down the stairs. Sath smiled sadly. "I will take care of her, Sir," he said to Ailreden, bowing his head reverently before his guild master. I will let no harm come to her, I swear it."

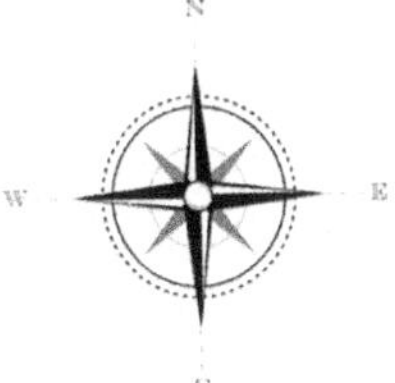

# Seventeen

After many uncomfortable months of traveling alongside Sath and the other Fabled Ones, Gin found herself one evening sitting on the marble floor of the grand hall, packing her things for a long mission. Ailreden had asked them come to the aid of a magician that had been a longtime friend of his. The magician, called Gaelin, was an elf from Alynatalos, so Gin was hoping that he might have some news of her friends from her childhood. It had been many months since any of the Fabled Ones had heard from the elderly mage, and Ailreden feared that Gaelin was held prisoner, so their job was to find and bring him home.

She studied the other members of her team warily. Ailreden had called them all together the night before in order to brief them on the mission, and she was still not sure she would remember their names. Well, save two…Gin was sure that she would never forget Sathlir Clawsharp's name. He had been her constant shadow since being "assigned" to help her by their leader. Elysiam was also familiar from back home in Aynamaede, but Gin had not seen her much after her banishment. She was not sure how Elysiam could stand to be in the same room with Sathlir, but there she was! How her old friend could have invited her to the guild without telling her that Sathlir was a part of it... Perhaps she bought into his story of seeking atonement, but Gin was not so convinced just yet.

Gin was glad to be hunting with Elysiam all the same. After the unpleasantness surrounding Nelenie and Elysiam's banishments, Gin had feared for her sister-druid. She was still young but she seemed to have landed on her feet. Elysiam now had a companion who had devoted his sword to protecting her: a gnome called Hackort.

Gin smiled as she looked at Hackort now, as he watched Elysiam's every move and made sure that all of her weapons were sharpened and ready for battle if needed. He clearly cared deeply for her, and Gin found herself a bit jealous. She giggled as Elysiam swatted at the gnome's hands when he got too close to her rations. "We are not taking ale," she snarled. "You can talk to the dwarf if you want some of his but I am not packing any, Hack," Elysiam hauled him out of her bag by his collar. "Don't you have someone else to annoy?"

"No one as fun as you," the gnome replied, beaming a grin at Elysiam, who scowled back at him. "Although Gin…Ginol…I'm sorry, what was your name again?" he asked Gin as he squinted up at her.

"Ginolwenye," she replied with a smile. He frowned.

"Nope, can't say that one. I'll call you Ginny," he said. Gin rolled her eyes.

"That's what we used to call her back home," Elysiam said softly. Gin stared at her sister-druid. Elysiam never let her guard down and was usually hard as stone. Hearing the longing for their home in her voice was surprising to say the least, especially after how the elders had thrown her out like so much rubbish.

Gin reached over and squeezed Hackort's tiny hand. "That's fine, Hackort."

"You can call me Hack," he said, grinning. "Just don't call me Teeny, that's Elys's pet name for me when we're alone, isn't it?" He fluttered his tiny eyelashes up at Elysiam who groaned loudly. "She doesn't like it when I announce it in public, though." Gin giggled as she looked around the room.

The only one that did not seem too interested in getting to know everyone was the dwarf warrior, Teeand, but he was apparently good friends with Sath already so Gin was not sure she wanted to know him. Rumors flew about the relationships of the races that made Orana their home, and often the dwarves were said to be even worse than the dark elves who still skulked about in the darker parts of the forest when they were not underground.

Gin had met Teeand before, once long ago when she had only just come to the grand hall of the Fabled Ones and she remembered how kind he had seemed in that brief encounter. Now he was cold and quiet, and he drank a lot of ale. Must be the association with that Qatu, she thought. That would drive anyone sane to drink.

"So we know our route and we'll be ready to head out at first light?" Teeand barked, rousing Gin from her memories with a start. "Steady there, druid, I didn't mean to scare ya," he said as he and Sath shared a grin. "I'm just asking because I'd like to have a bit of time to relax before we're off in t'morning, so are we good to go or...?"

"As long as you bring back a bit of the ale from the tavern to take with us?" Hackort said with a wicked grin. "That trail will be long and I feel like we might need it…"

"Of course I will, wee man, of course, that is if your lady friend there doesn't mind?" Elysiam answered Teeand by throwing a shoe at him and barely missing his head. "Ah, this will be fun, eh Qatu?"

The dwarf clapped Sath on the shoulder but the Qatu ignored him. He had been staring at Gin, still unable to believe that the one who wrote the words that had so inspired him was right there in front of him. He had not forgotten his promise to Raedea, but similarly he had not quite been able to give up the journal. *"Hello? Sath? Stop checking out our new druid or I'll teach her to speak Qatunari."* Sath started at the sound of his native language and then chuckled along with Teeand.

"HEY no fair talking in the growly grumblies!" Hackort shouted, and they all burst into laughter. Gin looked from face to face, finally locking eyes with Sath and quickly looking away. He took a deep breath and frowned at the fear he could smell from her. Hack looked back and forth between them, and then scooted over close to Gin. "Don't worry about the Qatu, Ginny," he said in an exaggerated whisper. "If he was still eating druids for lunch our Elys would have been an entrée ages ago." She grinned at Hackort with gratitude and then stood, pulling her pack onto her back.

"Right then! To the tavern?" Tee said, finally smiling. Gin shook her head.

"I'll just be off to say goodbye to my sister," she said. "I'll meet you all here in the morning to leave, if that's all right?"

"Don't blame you," Elys said, grinning at her. "You'll have enough time to spend up close and personal with this lot. Go get a good night's sleep in a bed. We will see you in the morning. First light"

"Yeah, let Elys have one more night with us all to herself," Hack said. He let out a loud OOF as she planted one of her boots in the middle of his back. "She doesn't like me telling THAT in public either." Gin was laughing as she opened the great hall door and headed for the tiny room at a local inn that she was currently sharing with her sister, Lairceach.

The Fabled Ones had set up in an old cathedral in the outpost near the edge of the Forbidden Sea. This body of water had become so acidic by the outpouring of magic that created the dragons that to put a toe in the water for most of the races of Orana would cause the skin to burn. The outpost here was different than most in that it existed due to a partnership among most of the races of Orana. There were representatives of the humans, dwarves, elves, and gnomes there who had formed embassies so that they could mediate issues that arose amongst their people. Notably missing were the Qatu and the Dragonkind, neither of which felt that they needed to mix with the others, and the dark elves who did not trust anyone but their own kind. Gin had sent word for her sister to join her there when she became part of the Fabled Ones, but since Lairceach was not yet ready to join a guild and she was still pursuing her training they lived in a room in a nearby inn.

After much laughter, storytelling, and a restless night, Gin found herself up well before dawn and headed back to the grand hall. She was surprisingly excited to be going on the mission, considering the variety of her traveling companions. Her sister had been shocked to learn that Gin was traveling with the Bane of the Forest, but after much discussion and assurances, she had accepted it and sworn on the memory of their parents that she would not try to follow Gin.

"You have many seasons of training ahead of you, Lairky,"

Gin had chided her. "Just think, you're so far ahead now, but how much better can you be with more training? You'll know more than your guild masters!" As she walked along the cobblestone path leading to the hall, she thought about the smile that had split her sister's face and grinned. Lairceach was going to be all right, and Cursik was there if she was not. Her family was safe.

Gin almost skipped up the ramp leading to the door of the massive great hall. She did not notice the cloaked figure behind one of the massive columns that followed her inside the lobby. The figure stayed with her until she got to the great hall door, but was not close enough to see the intricate pattern of shapes on the door that Gin touched in sequence. The spots in the door served as a password of sorts that allowed only members through the giant door, and without the correct order, the figure remained, swearing softly, in the lobby.

Her compatriots were still asleep, as she had thought they would be, and she was careful to step over them as she made her way to the pool of magical water that would rejuvenate her before the long trip. She stripped down to her tunic and trousers and slid into the cool water, saying a silent word of thanks to the All-Mother and marveling at how instantaneous the restorative effect was. Within moments, she was nearly asleep.

"You're up early," said a grumbly voice from the shadowed corner of the room that held the pool. Gin jumped to her feet and scrambled for her armor. "I'm sorry, wait, wait…" said the voice. Wide-eyed, Gin stared as Sath emerged from the corner. "Me, I can't stand that stuff. My race doesn't…care for water." He chuckled but then stopped when he caught the scent of her fear. "I'm sorry, I'll go."

"No, I lingered longer than my fair share in the water," Gin said as she backed out of the room, holding her armor up in front of her as a shield. "I understand that you may feel the healing benefits if you merely sit next to the pool, so if you…" Sath moved faster than Gin could turn and run, and was soon between her and the door to the main room of the grand hall.

"Wait. Please." He knelt slowly, his arms outstretched to show that he was unarmed, and looked her in the eye. "You have every right to be wary of me, Ginol…Gin," he began, his teal eyes pleading with her to listen. "In fact, I deserve every bit of anger you have toward me. I can only hope that you will come to know me as I am now, and not as the monster I was when we first met. I have so much to teach you, if you will trust me."

"You stole my things, injured me, and sent your terrible pet after me," Gin said, her tone accusatory and angry. "Granted, you did return most of my things, but still… Why should I trust you?"

"You shouldn't." Sath stood back up and sighed loudly as she dashed past him and into the main room. Gin strapped on her armor as fast as she could, and in the process got her hair tangled. It was light chain mail, and the tiny loops held her hair fast. She cried out in frustration before she could stop herself, and Sath was at her side in the blink of an eye. "Can I help?" he asked as he studied the mail tunic that she held aloft to keep the weight from pulling her hair from her head.

"No, I'm fine," she said, struggling to release her hair while not dropping the tunic.

"Let me help, I'm taller than you are and can use my claws," Sath said, not thinking about how that sentence would sound to her. Gin stilled, frozen in place, tears welling up in her eyes as Sath carefully picked the tangled strands of hair out of the neck of the tunic. "There. All fixed," he said before backing away from her, hands raised.

"Thank you," Gin mumbled as she pulled the tunic over her head. She released her hair from the ponytail and pulled it back up, causing a shower of what seemed to be sunflowers to assault Sath's nose. Did she always smell like that? He backed away another step to clear his head, and put his foot right on top of Hack's leg. The gnome screeched and scrambled to his feet, his giant axe already in his tiny hand. Elysiam was at his side immediately, her weapon drawn as well.

"What happened?" she barked, waving the scimitar about in front of her. "Did someone sneak in?"

"Sath stepped on me!" Hack wailed as he dropped his axe and rubbed his leg. Elysiam smacked him in the back of the head with her hand before returning her scimitar to its sheath. "OW!" Gin covered her mouth to stifle a laugh, and then noticed Sath was watching her. She managed to smile at him, amazed at the relief that flooded his face as she did.

"Well, I suppose we're off now, yeah?" Teeand said as he rose from his bedroll. He rubbed his head, frowning. "One of these days I'll meet m'match in that tavern, but that day was not last night." Sath grinned at his old friend. "What are you smiling at, Cat?" Teeand barked. "You were as much in the ale as I was last night, and yet, not a spot of a hangover."

"Qatu accelerated healing," Sath chuckled. "Also, I have a lot more room for ale than you do, my short friend." Teeand scowled at Sath as he got to his feet and stuffed his bedroll into his haversack.

"Right then, off we go?" Teeand asked. Met with nods all around, he headed to the door of the grand hall. "This is going to be a long trip," he muttered as he opened the door and took a long look over his shoulder at the rest of them. He shook his head. "A very long trip."

A robed figure fell through the door as Teeand opened it. Swearing, the dwarf kicked the lump of a person back out the door as he drew his sword. "On your feet!" he called out as the figure quickly sprang up and dashed out into the lobby toward the door. "Bloody hobos," Teeand said, re-sheathing his sword.

"Do you think he needed money or food?" Gin asked. "Should we have offered that instead of…" She snapped her mouth shut as Teeand turned to glare at her.

"You give them that and they never leave," he hissed. Gin stood her ground, staring back at the dwarf. They were almost the same height.

"You give them that because it is right to do it," she snapped back at him. Elysiam and Hack stared at the two of them, eyes wide, but Sath started chuckling. "And what is so funny?" Gin demanded as she glared up at the Qatu male, nearly twice her size.

"He treats them like he does his own young who are always hanging about, looking for a bit of money or ale from their father," Sath said. "Oh, don't look at me like that, Tee! You know it's true." Gin found herself staring at Tee in surprise. The boozy dwarf had a family at home. Her eyes narrowed, but then softened. He was probably out taking on work in order to support all those children.

The five of them filed out the door and then out into the streets of the outpost. They would take the long way around to Bellesea Keep, a place that Gin had heard of only in hushed and frightened whispers. Gin checked her map again as they made their way toward the front gates of the outpost. "Going to be our navigator?" Teeand asked her as he beamed a smile her way. Gin looked over at him, trying to smile back.

"Aye, we don't want to waste time by going too far out of

our way," she replied. "Though we could travel through the edge of the forest, to the other outpost. I understand it is lovely and would be welcoming to a…well, a mixed group such as we are." Emhlenor was a shared outpost between the humans and the elves, situated just between the forest and the grasslands with a clear view to the north of the foothills of the Volcanic Mountains. The views were amazing and said to represent the best of the homelands of both races that made it their home.

"Ah yes, the grand Emhlenor outpost," Sath said, his words dripping with sarcasm. "They don't exactly love me around there, don't forget." He regretted his words instantly as Gin and Elysiam shot him equally pointed looks. "A fact I'm working on improving, mind you ladies," he said, his best toothy grin on display. Elysiam chuckled but Gin held his gaze a bit longer. I will have to work doubly hard on that one, Sath thought.

Teeand clapped a hand on Gin's back as though she was one of his children. "There, there, flower, you'll get used to it." Mortified that he had noticed her discomfort, Gin swallowed hard and nodded in Teeand's general direction. They ducked into a cave due to a sprinkling of rain that set Sath hissing. "Now let's be having that map, if you please Pet?" Gin handed him the map and he spread it out on the root-infested floor of the cave. "Looks like we could go straight ahead into this cave as it leads to a tunnel, and then turn left at that junction there. I'll take the lead and Hack, if you will, bring up the rear in case we meet anyone of a more nefarious purpose."

They all agreed and soon were moving through the passageways as fast as they could. "Tee? Hold up a minute," Sath called out. The group stopped and turned their attention to the Qatu, who began speaking in a language Gin had never heard before. Bluish light seemed to flow from his claws and surround him, and when it faded, Sath was just about as tall as Gin and Elysiam! "Now we can move faster and I won't have to keep ducking."

"I think it suits you," Teeand remarked as they started again. "Pocket Qatu. I bet we could make a fortune selling little cats to people as pets." A growl from Sath shut Teeand up, but also made every muscle in Gin's body go rigid. She was walking right between the dwarf and the Qatu, and she did not like having him behind her, especially if he was going to be growly!

"Sorry, Gin…Ginol…wenye," Sath whispered. "I didn't mean to scare you."

"I'm not afraid of you," she hissed back. "And just call me Gin. I think Elys is the only one that can pronounce my full name properly."

After what seemed like forever in the dripping, dark cave, the light at the exit that led to the Outlands finally came into view. Bellesea Keep, where they were headed, was the ruin of an ancient dragon stronghold, said to be inhabited by ghosts. It teetered on the edge, between the Outlands and the mountain home of the dwarves. Gin had kept up her silence as they walked; only making a sound when she tripped over one of the giant roots that surrounded the walls and floor of the cave. She blinked into the near blinding light that reflected off the alabaster snowcaps just past the Outlands. Suddenly Elysiam's hand appeared in front of her face and Gin nearly fell over onto her sister-druid. "A bit of magical camouflage might be in order, don't you think?" Elysiam said with a grin. Gin nodded.

"That and maybe some levitation and a bit of speed?" Gin asked. She began the chant in Elvish and soon each of them felt their feet lighten, ready to zip across the desert plain. Elysiam joined in just as Gin was finishing and soon the five of them faded from view. "Well done, my sister," Gin whispered to Elysiam, who smiled. The group moved out into the boiling sun of the Outlands and made their way toward the imposing stone building just before the gentle slope of the mountains.

"That's the entrance, there," Sath pointed just before he realized that no one could see him. "The two stone structures with the statues in front of them. They are guarded by wyverns, but most of them cannot see as well as they can smell. If our invisibility drops, then…"

"If it drops? BAH! My spells don't drop, Cat," Elysiam snapped back at him.

"All I was going to say was that if it drops, run toward the entrance and don't stop. Tee and I will take care of those minor dragonkind if needed," Sath whispered back, making Gin jump. If he was imposing when she could see him, Sath was much scarier when she could not. She took a deep breath. "They walk upright though, and are bigger than I am. Don't worry. Those things are nothing new to me and Teeand." The dwarf chuckled.

"I can take them too!" Hackort wailed from the back of the pack. "You always forget me because I'm shorter than you two! Oof!" A giggle from Elysiam told the rest of the group that she had managed to kick the gnome even though she could not see him. "I'll get you for that one, Elys, once I can see you."

"How do we know if they can see us?" Gin said as they stopped directly opposite from the entrance to the ruin that had once been a magnificent castle. Wyverns stalked back and forth in front of the entrance, still adorned with carvings depicting the once powerful human empire that had dominated most of Orana. Giant statues of the conquerors, names long lost to history, stood like sentinels, ready to spring into battle against their enemies. Gin shuddered as she gazed up at the stone figures, and remembered seeing Dorlagar for the first time in Aynamaede.

"We don't, until they do," Teeand replied in a whisper. He sounded like he was right in her ear due to her inability to see him, and she backed up a step involuntarily.

"Oof, careful," Sath whispered. Gin could feel his fur up against the back of her neck and she shuddered before moving away from him.

"Sorry," she mumbled. She studied the guards at the door for a moment. "No sense in all of us having to waste energy on those wyverns is there?" she asked suddenly. "I mean there are two of us druids, so…" She broke into a run, straight up to the front door, only stopping when she nearly ran headlong into one of the wyverns, a large bluish-skinned one. Back at the group, the other four made various gasps and noises of disbelief and irritation at her apparent dash to the front door. Gin scampered back to where she thought the group was and skidded to a stop. "They can't see us, I ran right up to them and nothing happened," she said, grinning from ear to pointed ear.

"What in the Mother's name was THAT, Gin?" Elysiam hissed as Gin hung her head. "Well, clearly they didn't see you, so let's head inside. This air is starting to make my hair frizz." The five of them headed toward the entrance and slipped past the guards and through the massive stone doors. Once inside, they took a collective sigh of relief and as if on cue, their invisibility faded. "See, I told you, Cat, my invisibility spell doesn't fade until it's time," Elysiam sneered. Chuckling, Sath took a swipe at her, missing her by a mile.

"Right, so where is this Gaelin?" he asked, looking over Teeand's shoulder as the dwarf rolled out the map.

"Here, in the cells on the top floor," Teeand answered. "Or at least that's where Ailreden believes him to be, from…past experience."

"Aye," Sath said, his countenance grim. "We know right where those cells are, don't we?"

"You've been a prisoner here before?" Gin asked, wide eyed.

"Aye, Gin," Sath said. "It was during a darker time, wasn't it Tee? That was before Elys here found us and dragged our sorry hides back to the Fabled Ones."

"Not that long ago," Elysiam said. "I came to get Tee out and got this fur ball in the deal."

"You…brought Sath…the Bane of the Forest…?" Gin stared at Elysiam. It was too much to wrap her mind around. A wood elf druid saving the Bane of the Forest?

"Ginny, you are so wonderfully naïve," Elysiam said, a look of genuine affection on her face. "When I was exiled from Aynamaede, I broke all my ties to our home and its people…well, save you of course because you were kind to me. But then some time in another prison made me…shall we say more understanding of the flaws of others?" She looked each of them in the eye in turn. "And if you ever dare repeat what I've just said I will not only deny it; I will probably kill you."

"Probably?" Hackort said with a chuckle, and then dodged the business end of the staff that Elysiam was carrying. "Right, lead on, Tee! We've got wyverns to kill and wizards to save!" His axe swung up into his tiny hand as a wide grin split his features. With a nod, Teeand led the way into the dark ruin of a castle.

At the end of the shadowy entryway, they turned a corner and found the entrance to the castle proper, the actual Bellesea Keep, bounded on all sides by a moat. Two larger wyverns, both red-scaled with golden eyes, stood on either side of the drawbridge. "Do we sneak past them too?" Gin whispered.

"No," Sath replied, grinning as he noticed that she did not jump when he spoke. "We could but there are undead past them that pay no mind to our magic."

"What about the moat?" Gin said. "Can we just swim around to a better entrance?"

"Well, even if our feline friend here liked the water, that moat doesn't go all the way around," Teeand said. "It is very slight, but we are actually moving downhill the further we move into the castle. It's built into the ground and the moat just leads around to a wall." He swung his own giant axe into his hand and gripped the handle, cracking his knuckles as he did so. "Unless anyone here speaks Elder Dragon, I think we have to fight our way in, flower."

Gin found herself shrinking back to the rear of the group. All of the bravado she had before when she had charged at the wyverns guarding the door was gone now that she knew they could see her. She glanced over at Elysiam who had already unsheathed her scimitar and was clearly itching for the fight to come. Why hadn't she been born like that? "I guess I'll hang back and be the healer, then?"

"You'll have to, Pet," Teeand said. "We don't have a proper cleric with us, but I trust you and your magic to keep us alive." He leaned in close to her, indicating Sath with a nod of his head. "All of us."

"Of course," Gin stammered, flustered. It had not occurred to her that she would have to heal the Bane of the Forest, but she supposed that the sooner she stopped thinking of him in those terms, the better. He was part of the team and he was just as responsible for her safety as she was for his. Just then, Sath glanced around at her, the smile that parted his feline features spreading up and into his teal eyes. Gin looked away, speaking magical words that summoned Beau, her preternatural pony, and was soon sitting in the saddle, her hands fiddling with the horn as she always did when she was nervous.

"Right! Elys, if you will, use your magic to slow these things down so that Hack and I can have at them at our own pace?" Teeand said, returning his gaze to the target. "Then once we've engaged, Sath, your pet can join us and you can work your own magic to deter their attack." Sath nodded and Elysiam moved to the front of the group. She looked back over her shoulder at her sister-druid, mouthing the words *You got this, Gin,* in Elvish, and then charged ahead of them.

"HEY!" Elysiam cried out as she ran toward the drawbridge. The guards sniffed the air and then looked down at her, snarling. "Come and get me if you're not all talk!" She spoke ancient Elvish words as the two pounded across the drawbridge with heavy feet, turning to run only when her spell was complete. Though slowed down by magical tangling roots, one of the guards was quicker than she had expected and it managed to get a good swipe in on her before she could get clear. The hit sent her sprawling into the dirt in front of the advancing wyverns and sent Hackort surging out ahead of Teeand, his axe swinging madly over his head.

"Don't…hit… ELYS!" he bellowed, landing a good blow to the knees of the wyvern that had caught up to the druid. Gin gripped the horn of the saddle. To send healing magic to Elysiam too soon would get the wyverns' attention and they would be on her in a flash, but she could not just let her sister-druid lie there in the dust.

Sath spoke something in Qatunari and a small tiger appeared at his side, and then bounded into the fray, snarling and hissing as it attacked the slower of the two wyverns. He continued speaking in the strange purring-laden language and a cloud formed around his hands, and then moved swiftly to surround the heads of the two wyverns who immediately decreased the speed and ferocity of their attacks. Gin watched, fascinated by the sound of his language.

Finally, however, something deep inside of Gin snapped and she knew what she had to do. She focused her attention on Elysiam, still curled up on the ground, and channeled the strongest healing magic she had in the direction of her fallen sister-druid. Light surged from her fingers, surrounded Elysiam, who moments later was hauling herself up off the ground, and rubbing her eyes.

Elysiam snapped right back into the rhythm of battle, shouting out her spells in a mixture of Elvish and Elder Elvish, the language of the high elves. Gin smiled sadly. Elysiam must have learned that during her time studying with Nelenie. She surveyed the rest of the fight and was dismayed to see that while the two warriors were almost finished with the wyvern that had attacked Elysiam, the other one seemed to be making a mess of Sath as he took it on with only his magical tiger to help. She urged Beau closer and focused on Sath, forgetting who he had been and what he had done, and only thinking of making him stronger and well again. She spoke the ancient words in a whisper and soon the same white light shot from her fingertips and surrounded the Qatu.

Sath's attention almost ripped away from the wyvern in his face as he felt the curtain of healing warmth settle around him. "Oh, now that's better," he said to the wyvern just before his staff made sickening contact with its skull.

The guard stumbled; Sath's magical tiger took advantage of the situation, pounced, and ripped its throat open, leaving it a gurgling mass of scales on the ground. He turned back to the two warriors to find them standing above another wyvern corpse. Hackort was grinning from ear to ear and Teeand bore the semblance of a tired smile.

"Well done," he said as he surveyed the group. "Gin, you can move up closer now!" Gin did as told, still with a death grip on the horn of the saddle. "You'll want to dismiss your pony, Flower," Tee told her. "Some of these passageways are not friendly to horseshoes." The druid slid down from the saddle and moved close to the pony's head, whispering magical words as she stroked his neck. He winked out of existence with a whinny. A female hand on Gin's shoulder startled her back from her musing with her pony, and then spun her around into an embrace.

"Thanks," Elysiam whispered in her ear. "Do you think anyone noticed me using Nel's magic?"

"I did," Gin whispered back, "but that's only because I know Nelenie so well." She pulled out of Elysiam's hug and winked at her sister-druid. "It's all good, Elys. WE got this." The five of them moved further into the castle, across the drawbridge to four more of the waiting wyverns. Working together, they managed to end the lot of them, and took a moment to rest before moving deeper into the keep.

The robed figure that had been waiting outside of the great hall had made good time crossing the Outlands to the entrance of Bellesea Keep. Upon approaching the guards at the door, he spoke to them in their language, a deep and guttural form of communication that occasionally sounded like hissing and growling. "You saw no one?"

"No, my Lord, no one," the guard to the left of the main entrance replied. "Though it seems our brothers at arms have sounded an alarm inside. Perhaps we have a traitor in our midst."

"There is no traitor, you idiot." the robed figure snarled in response. "There are two druids in your midst, and now they are in the keep. Master will not be pleased." The wyverns hung their heads. "I will fix this but you can be sure that I will answer when your Master asks how a group of strangers made it past the front gate of his stronghold." Pushing past the guards, the figure strode into the castle. The giant stone door reverberated as it slammed behind him.

"Now, where are you, my little druid?" he said as he walked carefully through the entryway and stepped over the bodies of the dead wyverns at the drawbridge. "I can't wait to see my Master's face when I bring him a lovely little wood elf like you. Feisty one as well. All the better."

The trail of dead wyverns led him across the drawbridge and up the stairs to the ramparts where he found more carnage in the form of corpses of lookouts and piles of bones that surely had been animated by dark magic to guard the outer circle of his ruined castle. "What are they here for?" he mused aloud as he heard the sounds of battle just ahead. Pressing himself against one of the walls as he spoke ancient dark words, faded from view, and then moved closer to the group to listen.

"Did you just feel that?" Gin asked, shivering. "A chill just ran down my back. Strange." She looked around and at one point was looking right at the robed figure but his magic kept him hidden from her eyes.

"Nope," Elysiam said. "So, let's move on? More wyverns to play with between here and Gaelin's cell, yes?" The other druid was almost dancing; she was so eager to fight. The robed figure marveled silently at the difference between the two females.

"Yes, but we have to rest now and then or our Ginny

won't be able to keep us all alive, will you Ginny?" Hackort replied, smiling up at Gin. The robed figure scowled under his hood and invisibility magic. She is still only healing, he thought. Pity.

"I'm fine, Hack," Gin said, patting him on his helmet. The gnome beamed a smile up at her that made her laugh, a noise that threatened to undo the robed figure. "Can we check the map again though? I don't doubt Sathlir and Teeand but I just want to make sure that I know how to get around if we get separated."

"That's easy," the robed figure said, dispelling the invisibility magic and stepping into view. "You just cast an evacuation spell. You and those nearest to you will be whisked away from danger and back to the relative safety of the other side of the drawbridge." Teeand turned and glared at the figure.

"YOU!" the dwarf exclaimed as he rolled his axe back and forth menacingly in his hands. "Didn't I trip over you on the way out of our hall back at the outpost? State your business and make it fast." He brought the tip of the axe up under the stranger's chin and knocked back the hood of his robe. Gin gasped loudly.

"Dor?" she said, her face paling as she took a step back. Sath gaped for a moment; the resemblance to Raedea was uncanny. Her dying words to forget him rang in his memory and he shook his head to clear it. Instantly the other three stepped between Gin and Dorlagar protectively as Dorlagar held up his hands. Sath was still a moment, but then moved over with the others, not ready to reveal what he knew.

"No need for that, really. I'm quite impressed, though, that you seem to have landed on your feet, Blueberry," he said. Gin frowned at him. "Yep, same reaction to the name as always, my dear Gin, good to see that hasn't changed."

"She's not your dear anything, human," Hack bellowed.

"She's our Ginny and you still haven't told us what you want with her."

"I want nothing but to make right a debt I owe her," Dorlagar replied. "Gin and I have quite the history, and not all of it has been pleasant. Nevertheless, I seek to make amends. Surely, you," he said, shifting his gaze to Sath, "the Bane of the Forest, can't begrudge me that chance to right my past wrongs, can you?"

"How do you know...how does he know who I am?" Sath demanded, looking from Elysiam to Gin. Dorlagar smiled wickedly.

"*Your Ginny* talks in her sleep," he said. Sath growled low in his throat and gripped his staff, nearly snapping it in two. Dorlagar studied Gin a moment, reaching out to touch the scar left on her cheek from her first meeting with Sath. "Did he do that to you, Blueberry? Is that how you treat females, Qatu?" All of them drew their weapons and pointed them at Dorlagar, who kept his hands raised but took a cautious step backward. "I will kill you for that, CAT," he hissed under his breath.

"Okay, THAT is enough," Gin said. "Stand down; he's not going to hurt me. Dor and I hunted together many seasons ago." She looked over at Elysiam. "After Nel was exiled, she fell in with another disgraced daughter of the forest, Naevys." Elysiam sucked in her breath sharply.

"Gin, Naevys was sent away for...behavior not befitting a druid," Elysiam said, her eyes blazing. "Why was Nel with her?"

"I don't know, Elys, but Nel introduced me to her and they took me in for a time. I learned a lot about who I am while traveling with them. I had met Dor when he fell out of Aynamaede and nearly killed me."

"I still owe you one for that as well," Dorlagar said, unable to take his eyes off Gin. His Master would be so very pleased with her. She was just quiet and mousy enough that she probably would not fight back during the spell testing. Now if only that wizard in the cells would agree to help craft the spell…

"You don't owe me anything, Dor. I release you. I don't forgive you, but I release you." Gin turned to face Elysiam. "Naevys was good to Nel and as far as I know they still travel together. Don't worry." She looked back at Dorlagar. "In fact, I thought you were still with her. What are you doing here?"

"I have no idea where they are, Blueberry..." he began, but Gin cut him off mid-sentence.

"Gin."

"Yes. I'm sorry. Old habits die hard. I didn't go back after that day, the day you challenged me in Calder's Point. I have been traveling alone since then, trying to find a way to make amends for your parents' deaths and find out what I can about the death of my sister." Sath swallowed hard but continued to remain quiet. He could not understand how Raedea was related to this slimy human at all, let alone had been his twin! It made no sense.

Dorlagar hung his head. "The only thing I knew to do was to draw close to you and be there in case I could protect you in the way your parents should have been protected from me."

"So you have been following me? Come on, Dor, I would have noticed that," Gin said, her hands on her hips. Sath narrowed his eyes as he glared at Dorlagar.

"Maybe not," Sath said, a growl prominent behind his words. "Knights like this one are trained to be stealthy, to work in the dark rather than the light." He moved closer to Gin, again placing himself in between her and Dorlagar. Gin tried to push him out of the way, but Sath stood firm.

"Gin, you didn't tell me you had a pet," Dorlagar said. He locked eyes with the Qatu and his pupils shifted to a deadly blood red color while Sath's stayed a fiery teal. They both squared shoulders at each other like bulls about to charge. Gin threw her hands up in the air and looked to the others for help. Clearly, neither of them was going to back down nor listen to her.

"Knock it off," Teeand said to both of them. "If you're looking for an invite to travel with us, Dorlagar, I'm afraid the answer is no. We live in the light, not the dark. Now, if you'll be on your way, we've got a mission to complete."

"Aye, you seek the magician Gaelin, do you not?" Dorlagar said.

"Anything else you overheard that you'd like to share?" Elysiam said, tracing invisible patterns on her staff as she glared up at him.

"I can get him for you. I have…partnerships with some that dwell here in the keep, and for a price I can bring Gaelin to you, no questions asked, and you can walk out of here with him. No more fighting. What do you say?" Dorlagar asked, licking his lips nervously.

"What's the price, human?" Sath growled. Everything that Raedea had told him of her brother and all of her willingness to right his wrongs for him seemed hollow now. This human before him now was not worth one tiny bit of her good nature. Not one bit.

"Gin's forgiveness," Dorlagar said, trying to sound as honest as he could manage.

"Unacceptable," Sath replied. Gin placed a hand gingerly

on Sath's arm and then pushed him out of the way.

"I can answer for myself, Sath," she said quietly. "It is agreed, Dor. If you rescue Gaelin, bring him here to us AND ensure that we have safe passage out of the castle, you have my forgiveness for causing the death of my parents." A rumble of disagreement burst from the others behind her.

"Gin, a word?" Teeand barked as he grabbed her arm and pulled her off to one side. "Are you saying this human killed your parents?" Gin nodded. "He killed your parents, and now you're willing to make deals with him? To forgive him rather than just run him through?"

"Aye, but I know Dor and I have seen that he CAN be an honorable man," Gin replied. She looked the dwarf in the eye. "You're just going to have to trust me on this one, Teeand. Can you do that?"

The warrior scowled. "No, but I will go along with this for now. You should know that if he steps one inch out of line…well, I'll let Hack take that human off his list of people NOT to kill," he replied, stalking back over to the group. Gin stood there a moment, feeling stung by his reply but understanding his hesitance, and then she rejoined the group.

"Well?" Dorlagar said, waggling his eyebrows at Gin. "What's it going to be, Blueberry?"

"I told you, Dor, my name is Gin," she snapped. "We are agreed that if you can follow the terms I've set out then we have a deal. We will return to the entrance of the keep to wait for you and Gaelin unless you require assistance."

"Return to the…we agreed…wait, what?" Elysiam's eyes blazed, but Hackort laid a tiny hand on her boot and she stilled.

"I don't want any of us to get hurt, Elys," he said softly. "If the human doesn't live up to the bargain, we can kill him." He turned to Gin, his eyes lighting up. "Right, Ginny? We can kill him?"

"Let's just see what Dor can do first, Hack," Gin said, smiling at him. Her smile did not make it to her eyes. "Let's head back out to the courtyard where it's safe." She turned to leave with the others but stopped when Dorlagar placed a hand on her arm. His gesture was met by the sound of the other four drawing their weapons and Sath calling up his magical pet tiger.

"Easy, easy," Dorlagar said, taking his hand off Gin's arm and raising both of them in the air. "Here's the problem with your plan: I can't get in there alone. I need a prisoner with me so that the wyverns will let me get to the cells. If Gin goes with me, then she can transport herself and Gaelin out to you."

"That was not the deal, human," Sath snarled. "You were going in alone."

"And now I'm not," Dorlagar said, beaming a wicked grin back at the Qatu. It was taking all the willpower that Dorlagar had to keep the magic and bloodlust from creeping up and turning his eyes the color of blood. "Do you want me to take the risk that Gaelin is injured and I cannot bring him out alone without arousing suspicion? You of all should know the kind of…hospitality shown to prisoners here." He again locked eyes with Sath.

"It is fine," Gin said, stepping between them. "I will go with him."

"Not alone," Teeand interjected. "Sath, you go with them. Elys and Hack and I will come to you if needed. You're about the same height as those wyverns so if you put on your traveling cloak you might be able to fool them." Gin let out an exasperated sigh and threw her hands up in defeat.

"See? Now we're thinking!" Dorlagar exclaimed, and then immediately fell silent when five angry glares met his gaze. "Right. So I'm taking Gin and her pet cat with me." He turned on his heel and headed toward the inner part of the keep, pulling Gin along behind him as though she was his prisoner. Sath growled and ran to catch up, putting on his cloak and pulling the hood up over his head as he went.

"This is not going to end well," Teeand murmured as he watched them go. Elysiam said nothing, only stood and pouted.

"I hope not. I haven't added that human to my list yet, and I won't," Hackort said, grinning as he gripped the hilt of his axe. The three of them headed back for the entrance with Teeand lagging behind, watching over his shoulder.

"Not if I get to him first," Teeand muttered under his breath.

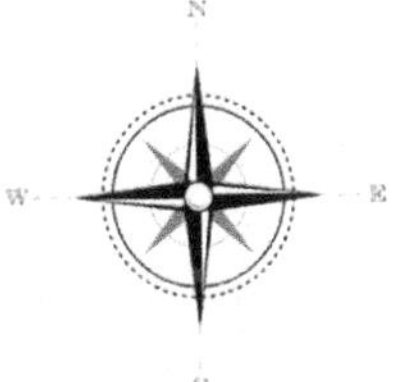

# Eighteen

"Slow down, human," Sath demanded.

"Having trouble keeping up?" Dorlagar taunted.

"Hardly." In two strides, the Qatu had lapped Dorlagar and came to a halt in front of him. Dorlagar's nose almost crashed into Sath's chest. "How many of those wyverns do you see walking that fast? If you don't blend in, you're going to give us away, you fool," Sath hissed.

"Fair enough. I can play the part," Dorlagar replied. Sath moved back around behind Dorlagar and Gin, still rumbling deep in his throat as he adjusted the hood of his cloak to make sure his features were hidden. Dorlagar released Gin's arm and withdrew a length of rope from his own cloak. "Never know when you might need this," he said grinning at Gin. "Your hands, please, Blue…Gin?" Gin narrowed her eyes but extended her arms to him and he quickly bound her hands together in front of her, leaving a bit of the rope for him to use as a leash. "Yes, this is MUCH more convincing," the human warrior said. He gave a quick tug on the rope and Gin stumbled forward but did not lose her footing.

"Watch it," Sath spat from under his hood.

"It's all right, Sath," Gin whispered. "We have to look authentic. Dor won't hurt me." She looked up as Dorlagar turned his head to meet her gaze, and swallowed hard at the red that was creeping in around the corners of his eyes. "I am trusting you, Dor."

"I know," he said, and for a moment she could hear in his voice the man that she had trained with and fought alongside, the man that would never use his life-tapping magical power on her, even when she offered in order to help him heal. She saw the Dorlagar that she knew to be a good man who had found himself in a bad situation and was heartbroken over the loss of his sister. However, just as quickly as that Dorlagar had surfaced, the dark knight in him recovered and his eyes glazed over with a bloodthirsty stare. "Now let's get moving, slave," he barked, yanking on the rope again. Gin swallowed hard and tried to keep up with him, but stumbled a few times due to the difference in the length of his gait.

They moved through the corridors as quickly as they could. Each time they approached another group of wyvern guards, Gin felt her heart leap up into her throat as they passed, as she was sure that one of them would think something was amiss and stop them. Nevertheless, none of them did. Some of them, she noticed with a lot of revulsion, nodded to Dorlagar as though they knew him. As she began to lag behind, he would yank on the rope and nearly bring her to her knees. At one particularly violent tug on the rope, Sath jumped forward and caught her, steadying her before he released her. Every muscle in her body tightened, letting Sath know that had been the wrong thing to do.

"Sorry," he whispered. Gin shook her head at him. Without thinking, he cracked his knuckles in the long sleeves of his robe and Gin winced. Dorlagar frowned and tugged again on the rope, this time before Sath could step in, and Gin went sprawling face first onto the stone floor. Sath immediately turned on Dorlagar, but was met with a blood red gaze from the human knight.

"Someone is coming, you fool. We are very close to the cells here and I can't be seen showing mercy to a prisoner," Dorlagar hissed at the Qatu. Sath clenched his jaw and nodded. With one vicious upward tug on the rope, Dorlagar pulled a squealing Gin to her feet and dragged her right up to his face. "Try that again and it will be the last thing you do!" he screamed in Elvish, his nose only inches from hers. "Do you understand me, wood elf?" Gin bit back tears and nodded at him as he deposited her back on the floor.

Sath, again shocked that this human was his Raedea's twin, bit the inside of his cheek to keep from ripping Dorlagar apart. He had no idea what the human had just said to Gin but he was sure that it was not polite. Luckily, it was only a few more steps before they were standing in front of a doorway that Sath knew all too well. He and Teeand were taken prisoner when they stumbled upon the wrong dragons out in the deserts of the Outlands, were brought back here, but had managed to escape with Elysiam's help. Images of the inside of the cells, the pitiful state of the inmates, and the sound of the voices of the wyverns that guarded the prisoners assaulted Sath's mind and he found himself reaching out for a wall to steady himself against the memories.

"Where is the prisoner called Gaelin?" Dorlagar bellowed

into the long hallway, lined on either side with crude cells. Gin fought with everything she had not to stare at Dorlagar as he spoke what must be the language of the dragons. He could barely pronounce her name! "I am to take him to our Lord Taanyth." He took a few steps in, then turned and handed the rope to Sath, who took it hesitantly. He had learned the dragon languages as a young one, and tried to wrap his mind around why Dorlagar was going off plan. Who was Lord Taanyth?

"Here brother, I do not want to lose this one to one of our guests," Dorlagar said, still speaking the language of the dragons. "She's a pretty one and bound to turn some heads." Leaving a very puzzled Gin with a very angry Sath, he walked down the row, peering into the cells. "You there, you are an elf. What is your name?" A red headed male sat in the back of the cell, huddled up in an almost fetal position. "Are you Gaelin?" The male looked up at him, and Dorlagar recognized him. "Bah, no, you certainly aren't."

"I am Gaelin," another voice said from across the hall. Dorlagar turned to see an elderly male elf standing in the back of one of the cells. His voice was commanding and resonant, but did not match the skeleton that stood before him, a red robe hanging off of his shoulders and stringy dark gray hair hanging loose about his face. The eyes were keen, however, and their dark depths flashed with life and seemed to pierce Dorlagar's soul. He broke eye contact with the figure and moved quickly to the cell door.

"You will come with me," Dorlagar said. The wizard was standing at the cell door before Dorlagar could blink, causing him to stumble back a step or two. "Easy there," Dorlagar said in an attempt to cover his fumble. "Hands out where I can see them." Gaelin complied, holding his wrists out in front of him.

Watching carefully, Sath shuddered a bit, remembering

the prisoners that had been there much longer than he and Teeand that had explained "the position" that one struck when the guards came to search the cells. He could almost feel the chains fastened around his wrists, and when he glanced down and saw Gin's tiny hands in the same fashion he almost roared in frustration before he got himself together. "Just a bit longer," he whispered to her. She did not respond.

Once Dorlagar was satisfied that Gaelin was bound tightly, he pulled the mage out of the cell by the rope. However, Gaelin, being considerably taller than Gin, never lost his footing. His slight frame belied a strong will. "I remember you," he said to Dorlagar. "You're the traitor that serves Lord Taanyth, aren't you?"

"Silence, slave," Dorlagar barked, his gaze immediately shifting to meet Gin's confused look. "Keep moving. We don't want to keep Lord Taanyth waiting."

"Hmm, twice in one day, I must be quite popular," Gaelin said, a smile spreading across his face and up into his eyes. Gin liked him immediately, though she was not sure if that was because he was a fellow prisoner or if he was genuinely a good soul. She also was mulling over Gaelin's words to Dorlagar: You are the traitor that serves Lord Taanyth, aren't you? She had heard Dorlagar say the word Taanyth before, when he was speaking the dragon language, but had not known enough of it to realize that was a name.

"Thank you for holding that one, brother," Dorlagar said, resuming speaking the dragon language as he approached Sath and Gin, hands outstretched toward Gin's rope. "I'll take that back now, if you don't mind?" Sath growled at Dorlagar but handed over Gin's rope.

"I suppose I don't mind," Sath replied in Elder Dragon,

causing Dorlagar's eyes to bug out a bit in surprise. He glared at Sath but yanked the ropes to draw attention away from Sath.

"As you were, my brothers," Dorlagar called out to the wyverns guarding the cells as he walked through the doorway, Gin and Gaelin in tow behind him with Sath bringing up the rear.

"Just get us to a clear space and I will port the three of us to safety," Gin whispered to him. Dorlagar nodded almost imperceptibly, his eyes blazing crimson. He led them back through the corridors with such rapidity that Gin was not able to keep straight which way they were going. Finally, they came to an opening and after some orders to the wyverns to send them away, Dorlagar turned back to Gin and Gaelin. He unbound Gaelin's hands first, and then slowly untied the rope around Gin's wrists.

"There. I have kept up my end of the bargain, I hope you will keep yours?" he asked as his eyes slowly faded back from their blood red color.

"Aye. Now if we can all gather in I will transport us to the rest of our party who are surely mad with worry by now," Gin replied. "I forgive you, Dor, for the murder of my parents. You are a good man who finds himself in bad situations, and I hope that you will improve the company you keep from here on out."

Sath moved around next to Gaelin who seemed to be having trouble standing and took the ancient wizard's arm. Gaelin beamed a thankful smile at the Qatu as Gin began speaking ancient Elvish words of transportation magic. "Safety," she said, the last word of the spell being the one that tells the magical portal where they were going. As she spoke that word, Dorlagar darted over close and threw his arms around Gin before she was taken away by her own spell.

"Sorry," he whispered in her ear just before clouting her

on the head. Everything went black as she lost consciousness.

Gin's eyes fluttered open, but she had no idea where she was. The walls were cold stone, and huge age-worn tapestries bearing strange marks and creatures hung everywhere. The room was lit by a few torches, but Gin's elfish vision could make out that she was lying on a huge bed. She soon spotted Dorlagar sitting in a chair across the room, and she sat up as quickly as she could, considering her hands, chained together in front of her. He had been leaning against the wall, and when he heard her moving he righted his chair.

"Hello again, Blueberry," he said. "I was starting to think you were going to sleep forever!" He crossed the room with large strides and sat down on the bed, a tray of steaming food in his hands. He placed the tray on the bed in front of her.

Gin resisted the urge to scoot away from him, and instead stared him down. "If you think I'm going to eat that, you're insane," she said. "I can't even use my hands, thanks to you and these ridiculous chains. What is the meaning of this?" She tried to sound as fierce as Elysiam when she stood down an enemy in their mission to rescue Gaelin. Gin's heart sank. They would not know where to look for her because even she was not sure where she was, but if they did find her it would mean certain death for them if they tried to rescue her.

Dorlagar laughed. "Silly Blueberry," he said. "I'm here to take care of you. Now, what will it be first? Apricot marmalade on buttered toast or some hot oatmeal with wild berries?" Gin merely stared at him, so he picked up the spoon and gathered a steaming spoon full of the oatmeal. "Now then, my dear, you have to eat and keep up your strength." Gin closed her lips tightly and shook her head. Dorlagar sighed loudly and replaced the now dripping spoon in the bowl. "You frustrate me so," he said through gritted teeth. "You make me do things I don't want to do." He carefully placed the tray on the table by the bed, and again scooped up a spoonful of the oatmeal.

Gin's eyes widened as Dorlagar closed his forefinger and thumb over her nose, pinching it shut and stifling her breathing. The chains were just short enough to keep her from shoving him due to their size difference. She held her breath as long as she could, and only opened her mouth as the room began to swim before her eyes. Dorlagar popped the mouthful of oatmeal into her mouth and quickly withdrew the spoon before she bit it. Gin gazed into his eyes and mimicked moving the oatmeal around in her mouth, as though tasting it. Unfortunately, it was good, but she could not run the risk that it had been poisoned or drugged. Dorlagar sat on the bed, seeming lost in her eyes. She leaned in close to him and spat the contents of her mouth in his face. Dorlagar roared at her, the back of his hand cracking against her cheekbone. She felt a fiery pain spread throughout the side of her face and up into her forehead, and her eyes watered.

"Starve then!" he bellowed, stalking out of the room. Gin heard the heavy bar fall on the other side of the door, locking her in. Still, no tears came. She mused briefly, thinking about how proud Ailreden would be of her bravery and ability to avoid showing Dorlagar how terrified she truly was. She had learned so much from him and her guild mates...her heart ached at the image of them discovering her missing.

"Please leave me here," she whispered. "Mother of us All, please guide their feet to safety and not here to me, please."

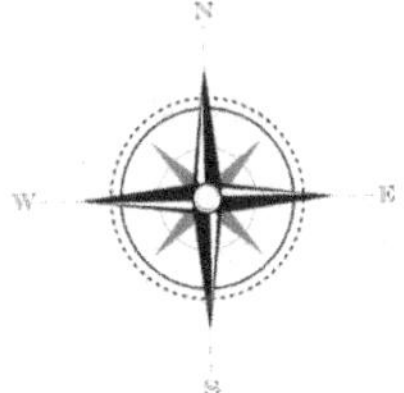

# NINETEEN

Taeben drummed his fingers absently on his spell book. The room was dim, and the leather-bound books blocked what little light came from the candle on the other side of his desk. It was also quite cold in the turret room, and the wizard found himself hunching over as though trying to conserve his own body heat. On the plus side, this was a step up from the cells in the ruins of the Keep, where he had been since his capture, but not much of one. He had been moved to the turret only the night before, after being passed over yet again in the cells by Dorlagar in favor of an older high elf like himself called Gaelin. He wondered, if Gaelin had been freed, what the elder wizard had done to be allowed release, but he knew in his heart that it was more likely that Lord Taanyth's spell research and testing had finally meant the end for the elf. He pulled his red hair back into a neat ponytail at his neck, struggling to tie the leather thong around it with his cold fingers. At least he had been warmer in the cell, due to its lack of a window.

"Research," he groused. Rubbing his forehead with his fingers eased the pounding headache for a moment. "Bah, why doesn't he just kill me?" He selected an ancient grimoire from the stack of books and opened it, frowning as the pain returned just behind his eyes. Taeben did not notice the door to the room open and close until a puff of air extinguished the candle. "Ikara's teeth!" he roared as he flew out of his chair. "Now I'll have to go all the way down to the..." He stopped short when he saw the form of an enormous dark green-skinned dragon hovering a few inches above the floor. Immediately the elf fell to his knees, his forehead only inches from the stone floor. "Lord Taanyth, forgive me, I did not know it was you..."

"Rise, Taeben," the dragon hissed. "How goes the research?"

"Not well so far, but I press on," Taeben said as he stood, being careful to keep his gaze on the floor. "If I had more books, it might speed the process a bit. Perhaps I could make a trip to the Great Library at Calder's Port in order to..."

"Taeben." Lord Taanyth's voice quiet but the tone was unmistakable. The young wizard had spent enough time in the cells to know when he had pushed his captor too far. Taeben tried to look up to catch a glimpse of the dragon, having been blindfolded when he was taken before and used for testing the spell he now researched. However, Lord Taanyth remained, for the most part, obscured by the shadows in the room. All Taeben could see clearly was one dark green clawed foot attached to a tree trunk of a leg. The high elf slowly twisted his head around and almost caught a glimpse of the shimmering scales across the dragon's nose, but looked away again when Lord Taanyth's burning amber gaze met his. "You will work with what you have and press on." With a sweep of his massive tail, the dragon lord had left the room, bolting the door behind him with a thump that shook the stacks of books and threatened to send parchment and quills flying off the tables.

With a growl of his own, Taeben hurled one of the books. It bounced off the heavy stone door with a slight thud, no match for the sound of that bolt that signified, again, that he was the property of the dragon just as he had been while kept in the cells with the other prisoners. The wizard sighed and sat back down at the desk. He pointed one ink-stained finger at the candle and murmured some words in an arcane language, smiling slightly as the wick burst forth with light. He then opened one of the volumes, dipped his quill in the ink, and began recording his notes.

After as much work as he could stand, Taeben crossed the room to the sole window in the turret. He started to pull it shut, but leaned out in order to fill his lungs with fresh air. He lingered there a moment, enjoying the cool night air and contemplating the distance to the ground below.

"Pleasant night, eh wizard?" Dorlagar said from behind him, making Taeben jump. He silently cursed the ability of those in the castle to move about undetected. The stone floors, walls, and doors absorbed the sounds of movement that would have been more prominent had they been made of wood instead. This would make twice in one night that he was surprised by a visitor.

"What do you want, Dorlagar?" Taeben said, his voice low and menacing. Because he was unable to cast any of his more damaging spells while in the castle, he kept a dagger hidden in one of the books on the desk, and slowly moved toward it as he spoke.

"Come with me," Dorlagar said, his voice pinched a bit. "You're needed elsewhere, Taeben." He strode over to the door and turned back to Taeben as he opened it. "Move it."

"I'll ask you again, Dorlagar, what do you want?" Taeben did not move.

"I heard you the first time, wizard," Dorlagar said. He crossed the room and grabbed Taeben by the arm, shoving him toward the door. Taeben glanced at the book that contained the dagger, lamenting its distance from his hand. He stumbled and gasped for air as Dorlagar smacked him between the shoulder blades, urging him forward and out the door. "I need you to keep an eye on something for me. The wyverns are no good for that; I need a magic-user."

Taeben sighed. "What is it, exactly?" He loathed the human, and found it hard to hide his feelings now that he was no longer under Dorlagar's thumb. He got to his feet in the hallway just as Dorlagar slammed the turret door and then grabbed Taeben's arm, leading him down the passageway.

"**It** is a she, Taeben, a new test subject for Lord Taanyth, and she is called Ginolwenye." At the mention of the name, Taeben felt his stomach churn. Could it be the same Ginolwenye he had known so many years ago in the forest, the wood elf that had been a playmate when they were children? The wizard bit his tongue to keep from angering Dorlagar further, though his curiosity was getting the best of him. "She is a druid and could cause trouble if allowed to cast on the wyverns that are guarding her," Dorlagar said.

Taeben's heart leapt up into his throat. It had to be the same Ginolwenye…Ginny. "Hmmm, seems to me that if she's yours she shouldn't need watching, should she Dorlagar? Are the cells with the other test subjects too good for her?" Taeben immediately regretted his words, but still managed a smile at the infuriated look that spread over Dorlagar's face. The elf braced himself for a certain blow from the human, but it never came.

They stopped suddenly in front of the door leading to the other turret. Dorlagar pulled a key out of his cloak and opened the door, then shoved Taeben through it. "Just do as you're told. If she moves, root her." With that, Dorlagar left the room. Taeben could hear the massive bolt click, locking the door behind him.

The room, poorly lit as any in the castle, was dim but Taeben could still make out the furnishings around him. A large bed loomed on the left side, directly across from a fireplace where a smoldering pile of ashes flickered. Taeben cringed slightly at the padlock on the window. His eyes narrowed as his gaze lingered on a lump of sheets on the bed. One tiny hand protruded from under the sheets, its wrist hanging limply in the shackle that connected it to another one still hidden under the sheet. Against his better judgment, the wizard crossed the room to get a better look. Moonlight poured through the window, casting a spotlight on the crumpled form. It was female, and she moved as though stretching, causing Taeben to jump back a step into a shadow as she sat up and the bedclothes fell away from her body.

First, an arm revealed itself, followed by a shoulder. Again, Taeben swallowed a gasp and bit the inside of his cheek as he caught sight of the face he had known since his own childhood in the Forest. Her face was swollen and bruised, and there were finger-shaped marks on her slender neck. Her brown hair was tied up in a braid, but wisps of it were starting to work their way free around her face. She turned toward him, and the moonlight caught her ice-blue eyes making them seem to glow. Those eyes that were so familiar pulled at the farthest reaches of Taeben's memory. He quickly looked away, pulling his hood back up to hide his features.

"And you would be?" she said, her voice strained and hoarse. No doubt from all the screaming, Taeben thought.

"No one. A bodyguard," he said, keeping his voice low and making sure to remain in the shadows. To his surprise, the female chuckled at him.

"A bodyguard? You? Speaking the common language?" she snorted. "You're nothing but an elf like me. Dorlagar's got those wyverns outside for bodyguards." She tilted her head to the side slightly to get a better look at him, wincing at the movement. "Why don't you come out of the shadows? You afraid of something?"

Taeben stepped out into the moonlight just enough for the side of his face to show. "Hardly," he said. "Least of all a wood elf druid." The expression on her face changed and Taeben felt a tiny twinge just under his heart. Had she recognized him? "I'm to make sure you don't use your magic on the guards out there, is all," he said quietly as he moved to the fireplace, careful to move in the shadows so that she only caught a glimpse of his red hair. A chill had settled on the castle, and he found himself shivering. "Are you cold? Shall I call one of the wyverns to blow into the fire a bit?"

The female furrowed her brow. "Pffft, I can summon a simple bit of fire." She turned her gaze to the fireplace and struggled to get to her knees so that she could see it clearly over the end of the bed. She spoke words in Elvish that Taeben recognized, but she did not have the strength to finish the spell.

Taeben stood watching her, transfixed on the verge of laughter and tears at her plight. She tried again, this time making it to the last line of the spell before her energy gave out. "Ikara's teeth!" she shouted angrily as she tugged at the chains.

"Stop that now," Taeben said like a father chiding a child. "You'll only make yourself bleed, you silly child. You can't hope to summon any magic in the state you're in at the moment, now can you?" He turned back around to the fire and pointed a finger at it. Upon murmuring the words, tiny flames shot from his hand into the fireplace, igniting the scraps of wood left there. He sighed, lamenting whatever spell it was that Lord Taanyth had ordered that rendered his damaging spells useless. Parlor tricks were all he was good for here.

"Thank you," Gin said from behind him. Her voice sounded small and tired. "You're right about the bleeding, and I can't even properly bandage my wrists with these cursed chains around them."

Taeben laughed aloud. "So come and take them off me, kind wizard, so that I can root you to the spot with my magic and jump out the window there, or better yet, magically transport myself to somewhere safe?" Her gaze narrowed, causing the wizard to laugh harder. "Figured you out did I?"

He moved out of the shadows into the moonlight, drawing himself up to his full height to tower over her. "I am not one of those creatures outside the door, my dear lady," he said, nearly hissing the words. "It was a valiant yet insulting try." He moved a bit closer to the bed to stare down at her. "Make yourself at home, my dear, it seems your Dorlagar would keep you here for quite some time...though with that temper I can say I have no idea why."

Gin lunged at him as he turned his attention back to the fire. He winced slightly when she cried out as the shackles Dorlagar had put on her ankles cut into her flesh when she toppled over. "He's not my anything," she spat as she tried to right herself on the bed. She fell silent for a moment before she continued speaking. "So, what brings you to this horrible place?"

"What brings you?" Taeben did not turn around, his sharp response cutting through the cold night air. "Oh, I forgot,

Dorlagar. What did you do to make him so angry, my dear? Did he catch you plotting to run away with someone else?" She was silent, and he found her non-responsiveness irritating. "Or worse, eh? Came home and found you with..."

"Shut up." Her voice was cold and quiet. "You don't know what you're talking about." When he turned to face her, he found her eyes on him. Her gaze cut through to his soul, and he steeled his resolve against it.

"Hmmm, touched a nerve, did I?" Taeben moved closer, smirking slightly, trying to diffuse the situation before she could figure out who he was. "Is that guilt I see boiling in your eyes, little one?"

"My name is Ginolwenye," she said, her eyes not leaving his.

"I see. Touched a nerve, did I, Ginolwenye?" Taeben raised an eyebrow. "You seem to have an answer for everything else but not for that, so why don't you tell me why I'm here?"

"How would I know that? You have not answered my question about why you are here. You have not even told me your name, though your voice is very familiar, and I think I already know who you are," she said softly.

"My name is irrelevant," he said, his expression blank. "I am sure you do not know me." He pulled the robe closer around his face.

"And do you work for Dorlagar?" she asked. "Or for Lord Taanyth?"

"And do you always ask this many questions, Ginolwenye?"

She let out an exasperated sigh. "Call me Gin, please;

you've never called me by my full name anyway, BEN." Taeben turned away quickly to keep her from seeing the smile that spread across his face. She had recognized him. In all the long nights kept in the cells, he had not ever dreamed that he would see anyone from his home again.

"Apologies, Ginolwenye, I wondered if you had recognized me," he said, chuckling. "I suppose you could say I work for your Dorlagar; it was he that brought me here to keep you from roasting everything in sight."

"He brought you here, meaning you didn't come of your own free will?" Gin said as Taeben cursed himself for letting that detail slip. "So you are a prisoner, like I am?" Taeben remained silent. "Are you? Please, it's so good to see a familiar face, to hear a voice that isn't a wyvern or worse…tell me what has happened to bring you to this awful place?"

"You do ask too many questions," Taeben barked at her. "Yes, I am a prisoner here. I research magic for Lord Taanyth. I am here because I was adventuring here and my party was ambushed." He paused a moment and took a deep breath. "Some of us made it out. It is my understanding that my female companion made it out. I did not and she never came back for me. Any more questions?" A vision of a female elf of his own race danced before his eyes as he turned back to the fire. He gripped the mantel above the fireplace as memories flooded his mind of her blue eyes and light blonde hair.

"You mean Nel, didn't you? Is she alive?" Gin said, hopefully. Taeben did not answer her, but merely stared straight ahead, his gaze threatening to bore a hole in the wall opposite him. "Ben?"

"Yes, I do mean Nelenie and clearly I am not dead, so you may pass on the happy news," he spat, unable to contain his anger, "and do be sure to give her my best when you…oh, wait, you're not going back home, **ever**, are you?" He did not have to look at her to feel the shock and hurt in her expression, it rolled off her in waves. Taeben's stomach churned slightly as he remained silent, marveling in horror as he thought of Dorlagar. Could he not see the bruises he had left on her? Was he deaf to her screams when the chains cut into her wrists?

Long forgotten feelings surfaced in the back of his mind as he finally looked over at her. He recalled her as a young girl, laughing at him and Nelenie; he remembered the times he had caught her staring up at him as he told stories. But the cruelest memory of all? Nelenie wrapping her long arms around him as they ported, and her trust in him that shown through her blue eyes as she looked at him from the cell next to his.

"I will make it worth your while if you help me escape, Ben," Gin said, obviously trying to soften the wild look in her eyes as she clambered out of the bed, hindered by her chained wrists. Taeben shook off the memories and glared at her. "We could escape here together, and go back home…to the Forest…together."

"Don't be ridiculous, Ginolwenye," he said, ignoring her suggestion. How anyone could leave one with her spirit here to rot was beyond him. This was not the simpering child he had known when they were children. Taeben shook his head to clear it, and focused on her once more. It would do him no good to feel anything for her if he intended to get any work done for Lord Taanyth and possibly earn his freedom.

"You used to call me Ginny when we were kids," she whispered. Taeben winced. Names were a hindrance. Names gave familiarity, bred sympathy. Names made you weak. The wyverns probably had names, but he did not know them. He did not want to know them. It was easier to hate them without names. "I can help us both get out of here if you will let me."

"I know you can, for you are the price I pay for my freedom from this place, Ginolwenye," Taeben said, pronouncing her name very carefully. "I am researching a spell for our host, Lord Taanyth. It just seems to have run into one snag, however." Gin walked toward him, slowly due to the shackles on her ankles, and then stumbled and fell, tripping over her own feet. He helped her stand, holding her hands a little too tightly and looking her in the eyes. "Druids seem to have a nasty resistance to the spell, so I have to figure out why and fix it." Her eyes widened, and Taeben bit the inside of his cheek to avoid letting the fear in her eyes sway him.

"What kind of spell?" she asked, her throat clearly dry.

"It's wickedly beautiful, really," Taeben said. "Something that no magic user has ever been able to do to a living creature, at least not on this scale. The spell commands its target to do the caster's will, but has the capability to work on a massive scale. He could enthrall whole cities at once if all the inhabitants are within the area of effect. Should they resist…well, the effects are most unpleasant."

"And druids are resistant?"

"Aye, as were other magic users with the ability to charm and bend lesser beings to their will. He solved the problem with most of them, however," he said, his features darkening as he remembered the young high elf female that was housed with the other test subjects. Tairneanach was her name, another friend from childhood who had been a shining pupil of Alynatalos's magic guild when Lord Taanyth captured her.

"But I digress. You will be the first druid to test the spell since I have taken over the research, and hopefully the last, once I figure out why you druids are so resistant." Taeben paced over to the fireplace, his slender hands clasped behind his back as he spoke.

"What did you do to the others?"

"What?" Taeben turned around to face Gin. "What do you mean by that?"

"Just what I have asked you. What did you do to the others? How did you test your theories on them?"

"I did nothing, I have only just begun my work, but I have Lord Taanyth's records detailing the process. I do not suppose it would hurt to tell you. Tairneanach, for example, had a gift for..." Taeben stopped as he saw the color run from Gin's face. "Are you ill?"

"Tairneanach. I know her...Tairn! Ben how could you? Nel's little sister? An elf like you..."

Taeben bit his cheek again before speaking. "I am hoping for a bit more resilience from you, Ginolwenye."

"You killed her?" Gin's voice was barely a whisper.

"I DID NOTHING!" Taeben took a moment to regain his composure. "It is all for the cause, Ginolwenye," he said, again turning his back to her. Curse that druid for affecting him this way! "All for the cause. As my sworn deity, Indarr, would tell us, it is in our death that we prove ourselves worthy." He swallowed hard, silently asking for strength.

Gin fell silent and Taeben remained by the fireplace until Dorlagar returned with a wyvern guard that escorted the wizard back to his spell work. He settled back in and managed to keep his mind on the task at hand by making an effort to keep Gin's image from lingering too long before his eyes. It did not matter that the druid he was to test was someone he knew. Names bred familiarity, and that was something Taeben could not afford.

Weeks went by and he finally had a rough outline to show to Lord Taanyth. He alerted one of the wyverns, and waited for a response. It came in the form of an escort back to Gin's quarters and an order to bring her and the outline with him to an audience with the dragon.

The wyvern opened her door and stood there, silently, as Taeben planted his feet and crossed his arms across his chest. "Get her," it said in the language of the dragons as it shoved him into the room. Taeben recovered himself, imagining how easy it would be to cast a freezing spell on the smelly creature and then tip it over so that it shattered into a million pieces. He was still smiling at that image when he made eye contact with Gin.

She smiled back at him. "So what are you planning to do with me?" she said, her voice regaining a bit of strength.

"I do nothing but deliver you and the revised spell to Lord Taanyth, then watch the results and make notes as we go. And speaking of," he said as he patted his robe, underneath which was a bag containing several scrolls, "we'd best not keep him waiting." Gin opened her mouth to protest, but then snapped it shut again and moved past him and out into the hallway. The wyvern that had brought him was joined by another and the second one took one of her arms in its scaly hand, dragging her down the hallway before slinging her up and over its shoulder. She bounced as it walked, and dirt rose in clouds out of the ragged tunic that the creature wore. Taeben noticed that she was not fighting them. *Pity*, he thought. *I had not reckoned her that easily broken.*

The wyvern that carried Gin over its shoulder led the procession through the winding passageways to the arena where Lord Taanyth would be waiting for them. As they passed the cells where prisoners languished in various states of despair and injury, Taeben forced himself to remember his own time in those cells, only mere weeks ago. His thoughts flew back to Nelenie in the cell next to him, beaten and bleeding but promising him she would help him escape. The wizard frowned. *When it came to it, you made no attempt to save me, my oldest friend,* he thought. Taeben felt his blood boil. Why had she not come back for him?

Looking to the wyvern in front of him, Taeben focused on the wood elf over its shoulder. Her hands were still bound and as he stared at her, he imagined her tangled brown hair turn a silvery blonde. Her dirty, oaken-tinged skin smoothed out to become the porcelain-like cream-colored skin of high elves. No longer did Taeben see Ginolwenye, wood elf, druid…but rather he saw only Nelenie who had left him there to rot. The wizard smiled.

They entered the arena and Lord Taanyth was in the back, levitating as he meditated. An ancient book was in his clawed hand, flipping the dark-stained pages in an annoyed manner. The ancient dragon's head snapped upward as they neared him, and Taeben took a moment to take in the dragon. The creature was covered in dark green scales that caught the flickering light from the torches, causing some of them to shine like emeralds. As always, Taeben could not tear his gaze away from the dragon's face, the massive snout that held those horrible teeth, and the amber eyes that seemed to glow from an inner light He swallowed hard and then cleared his throat, catching the dragon's attention.

"Wizard," he said. "Have you brought me another spell to test?" His voice filled the room, reverberating off the stone walls. The wyvern had stopped just outside the door, but still held Gin over its shoulder.

"Aye, my Lord Taanyth," Taeben said, forcing the words out through his clenched teeth. No one had ever received that kind of submission from him without earning it before, and it pained him every time he had to refer to this monster in that way. "I must first thank you for allowing me space for my work, the cell was…not conducive to work. After reading your solutions to previous problems, I hit upon another snag, as you know. Druids seem to be also resistant to your thrall." He nodded to the wyvern who entered the room and then dropped Gin onto the stone floor. "We have a druid here that is willing to help us test the spell as I have written it, to discover what causes the resistance so that we may overcome it."

"Excellent!" Lord Taanyth held out a scaly claw to Taeben after studying Gin for a moment. He inhaled deeply and then seemed puzzled, but then recovered and grinned down at the wizard. "Quickly, I shall have it now, so that we may begin the testing." Taeben held out the scroll and winced as one of the dragon's deadly claws grazed his hand. Once he had finished reading, Lord Taanyth looked back at the wizard, smiling. "Shall I begin, wizard?" he asked, salivating a bit. Taeben bit the inside of his cheek, disgusted.

"On your call, my Lord," he managed, then stepped clear of area where the wyverns had left Gin. "There are several spells there, meant to test her resistance to fire, cold, and magic. Today I think we shall start with fire." He again tried to call up the image of Nelenie, but found that it was only Gin before him, screaming in pain when the dragon lord began his spell casting. "Stay down, you foolish elf," he hissed under his breath. "He will stop if he thinks you are spent. Stay DOWN!"

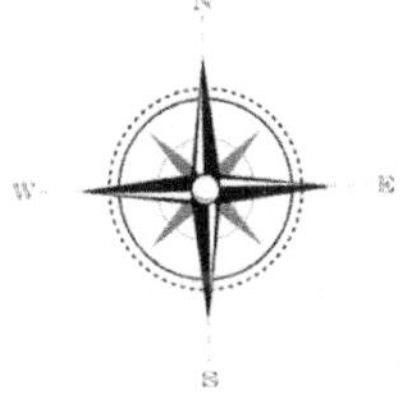


# TWENTY

For weeks, Sath and the other Fabled Ones watched and waited for word from Gin about why she had not joined them when they left the Keep with Gaelin. They looked for her to appear in the grand hall but she was not there. No one had seen her. Teeand, Hackort, and Elysiam had set out in different directions to search for her on Ailreden's command but had regrouped when their solo attempts produced no information. Sath had just about decided to brave a trip to the tree city when a mysterious messenger approached him on the street in front of the grand hall.

"Sathlir Clawsharp? Sathlir of the Fabled Ones?" a deep and raspy voice asked. The stranger was clad in a hooded cloak that obscured his features, but he was easily two heads taller than Sath, no small feat considering the considerable size of the Qatu.

"Aye, I am Sathlir," Sath responded, eyeing the stranger dubiously.

"I have a message for you." The stranger extended what looked like a clawed, winged arm that was clutching a sealed scroll. Sath took the scroll from him.

"You've delivered your message, be on your way," Sath barked at him. Something about the stranger raised the hairs on the back of Sath's neck, and he wanted rid of this hindrance so he could continue on his way. Thoughts of his reception in Aynamaede caused his stomach to lurch.

"I'm to stay for a response, Qatu," the stranger said, his voice equally curt. Sath sighed loudly and unrolled the scroll to read.

*"This is to inform you, Sathlir, and the Fabled Ones of the fate of the wood elf called Ginolwenye. I told you before, Qatu, that I would have my revenge for the mark you left on my Blueberry's face, and I have done so...for I have delivered Ginolwenye to my master, Lord Taanyth. Do not return here, for she does not wish to see any of you, ever again."*

Sath gripped the scroll, nearly piercing it with his claws. "Filthy human," he muttered, then continued reading. *"I would wish you all a long life and good hunting, but ones such as you deserve punishment for the torturous life to which you once doomed sweet Gin. Cross me not, Fabled Ones...for it will mean her death as well as yours...and while I would dispatch you quickly, I fear that her demise would be a bit more involved..."*

Sath took a deep breath and then turned to face the messenger. "Remove your hood, sir, and let me see that you are not Dorlagar."

The messenger chuckled. "Nay, I am not that stupid human. I am a bodyguard of the Warlord, Protector of Lord

Taanyth and Bellesea Keep."

"Ah, the Keep...so that's where he's holding her, eh?" Sath beamed an evil smile at the bodyguard. "Here is my response: Tell your master Dorlagar that if he harms one hair on Ginolwenye's head he will regret it." Sath paused a moment. "Never mind, I'll tell him myself!" The giant cat broke into a run toward the gates of the outpost, with the bodyguard hot on his tail. *Just keep following me,* Sath thought as he ran, *so that I may kill you when we are outside of the outpost.* Sath spun around as he passed under the giant stone arch that served as the gate to the outpost to see the messenger close behind him. He charged at the still hooded figure and knocked him off his feet. The hood fell away and Sath's suspicions confirmed. The dragonkind male made no sound, but launched himself at Sath, clawing frantically at the Qatu's armor and fur. Sath managed to grab the weapon strapped to his breastplate and swung the large hammer, making contact with the dragonkind's skull and splitting it in half. The bodyguard sunk to the ground in death.

Grimacing slightly, Sath set to work on his next task...a message to the human, Dorlagar. Placing his hammer on the ground, Sath retrieved his claw-weapon from his pack and slid the shining blades over his hand. He took a deep breath and plunged the claws into the dead male's chest, ripping a large hole through its carcass. With the other hand he rummaged around inside and found the beast's heart.

Luckily, Sath had an empty pack with him. He dropped the heart into the pack, lamenting the rate with which its blood was beginning to saturate the fabric. Quickly grabbing a blank piece of parchment from his other pack, he dipped his claw in the pooling blood in the dead bodyguard's chest and began to write, "Please receive this gift from the messenger you sent to me, and know that you are next." He stood up and, after donning the hooded cloak of his downed enemy, began his journey to catch up with his compatriots. "Next time it will be your black heart, Dorlagar," he swore under his breath as he ran, heading for the Outlands and that cursed Keep.

The other Fabled Ones, minus Sath, had camped out on the edge of the Outlands, almost in the Forest. Once it was discovered that Gin was missing, they were sent by Ailreden to wait there, possibly to raid the ruined Keep to look for her but more likely to keep Sath from doing anything stupid. He felt personally responsible for Gin's disappearance in a way that only Ailreden seemed to understand, but the others were happy to do whatever was needed to protect a member of their little family. They had been there for many days now, and as Sath ran up on them, he felt his heart would burst with relief and happiness.

"Hail, friends!" he called out, forgetting that he was still dressed as the messenger. Immediately Elysiam turned on him.

"Hack!" she shouted. "We've got another one, magic user from the looks of his robe, coming in hot!" She raised her arms and chanted loud words in Elvish. Ailreden had taught Sath enough of the Elvish language for him to recognize the spell that called up roots to spring from the ground and slow his movement. He headed straight for Elysiam to show her who he was, but was quickly intercepted by Hackort who was swinging his axe straight at Sath's knees.

"Leave the druid alone, scum!" Hackort bellowed at Sath. Inwardly Sath was pleased that he had not summoned his magical pet, for the tiger would have attacked his friend without a second thought.

"Wait..." Sath said, fumbling to remove the hood from his head. A blow to his back knocked him to his knees and knocked the air from his lungs.

"Well done, Tee!" the gnome called out to the dwarf that had cracked his staff directly in the middle of Sath's back. "Elys! Now! Fry the rat-bastard!" Sath glanced upward to see Elysiam once again raising her arms, and though he hated to do it, he quickly recited the words to a spell that caused a swarm of magical insects to form around the druid. Her casting interrupted, Elysiam swatted the insects away and Sath scrambled to his feet. "Mighty strike incoming!" the gnome shouted as his axe hit Sath squarely in the stomach. The giant cat fell over backwards, unconscious, the hood falling back from his face and Hackort's axe stuck in his armor.

"SATH!" Teeand shouted. "Stop guys, stop!" Quickly the dwarf knelt and placed his head on Sath's chest. "Oh, for the love of…He's still alive," Teeand said, "but just barely."

"What the...?" Elysiam ran to Sath's side and knelt, placing her tiny hands on his chest and reciting healing spells. Finally, the Qatu's eyes fluttered open. "Mind telling us what that was all about, Kitty Cat?" she said, her voice stern.

"Only if you tell me why in the nine hells you attacked me?" Sath said, his voice sputtering as he dusted himself off. "Oh...the robe..." He closed his eyes a moment, the world still slightly spinning around him. "Thanks for the healing though, Elys." He opened his eyes and smiled charmingly at her, but the druid still glared down at him.

"You were lucky," Hackort said as he retrieved the axe from the front of Sath's armor. "One more strike from me and you'd be nothing but a furry bag of bones." The wee man held out his hand. "Can I help you up?"

"I doubt it, but thank you anyway," Sath said as he rolled over on his side. Pushing himself up into a sitting position, he smiled. "I am glad to have run into you though. I have a...

problem I need some help with, if you don't mind."

Hackort waggled his eyebrows. "Why do you think we're out here, Sath? Ailreden knew you'd be up to something stupid once he found out our Ginny was missing. We've just been out here waiting till you showed up to help us." He grinned broadly, as Teeand chuckled. Sath's solemn expression soon put an end to the frivolity, however. "Hey, buddy, I'm sorry...what's wrong?"

"You are partially right, Hack. Gin is the focus of the problem." The Qatu took a deep breath before he continued. "Do you remember Dorlagar, the human that she used to run with before she met us?"

Teeand grumbled. "The rat-bastard hobo that tried to help us free Gaelin? Aye, I remember him," the dwarf said. "What of it?"

Sath's brow wrinkled as he spoke. "He has Gin, Tee. He's holding her in the Keep, and I've got to get her out of there. He says in this letter that he has handed her over to his master."

"Bellesea Keep? Are you insane?" Elysiam said. "We'd have to gather an entire raiding party for that, Sath, or a small army! We never would have gotten Gaelin out without that idiot's help…if you can call it that."

"I don't care, Elys. Gin is in trouble and we have to help her." Slowly Sath got to his feet and walked over to Elysiam as he spoke. "We'd do the same for you, or for any of us if needed." She nodded, grimacing.

"I think we can manage it," said a deep voice from Sath's right side. Gaelin had finally joined the conversation. His age and demeanor commanded the attention of everyone around when he spoke. "I am much rested from my ordeal and in truth, I would not mind a chance for a bit of revenge. My magic longs to be used." His eyes twinkled maliciously.

"Aye," Sath said, "and I'm glad you didn't use it on me just then."

Gaelin chuckled. "I was just about to when your hood fell off, you know."

"So, I suppose I can thank Teeand for that?" Sath grinned. "Will you help me?" Hackort and Teeand looked at each other and grinned.

"Any fight is a good fight as far as I'm concerned," the gnome said. "I've got a bone to pick with those wyverns anyway. I'm in!"

Teeand nodded. "Aye, count me in as well. Ailreden sent us for this very purpose. Protecting the innocents is part of what we do..." He paused a moment and studied Sath. "I have to ask you this, my friend, please understand...are we sure that Gin wants to be rescued?"

Sath stared at Teeand. "Well of course she does! She's with Dorlagar so she can't have gone there of her own free will...could she?"

"I would hope not," Elysiam said. "Humans and wood elves..." She shuddered at the thought. "But we should be sure, Sath, because that's a dangerous place to burst into only to have to say 'Whoops! Sorry about that!' and then head for the door."

Gaelin raised a finger and everyone fell silent. "What do we know of how to defeat his master, this Lord Taanyth mentioned in the letter sent to us and to Sath?" Sath gaped at Gaelin first and then at his own empty fist. "It fell out of your hand when our warriors here put you on your back, friend, and I thought it might be important."

"Lord Taanyth is a dragon lord," Teeand said, his voice pinched with worry. "I'm thinking that might be too much even for us. He's no drake, he is a full grown magic using fire breathing dragon lord!"

Hackort fidgeted. Gnomes were not known for their patience, and warriors were even less so. "Let's just go kill the wyverns and get Ginny! If she doesn't want to leave with us after we've laid waste to the Keep minus the big bad dragon, we can just leave her there." Hackort caught sight of Sath's pained expression and was silent. He wandered over to Sath and laid a miniscule hand on the Qatu's boot. "I'm sorry, Sath." he said. "We all love Ginny, really, but…"

Elysiam fiddled a stray thread on her tunic. "We need a plan then," she said. Sath marveled for a moment at how different Elysiam and Gin were. Though both druids and wood elves, Elysiam possessed a hunger for battle that Sath had never seen in Gin. On hunts in the past, Gin would hang back, astride Beau, as Elysiam ran straight into the fray, dealing out fiery magical death to their opponents.

"May I make a suggestion?" Gaelin asked. His solemn demeanor was quite a contrast to his abilities in a battle. Sath glanced over at the elder wizard and nodded. "Keep that robe on, Sathlir," he said. "You're almost tall enough to pass for a small wyvern, as evidenced by our attack earlier." Hackort chuckled, but Elysiam had moved in behind the gnome and soundly bonked him on the head. He whined in complaint but then fell silent, again listening to Gaelin. "We can cast invisibility on you and head into the Keep's outer courtyard. Have you any idea of where Ginolwenye is once we're inside?" True to his slightly haughty, high citadel-raised elven nature, Gaelin always referred to his compatriots by their full names.

Sath shook his head. "Nope, only that she is there...and I

am here." The Qatu frowned and sat down next to the wizard, who patted Sath's shoulder in a fatherly manner. Teeand joined Sath in a frown – why was his old friend so concerned over this one wood elf?

"Then that information will have to be enough," the wizard said. "My suggestion is that the four of us work our way in to the courtyard, with you alongside us, but under a spell of invisibility. Once we have moved to the second floor, you will move to a safe distance from us and remove the invisibility." Gaelin shifted slightly, stretching his long arms. "With the hood up to conceal your identity, you will make haste to all the sentries and bodyguards within, warning them of the intruders on the lower levels. They will flock to us, of course, leaving you free to find Ginolwenye. The two of you can then magically transport to safety and we will do the same." Gaelin was silent, but nodded, as though in agreement with his own plan. "You will not have much time," he added, "but I feel that this is our only option."

Sath considered Gaelin's words for a long time before a smile spread across his face. "I think this is a wise plan, Gaelin," Sath said. "There is just one thing I must do in preparation. Make yourselves safe, I will return to you in a moment." With that, the cat replaced the hood and set out toward a wyvern that had appeared on the hill.

"How now, brother?" he called out as he reached the crest of the hill. The wyvern turned in Sath's direction and grunted a greeting in the dragon language. "I am in need of assistance," he said. "Take this to the human that dwells in the castle...tis the heart of an enemy, and he will understand the meaning." Sath held out the still dripping backpack and the note, and the wyvern took it, sniffing it slightly. "Be on your way, brother, you know the influence Dorlagar has with the Lord Taanyth." The wyvern nodded and took off running for the castle, flightless wings flapping in the arms of the robe it wore. Sath turned and headed back toward the adventurers. "Soon, Gin, you will be safe," he whispered. "I will snap that human's neck with my own hands if he has hurt you. This I swear."

Teeand held up his hand, silently signaling for the group to stop. "Let's take care of the two on the outside first," he whispered. "I'll try to only bring back one at a time, but you never know." Sath chuckled under his hood at the dwarf. Everyone knew very well that Teeand would only come back with one of the wyvern guards trailing. The group members took their places as Teeand ran off after the guard, bellowing obscenities in its direction.

Elysiam backed up to the rear of the group so that she could heal the others without being attacked herself. Gaelin moved to the right and slightly in front of Elysiam and sat down, meditating to raise his magical energy. Only Hackort stood in front, axe in hand, ready to take down whatever followed Teeand back to the camp.

"Sath," Hackort whispered, "don't forget that you're invisible. No magic pet, no fight."

Again Sath chuckled. When the group hunted together Hackort often complained that he never got to be the one that actually killed their opponent because of the wizard's magic, the two druids and their magic, and himself casting spells on the monster. The two druids... Sath's mind wandered a moment to Gin, and he growled. "Hey, I'm just trying to help," Hackort said.

"That wasn't at you, Hack," Sath mumbled.

"Incoming!!" Everyone took their positions on hearing Teeand shouting as he rounded the corner with a large and angry wyvern hot on his heels. Teeand had taken a few blows on the run back to the where the group was waiting, so Elysiam immediately recited a healing spell for him. The wyvern stopped suddenly, sniffed the air, changed direction, and headed straight for Elysiam. The druid merely tightened her grip on her club and smiled. Just as the wyvern's claws were about to rake her face, the creature spun around to face the other direction. Hackort was standing behind it, bellowing at it as loud as he could and whacking it in the backs of its legs. While Hackort had its attention, Teeand began attacking with his broad sword. The wyvern's attention soon shifted to Teeand, who had started to bellow horrible things about its mother. Hackort slashed at the monster with his axe until it turned back to him.

"This is taking too long," Gaelin muttered, an amused smile on his chiseled face. Hackort and Teeand were soon joined by searing flash of magical light that coalesced into the form of an air elemental, who flew into the melee and quickly dispatched the wyvern.

"Aw, Gaelin, we warriors never get to have any fun with that pet of yours around!" Hackort complained. "This is how we always take down baddies, first I start with bellowing at it and then..."

Gaelin held up his hand, smiling at Hackort. "We are without the assistance of our friend Sathlir, who would be casting detrimental spells on the monster while you two are playing catch with it." Hackort nodded his head. "Now, then, Teeand, if you will be so kind as to bring us the other guard?"

Teeand grinned and ran off after the other guard. The fight followed the same plan as the first, and the wyvern soon fell at the hands of Gaelin's magic. "Okay, I get to burn the next one right?" Elysiam asked. The others laughed as Teeand ran off to see what would be next.

"Of course you do," said Hackort, "as soon as you're done keeping us alive, silly druid." He turned his back to her and once again, she landed a blow on his head with her club. "Oweee!" he exclaimed, rubbing his head.

"Incoming!!!" Teeand soon rounded the corner with yet another guard. "Sorry I couldn't scout it first guys, but this one decided he wanted to play." Elysiam cast a spell that snared the wyvern's feet, and then unleashed deadly spell after deadly spell as it advanced on her. Finally, she let fly her worst magical fire, and the wyvern melted into a fiery puddle in front of her.

"It's good to be a druid," she said, her voice low and menacing.

"Perhaps we could just send Elys in and the rest of us can wait out here for her to clear the castle?" Sath whispered, chuckling.

"You'd better hope I can't see invisible things, kitty cat," Elys snarled. Again the group burst into laughter.

"Entrance is clear, move up to me," Teeand called out. The group advanced, and repeated the battles again. Soon they were standing on the drawbridge leading into the castle, surrounded by corpses. "Okay, once we're in the courtyard, let's start with the left side," the dwarf whispered. "I think while we're engaged in that room, Sath will be able to start running into the Keep proper to sound the fake alarm."

Gaelin nodded. "In fact, Sathlir, why don't you run on ahead now?"

"I'm on my way!" Sath said, and ran down the drawbridge. He turned to the right at the end of the passageway, and passed unnoticed through the open courtyard where several sentries were standing guard. "I'm coming, Gin," he whispered as he started up the nearest staircase.

Once at the top, he found a row of cells with a wyvern standing guard. The heart wrenching and piteous cries from behind the bars caught his attention. Gin would be begging us to set them free, he thought, if she were close enough to hear them. He decided to scout out this floor of the Keep a bit more before revealing himself and passed down the line of cells. Making a left, he froze in his tracks at the sound he heard.

"You cannot make me do that!" Gin screamed. "Dorlagar will be furious with you!" Her shouts were followed by the grunting and hissing sounds of the dragon language, and though Sath both knew the language and strained his ears he could not make out what it was saying to Gin. "Dor!" she screamed again. "Help me!"

Sath's stomach twisted. *She's calling out to that human for help?* he thought. He stifled a growl and turned his keen hearing toward the direction of her cries. With his back turned he didn't see Dorlagar come running down the hall and pass right by him as though he was not there.

Dorlagar stopped a moment. It felt as though he had just passed through cold water. He turned back around and looked down the hall, but saw nothing. Gin's stifled screams roused him and he headed for the room where she was held.

Forcing his feet to move, Sath followed the human. He passed through the doorway just as it swung shut behind Dorlagar. The sight that greeted his invisible eyes burned him to the core. The wyvern was on top of Gin, who was kicking and struggling against it. Dorlagar leaped onto the bed and tossed the guard off and onto the floor. The guard sat up and shook his head, then sprang to his feet to attack. When he saw who had removed him from the bed, he froze, hanging his head.

"Forgive me, Lord Dorlagar," the wyvern grumbled. "The wood elf was trying to escape, and I was merely trying to..."

"SILENCE." Dorlagar said, his voice echoing off the stone walls. Sath noted again that the human had a good command of the dragon language – he had been here a long time. "Get out of my sight, and tell the Warlord I require a new guard for my property." Sath swallowed a growl. Dorlagar moved to the window as the wyvern scurried out the door, giving Sath a better view of Gin's condition. He had to work hard to remember that she had only been here a few weeks.

The shackles on her wrists that bound them in front of her had dug into her flesh, and her hands were caked with dried blood. She was sitting with her legs straight out in front of her, and equally heavy chains kept her ankles bound together. Her left eye was swollen and there was a bluish ring underneath it. A cut was visible on her bottom lip, and there were various scratches on her neck and chest.

Her armor was piled in a heap in one corner of the room. Sath took a few steps back and clenched his fists. Now was not the time to reveal himself because he had not yet sounded the alarm. He turned his back to leave, but found to his chagrin that he was trapped in the room. The door was closed, and if it opened on its own, it would catch Dorlagar's attention.

"Did he hurt you?" Dorlagar asked, still looking out the window.

"No more than you and your master, Lord Taanyth, already have," Gin hissed.

"Do you think I enjoy this?" Dorlagar asked as he turned to face her.

"It does seem that way," Gin said. Sath noticed the

sadness in her voice, and his anger threatened to burst out of his chest. "Get out of here, Dorlagar, I don't want to look at you." She settled back as well as she could against the pillows, and Sath saw that the chains were too short to allow her to truly become comfortable. She was clearly exhausted, and that was why she had not healed herself, he thought. Magical ability requires energy from the user, not just the power given to them by Orana. Dorlagar turned on his heels and stalked to the door with Sath right behind him. I could just take her now, while he is out of the room, Sath thought, but quickly changed his mind. His friends were depending on him to follow the plan, and that was exactly what he had to do.

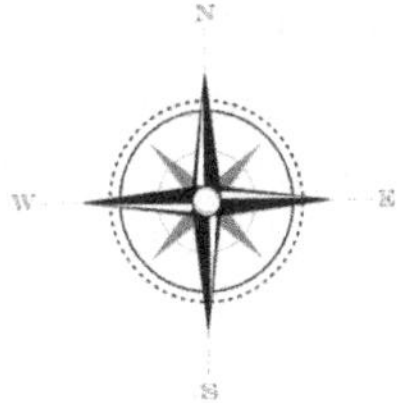

# Twenty-One

Elysiam shifted in her seat as she meditated. "I hope nothing's happened to Sath," she said. "We should have had a ton of wyverns on us by now." Gaelin stood up.

"Perhaps I should summon him back to us, for I too fear that something has gone wrong," he said. Teeand nodded, and Gaelin took a small stone from his backpack. Focusing his energy into the gem, he spoke in Elder Elvish. "Sathlir!" he said, and soon Sath was standing in front of him.

The Qatu blinked. "What happened?" he said.

"Are you all right Sath?" Hackort asked. "You were gone a long time, and no screaming wyverns came to kill us, so we wanted to make sure you were still all right."

"But how did I…?" Sath began, and Gaelin held up his

hand.

"I used the magic in this gem to bring you back to us," he replied.

"So you could just bring Gin to us and then we can get her to safety?" Sath said hopefully. Gaelin frowned.

"Sadly it does not work that way, Sathlir. I can bring you to us because I have an idea of where you are. I would have to locate Gin first, and then I could bring her here. You see, the magic in the gem is tied to…" He looked down at Hackort who was making loud whining noises. "Something troubles you, Hackort?"

"Finally! I did not think you would stop talking. Sath, are you all right?" Hackort replied.

"Aye, I am just fine." Sath sounded slightly annoyed. "I found her," he said, gritting his teeth. "He's hurt her, and is keeping her bound so that she can't cast any spells." Unconsciously Sath cracked his knuckles. The popping sound startled Elysiam, who let out a derisive snort as Sath took off running. This time he stopped at the top of the stairs. *"Brothers, to arms!"* he shouted in the language of the dragons, Eldyr. *"Invaders just over the drawbridge in the courtyard! Attack!"* His shout was greeted by a flurry of wyvern speech that seemed to come from everywhere at once and was followed by the thundering sound of the sentries flocking to the drawbridge to defend their master's Keep. The Qatu hurried past the cells and turned the corner toward the chamber at the end of the hall. He carefully turned the knob and entered the room.

Gin did not look around when the door opened, assuming Dorlagar had returned. "I told you to get out, Dor. I heard one of your guards shouting; perhaps you should go see what is going on," she said. Sath moved into the room, his hood still covering his features. He began searching for the keys to her shackles. "Ah, it's one of you," she said. "You must be the new guard, but aren't you a little too short to be a wyvern?" Sath bit his lip and nodded his head, continuing his search. "Listen," Gin said, her voice softening. "You and I could make a deal. I wouldn't tell your lord Dorlagar anything about it."

Sath tried to make his voice sound gruff. "What deal?" he said, hoping that she did not recognize his voice just yet.

Gin cocked her head to the side a moment, but then shook it before speaking. "Let me out of here. I have money and weapons in stores. Please," she said, her voice strangely hollow, "I'll do anything, just let me go. The keys are in the chest under the window."

Sath closed his eyes a moment, then opened them and started over for the chest. He opened it, and found a large ring with only two keys. Fumbling with the ring, he moved back to the bed and started to unshackle her legs. Gin stared at the hood.

"Please, remove that hood, I wish to see your face."

"Nay, wood elf, I cannot," Sath said. He couldn't run the risk that she might botch the plan if she knew who he was and who was with him in the Keep. Gin was just as likely to run out ahead of him and get herself in trouble as she was to agree to stay there in order to ensure the safety of the rest of the group.

He released her legs and then moved up to unlock the cuffs at her wrists. After the first one was free, Gin reached up quickly for his hood. Hating himself for doing it, Sath grabbed her wrist before she could knock back the hood, knowing that he was pressing on the wound left there by the shackles. She yelped. The giant cat released her other hand from the shackles, then shoved her backward. "Stay here and stay quiet," he said. Sath crossed the room to the door and stuck his head, still hooded, out in the hall.

Gin saw her chance. Silently she slid out of the bed and crept across the floor to the pile of armor. Her sword was next to the pile, and she quickly snatched it up and ran at the hooded figure. Her melee skills were lacking, however, and her blade sliced through the side of the robe. The tip of it did graze Sath's side, however, and he roared in pain. As he spun around to face her, his hood fell back.

Gin dropped the sword with a clatter onto the stone floor. "You?" she said in disbelief. Her voice was barely a whisper and he could not tell if she was afraid to see him or not. "Am I…dreaming…are you real, Sath?"

"Aye, Gin, now get behind me and keep quiet," he said as gently and quietly as he could.

"You've got to get out of here, he'll kill you Sath!" Gin hissed. "Here, I'll port us both out so that you're safe, and then..."

"You'll do no such thing," Sath said. "Others of the Fabled Ones are downstairs, Hack and Elys, Tee and Gaelin, and we've got to go help them."

"Did you bring them all here?" Gin asked eyes wide.

"Aye, couldn't have gotten in here without them," Sath replied. "Ailreden sent us after you, actually," he added, not yet ready to take any credit for her rescue.

"Then let's go help them!" Gin shouted as she darted past Sath into the hallway. Sath cursed himself under his breath for setting her free at all, and then followed her down the stairs.

The steady stream of wyverns defending the courtyard had slowed a bit, but the Fabled Ones were starting to show signs of wear and fatigue. Elysiam was doing nothing but healing the group. Gaelin had used most of his magical energy and had to meditate in a safe place before he could be of any help. "Where is that cat?" Elysiam hissed as another wyvern corpse fell at her feet.

"I don't know, but he'll be here," Teeand said. "Sath would never leave us hanging like this on purpose." The dwarf continued swinging and slashing at the wyverns and other creatures that advanced on them, all under the control of Lord Taanyth.

"Maybe he stopped to kill that twit Dorlagar," Hackort said. The group managed a hollow laugh.

"I'm out of gems," Gaelin said, "and further, INCOMING!" He moved over behind the warriors as the ghost of a dragonkind warrior ran at him. "I can't summon him. We are just going to have to wait. Did we know there were spirits in this Keep?" The elder wizard grumbled as he returned to his corner to meditate while the others fought on.

"Come back here!" Sath bellowed as he ran down the stairs after Gin. He had thankfully remembered to pull the hood back up over his head so that he could be mistaken for a wyvern if spotted. "Gin!"

Gin continued down the stairs and out into the courtyard. She spotted the Fabled Ones across the drawbridge, engaged in battle back toward the front gates of the Keep. They were separated from each other, and each had an attacker advancing. Stopping in the doorway, Gin began casting healing spells on each of them in turn without alerting the enemies to her presence. Sath had almost caught up to her when she darted into the middle of the fighting. Pulling the robe off, Sath flung it to the ground before chasing after her.

"Ginny!" Hackort glanced over at her between swings at a giant hand that seemed bent on squishing him like an insect. "Hi! Now…oof! Get out of here! We're..." he ducked as the hand swatted at him, "fine!"

"Elys, can you draw their attention with magic for a moment?" Gin shouted.

"Can't, got to keep fighting," the other druid shouted back. "Just get out of here, Gin!" She continued swinging at the wyvern that was on her. Gin swore under her breath and started running around, smacking the different monsters as she passed in the hopes they would chase her. Some of them followed her, but most were too interested in their prey to notice.

"Gin! STOP!" Sath shouted, though he knew that she was too stubborn to heed his words. He watched her for a moment, his annoyance turning to admiration. He had never seen her be this brave. She darted past him, planting the hilt of her weapon in his chest as she did and knocking him off his feet. She dashed back toward the others, but Sath was ready for her this time and scooped her up as she ran past him. She kicked and struggled, but Sath's height and strength won out. "You do not have the strength for this, Gin, please…," he hissed in her ear, grimacing as she hit the spots in between his pieces of armor.

"Get her to a safe place, Sath, we'll transport out of here as soon as you're clear," Elysiam said. Sath nodded and began running for the drawbridge.

Elsewhere, a wyvern knelt before Dorlagar. "I have a message, my lord," it said, and held out the backpack, now caked over with dried blood. Dorlagar took the bag and opened it. The rancid smell that greeted him nearly turned his stomach.

"It's a heart. What does this mean?" he asked. The wyvern said nothing and handed Dorlagar the note. Dorlagar's face paled a bit as he read it. "Insolent cat," he growled. "I'll lay out his hide on the floor in front of my fireplace." He looked up suddenly, noticing that the wyvern was still there. "Do you require a reply?" he asked curtly.

"Nay my lord...but it seems that we are under attack," the creature replied. "One of our brethren...a runt, it seems, for he was quite short... ran through the halls sounding the alarm. Most of our numbers are engaged in battle between the courtyard and the drawbridge."

"No!" Dorlagar pushed past the wyvern and out the door, certain that the "runt" was Sath. He flew down the hall, the sounds of battle and death growing louder as he ran. He finally came out onto the parapet above the drawbridge. He could see a battle to the right, with a small group of adventurers clearly outnumbered. He smiled, but the smile faded when he saw a giant cat running across the drawbridge with Gin thrown over his shoulder. "No!" he screamed, and jumped off the parapet into the moat. Quickly swimming to land, he barked orders as he ran. "Stop them! Kill the Qatu! Bring me the wood elf!"

Sath skidded to a stop, replacing Gin on the ground but keeping his arm firmly around her neck. "This wood elf is not yours to have, Dorlagar," he said, his voice booming across the front of the castle. As Dorlagar stopped in front of Sath and Gin, Sath inclined his head slightly and whispered in Gin's ear. "Follow my lead, Gin. No matter what. I will not hurt you if I can avoid it, do you understand me?" Gin nodded slightly.

"Hand her over, cat," Dorlagar demanded. "No need to

die over this. She was mine, she is mine again, and if you give her to me my master Lord Taanyth will let you leave alive!"

Sath beamed an evil smile at Dorlagar as he flexed his hand that was wearing clawed armor. The blades glinted in the sun as Sath deliberately wrapped that hand around Gin's neck and jaw.

She gasped, but held very still. Dorlagar stopped and stared. Sath drummed one finger lightly against Gin's face, simultaneously enjoying the look of horror on Dorlagar's face and fighting the revulsion at what he was about to do. *If I can get her and the others out of here, I will worry about their forgiveness then,* he thought.

"Let her go, Sathlir," Dorlagar hissed, not daring to move.

"Hmmm, no, I don't think so," Sath said. "I used to make a good living killing druids just like her as you well know...got quite good at it, as a matter of fact." He took a deep breath and drew the bladed finger down the side of Gin's face, leaving a tiny trail of blood. Gin cried out and Dorlagar roared.

"Final warning, cat!" Dorlagar screamed at him as he drew his blade. Sath merely smiled at him and tightened his grip on Gin's throat. This was going exactly as he had hoped. Dorlagar would lunge at him, he would toss Gin to safety to run to meet the others at the entrance, and he would hold Dorlagar's heart in his giant hand, squeezing the last drop of blood from it. However, Dorlagar did not lunge. "You see, my Blueberry, how he treats you? You are a snack to him, not an equal! I would never hurt you like that, never!" Though bellowing, Dorlagar stood fast, his giant blade aimed at Sath's head. His eyes glowed red as strands of his gray hair, still wet from his swim in the moat, stuck to his forehead and cheeks.

"Ah, you've figured me out," Sath replied, barely able to

form the words. "Tis none of your concern now, Dorlagar. Go play with your drakes over there." He took a step backward, hoping that would prompt Dorlagar to move. Dorlagar stood still, just staring. Over Dorlagar's shoulder, Sath could see the blonde top of Elysiam's head sticking out into the hallway leading to the drawbridge. *Not yet, guys,* he thought, but had no way to call out to them without revealing their presence.

"What's going on out there?" Hackort said, tugging on Elysiam's leg. The druid turned to him, a harsh expression on her face.

"Could someone put a leash on the gnome here?" she said. "I can barely hear what's going on as it is!" She inched up a bit and could finally see clearly around the corner. She gasped when she saw Sath holding Gin by the throat. "I think the kitty's been charmed," she hissed. "He's got Gin!"

Hack started to charge forward, but was stopped by Gaelin laying one slender hand on the gnome's shoulder. "Stay put, Hackort," Gaelin said. "We have to remain hidden until we get the signal to evacuate. That was Sath's plan as well."

Hack peeked around the Elysiam's legs. "She's bleeding, Gaelin! This wasn't part of my plan," the gnome whined, wiggling free of Gaelin's grasp and darting out into the hallway. Elysiam grabbed for him but he ducked under her hand as he ran.

"Plan B?" Teeand asked, sighing deeply.

"Aye, and hurry," Gaelin said. "Elysiam, you hang back for heals yes?"

"As usual," Elysiam said. The three of them ran after Hackort.

"Never fear, Ginny, your gnome is here!" shouted Hack as he ran up behind Dorlagar.

"Stop, gnome," Sath said, inwardly pleading with Hackort to back off. This was NOT part of the plan.

"Sath, I know you're charmed and it's not your fault, but I can't let you hurt Ginny," Hack said. Dorlagar turned slightly and took a swing at the gnome with his sword. Hack dodged the blow. "I can't let you hurt her either!" he shouted as he charged on Dorlagar.

"Root Hack, Gin," Sath whispered. Gin made neither move nor reply. Sath sighed deeply. "Root him. NOW," he hissed in her ear, tightening his grip on her neck. Biting her lip, Gin recited the Elvish words that caused roots to weave around Hackort's feet.

"Hey!" the gnome exclaimed.

"Dorlagar is mine, gnome," Sath barked. "Call your friends and get out of here. You're not needed anymore." Hack cocked his head to one side and looked at Sath quizzically.

Suddenly Elysiam smiled. "He's right, Hack," she said.

"What?" said the other three in unison.

"We're not needed anymore. We should leave while we still can," the druid said, winking surreptitiously at the Qatu. She moved carefully up to Hack and began reciting the words for a spell that would take them to a safe place. Gaelin and Teeand ran up to her just as the four of them disappeared, and Sath could just imagine the tongue lashing that Elysiam would get when they landed.

*At least she understands what I am doing,* Sath thought. *I just hope Gin does. I will not let her become a cold-blooded murderer by killing Dorlagar. I will do it for her.*

"Your friends are gone now, Qatu," Dorlagar said coldly. "Let her go and be done with this game.

"Negative." Sath tightened his grip on Gin's throat, and she gasped as the points of his claws pressed into her flesh. Dorlagar winced. "She and I are leaving now." Sath turned but focused his keen feline hearing behind him so that he would know when Dorlagar was about to attack. Sure enough, as soon as his back was turned Dorlagar charged after him. Sath slung Gin as far as he could out in front of him. "Run, Gin!" he screamed as he swung around to face Dorlagar, weapon drawn.

Gin hit the ground with a thud and slowly got to her knees. She stood unsteadily and turned back around toward Sath and Dorlagar. The human had already cast a deadly spell on the Qatu, and dark clouds of black and red distorted their images. After reciting a spell to heal her wounds, Gin changed her mind suddenly and ducked down at the last moment, interrupting the spell casting. She wanted the wounds to stay until this was done.

She would have answers from Sath as to why he had resorted to such a dangerous trick. If she had not known better, she would have thought him every bit the Bane of the Forest once more, and she wasn't really sure that she did know better. However, Elysiam had known something or seen something that made her take the rest of the group to safety. All Gin could do was trust her sister-druid, or her questions would get the best of her. No time for that now, she thought as she ran at the two combatants.

Sath and Dorlagar were locked in a struggling mass of arms, armor and weapons. It seemed hard to discern where one stopped and the other started! Gin swung her weapon around and raised it above her head. "Don't hit Sath, Don't hit Sath, Don't hit Sath," she muttered, and drove the blade downward.

"What did you do that for?" Hackort demanded, waving his axe in the air angrily. "I was about to take him!"

"I was following the plan, Hack," Elysiam said, her voice stern. "We have to stick to the plan. Gin ran in and threw things off kilter for a moment, as she is well known for doing, but now we're back on track." She sat down to meditate, facing the entrance to the castle. "Gin should be coming out of there with Sath at any moment, and we need to be ready to provide cover."

Hackort snorted. "Provide cover? We should be in there helping Sath. You know that Dorlagar is going to call that entire Keep down on them and they'll need the help."

"Gin will transport them out, Hack," Elysiam said.

"You know, the gnome might have a point there," Teeand said. He tugged at his beard as he pondered. "Gin did botch the plan to begin with by running away from Sath." The dwarf's face became troubled. "Guys, what if I was right and she does want to stay there with Dorlagar...we've just signed Sath's death warrant."

Hackort began pacing in circles. "I can't just sit here," he said. "If Teeand is right I can't just sit here and let Sath die." He swung his axe around. "And if I find out that Gin had anything to do with Sath's death..."

"ENOUGH." The one word from Gaelin stopped all of their arguing. "While I agree that this may be a dangerous idea and it did stray from the plan... I think that the gnome is right," the mage said slowly. Elysiam spun around to face him.

"What? This was your plan to begin with, Gaelin!" She bit her lip, obviously furious. "Now you want to run back in there? We'll all be dead if we do."

"Hackort, you are not to harm Ginolwenye, do you understand me?" Gaelin said as he knelt to look Hackort in the eye. The gnome nodded. "Not that I think you would, but we're all worried about Sathlir and we must keep our heads."

Elysiam tightened her grip on her weapon. "And just what will we do when we get there, Gaelin?" she asked.

"One way to find out," Gaelin said as he took off toward the Keep's entrance, grinning all the way. The others followed with Elysiam bringing up the rear and swearing loudly.

The Qatu roared in pain as Gin's blade sliced into his leg. Gin immediately yanked the blade back, nearly causing Sath's knees to buckle under him. "A well placed hit, my Blueberry!" Dorlagar called out.

"Gin, I told you to RUN! Do as I SAY!" Sath snarled at her. Ignoring him, Gin ran at Dorlagar, swinging her blade madly. Dorlagar reached for her just as she swung, and her blade left a deep gash across the palm of his hand. The human balled up his fist and swung at her, catching her squarely in the back and knocking the breath out of her. She doubled over but Dorlagar yanked her back up by her arm, placing her between himself and Sath.

"Careful, Cat!" Dorlagar said. "Don't want to hurt her, do you?"

"Let her go, Dorlagar," Sath said, a low growl forming behind his words. "This is between you and me now."

He took a step forward, but Dorlagar managed to position Gin so that any blow Sath dealt would hit her first. *So it has to be,* he thought. *Forgive me, Gin...* Sath balled the claw weapon and backhanded Gin out of Dorlagar's grip. She flew across the ground and landed with a sickening crack on the ground. Sath ran at Dorlagar, cursing himself inwardly for not casting a pet as soon as the battle began and hoping that Gin was still breathing.

Hackort entered the area just in time to see Gin fly through the air. A low growl rumbled in the gnome's chest as he ran at Sath and Dorlagar, his axe raised to strike. Gaelin was right behind him, keeping a close eye on the angry gnome. "Which one of you hit Ginny?" he demanded as he skidded to stop in between Sath and Dorlagar. "I want to know which one of you to take off my Do Not Kill List."

Dorlagar beamed a smile at Hackort. "Your friend the Qatu can take the credit for that blow, but I'm afraid you'll have to step back, gnome. Sathlir is mine."

"Then I guess it will have to be you," the gnome said, grinning at Dorlagar. "I had hoped it would be you. I really don't like you." Hackort charged at Dorlagar, bellowing with all the might his tiny lungs would afford. "This human needs killing, and we're the ones to do it!"

"Wonder if my magic could take him alone," Gaelin mused as Elysiam and Teeand nearly careened into the magician's back. "Ah well, one way to find out!" Quickly the mage directed his magic at Dorlagar with ferocious speed.

"Well what am I doing just standing here?" Teeand chuckled, and then ran into the melee, taunting Dorlagar as he advanced.

Elysiam sat back at a safe distance, watching the fight. At the same time, she was scanning the immediate area for other combatants that might want to join the party…like that wyvern that was advancing on them from the south. "We've got one coming in from the south!" she shouted, but the others were a bit too far away to hear her. "Well then," she said, smiling, "you guys stay over there, I'm going to try something."

Raising her arms high, she cast a magical snare on the wyvern. The monster turned toward her suddenly as though an invisible hand had snapped its neck around and charged toward her, its pace slowed by her spell as surely as though it had been caught in a physical snare. Again reciting magical words, Elysiam caused a system of engorging roots to form out of the ground beneath the wyvern's feet, and he stood fast.

"Now then," she said, "were you coming to say hello to ME?" More magical phrases and the wyvern was surrounded first by a swarm of deadly insects, then by flames that seemed to cascade over him in smoldering white hot waves. He weakened and Elysiam backed up a bit, and then channeled the magical energy of the wind to slam into the wyvern. It stumbled toward her, having broken free from the enchanted roots at its feet, but made it no more than a few steps before the breath of Kildir himself, through the fingers and words of Elysiam, drove it to the ground in death. Elysiam then turned her attention back to the fight between the drawbridge and the courtyard.

Hack was staggering. Teeand was sitting to the side and binding his wounds with bandages as Sath and Dorlagar continued to swing and cast at each other. Slowly Gin roused and got to her feet, still very dizzy and off balance. She looked around at Elysiam and motioned for her fellow druid to move closer. Elysiam did as requested.

Gin raised her arms as high as she could manage and began reciting softly strained words in Elvish. Elysiam recognized the words and joined in but it was too late: the party was already being magically whisked off to the outpost. As soon as they had all recovered from the transporting, Elysiam looked around for Gin but did not see the other druid anywhere.

"Sath?" she said, moving to the broken and bruised cat on the ground ahead of her. She quickly cast a healing spell or two and soon Sath looked as good as new. "Where's Gin?" Elysiam asked, fearing the answer.

"She's not here?" Sath growled as his eyes widened. "That's not possible, she cast the spell that brought us here. She has to be here."

"Ely's right," Hackort said as he dusted himself off. "I don't see Ginny anywhere." Sath's face darkened with fury as Hackort dashed about, searching the immediate area. Elysiam also joined in the hunt, then stopped when she noticed Teeand sitting on the ground next to Gaelin.

"She stayed behind," Teeand grumbled, irritation clearly audible in his voice. "I don't know why or how, but as we were ported I saw her run from us back to Dorlagar."

"Not possible," Sath repeated.

"Could be some sort of enchantment, perhaps?" Gaelin suggested. "Elysiam, you were the closest to our Ginolwenye at the time, did you see or hear anything out of the ordinary?"

Elysiam thought very hard. "No, I saw her get up and motion me closer, so I came over to where she was. She started chanting, and I moved closer to hear what spell she was casting. I started chanting along with her, just in case she was too weak to finish, and…"

Sath ran over to Elysiam, grabbing the druid by her shoulders and yanking her up to his height. "You did WHAT?"

he demanded.

"Geez, Sath, put me down!" Elysiam demanded. "I said I started chanting with her in case she was too weak to finish or recite the spell correctly." She wiggled in Sath's grip and he released her, causing her to fall with a thud to the ground. "OW, I said put me down, not drop me on my…"

"Enough!" said Teeand, in an uncharacteristic fit of anger. "I think we all know what happened. When Gin heard Elys start casting the port spell with her, she stopped and ran back to Dorlagar so that she wouldn't be transported along with us." His eyes seemed to boil as he stared off into nothingness. "She didn't want to come with us, Sath. We warned you that she might…"

"No!" Sath bellowed, again interrupting Teeand before he could make the suggestion that Gin wanted to stay with Dorlagar. The giant cat turned his back to the dwarf before stalking off toward the bank. His mind was spinning with memories of Raedea, comparing her to her twin Dorlagar, and intertwining with his feelings for Gin. He felt sick for a moment, but then his head seemed to clear as his heart hardened.

Hackort looked up at Gaelin; though the mage was sitting in the grass, the gnome was still considerably shorter than his Elvish stature. "Ginny didn't want to come back with us?" Hackort said, obviously befuddled. "Why wouldn't she want to come back with us?" He walked over to where Sath had sunk into the ground and laid one small hand on Sath's shoulder, even though it meant standing on his tiptoes. "We'll get her out of there, Sath," he said. "Dorlagar's been taken off my Do Not Kill list, don't you worry."

"Bah," Sath said. He felt the last twinges of feeling for Gin, for Raedea, for anyone fading from his heart. What good was atonement for sins if this was how it ended? He didn't need the

Fabled Ones now any more than he had before, and he had certainly learned a lesson about dalliance with wood elf druids like Gin. Thankfully, there was no relationship to untangle; he could easily make a clean break and get back to the life that made sense. "Let her stay if that's what she wants." The Qatu rose, and stalked off. "I'm sorry, Rae, but your wishes cannot be. Let Gin wallow in her vengeance, I cannot care any longer," he muttered.

Hackort was on his feet to follow when Elysiam stopped him, stepping in front of him. "Let him go, Hack," Ely said. "You'll only make it worse."

"No I won't!" Hackort exclaimed, suddenly spinning around to face the group on his tiny gnomish heels. "We'll get her back. That will make it better. And this time, Sath won't know about it and won't go, so he can't get charmed," he said, matter-of-factly. "I just know that's what changed Ginny's mind, she got scared when Sath went all Dorlagar on her, but we'll go without him and rescue her!"

"Do you really think we can just charge into the Keep and pick Gin up like a backpack of supplies and then ride right back out the front door?" Teeand glowered at Hackort. "Have you learned nothing from our past trips to that cursed ruin? You gnomes really are insane. What if you are running through the halls and come face to face with Lord Taanyth himself? Not happening, at least not in the name of the Fabled Ones." The dwarf stood, dusted himself off, and headed for the entrance to the grand hall. Gaelin stood slowly and followed him.

"Well," Hackort said, taking a deep breath, "there's only one way to find out!"

Elysiam sat down on the ground and opened her spell book. Hackort looked hopefully at her but she shook her head. "Hack, there is no way. I am sorry, I love Ginny as much as you do, but it is over. She's made her choice."

Hack plopped down next to her. "I suppose. It was a dumb choice, but it was hers." He began cleaning his weapon and leaned against Elysiam, who for once did not shrug him away.

The scene in the Keep was equally tense. "Dor?" Gin whispered. They seemed to be alone on the drawbridge, but she knew that the eyes she felt upon her belonged to the wyverns that stood at the ready, surrounding them. Dorlagar stood with his back to her, his arms folded across his chest. Perhaps he hadn't heard her? "Dorlagar," she said, her voice unwavering despite the choking fear that held fast to her chest. Slowly, as though moving through water, Dorlagar turned around to face her.

"You're not real," he whispered, his voice hoarse and pinched.

"I am very real, Dor, sweetheart," she said, hoping the use of the nickname would convince him before it made her nauseous. Forgive me, Fabled Ones, she thought as she moved closer to Dorlagar, who took a quick step back.

"I don't know what magic this is, but you can't be real," Dorlagar hissed at her. "Now leave me, I have work to do."

Gin took a deep breath before she spoke. "If I am not real, then touch me and prove it," she said. He cocked his head to one side for a moment, staring at her, and then gingerly stepped forward with his left hand outstretched. Gin braced herself for the revulsion that would come with his touch. His fingers barely brushed her cheek and his eyes grew wide. He gripped her chin suddenly, tears forming in his eyes, and pulled her closer. Gin gasped but held her eyes locked on his.

"Why…why are you here?" Dorlagar said, choking on the words. "Do you…did they leave you?" He released her chin but remained very close to her, staring down at her in disbelief. "Are you here of your own doing?" he asked, his voice barely a whisper.

"Aye, Dor, I am," she said. Before she could breathe, Dor swept her up in his arms, crushing her to his chest.

"I'll never let you go again," he mumbled.

"Aye, you'll never have to," she said. *Because I will end you, provided I can keep Sath and the others away from here, she thought.* Images floated through her mind of the scene in the Outpost when the party arrived without her, and a tear escaped from her eye. Her time with the Fabled Ones might be at an end, but her wait to avenge her parents would be as well, and that was what mattered most.

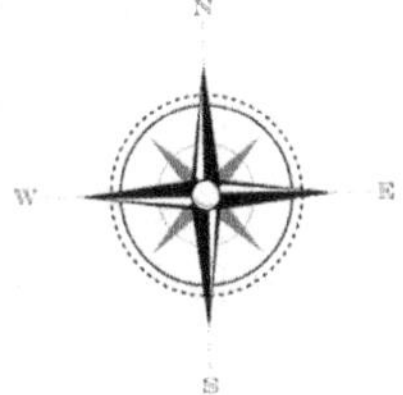


# Twenty-Two

Dorlagar stood for a long time on the drawbridge, his arm locked around Gin's shoulders, holding her fast to his side. She swallowed hard with revulsion. "I can't believe you're here," he whispered repeatedly. She looked up at him and forced a smile.

"And yet I am," she said. "I suppose you should again deliver me to that wizard so that we can get the spell ready and escape this cursed place?"

"And you will take me with you?" Dorlagar asked. The childlike quality in his voice since he began to believe that she had stayed purposefully was tugging at Gin's heart, but she knew that she must not let it affect her. This must be how he was before he lost his sister.

"Of course. You will be free as well, Dor," she said.

"Hold out your hands," Dorlagar ordered, his tone suddenly rough. Gin looked up at him, confused.

"Why?" she asked.

"Prisoners don't walk around here free, Gin, remember?" he whispered. "It will keep you safe." Gin took a deep breath and held her wrists out in front of her. "Much better." He secured her hands with a piece of rope he had removed from his belt and gave it a little tug. "Just like before, only this time you can be sure that filthy Qatu won't put his grimy paws all over you. I should have killed him for that. I may still."

"Don't worry about Sath," Gin said, swallowing hard. "After my performance I doubt he will want anything to do with me…not anything good any way." Dorlagar startled and looked back down at her.

"I will never let him hurt you again, my Blueberry, I swear it," he said, and the honesty in his gaze nearly brought her to tears.

"I know." Gin bit her lip as he tugged on the rope, leading her to the turret where Taeben was being held.

She struggled with some of the stairs but finally made it, near total exhaustion. Dorlagar did not knock but flung the door open to find Taeben hunched over his journal again, writing furiously.

"Oh, you again?" the wizard exclaimed as he looked up and saw Gin. "I can't imagine that Lord Taanyth wants her again, Dorlagar, she was all but used up before." He searched Gin's eyes and face, his eyes lighting on the scratch down the side of her face. Frowning, he shook his head. "She does seem a bit worse for wear, perhaps there is something more suitable in the cells?"

"It is to be her," Dorlagar said. "Our Gin has volunteered." He beamed a proud smile that caused Gin's stomach to lurch. "You will come with us. Hands out."

"I will do no such thing, I have work to do and…"

"HANDS OUT!" Dorlagar dropped Gin's rope and moved quickly across the room, a cloud of blackness and death coalescing around his hands as he moved. The moment he touched Taeben's robe, the wizard shrieked in pain and his knees buckled. Dorlagar grabbed both of the elf's slender wrists in his meaty hand and quickly tied them together. "Now then, shall we?" he said as he yanked Taeben up to his feet.

"You will pay for this," Taeben hissed. Dorlagar laughed and pulled both of them through the door. *"Have you lost your mind, Ginny?"* he whispered to Gin in Elvish, hoping that Dorlagar didn't speak it. The human's bloodlust had already begun to creep in around his vision and he paid them no attention, motivated only by getting them to the arena and to his master.

*"No, and if you'll do as I say we will get out of here. As soon as he cuts our ropes in front of Lord Taanyth you distract him and I will kill Dorlagar,"* Gin replied, her voice barely audible. *"Then return to my side and we transport away, safe and sound."*

*"That is a ridiculous plan,"* Taeben whispered back. *"How about once we get there we both just port out?"*

*"Because Dorlagar needs killing,"* Gin said, smiling gravely as she thought of how many times she had heard Hackort say that very phrase in the relatively short time she had known the gnome warrior, *"and I'm the one that has to do it."*

*"You're the one to do what? Whimper? Bat your eyelashes?"* Taeben asked angrily. *"You are no more able to kill that human than you are the rat that just ran over your foot."* Gin jumped, kicking the foul creature off her boot and nearly pulling the rope out of Dorlagar's grip.

"That's no use, Blueberry," the human growled as he stopped walking and turned to face her. "Naughty girl, trying to get away."

"I wasn't, Dor, I swear," Gin pleaded, but soon fell silent at the sight of his eyes, blood red and seeming to glow as he glared at her. She remained silent the rest of the way to the dragon's chambers in the belly of the Keep, but could not stop shaking the closer they got. Images of the Fabled Ones settled in her mind; she saw Sath bravely charging toward an enemy and the two warriors bellowing curses as they ran, weapons raised. But more to the point, she pictured Elysiam, her eyes blazing rather than hollow or afraid, regardless of what she had been through. "I need your strength, Elys," she whispered as Dor loosed her hands and then, after a long glare at Taeben, crossed the room to call for Lord Taanyth.

After leaving the group, Sath had headed for the room Gin and her sister rented above the tavern in the outpost. It was lucky that when he had burst through the door Lairky was gone, or he might have started with her to soothe his wounds. He could find no clear reason why Gin would have stayed behind, and the absence of an answer combined with the voice in his head wondering why he should care at all was driving him mad. The Qatu paused for a moment by the bed, picking up one of the pillows. He buried his face in it for a moment, breathing deeply. "Gin," he whispered, and then his face contorted with rage. His claws ripped the pillow to shreds in only a few swift motions, and then began to ravage the bedclothes. When the bed was bare save scraps of fabric, he lifted it off the floor and threw it up against the wall. The wooden frame shattered into splinters.

Sath moved next to the backpacks hanging on pegs next and tore them easily into tatters. He paused for a moment as his paw rested on the magical bridle that Gin used to summon her enchanted pony, Beau. He spoke the words that he had heard Gin speak hundreds of times, but the horse did not appear. Flinging the bridle to the ground, he continued to tear apart everything he found until his eyes lit on a faded leather journal that had fallen out of its place, tucked into his tunic.

Sath sank to his knees, holding the precious book to his chest. It was because of this journal that she had come into his life in the first place. "An interesting experiment, the attempted taming the Bane of the Forest," he said, steely coldness settling in his eyes. "But it is over."

A pounding on the door roused him, and he walked over to answer it after carefully placing the book back in the one remaining backpack. When he opened the door, an angry looking human stood glaring at him, muscled forearms emerging from his rolled-up sleeves as he crossed them across his chest. "Erolith…apologies for the noise," Sath said.

"It's not the noise," Erolith, proprietor of the tavern and the inn above it, said harshly. "You'll be paying for the destruction of my property, I suppose? Where are the wood elves that live here? Why, I knew I should not have let you come up here, but that Gin seemed so sweet and if you are a friend of hers…. Well, I could not say no. I should have my head examined! Now, that will be ten platinum pieces for the furniture, next month's rent in advance, hmm…"

Sath interrupted the Erolith's calculations by shoving a sack of platinum pieces at him. "There, that should cover it."

The man stared at the sack and dumbly nodded his head. The door shut in his face before he could ask about the pretty elf's plans, so he turned and descended the stairs. He would ask when that sack of money ran out.

Days went by and the Fabled Ones had no word from Sath. Sent to track him down, they reluctantly complied. "This is a bad idea, guys," Teeand mumbled as he followed Hackort and the others up the stairs to the room that Lairceach and Gin were renting above the tavern. "You heard the landlord, Sath's in a state right now, and I can't say as I blame him." They had answered the summons to the tavern, and Erolith was quick to tell them about the Qatu laying waste to his property upstairs.

"Hush, Tee," Hackort said as he hopped up the stairs. "Curse the minds that designed the buildings in this outpost for not thinking of gnomish legs!"

"Do I need to carry you, wee man?" Elysiam quipped as she followed the gnome. Hackort glared over his shoulder at her and then continued his hopping. "Gotta say that I agree with Tee though…Sath's either going to want to go hunting with us again or he's going to knock the lot of us for a loop for even turning up here."

Gaelin smiled. "He will have the opportunity to do neither," he said, his voice calm and even as always. "I will see to that." They reached the top of the stairs and the mage laid a hand on the gnome's head. "A moment, Hackort, before you burst through the door?"

Hackort shook Gaelin's hand off his head. "I wasn't going to burst through the door," he said, clearly irritated. "What is it?"

Gaelin spoke some words quietly in a long forgotten language, and a water elemental appeared next to his shoulder, taking the group aback slightly. The creature wore a stern expression and carried a large scimitar. "Now then, knock."

"Is that really necessary, Gaelin?" Teeand asked, his own expression matching that of the elemental.

"I think it may be, yes," Gaelin said.

Hackort knocked on the door. "G'way! I paid ya yer money, ya stinkin hoomin!" Sath's voice bellowed from the other side.

"Great, a drunk cat," Elysiam muttered. "Glad you pulled the elemental out of your bag of tricks, Gaelin, this could get ugly."

Hackort snarled at Elysiam and knocked again. "It's just us, Sath," he said, trying to hide the annoyance in his voice.

"I sed g'way!"

"See if it is unlocked, Teeand," Gaelin said.

Teeand glanced up at the wizard. "Are you insane?" he said.

"Tee? Zat you?" Sath said, the sound of his voice moving closer to the door.

Teeand glared angrily at the others. "Aye, Sath, tis me."

"I'll letchoo in but tell the others to stay outside," Sath said as he fumbled with the lock on the door.

Teeand stepped up to the door. "Now who's insane?" he said as Hackort spat something under his breath, but Teeand shot him a look that silenced the gnome. The door opened a crack, and Teeand pushed his way in just before one of Sath's giant clawed hands slammed it shut behind him.

"Now what?" Hackort said impatiently.

"Now we wait," Gaelin said, speaking to the gnome as a father would to a child. A wave of his long, manicured fingers dismissed the elemental. "Have a seat, wee man; this may take a long while."

The room was in shambles. Teeand drew in his breath sharply as he scanned the scene before him. "What happened here, Sath?" he said slowly.

"I happind," Sath slurred, sinking back down on to the floor, his back against the door. "Whatuvit?"

Teeand thought for a moment before he spoke. "What can I do for you, my old friend?" he said as calmly as he could as he walked over to stand in front of Sath, looking him in the eye.

"Nuttin," Sath said, taking another swig from the bottle he held with a grip like a vice. "I'll be okays, dontcha worry none." He raised the bottle again to his lips, and the pressure of his grip shattered it. "IKRUHZ teeth," he muttered, "thass the fourth one." Teeand looked to the right of the cat and saw a pile of shattered glass in a puddle of warm ale. "Isss okay tho, I've got nuthers," Sath said as he struggled to stand. Forgetting about the glass on the floor, Sath placed one giant hand right in the middle of the pile to push himself up from the floor and howled as the shards tore at his skin.

Teeand stood still, fighting the urge to call Elysiam in to heal Sath's wounds. He wondered for a moment if her magic would work through the door. "You don't look very okay to me, Sath," he said, wrinkling his brow. "In fact, you look pretty pitiful and drunk, and coming from a dwarf that's saying something."

Sath glared down at Teeand, holding his injured hand to his chest. "Be glad I hurt muhself, dorf, or I'd backhand ya one," he snarled. Teeand rolled his eyes but took a step back.

"So, what are you going to do, Sath, drink until she either

comes back or you die?" Teeand hissed at him. "Either way, not a pretty sight and not one I'd care to hang around and witness." The thought of telling Sath that Hackort wanted to rescue Gin entered Teeand's mind, but he quickly thought better of it. Sath was in no state to fight, and he would only get himself and the gnome killed if he tried.

"Just lemme alone, dorf," Sath said as he searched for something to bandage his paw. "Take the others and lemme lone."

Teeand scratched his jaw a moment. "Fine, if that's what you want," he said as he moved toward the door.

"I want her dead," Sath whispered. "Thass what I want, dorf, her and that human dead." Teeand winced at his friend's words. Sath was definitely not fit to come with them yet, and especially not under the banner of The Fabled Ones.

"You don't mean that, Sath," Teeand said quietly as he placed a hand on the doorknob. As his fingers closed around it, he mused briefly that it seemed to be the only thing left intact in the room.

"Aye, I do means it, and if you'uns plan to steal dat kill frum me I'll kills all of you too!" Sath bellowed. Teeand swallowed hard, opened the door and walked slowly through it. "I mean it dorf!" Not finding any bandages, Sath hurled the remains of a backpack after Teeand. He growled as it bounced off the now closed door.

"Okay, change of plans, guys," Teeand said. "Gaelin, could you please leave your elemental here to guard Sath? He is not to leave this room until he is sober and thinking clearly. Letting him loose right now would be dangerous to the public at large."

"I'm afraid I can't do that, Teeand," Gaelin replied, his tone somber as he spoke. "If you and yours hold out any hope of regaining a friendship with the Qatu Sathlir, you must leave this alone. The druid has made her choice, and you must honor it, just as you must give him time to get past his anger."

"We can't just leave Ginny there," Hackort whined. "She can't have made that choice on her own!"

"You know, as much as I love a good fight," Elysiam said as she laid a hand on the gnome's head, "we have been in there twice now. We have fought well but I know that I am not the only one that may need time to heal before we go in again. Teeand made the decision, Hack. We are not going back." Hackort looked up at her to protest but stopped as her gaze met his. "If our Ginny has made the decision to stay then going in and getting hurt again will not make her leave. Gaelin, as much as it pains me to agree with a high elf, on this you are right." She picked up her bag from the floor and gathered her things. "I'm going to go to the great hall. I need some time to think." She left the tavern and after a moment or two Hackort followed her.

"It is for the best, Teeand," Gaelin said, turning his gaze back to the dwarf warrior at his side that was positively radiating with anger.

"I did not want to rescue the wood elf," Teeand hissed. "I was going to end her. Just me, not us, not under the banner of the Fabled Ones. She has, in her short time with us, somehow destroyed all that was my friend, Sath, and turned him back to the Bane of the Forest…he is exactly what she expected him to be, and for that I cannot suffer her to live."

"This I knew, Teeand," Gaelin said, bowing his head sadly. "You must not waste your time on such endeavors. Your friend

Sathlir needs you, and you must go after him and keep him from ruining all the good he has done. We in Alynatalos knew of the Bane of the Forest just as the wood elves did, and I must say upon meeting him I was pleasantly surprised by Sathlir's devotion to Ginolwenye. I think he still has it in him, but it will take a true friend to help him find it again."

"Aye," Teeand agreed, tugging on his beard. "I should also make a stop in at home if I know what's good for me. Nehrys has sent letter after letter. My children need their father…and perhaps a bit of time with my brood would be just what our feline friend needs to sort him out." He extended his arm to Gaelin who grasped it just below the elbow, a common greeting and parting. "May your travels be wondrous and safe, my friend," Teeand said.

"Aye, and yours as well, Teeand. May there always be a pint of ale, a warm welcome, and a bowl of stew at the end of your journey." Gaelin smiled affectionately down at Teeand. "Should our paths not cross again, I will be proud to say that I fought with the Fabled Ones, and I owe them my life."

"Of course they will cross again, Gaelin, don't be daft," Teeand chuckled. He picked up his pack and headed back for Sath's door. "Well, unless I get eaten by that cat in there, that is." Gaelin smiled a sad smile and turned to leave, seemingly floating across the tavern floor.

Once outside the tavern, Gaelin pulled out his spell book and thumbed through the pages until he found a spell of transportation. "I fear you are wrong, brave Teeand," he said as he scanned the page with his long finger, nodding. "But I meant what I said, I owe the Fabled Ones my life, and I will start paying off that debt by setting the druid and that poor wizard free…or I shall die trying." Gaelin's voice was low as he read the words of the spell, and then snapped the book shut as he spoke the final word that determined the destination. "Outlands."

The ancient mage threw on a magical cloak of invisibility as he drew close to the entrance of the ruined Keep. Gaelin mused on the irony that for months, he had only wanted to be free of the place and now he was walking back in the front gate on his own, AGAIN. The ancient mage progressed silently across the stone floors, almost levitating as he moved. His robes, the color of the blackest night, hung absolutely still on his emaciated frame. He had completely ensconced himself in the magic that kept him moving as well as kept him virtually undetected. There were benefits to having been alive as long as he had been.

He concentrated on the wood elf druid that had come with Sathlir to rescue him from the awful cells in the Keep. Sending out tendrils of magical power, he searched the ruin for her energy. Gaelin smiled sadly as he searched. Had he tried this before, they would have been able to snatch Gin away from danger and get all of them out safely, but the All Mother moved in her own mysterious ways.

Gin was farther in than the drawbridge, past the parapets of the castle, near the…ah, there she was. He had only to focus on the wretched slaves still held in the cells and he managed to pick up Gin's energy nearby.

Without any hesitation, Gaelin removed a dark stone from the pack at his hip and held it between his palms. Almost immediately, the gem began to feel warm, and as he spoke the words in Elder Elvish to cast the spell, he focused on Gin's face and her energy. "I cannot hide from you, Ginolwenye," he whispered, and with that, the spell cast and Gaelin disappeared.

He reappeared in the arena in the center of the Keep and spotted Gin across the room, standing defiantly in front of the massive indigo dragon. Gaelin ducked back into a hallway to the side of the great room, moving quickly even though there was no indication that anyone had seen him. He looked back in time to see the antediluvian reptile lower his head and stare at Gin, then felt more than heard the rumble of Taanyth's voice as he spoke the words of the spell.

Gaelin looked across the room from where he hovered and spotted Dorlagar. The human was watching the dragon carefully and Gaelin wondered for a moment if he was under the thrall of Taanyth's spell. Next to him stood Taeben, and Gaelin smiled sadly at the high elf whose sole attention was on Gin. By all rights, he should have been watching the spell work, hoping that his research would please the dragon. Gaelin had been in Taeben's shoes, forced to research the spell for Lord Taanyth, and had borne the brunt of his own inability to figure out certain aspects of what the dragon wanted to do. Instead of being visibly concerned for his own safety, however, Taeben appeared moved by what Gin was enduring. Perhaps he wasn't the heartless creature Gaelin had thought him to be back in the cells.

Gin held her ground, her eyes closed and her hands fisted at her sides. Gaelin, by the sheer amount of time he had walked the face of Orana, could see the magic flowing from the dragon. It was black, as black as the robes Gaelin wore, and it began to obscure his view of the wood elf. He heard her cry out from the center of the dark cloud of magic, and then watched as it dissipated. She was still standing. "Good girl," Gaelin whispered as he made his way across the room, imperceptibly stopping just behind Dorlagar as the human crossed to where Gin stood and rebound her hands. He noticed Taeben following along behind as Dorlagar led his prisoner away from an angry Lord Taanyth.

"Wizard!" the dragon rumbled as sparks began to appear around his huge nostrils.

"I will fix it, my lord," Taeben responded, taking care not to look up at the dragon.

"Yes you will!" the dragon roared as a curling bolt of flame shot from his nose and danced along the floor toward the three of them like a lit fuse as they moved out of its path. Gaelin followed along, finding himself marveling at the magic possessed by the enormous creature. They were kindred spirits in a way, and had been at this business of magic for a long time. However, unlike the dragon, Gaelin had only ever sought to use his power and training for good.

"May you never realize your dream, Lord Taanyth," he whispered as he followed the trio out the doors and back along the corridors, assumedly headed for the room where Gin had been kept.

"Keep moving, Gin," Dorlagar barked. "You could at least show some fear when you are being tested. Something to make Lord Taanyth think he is getting somewhere since this one," he said, shoving Taeben forward, "isn't making progress on the spell."

"I won't play your game," Gin replied, her voice tight and pinched. The spell had done some damage, but she seemed unwilling to reveal that. Gaelin was again very proud of this little wood elf, and thought how proud the Fabled Ones would be of her if they knew. "I wasn't afraid."

"She wasn't afraid of Taanyth," Taeben snapped. She was just disgusted by you," Taeben said, and even as he spoke, he wondered why he was sticking up for the druid.

"As are we all, in truth," said Gaelin as he appeared behind them. Dorlagar nearly toppled over backward in surprise, giving Gin the advantage she needed to grab for his sword with her still-bound hands and push him down with her boot. The elder wizard smiled at her, and then pointed a slender finger at Gin's wrists and the rope burst into flame, freeing her. "Well done, my girl. Now then, for you," he said, turning to Taeben as Gin leaped on top of Dorlagar, sword raised.

She took a deep breath and without another word, plunged the sword downward into a very surprised Dorlagar's neck, leaving him gurgling and staring up at her in confusion. As she tightened her grip the hilt, she leaned down close to him and smoothed the hair off his forehead. "Go, be with your Raedea," she whispered as she tugged at the blade, removing it from the wound as the light went out of Dorlagar's eyes. She stood still a moment, looking down at him and imagining him reuniting with his sister on the other side.

After tearing his gaze away from the carnage behind him, Taeben rubbed his wrists. "I appreciate that, Gaelin," he said, eyeing the mage cautiously, "but I do not understand why you have done it."

"You are my kin; we are both sons of Alynatalos. You are a prisoner here, just as I was, Taeben," Gaelin said. "I could not leave my brother wizard to rot if I had a chance to make it right." He leaned in close to Taeben, changing his language to Elder Elvish so that Gin would not understand him. *"You have a chance to make right the wrongs you have committed while being held here, my brother. Do not help the evil of Lord Taanyth and the dragonkind that follow him to spread any further. Do not forget the lessons learned in the Forest Wars. Take this wood elf back to her kind and then use your freedom to do good things."*

*"I am sure that I have no idea what you mean,"* Taeben said as he stepped in between Gaelin and Gin, who was still standing over Dorlagar's body, a solemn look on her tiny face. *"What else would I do but take care of her?"* Her eyes were vacant. "Ginny, you need to transport yourself out of here, yes? If they find you here

with his body they will kill you." He took her shoulders and turned her around. "Do you hear me? I will take care of myself and Gaelin. Just go." She stared up at him, eyes blank and unseeing for a moment. "Never killed anything before, have you?" he said, clucking his tongue and then spoke magical words of transport to the Forest, just below her tree city home. A ring of fire appeared around Gin's body and then she just disappeared. "Now then, you were saying?" he asked as he turned back to Gaelin.

"What are you playing at, Taeben?" Gaelin asked as he raised an eyebrow at his fellow wizard.

"Nothing, Gaelin. I am just tired of being left behind when rescue parties come, I guess. What made you so special that they took you and not me? Why did Nelenie make it out of here in one piece," he said, clenching his fists by his side as his voice rose, "and I stayed here to suffer? Do you know what they do if you do not comply, Gaelin? Of course you do, you were a test subject." Taeben smiled menacingly. "A particularly tenacious one if I remember correctly." He took a step toward Gaelin and frowned when the older wizard did not back away.

"You are free now, my brother. Your choices are between you and your deity now," Gaelin said as he smoothed out his robes with his willowy hands, their near translucence a stark contrast with the ruby red color of his robes now that the protection of his magic had dropped away. "I do not need you to port me out, I can do that myself. Have you enough strength to get yourself to freedom?"

"Alas, I do not," Taeben said, licking his lips and smiling at Gaelin. "Will you permit me to cast a spell that will allow me to use some of yours?" Gaelin nodded, a suspicious smile on his face. He held out an arm, watching Taeben warily. Taeben took Gaelin's arm in his hand, then closed his eyes to recite the spell.

For a moment, both of them stood still, eyes closed, as magical energy flowed between them. Suddenly Gaelin's eyes flew open.

"Stop this, Taeben," he commanded, but Taeben held fast to his arm. "STOP! You are taking too much!"

"No, just enough I think," Taeben whispered, his eyes still closed. As his grip tightened, Gaelin struggled but could not free himself. Taeben's eyes opened and his gaze held Gaelin's own. His silvery eyes blazed and his face split into a maniacal grin. "Just enough. Goodbye, Gaelin," he said as he let go of the arm of the now dead mage. "You're right, my choices are my own." He kicked the corpse to the side and then spoke magical words that would transport him to the forest. He had much work to do and he needed the druid. "See you soon, Ginny," he whispered. "Forest!" Clapping his hands above his head, he disappeared in a flash of light and flame, leaving Gaelin's body to stare with its dead eyes up at the night sky.

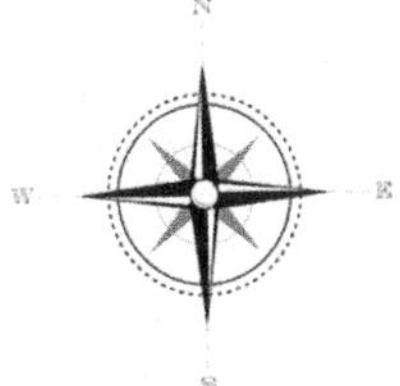


# TWENTY-THREE

Gin lay in the grass in the forest for a long time. When she found that she could close her eyes and not immediately see Dorlagar's dead eyes staring at her in her mind's eye, she sat up. She had taken lives before while hunting with Naevys. That part was not new. However, she had never taken the life of one unarmed…or one that was a friend. But was Dorlagar a friend? Gin rubbed her eyes with the heels of her hands. She felt as though the fabric of her soul had been ripped to shreds.

Everything that she knew, everything that made her who she was had been destroyed in that one moment, that one act. She couldn't even remember making the conscious decision to attack him. There was no memory of the planning of the attack, no thought to make sure she would knock him down. She had seen her chance and known what she had to do and that was all there was to it.

What did that mean for her now? Was she a killer? Was

she a martyr? Was she a hero? Gin moved her hands from her eyes and focused pressure on her throbbing temples with her fingers. As she continued the small, circular movement, she let her thoughts wander to Taeben.

Admittedly, her memories of him were through the filters of childhood, so the coldness of his demeanor may have seemed more exaggerated than it truly was. In addition, to find that he had been hunting with Nelenie before she was banished… Gin recalled long nights huddled around the campfire with Nelenie and Dorlagar, swapping stories of their past. She never had much to add, but the others had fantastical tales of glory in battle. Had Nelenie ever mentioned Taeben by name? She honestly could not remember.

She remembered how taken she was with Taeben when she was only a child. Often, if she was playing with Nelenie and Taeben joined them, Gin would become so enthralled with him that she could not speak, and he would tease her about it. As they grew older, she saw his attention turn toward Nelenie, and then he was gone for his training. She hadn't thought of him in ages, but now here he was…his part in the dragon's plot troubled her greatly.

Gin's mind swam. It was all too much. All of these different parts of her life were converging, like streams running toward the sea, and at the joining points, there seemed to be the most awful turbulent waters. Nelenie had been in those dreadful cells like Taeben and Gaelin…and Teeand and Sathlir, apparently, if their tales were to be believed.

Sath. The sparkling teal eyes appeared in her mind's eye now, pleading with her to trust him, to forgive him. However, right on the heels of that memory was the vivid recollection of the scene on the drawbridge, the showdown between Sath and Dor. Every bit the Bane of the Forest in that moment, she had seen Sath for what he truly was…and wasn't. Why had he warned her before he struck? Why had he come for her when Dor held her prisoner? Was he just trying to make right an age old wrong between himself and her kind? She was certain that he was not just trying to gain an advantage over her so that he could return to his former ways and kill her. The thought of Sath harming her on purpose caused a strange pain in her chest that she had not felt before. However, that pain was nothing compared to what followed when she realized how her choice to stay behind in the ruined castle must have appeared to her friends…to Sath.

This had to be put right, but how? Gin gnawed on her fingernail for a moment, losing herself to a memory of her mother correcting her for that bad habit. "How will you attract a mate when you act like an animal, Ginolwenye?" she whispered, a melancholy grin spreading across her face. "I suppose you will take up with the beasts before you will find a good wood elf male!"

Again Sath's face barged in on Gin's musing. He was not a beast, not really, even though she had accused him of that more than once. He was a good male, a male of much worth, and she had to be fooling herself to think that her actions had made a bit of difference in his life. He and the Fabled Ones were probably at the tavern in the Outpost right now, laughing over pints of ale and planning their next adventure…without her.

Gin glanced back over toward the towering edifice of Alynatalos and noticed someone on the path. Her heart caught in her throat as she recognized the voice. It was Taeben, and he was free! He had not noticed her yet. She was not sure if she was ready to approach him, though; his deeds at the behest of that dragon were still fresh in her mind and she found that now, looking at him, she was a bit afraid of him. She quickly spoke magical words of camouflage and blended into the background so that she would be able to move closer, and nearly gave herself away, for when she saw the condition that Taeben was in she gasped. He looked up, but seeing no one returned to his musing.

His hair, as red as the crimson berries that Gin had collected as a child for her mother's oatmeal, was now a shock of white. His face was pointed and sunken, as though he had not eaten in some time. His robes hung on him, much the way that Gaelin's had when they found him. Gaelin. Gin's mind raced. Why had Taeben transported her out without the elder mage? She was not able to understand what they were saying to each other in the Keep because they were speaking the dialect of the high elves, but she had felt that something was wrong. Now, to look at Taeben from a distance, she could have mistaken him for Gaelin. As she pondered that thought, he dashed off into the forest. Gin decided to follow him.

She kept up with him until he ran into the cave cut into the mountain that joined the Forest to the Grasslands. Gin doubled back and darted into the cave, almost colliding with Taeben who was seated there in the dark, meditating and chanting in a low voice. The words were an elder form of Elvish, and she was frustrated that she could not understand all of them. Finally, he stood, his chanting growing louder, and a bright white light began to coalesce around him. It started as a cloud clinging to his feet, then spread until it covered the whole of his body. Gin stepped back a bit, shielding her eyes from the unearthly glow. Finally, it faded and she gaped at what she saw.

Taeben stood before her; red hair pulled back in a ponytail and his deep blue robe hugging the contours of his now healthy and filled out frame. He stared right at her as though he could see her. Gin started to suspect that he could, actually, and began backing out of the cave. He smiled at her, holding up one of his slender hands.

"I can't let you just leave after what you've seen, Ginny,"

he said, his voice seeming to resonate in her mind rather than her ears. "No one would believe tales about a wizard that can do what I can do, now would they? Far too dangerous." He moved toward her, his hands up and palms open, and then there was a bright flash of light. When Gin next opened her eyes, she was again in the grass where she had been before.

"Could I have dreamed…what did I…?" Gin wracked her mind but drew a blank. There was something clinging to the edge of her consciousness, a memory of…Taeben? She hoped that he and Gaelin had made it out of the ruined castle. Gin shook her head to clear it, got to her feet and pulled out a map to plot a journey to the Outpost. There was much to apologize for with the Fabled Ones, and her first stop would be the great hall. The image of Sath coming out of the shadows in the healing pool flitted through her mind, and for the first time Gin felt safe and warm in that memory. Perhaps her amends should start with the Qatu.

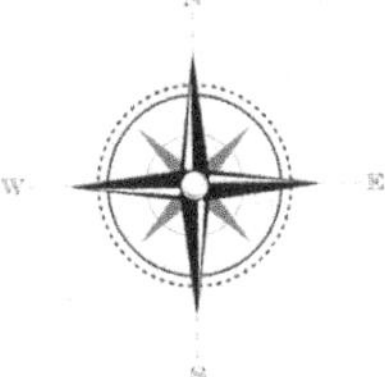

## Several weeks Later…

Shhhink. Shhhink. The room was silent, save the sound of the sharpening stone honing the blades of Sath's clawed weapons. A single candle illuminated the corner of the room in the great hall where the Qatu sat, hunched over a table. Spread out before him was a collection of weapons, all sharpened to a deadly accuracy.

Shhhink. Shhhink. Gin's image floated through his mind for a moment, and he paused his work to consider her. Into the scene in his mind entered Dorlagar, and Sath watched as the human wrapped himself around her like an octopus. A low growl emitted from Sath's throat as he clenched his fist, not noticing as the blades cut into the tender flesh of his hand. The image faded as the pain shot up his arm, catching his attention and causing him to howl in pain. He threw the stone to the ground next to where he had already dropped the weapon, then grabbed a tunic lying close by to stop the bleeding.

How had that wretched wood elf wormed her way into his soul, her tiny fingers nearly clutching his heart? Sath knew how. He had read her diary so many times and been seared to his core by the emotions she had written about. He too had lost his family, and had been lost in the world. He too had been seeking some way to make that wrong right, and had taken many wrong paths in that quest. Raedea had seen that lost young one still in him and had helped him get started back on the right path, but he had failed her. How Elysiam, who found him bleeding at the lift at by Aynamaede, had managed to see through her own fear to bring him to the Fabled Ones was a mystery.

No mystery, really, Sath mused. Elysiam isn't scared of anything. How different she was from Gin. Again, the image of the druid filled his mind and heart and he ached to see her again. He could not imagine how she could stay with that human. His thoughts shifted to Gin as prisoner in the Keep; and to what the human had done to her in the name of his dark Lord, Taanyth. *We went in to save you from that, nearly got ourselves killed, and you thank us by staying,* he thought. The familiar bloodlust creeped in around Sath's vision and his teal eyes narrowed. *If we find that you have escaped from your human lover, we should make* ***you*** *pay, Gin,* he thought, ignoring the pain in his chest that accompanied the thought. *I will make you pay.* Suddenly the hair on the back of his neck stood up, indicating that someone was watching him. "Be gone," he grumbled without turning around.

"Looks like you've sharpened that one quite enough, Sath," a familiar female voice said from behind him. Sath closed his eyes, willing himself to be calm before he turned around.

"I said, be gone, wood elf," he snarled. His heart felt as though it would split in half. Part of him wanted to run to her and grab her up in his arms, but an equally insistent part of him wanted to rip her to shreds. He kept his attention on the sharpening stone in order to keep from closing the space between them, but his heart was in his throat.

"I only want to talk to you, Sath," she said, taking a

hesitant step closer to him. "If you hear what I have to say and still wish me to leave, I will."

"I have nothing to say to you, Gin," Sath said, his voice not much more than a growl. "Say what you came to say and then leave." He finally turned to face her, and nearly dropped to his knees at the sight of her.

She was clothed from head to toe in what looked like black chain mail armor. Tiny vines of carefully crafted steel wound around her arms, and the same vines coiled down her slender legs on her boots. As she moved, he now noticed, the soft chink-chink of her mail tunic almost sounded like tiny bells. Her hair was loose, out of its standard ponytail and flowing down her back. All of the wounds inflicted at the hands of Dorlagar, Lord Taanyth, and even Sath himself seemed to be healed. She took a step closer, and he tensed, flexing his injured hand. "Does that mean you will listen to me?"

"Do I have a choice? And how do I know you're who you say you are, or that you've returned to do anything more than kill me where I stand? Perhaps it would be safer," Sath snarled, "for BOTH of us if you return to your human lover and leave me be, as I asked?"

Instead of running as he hoped she would, she took another step closer to him. She cocked her head to one side, studying him. "What's with the black armor, Sath?"

Sath smiled. "Ah, you noticed that. Dyed black, compliments of the blood of more wood elves than I'd care to count, my dear." He grinned as she paled at his comment, though a pain shot through his heart. "It seems that your kind aren't as generous and honest as you made me think, my dear Gin. If one I loved…we trusted as much as the Fabled Ones trusted you could betray us the way you did, then it seems we are safe from none of them."

"How many?" she asked, her voice barely audible.

Sath grinned as he took a step closer to her. He had never noticed it before, but he could smell the fear on her. "Many," he whispered. "Many such as you, pretty little druids and rangers." He took another step closer, a bit annoyed that she was not moving away. "All of them dead, as dead as you are to me."

She took a deep breath. "May I speak now, Sath?" she whispered, fear quaking in her voice.

"I can't believe you've held back this long," Sath said as he sat back down at his work. Shhhrink. Shhhrink. "Well?"

"I didn't stay behind because I wanted to be with Dor," she said slowly. "I stayed behind to kill him."

Sath erupted in laughter, which slowly turned into a menacing growl. He did not look up at her. "You do not have it in you to kill anything! Do you think I'm a fool?"

"No. I know you are not, and that is why things happened as they did. You're quite tough to outsmart, Cat," she said. She paused a moment to get her heart under control before it burst from her chest, giving Sath the chance he needed. Before she even saw him move, Sath grabbed her by the throat, lifting her off the ground. She kicked at him and struggled, but his grip was like iron as it closed on her windpipe.

Sath brought her close to him, ignoring the blows landed by her flailing legs and arms. "I may be tough to outsmart, but you will be easy to kill," he hissed at her, again tightening the grip on her throat. She felt her eyes bulging from their sockets as she gasped for air. "Look at that, you even got rid of the scar I gave you." In one deft movement, the clawed weapon was on his other hand, its blade twinkling in the candlelight.

"Sath…please…" She could barely speak as she tugged at the fingers around her throat. She began to kick harder as Sath ran the back of one of the lethal blades down the side of her face. "Don't…"

Sath flexed the clawed weapon, allowing the bloodlust he had held back to flow freely. "Hmm, shall I be merciful and do this quickly? Bah, what's the fun in that?"

Tears rolled down her cheeks. She scanned the room that was beginning to darken around the edges. She found it difficult not to stare at his fangs, which were only inches from her nose. "Please…" she whispered, her voice hoarse from lack of air.

As suddenly as he had grabbed her, Sath released her. She fell in a heap on the floor, gasping for air. He turned his back to her and tried desperately to free himself from the sound her voice. "Say what you came to say and get out," he said, his voice low and menacing.

"I…" she started to speak but could only cough and sputter until she got her breathing under control. When she recovered, she continued, "I killed Dorlagar. He is dead. I suppose," she paused to cough, "that's all you need to know." She stood slowly, the room still spinning a bit from her previous lack of oxygen.

Sath nodded slowly. "So now you've come for me, have you? Going to give all of your companions a taste of your blade before you rest?" He turned back to face her. "Here, do it quickly, because you will have but one chance before I strike back." He knelt in front of her, again carefully avoiding looking her in the eye.

Her face knotted in frustration. "You're not listening to

me!" she exclaimed, sounding more like a small child than the woman that she was. "You never did listen to me; you only heard what you wanted to hear." She stamped her tiny foot in frustration, nearly causing Sath to laugh in her face.

"Aye, I have heard every word you've said, Little One," he said. "You've killed your lover. What business is that of mine unless you've come to kill me as well?" He leaned in a bit closer to her. "I suppose there is a line of them, just waiting for you to return and…"

She silenced him by slapping his face as hard as she could. Sath roared and once again grabbed her, but this time by the shoulders.

"That was a mistake, druid," he hissed.

"You're making a mistake," she blurted out. "I'm not…I mean; you don't understand…" Sath pulled her close to him to snarl at her, but suddenly stopped cold as he looked into her eyes.

"They're dark," he murmured, as though in a trance.

"What?" She struggled against him, using his momentary pause to her advantage. She wiggled out of his grasp and dashed toward the door, but stopped short as he growled low in his throat. She looked back at him, her hand reaching for the door behind her.

Sath turned slowly to face her, and the rage in his eyes made the wood elf weak in the knees. "Your eyes, wood elf, they're dark. My Gin's eyes are blue. Who are you?"

He advanced on her, but stopped short of grabbing her. Instead, he held the tip of her chin on the point of one of the bladed claws as the other one reached past her to hold the door closed. "You have thirty seconds to tell me who you are before I slit your throat."

The wood elf's eyes were wide with fear. "I told her that this wouldn't work," she said, her voice quaking with sobs. "I told her that you would know the difference, but she said that I was to deliver the message and leave but you wouldn't stop talking, and I couldn't get you to stop talking without slapping you and by the way I'm really sorry and…"

"Silence!" Sath roared. "Your thirty seconds are up." He smiled at her, making sure that he showed his fangs. "Say goodnight, wood elf."

"Gin sent me!" she shrieked, her eyes wide with fear. "Gin sent me!"

"That's better…but I don't believe you," he said as the tip of the claw pierced her skin.

"Her tunic was tangled in her hair…Sathlir please!" The wood elf found herself unable to move, praying to any deity that was listening that the memory Gin had told her to use her would work. She couldn't remember what the elder wood elf had told her it meant, but she had said that Sath would recognize it.

"What did you say?" he whispered, frozen in place.

"She…she said you'd recognize that memory, something about her mail tunic getting tangled in her hair, but I can't remember what it means." Sath sighed audibly.

"It was the first time that Gin saw me as something other than a monster, I think. What's your name, little one?" he asked, his voice softening.

"Lairceach," she whispered. "Gin is my older sister."

Sath nodded. "I see the resemblance," he mumbled,

backing away from her. "Where is your sister now, Lairceach?"

"I…can't tell you that," she said. A low growl erupted from the Qatu's chest, but by the time he had lunged for Lairceach she had disappeared through the doorway.

"Where are you! You can't hide from me, druid!" he roared as he burst through the open doorway.

Her laughter seemed to come from behind him, or was it behind the wall? He could not tell. "Yes I can, Sathlir." He heard tiny feet scampering down the staircase to the ground floor of the grand hall, but decided not to follow her.

"Gin will be back," he said quietly, nodding his head. "Then we will finish this."

"Gin!" Lairceach screamed as she entered the room at the inn and pounded up the stairs. "Gin!" The wood elf threw open the door to find her older sister sitting on the floor, meditating over her spell book.

"Lairky please," Ginolwenye said softly. "I'm busy."

Lairceach stormed over and put one of her boots firmly in the middle of Gin's spell book, nearly ripping out the pages. "Not anymore you're not," the younger sister ordered, her voice shaking a bit around the edges. Gin slowly looked up at her sister, her ice blue eyes betraying her anger.

"Remove your foot," Gin said, her voice still and cold.

Lairceach hesitated a moment, then did as she was told.

"Now," Gin said as she closed her spell book reverently, "what is it? Did you deliver the message to…Ikara's teeth, girl, what is that scratch on your chin?"

Lairceach sank down to her knees in front of her sister. Tears welled up in her dark eyes. "He was really angry, Gin, not like I'd ever seen anyone before." The illusion was starting to fade, and Gin could see traces of her sister's black hair peeking out from behind the brown locks that resembled her own. "He's not himself. You shouldn't go back to him."

"You know I can't do that," Gin said. Her composure was fading fast at the thought of Sath hurting her sister. "Now tell me what happened."

"He figured it out, but he had already tried to kill me before he knew I was me and not you so really he was trying to hurt you!" The younger wood elf's words came out in a rush, only moments ahead of sobbing tears. Gin gathered her sister in her arms, letting the young one sob as much as she needed. She smoothed Lairky's hair, which now had turned back to its natural inky blackness. Gin lightly touched her sister's chin with her forefinger, and spoke soft words in Elvish. The wound on Lairceach's chin dissolved into healthy skin, leaving not so much as a scar.

"I will deal with this, Lairky. I am sorry that I sent one as young as you are. Had anything happened to you…well, I cannot believe that Sath would kill you, but…"

Lairceach jerked her head back. Her face was red from sobbing and her normally wide eyes were pinched with swelling. "Believe it," she said through choking sobs. "He's the one that's been doing it, Gin!" The girl wiped her nose on her sleeve, making Gin wince a little. "The return to having a curfew, the fear of leaving the city at night, it's all because of him!"

Gin smiled at her sister as she smoothed Lairceach's now-black hair away from her face. "No, little one, that was a long time ago. Those are legends best left untold."

Lairceach snorted. "Legends indeed. Gin, was Sath's armor black the last time you saw him?"

Gin knotted her eyebrows. "No."

"It is now, and when I asked him about it he said it was dyed courtesy of the blood of my kind…OUR kind, Gin, wood elves. Druids and Rangers!" She sniffed loudly before she continued. "He said that if you would betray him then he can't trust any of us, so we're as good as dead."

Gin's face paled. "He actually said that?" she said, her voice barely a whisper.

"Aye." Lairceach took Gin's hand in hers and squeezed it. "You must promise me that you will not go after that Cat, Gin, please? I couldn't stand it if I lost you. Now that Cursik has left us and not sent word or come home…well, I'd be all alone and I'd die!" The sobs once again overtook the girl, and she fell back into her sister's arms. Gin stroked her sister's hair, but her face was still paled with shock. *Killing druids and rangers,* she thought. *Sath… He is angry with me, and I must put this right.*

"Lairky, listen to me. I want you to go lie down and try to sleep, and put all of this out of your mind," Gin said softly. The younger wood elf finally nodded, her eyes half closed, then stood and went to her pallet on the floor. Gin considered her sister for a long moment, and then crossed the room and pulled on her cloak. "I'm going to go…clear my head with some fresh air, but I'll be back very soon," she said. She barely heard the door slam behind her as she dashed off to find a courier to take a message to the grand hall of the Fabled Ones.

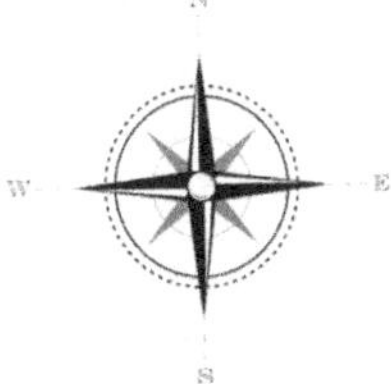

# Twenty-Four

Sath was waiting at the front door to the grand hall when Gin arrived. He was sitting on the ground meditating, with his magical pet by his side. The tiger scanned the area in front of its master, watching for signs of danger. Gin could hear it start to purr when it saw her draw close. She smiled at the magical beast. How many times had that creature put its own life in danger to protect its master… or her?

"Close enough, wood elf," Sath said, his voice rumbling like a growl. He had not had to open his eyes to know that his warder was purring at Gin. The smell of sunflowers had hit him in the nose like a roundhouse punch. Nevertheless, he was still angry at her, even more so now for the deception involving her sister, and he was not going to let her off easy. Better to let her reveal herself first, and then he could figure out what to do with her.

"Hello, Sath," Gin said softly, cursing herself for not coming up with anything better to say. "I've come to talk."

"Bah, you think you can fool me again? I should have killed you before when I had the chance." He remained seated, his eyes closed.

"Sath, look at me," she began, but he cut her off quickly. The Qatu sprang to his feet and in one movement had her by the shoulders, pulling her close to his face. Gin did not struggle, only locked her eyes on his.

"They're…blue…" he said, and dropped her as quickly as he had grabbed her. He turned his back quickly as she got to her feet. "What do you want, Gin? Did your sister not relay my words to you?"

"Aye, she did, and I suppose I should thank you for not killing her," Gin said, swallowing the anger rising in her at the thought of Sath hurting her sister.

"Bah, she's just one more ranger. I'd reached m'quota for that day." Sath winced at the gasp he heard from behind him, thankful that he was not facing her.

"So it's true then?"

"What's true? That I have once again become the bane of the wood elves of the forest? That I sneak about in the trees at night, snatching up the young and the slow?" Sath turned around slowly and looked down at Gin. "That my armor is dyed with the blood of those unfortunate wretches? Aye, my dear wood elf, our Ginny, tis all true." He held his breath a moment as he resumed his meditating, waiting for the out lashing of anger that he knew would come…but none did.

"Why?" Gin said.

"Why? That's all you have to say is 'why?'" Sath roared as he stood again and looked down at her. "I'm killing your kin,

Ginolwenye! Murdering your cousins and their children! Tasting the blood of your neighbors and friends! And all you can say to me is why?"

"Aye, that is what I wish to know. Why?" she said, her voice more calm and solemn than he had ever heard her.

Sath smiled and flexed his hands. "Your sister didn't tell you? Tis nothing but revenge, *darlin,* revenge on the race that bore the banshee that betrayed me and the Fabled Ones." He leaned down until he was again looking her in the eye. "And I suppose you have come to beg me to stop this? To plead for your wretched kind?"

"No," Gin said carefully. "I have come to ask for your help, Sath, for I find myself yet again in a bit of trouble. It does seem to follow me…"

"Help you?" The Qatu roared in laughter. After a moment, he was again able to speak as he wiped tears from his eyes. "Oh, forgive me, but that's the best laugh I've had in ages," he said through returning giggles. "Why in the name of your Mother Sephine should I help you?"

"Because you are a good and kind soul, Sath, and you would die for one of your friends," Gin replied. "And if I am nothing else to you, I would hope that I can still be counted among your friends after you hear what I have to say."

"Always with the talking," Sath grumbled. "Well, get on with it, I'm already getting bored."

"Can we go somewhere more private?" Gin asked, hoping that he would not misunderstand her question. She scanned the area around them, and though she saw no traces of malicious presence, it would still be safer to speak indoors than on the parapets of the grand hall with the warriors hanging about at their posts, guarding the citizens within.

Sath clearly was taken aback by her suggestion. "Whatever you have to say to me can be done here," he said gruffly. Gin moved closer to him, and he noticed that the fear he had smelled on her… on her sister earlier was gone. His heart lightened just a bit at that realization. I nearly killed her sister and have murdered half of her kind, and yet she still does not fear me as she did before. What has changed?

"I need for you to know why I stayed behind in the ruined Keep, for I fear that you and the others have the wrong idea. I am also concerned for the safety of one of the Fabled Ones, Gaelin…" She paused a moment as a fuzzy memory tugged at her, but finding it unable to coalesce she continued. "I fear that he did not make it back out of the Keep with the wizard."

"What? I don't know what you're talking about, female, and I don't particularly care to hear the details of your little tryst with that human," Sath said, intentionally avoiding her gaze. He scanned the ground at his feet. "At least sit down, will you? Your pacing is going to set off my pet here." Gin sat down very close to Sath, causing his mind to spin and grow a bit fuzzy. "See? Not like I'm going to bite."

"I'm not so sure about that, from your own admission," Gin said, trying to stifle a grin. She remembered then that Sath had an uncanny ability to put almost anyone at ease, an odd thing for one as large and clearly dangerous as he, and she relaxed a bit before she began speaking. "Sath, I stayed behind because I needed to finish things with Dorlagar. He was responsible for my parents' deaths, as you may remember."

"Go on." Sath continued to stare at the ground, now and then picking at a frayed edge on his boot. "I am not sure why I should care, but go on."

Gin paused a moment before she spoke, choosing her words carefully. "I did not defeat him in the arena many seasons ago, just before I…ran into you for the first time." Sath raised his gaze to meet hers as, unconsciously, her fingers found the scar on the side of her face. The gesture sent a painful twang through Sath's heart as he watched. He had hurt her, hurt GIN. He was no longer just a legend to her but a monster. Bane of the Forest.

"Yes, I remember. Excellent marmalade sandwiches," Sath said, trying to lighten the mood, a grin spreading across his feline features faded as he watched the color drain from her face for a moment. She chewed on her fingernail until she had regained enough control to continue.

"When we first met, I had come from the arena in Calder's Port. We were there with Naevys and Dor had been out all night drinking the night before. I challenged him to a duel to avenge my parents but when it came down to it…I couldn't kill him." Gin hung her head in shame. "Naevys was right, you know, I was not fit for much save healing from a safe distance. After I…well, let's be honest, after you ran me off with your pet, I was lost. I don't mean physically lost; I knew where I was. I mean that I had no purpose. It wasn't until Elysiam brought me into The Fabled Ones that I found a home and a reason to wake up in the mornings."

Sath sighed loudly, to try to stop her from talking for a moment but failing. He was having trouble focusing on her story, finding himself instead remembering their meeting in the tunnel and how he had immediately been sucked into reading her diary from the first words on the page. What was happening to him? She wasn't Qatu. She was an elf, a wood elf at that.

Strange warmth spread throughout his chest as he looked at her, and it crackled and popped like a firework in his heart when she met his gaze. He shook his head to clear it and found her to be staring at him. He realized with a start that he had not heard a word she had said and hoped she had not ended with a question. "Am I boring you?" she asked. He could not tell if she was annoyed or amused.

"Well, you do tend to rattle on," he said, beaming a toothy grin at her, then remembering that he was angry at her and turning it into a scowl. "I should have known that wasn't you before, Lairky is…"

"Lairceach. Don't use her nickname," Gin snapped, glaring up at him. "You nearly killed her."

With that, Sath snapped out of his lovesick kitten demeanor and was instantly the Bane of the Forest again. There was no way this tiny druid before him was going to charm him, as she seemed to have been doing. He leaned in close to Gin, making sure that his fangs glistened just inches from her nose. "No, Gin, I almost killed YOU. That is who she was supposed to be, right? THAT was my intention, and still might be." He inhaled sharply, growling a bit in his throat. She was still not afraid of him.

Gin closed her eyes a moment and took a deep breath. "That remains to be seen," she said. "Before we get to that, though, may I continue?" Sath leaned back, scowling and waving her on, so she resumed her tale. "Thank you. I need for you and the others to know that I have found myself in the Fabled Ones. You…they are my home and my family. I have no need of my kin in the trees of the forest." She placed a hand on Sath's arm; he could feel a tremble in it when he rumbled deep down in his chest, but she did not remove it. "Will you help me convince the others that I am worthy to come back? They will listen to you, Sath."

"Why should I help you? Why shouldn't I just kill you?" he said, baring his teeth. There was no fear at all from her as her hand remained, tiny fingers winding into his fur.

"If I thought that my death would keep you from killing any more of my kin, I might consider it. Seems you're not going to help me anyway," she said. Her voice was tight with barely controlled anger. "I tried going to Tee, Sath. I don't know what you said to him, but when I found him in the tavern here, he sent me away and I got the feeling I should consider myself lucky that is all he did." She frowned, clearly distressed by her interaction with the dwarf. "I can't find Elys and Hack. Ailreden says that they are off on another mission but he won't tell me where, and he says Tee has returned home to the mountains."

Finally, she removed her hand from his arm and stood up. Sath mused a moment at the fact that while he sat and she stood she was still only a bit taller than he was. "You were my last hope." Sath looked up at her and his chest tightened at the deadness in her gaze. "If you will promise that you will leave my kind alone, especially my sister whom you have terrified beyond reason, then I will do whatever you ask of me. I will become your personal healer. I will fall on my tiny little sword, whatever… I will leave and not trouble you again." She took a step back from him. "In fact, if you want to take revenge, I will not fight you. I am tired of fighting."

"Wait." Sath snarled under his breath. "The truth is I have no wish to kill you. Ailreden has sent word to me that he is planning to leave the Fabled Ones and…he has asked me to take his place." Gin looked up at him, surprised. "I know that he had thought of you for his successor, but when you stayed behind…" She smiled at him and he looked at her quizzically. "Why are you smiling?"

"Because you will make a good guild leader, Sath," she said. All of the feelings for Sath that had been floating around in her head since leaving the ruined Keep solidified into a soothing warmth in the middle of her chest that spread out to her arms and made her feel like she was swaddled in a warm blanket. "You are a good male, a trustworthy friend, and I believe that you will never return to your days as the Bane of the Forest, regardless of your posturing before. You can huff and puff and stomp around and grab me up by my chin as many times as you like, but when it counted you did not hurt me. You will not hurt me, and I know you will not hurt any of my kind again." Sath looked away from her and she scrambled around until her ice blue eyes again searched his. "Sathlir Clawsharp, head of the Fabled Ones…just as it should be. You were born to be a leader, Sath," Gin said, her voice soft.

Her words jarred him visibly, and for a moment, she was not sure what to do in response. She reached out and touched the side of his face and before he realized what he was doing, he wrapped a hand around her hand, pulling it to his nose and inhaling deeply. His eyes opened, expecting to see her horrified expression, but instead she was smiling at him. Another tiny hand came to rest on his hand, and she pulled it over to her face, resting against her scarred cheek. He winced a bit and she shook her head at him.

"You asked me once if I could know you for who you have become and not the monster you were. I would contend now that you were never really a monster. I think you were just alone and a bit lost, and I want to help you find your way," she said. Sath's eyes widened but he didn't break eye contact with her. Raedea had spoken almost the identical words to him. "You came for me when Dor had me in that wretched place. Why?"

Sath swallowed hard. "I will always come looking for you when you are lost, Gin," he said softly, his words almost a purr. "I…mean it. Just as I would for any of the Fabled Ones." Inwardly he cursed himself for not admitting his feelings to her, but something in his gut told him she did not feel the same way.

She smiled at him.

"And I will always need you for that, I'm afraid," she said, her muted smile spreading into a grin across her freckled face. "Now then, I need to make some amends, it seems. Shall we see what trouble we can get into?"

"Aye, there's only one way to find out I suppose. First, we need for you to make amends with Tee and then we can look for Elys and Hack. I'll not go into battle willingly without them at my back," Sath said, his face darkening. "Perhaps our first adventure will be traveling to the dwarves stronghold in the mountains and winning back the heart of a very surly dwarf?" Gin nodded, still grinning. "Good. Tell me, can you use your transport magic to send us anywhere?"

"Yes, where would you like to go?"

"Calder's Port. We can take a boat up the coast and then cross the Outlands into the mountains. That will give us some time for me to teach you some Dwarvish," Sath said. Gin cocked her head to one side, looking puzzled. "He's much easier to understand when you can swear back at him in his own tongue, Gin," Sath said, chuckling. "And maybe I can teach you some Qatunari as well, if you'll teach me some of that strange language of yours?"

"Deal," she said, scowling a little, "though I'm not sure how you can call MY language strange when yours sounds like growly grumblies." She tried to keep a straight face but both of them burst out laughing.

"First, though, I need to make good on a debt I owe to an old friend," Sath said, his eyes narrowing a bit.

"Tee?"

"No, I wish it was that easy. When you and I first met, way back on that day in the tunnels, I was traveling with someone, a very good friend. It was a human woman that I met in a tavern right outside of Calder's Port." Gin's face flushed and she looked away.

"Was she…were you…I mean, it doesn't matter, but…"

"No," Sath said, chuckling sadly. "No, nothing like that. But she was my friend, my first real friend that wasn't getting close to me because of my…well, she didn't want anything from me."

"What was her name, Sath?" Gin asked, intrigued.

Sath frowned. "Well, this is the tough part, Gin. Her name was Raedea." Gin stared at him, slack-jawed and saucer-eyed. "Before you say anything, I know that she was Dorlagar's sister. I know that she was the person that he was looking for, because I read it in your journal." He reached into his pack and retrieved the precious book, and after a moment's hesitation handed it over to her. Gin took it, running her fingers over the cover in disbelief.

"You've had this the whole time?"

"Aye." He hung his head for a moment. "Rae died when her past caught up to her, Gin, and I wasn't there to protect her. She made me promise to find you and to tell you…" He paused a moment as he clenched his fist. Gin placed a tiny hand on his arm and when he made eye contact with her, she nodded at him, encouraging him to continue. "She made me bring your things back to you that day in the tunnels, but I kept the journal in my bag. She found it while I was returning what I had stolen and found out what Dorlagar had done to your family…and to you."

"Oh…" Gin placed her hands over her mouth.

"So she said that I was to find you and return the journal, let you know that her death would wipe clean the actions of her brother toward your parents and…and to look after you because, I guess, she thought you would keep me honest and help me atone for being the Bane of the Forest."

Gin bit her lip. "She sounds amazing," Gin said. Sath nodded. "Dorlagar could have been just like her, but he got lost when he thought he had lost her." Sath rumbled low in his chest. "I'm sorry," Gin said. "I wish I could have met her."

"You two would have been great friends," Sath said. "Do you forgive me for keeping your journal?"

Gin frowned. "I don't understand why you did, Sath, and why you waited so long to tell me that you had it when you knew how hard it was for me to trust you. If you had told me about Raedea sooner then I might not have…" She paused for a moment, chewing on her thumbnail. "I would still have gone after Dorlagar, because it was nothing to do with your sweet friend. She could not take away what her brother did. Perhaps one day I can forgive you for this lack of trust, but not yet," she said. "I suppose this makes us even, in a way. Now…shall we?" Sath nodded and she began casting a spell that would take them close to Calder's Port. Sath looked down at her as she spoke ancient Elvish words and frowned a little. *Oh, I hope Tee will be as easy for you to win over as I was, Little One,* he thought. *Only one way to find out…*

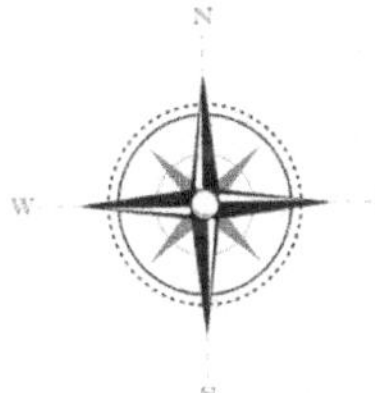


# TWENTY-FIVE
## (MANY SEASONS LATER…)

The moon hung full and bright in the sky, casting shadows over the plains of the Outlands. A small campfire crackled as it glowed, providing heat for the five travelers as they huddled around it. This was not their first journey out into the wilds, and they were taking turns keeping watch.

It was Gin's turn to sit up and she lazily scrawled drawings and notes in her leather-bound notebook as she scanned the area around their campsite. She could see the mountains off in the distance to the north, and the Highlands just past the edge of the Outlands. Now and then, a rumbling growl would catch her attention, letting her know that one of the lions that roamed the plains was getting close to the campsite. Usually, they would smell Sath or his magical pet, which slept between his master and the wilds, and keep on moving. This one was no exception.

Hackort stirred in his sleep, and then rolled over, snuggling up against Elysiam. Gin giggled. The druid would be so angry if she woke up to the little man even close by her, let alone touching her. Gin leaned back on her elbows to stretch her back a moment and gazed up at the stars and the moon, sighing contentedly. Tiny points of light, probably torches or bonfires, illuminated the outline of Qatu, the island home of Sath's kind.

"It's really beautiful, isn't it?" a rumbling yet purring voice said from behind her. Gin's face split into a grin.

"Aye, Sath. I can't imagine what it was like growing up out there," she said, not taking her eyes off the night sky. "At least you didn't have to worry about falling out of your home city!" His laughter warmed her. "Now go back to sleep, it's not your turn yet."

"Oh, Mama Gin," he said, smiling a toothy grin as she giggled at his use of the nickname. "You go on to sleep, I'll make sure your boys and Elysiam keep safe." Gin playfully punched him in the arm and he honorably pretended to be wounded by the strike, even though he had barely felt her tiny fist make contact with his fur. She wound her fingers into the fur on his forearm for a moment and then stood up, stretching her arms toward the sparkling sea of stars above.

"Fine. I could use some sleep if you and Tee are planning another hilarious round of Let's Test Gin's Abilities with Healing Magic like we have seen lately," she said, her voice more affectionate than snarky. Sath chuckled.

"I think that's a good bet," he said. "Now off with you. Take my bedroll if you like, it's warmed up already." Gin crawled into the bedroll he had just left and his pet looked up at him questioningly. "No, old friend I'm fine, you keep an eye on her. Don't let her run off," Sath said. The tiger positioned himself next to the wood elf and stared down at her.

"SATH!"

Sath laughed, a deep and rumbling sound. "At ease, old friend," he said and the tiger circled a time or two before lying down next to Gin. She patted its head and then snuggled down into the bedroll to sleep. Sath's attention was drawn suddenly to the south, where there seemed to be a scuffle underway. His enhanced sight, a birthright of his race, allowed him to make out human guards attacking a dark figure that seemed bent on passing through the checkpoint. He watched, fascinated, as the guards fell to the dark figure one by one.

It was only when he realized the figure was headed their way that he leapt to his feet to wake the others. "TEE!" he said, sternly shaking the dwarf who slept just to the right of Gin. "Get up! Incoming!"

The diminutive warrior was on his feet in a flash, though he had a bit of trouble keeping to them. As was the custom of his kind, Teeand had consumed a bit too much ale earlier as they'd all swapped favorite stories in the firelight, and now he was just the worse for wear as he struggled to strap on his armor. "What is it, Sath?" he stammered as he finished buckling his armored boots and came to stand at Sath's side.

"Dunno. Dark. Moving fast. Just took out all the guards at the southern checkpoint," Sath said. Tee winced and wrinkled his forehead as he stared in the direction Sath was pointing. "Wake the others, Elys and Hack, but let Gin sleep, she's just come off watch. I'll leave my pet with her." He glanced over at her and smiled as she wiggled in the bedroll and rolled over onto her side, then winced as her hair fell away and the scar on her cheek became visible.

"When ye gonna forgive yourself for that one, eh Sath?" Tee asked, patting his old friend on the arm. "She's forgiven you ages ago."

"Aye, she has," Sath muttered, turning his face back to the south. The figure was inexplicably closer than it had been before. "Ikara's Teeth, Tee, whoever that his has gained unholy amounts of ground in no time at all!" Tee strode over to Elysiam's bedroll and lightly touched her arm.

"Stand back! Who is it! What's wrong?" Elysiam exclaimed as she sprung from lying down to standing in seemingly one motion. Tee stifled a laugh as he jumped out of the way of the blade she waved wildly out in front of her.

"Sssh you'll wake Gin. She's just come off watch. We've got something incoming from the south at top speed. Dispatched the entire guard at the southern checkpoint," Tee said in a conspiratorial whisper. Elysiam rubbed her eyes and pulled her wild blonde hair up under her helmet.

"Have you kicked the gnome yet?" she whispered back, grinning.

"No. Be my guest," Tee said as he clapped her on the back. Elysiam's face split into a wide grin as she planted one of her boots in the middle of Hackort's back.

"HEY!" the gnome cried out. "What was that for?" He scrambled to his tiny feet and looked from face to face. "Who kicked me?"

"Guess," Tee said, chuckling.

"All right, the lot of you, look over here." Sath waved his arms and then pointed in the direction of the oncoming stranger.

"Tee, he's tripled his speed and will be here in moments!" Sath no longer cared if he woke Gin. "Guard her," he called out to his tiger as he and the other four set out on a course of interception with the dark stranger.

Gin opened sleepy eyes and sat up. "Guard who?" Sath's tiger nudged her and placed himself in between her and the others who were now running away from her and toward the stranger. "What's going on? Sath?"

"Gin! Stay down!" Sath called over his shoulder as he and the others sped to intercept the stranger that was now bearing down on them. "YOU!" he bellowed at the figure. "State your business!"

The stranger made no response, but instead kept up course and pace. Sath motioned to the others to huddle up, and they assumed a familiar formation before advancing on the stranger again. Tee and Hack took the lead, bellowing insults at the stranger. Sath followed close behind them, shouting out magical words in an ancient dialect of Qatunari that slowed the stranger's pace, but only just. Elysiam was just behind Sath, narrowly avoiding his swinging tail as he ran just in front of her, readying her fingers to release the healing magic her team would require to carry on if the interaction with the stranger went badly.

"Now, Elys?" Teeand called out and Elysiam skidded to a halt, magic flowing from her hands in the form of roots that rose up from the ground and wound around the stranger's legs, slowing the pace but not stopping the progression. The stranger swore loudly in modern Qatunari and reached down to pull at the growths.

"Hold up," Sath said. *"Who are you?"* he called out in Qatunari. The other three waited, watching Sath. *"Answer me! I know you're Qatu!"*

*"Who are YOU?"* came a female voice in response. *"Why should I identify myself if you do not?"*

"Now we're getting somewhere," Sath muttered. "Let me handle this a moment, but watch my back, yeah?" The others nodded and he approached the stranger alone, pulling the hood up on his cloak as he walked. There was nothing gained if the female recognized him. *"My name is Sathlir. We mean you no harm, but we were on alert after your spectacular performance at the guard tower just now,"* he said, switching to Qatunari just in case.

*"Saw that, did you?"* the female responded, her tone decidedly pleased. *"My name is of no consequence to you, but I am pleased that I have found you for it is you, my Prince, that I seek."*

With a roar Sath was on the female, knocking her to the ground, one giant clawed hand covering her mouth. *"Shut your mouth, female!"* he hissed at her. *"No one here knows who I am, do you hear me?* ***No one****."* Sath paused a moment as he signaled to the others to stand down, his eyes burning into the cool green ones beneath him, and the female nodded her head. He removed his hand from her mouth but held her fast under him. *"Why are you looking for me? Is it my father? Mother? Kahzi?"*

*"Your bastard of a father, our Rajah, is just fine, your highness,"* the female responded, a growl clearly present in her words that made Sath want to grin. *"Your mother, our First Wife, also is healthy. It is your sister Princess Kazhmere, who is in great danger."* Sath growled loudly and sprang to his feet, pulling the female up with him. *"PLEASE! Your highness…"* she choked back a sob that gave Sath pause. *"Please, Kahzi is my best friend and I fear that it is my fault that she is in danger!"* Tears welled up in her emerald eyes and Sath immediately changed his tactic.

*"It's all right,"* he said, gently replacing the female on her feet and forcing the anger boiling in his eyes at the thought of his

sister being in danger back down into the pit of his stomach. He managed a less than toothy smile and purred a bit at her. *"Tell me what has happened."* Over his shoulder, he could feel the stares from his friends, and waved them over. *"Do you speak Common Tongue?"*

"Ugh, of course I do, but why?" she asked.

*"Because these are my friends and I do not feel like translating this eve,"* Sath said, chuckling. "If we are to help my…Kahzi, then we must all be on the same page, yes?" he said in Common Tongue as he shot a look at Tee, begging that the dwarf would keep his knowledge of Qatunari to himself. Tee nodded, his eyes narrowed at Sath.

*"They don't know you have a sister or who you are. Trusted friends, indeed, Highness. Fair enough."* The female looked past Sath and addressed his friends. "So, you are the compatriots of my…long lost friend Sathlir?"

Tee gripped the handle of his axe. "Aye, Cat, we are, who is asking? I presume you and Sath were discussing why you were thunderin' up on us like you were?"

"Cat. What a horrible word. I suppose I'll have to tell you my name so that you'll call me something that sounds less…grating than your common word, 'cat'," she responded. "My name is Annilanshi but you lot may call me Anni."

"Annilanshi?" Sath said, the name prompting a long-forgotten image of a young female playing with his sister in the nursery to flit through his memory. "Anni, you said?" She nodded, smiling up at him as she saw the recognition in his eyes.

"Hello, Anni, I'm Hack," the gnome warrior said, pushing his way past his taller companions. "I understand that you're a friend of our Sath's here, but I need more than that to keep you on my list of People Not to Kill." Anni looked down at Hack curiously.

"What are you, exactly?" she said, her eyes filled with wonderment and, to Hack's surprise, hunger. Her countenance changed to that of a predator as she squatted down to his level, sniffing him and looking him over. She stopped abruptly as the tip of Elysiam's scimitar poked into the underside of her chin.

"Hands off the gnome, *CAT,*" Elysiam said. "I'm the only one around here that gets to look at him like he's off the list!" Sath stifled a giggle as Elysiam's face turned red at the realization of what she had just said. "Shut it, Kitty," she hissed at Sath.

"Hackort is a gnome, Anni. More than that, he's my friend and we don't eat friends around my camp," Sath said, pulling the female Qatu back up from the ground. "The dwarf there is Tee, finer warrior you'll never find." Hackort punched Sath in the leg with his tiny fist. "OOF! Sorry, wee man, I mean other than Hack, of course. Both these warriors have saved my hide more times than I'd like to count."

"And the other one? Do we eat her?" Anni said, her voice full of innocent wonder more than malice as she pointed at Elysiam. Elysiam beamed an evil smile back at her.

"I'd love for you to try," the elf said, twirling her scimitar in her fingers as sparks of magic gathered around her hands. Sath and Tee roared with laughter.

"I've gotten my fur singed by that one when she WASN'T trying to defend herself, Anni. I would not try it if I were you. This here is Elysiam, she's a druid and she's your best bet for raining fiery vengeance from the sky," Sath said.

"Aw, Sath, what a sweet thing to say. I see now what Ginny sees in you," Elysiam said, punching Sath playfully on the arm. He snarled back at her through a toothy grin, sending her into fits of laughter.

"Ginny?" Anni said, her brow furrowed. "What is a Ginny?"

"I am." Unnoticed by the others, Gin and Sath's pet had approached the group silently. With a wave of Sath's clawed hand, the magical tiger faded into nothingness. The wood elf now stood, her arms folded across her chest, staring at the back of Sath's head as though trying to bore a hole through it with her eyes. "And it's Ginolwenye, thank you. Who are you?"

Sath chuckled uncomfortably. "Gin, this is Anni. She is someone I grew up with and a…friend we have in common is in danger. She's come looking for my help…our help," he said, moving closer to Gin. She took an obvious step back from him and he sighed. "I think we should hear her out," he said, flopping to the ground. One by one, the others took seats near Sath and finally Anni joined them.

"Well?" Gin said, clearly sounding annoyed. Sath wasn't sure if it was because of the earlier joke with his pet or being left behind or…was she jealous? Ridiculous. He shrugged off that idea and nudged her with an elbow, grinning at her. She scooted closer to him and he couldn't help purring.

Anni watched the two of them suspiciously. *"So none of you here save Sathlir speak my language?"* she asked in Qatunari. Sath answered her with a warning growl. "Fine. Common language it is then. What I was telling Sathlir is that his…friend, *Kahzi*…err, Kazhmere is in grave danger. She and I joined a hunting party to explore Salynth's Tower and I fear that she was separated from the rest of us and is still there…" Anni swallowed the sob that threatened to send her into a blubbering mess in front of her Prince. "I fear that she is still there at the mercy of the tower's inhabitants…and I ask humbly for your help to rescue her."

"That's good enough for me! How do we get there?" Hack shouted as he hopped up to his tiny feet. Elysiam kicked him squarely in the back and he fell over, shouting awful things about her and her family in gnomish as he went. "What was that for?" he said, rubbing his head. "Don't you want to go kill things rather than just hang around here staring at each other and watching Ginny sleep?" Gin shot him a pointed glance and he bit his lip. "Sorry, Ginny."

"It's okay Hack, just don't call me that," she snapped back. He hung his head a moment, and then came over to sit next to her. Gin smiled down at him and patted his arm, and he beamed a smile back up at her.

"Amazing ability to charm a gnome you have," Anni said, looking pointedly at Gin who stared back at her. "Are you a wizard of some sort?"

"I'm a druid, Anni, not a wizard. And I don't charm, I simply…am," Gin said, struggling to find an answer for the strange question. "Your old friend Sath has been very helpful as I progress in my studies as a druid."

"Just Sath? What's a guy gotta do?" Tee said, grinning evilly at Gin.

"Stop trying to get me killed?" Gin said, her serious demeanor soon dissolving into giggles. All of them save Anni joined in, and she watched the five of them carefully. The Prince was still as handsome as she remembered him when they were all children in the royal nursery. That gnome and the other elf druid seemed quite friendly. She did not know what to make of the green dwarf other than he was quick with a blade but not with his tongue like the gnome. Then there was Ginolwenye, the one they called Ginny, much to her displeasure. Why was the Prince so concerned with one such as that? Anni studied the druid. There could not possibly be anything between them. Ridiculous.

"Sorry, Anni, please continue your tale," Tee said, wiping tears from his eyes. "We tend to get a bit off track from time to time, and sometimes it's nothing to do with the druids getting lost at all!" He fell backwards to the ground, rolling about and laughing as Gin and Elysiam rose from their seats to attack him with their tiny fists. "Sath! REEL in your woman!" he cried out in mock terror as the others continued laughing.

*"Your…woman?"* Anni asked in Qatunari. Immediately Sath ceased laughing and shot a look of warning at her. *"What does the dwarf mean, your Highness?"*

*"You and I will talk and then I will fill them in on what they need to know,"* Sath said to her in Qatunari. "Let me go talk to Anni so that she doesn't have to rely on her second language to tell us the details and then I will let you all know what she says. Yes?" He avoided Gin's gaze and stood, offering a hand to help Anni up off the ground. The female looked as though she would faint as she accepted his help, and Gin thought that she might have lingered a bit too long and a bit too close to Sath.

"I'll tell you what I think," Hack said, once Sath was out of earshot. "Not that anyone asked, mind you. But I think that female is nothing but trouble, as usual. No offense, Ginny and Elys."

Tee rubbed his beard as he watched Sath having an animated conversation with Anni. "For once I agree with you, wee man," he said to Hack. "Nothing good is going to come of this *"Anni"*. I can feel it in my bones."

"Have all of you lost your minds?" Elysiam erupted suddenly. "This is a quest. A challenge. A chance to FIGHT

THINGS. Isn't that what we do?" The other three stared at her. "Come on! If you think she's got the hots for tall, dark and furry there, Gin will put an end to that, won't you, sister?"

"Careful, Elys," Gin hissed.

"Bah." Elysiam brushed Gin's warning off with a dismissive wave of her hand. "You're good enough with a fire bolt. I'm not the only one's singed the Cat's fur." She pulled her blonde hair up into a ponytail and dug around in her bag for her helmet. "All I meant was that Sath knows who he belongs to and it isn't that other Cat there. ALL of us know who claims Sathlir Clawsharp." Gin smiled at Elysiam.

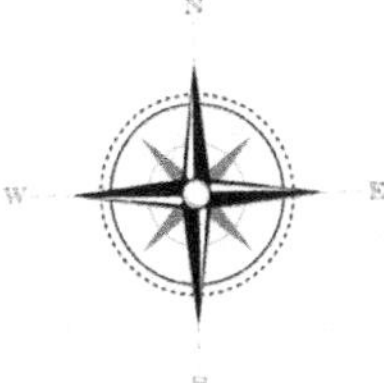

# TWENTY-SIX

*"You will not address me as your Highness or anything of that sort in front of them, do you understand me?"* Sath hissed at Anni once he was sure they were out of earshot. *"Some of them know some of our language and it won't take them long to start asking questions."* Anni fell to her knees as was the custom in Qatu'anari when in the presence of the royal family, but Sath yanked her up by one arm before her forehead could hit the ground at his feet. She glared at him. *"None of that either, no one bows before me like that. I am not my father. They only know me as Sath and I'd like to keep it that way."*

*"You mean the wood elf? Ginny?"* Anni said, spitting Gin's nickname as she said it. *"I know it is not my place to ask, your Highness..."*

*"SATH."*

*"Yes, sorry. Sath. What is the nature of your relationship with her? Is that why you no longer return home? Is that why your mother, our First Wife, cries out your name from her bedchamber and can barely look upon your sister, our Princess Kazhi?"* Anni knew she was pushing a boundary but she pressed on, genuinely confused about the prospect of a Qatu having…feelings…for a wood elf. She was also not convinced that they were so far away that the wood elf couldn't hear them. She had heard tales about the magic and preternatural abilities possessed by that race.

*"My relationship with anyone is none of your business, Annilanshi,"* Sath whispered, his voice low and dripping with warning. *"You know as well as anyone why I no longer make Qatu'anari my home. Now, tell me how we may save my sister. How did she end up in Salynth's Tower? That has been barren of life for years. Why would you hunt there?"*

*"You may not remember, Maj…Sath, but your sister is not one to let go of something once she's set her mind to it,"* Anni replied, smiling a little at the memories of Kazhmere dancing through her mind. *"She wanted to explore from the first day we set foot on that cursed icy land at the edge of the Highlands."*

*"Why is my sister not on Qatu'anari where she is safe?"* Sath demanded.

*"Again, you know your sister. She's been sneaking out since we were all in the nursery."* Sath rubbed his chin, grimacing. Anni was right, he did remember his sister being dragged back to the nursery by their father's *Qal'Dai,* the royal guard, having been caught out sneaking around in the wilderness alone. He could vividly remember his father bellowing at Kazhi for being too inquisitive and acting dangerously. His mother had told Sath repeatedly that their stubbornness had come from their father's side, but he knew that it was her stubbornness that had seen her become First Wife. He remembered with a pang the row she had

with his father when she learned that it was announced that Kahzi had been born dead since she was not a male and therefore could not ascend to the throne. He shook off the memories and focused his attention back on Anni. *"She convinced me to go with her to the Highlands, Sath, to hunt there rather than the lands our masters taught us were good for hunting for those of our inexperience."*

*"Masters? What guild has taken in my sister, if I may ask?"* Sath said as the fur on the back of his neck started to rise. One of his sister's extraordinary stubbornness and tendency to forgive but not forget would be, to a fighting guild, both a valuable and deadly asset.

*"Your sister follows in your majestic footsteps, Sath,"* Anni said, unable to hide the hero worship that dripped from her words onto Sath, making him immediately uncomfortable. *"She has taken up the path of the hunter."*

Sath shuddered under the weight of Anni's gaze. *"And you? You are progressing in the same path I assume?"*

*"No your…Sath,"* she said, smiling brightly. She had a lovely smile when it was genuine, Sath thought to himself sadly. *"I am learning the ways of the bard."* Bards were not unique to Qatu'anari, as every race had members who composed epic songs to serve as records of their histories. But Qatu bards were different. The magic that Orana had placed in them came out in the music that they composed, and could be used for anything from healing wounds to increasing movement speed to charming others to bend them to the bard's will. It was a tough path to walk, and Sath had to admit to a bit of appreciation for the Qatu female before him.

*"Ah, the magical speed, of course you are,"* Sath said, admiration heavy in his tone. *"Is that also how you were able to dispatch all of the guards at the southern checkpoint?"*

*"Aye."* Anni blushed to the roots of her fur. *"To be honest though, they were merely humans. No match."* Sath joined her in a hearty laugh, and then thought better of it. Gin would never approve of that, even in jest. *"Kahzi wanted to explore and I couldn't bear to see her go alone,"* she continued, her face sobering.

*"I can appreciate that, Annilanshi,"* Sath said. *"Did you have a target in the Tower?"*

"I *thought she was just exploring but I believe now that she had a target, sir,"* Anni said. *"She was driven to get to the very top floor because of stories of the fantastic treasures kept there by a sorcereress in ages past. I believe that was her target."*

Sath grimaced. He had heard the same stories when he left his home and began exploring the rest of Orana, and had attempted a few failed investigations of the tower on his own and with others. In fact, he and the Fabled Ones had been discussing a similar expedition but had not pursued the idea. *"I see. So you and my sister gathered a group together and set out to explore the Tower?"*

*"We should have, aye, but she wanted to go alone,"* Anni said, lowering her eyes against the onslaught of temper that she knew was brewing in Sath. *"I eventually talked her into letting me come along since I might be helpful with taming anything that we met inside the Tower. It was there that we joined a group already making their way inside."*

*"Come now, Anni. You didn't want to go just so that you could charm them to attack my sister and then flee with her loot?"* Sath asked, leaning in close and looking Anni in the eye. She gulped and he could smell the fear radiating off her so he averted his gaze.

*"No, Majesty…Sath, no! Of course not! Where would I be without Kahzi? Sent off to keep the rituals at the fires? Or worse, sent to the back alleys of Qatu'anari?"* Sath growled loudly at her and she shut her mouth quickly, her lips forming a line. *"Of course I*

*would not betray her, not ever."*

*"I'm glad to hear that, Annilanshi,"* Sath replied. *"I will expect that same level of loyalty from you and I further expect that you will extend it to everyone that travels and fights with me. Is that clear?"* Anni looked up at him, a mixture of relief and puzzlement on her face. *"Including the druids."*

*"Of course, your Highness,"* she replied.

*"Sath."*

*"Yes, Sath. Now, which of your companions can speak Qatunari?"* she asked.

*"Why?"*

*"Because I thought it might be helpful to teach all of them to speak it. It might help when we rescue Kahzi,"* she said.

*"I don't think there is a need,"* Sath replied. *"Tee is fluent, and Gin is…well, she's getting there,"* he said with a smile that turned Anni's stomach. He was in love with that wood elf! *"It's a hard language to learn, just like Elvish."*

*"You speak Elvish?"* Anni asked, forgetting her place, as her tone changed and filled with revulsion. *"Apologies, Sath, but why would you bother?"*

Sath felt a growl growing in the back of his throat but he swallowed it. He tried to remember how he felt about the world when he first left Qatu'anari. He remembered how alien the other races had seemed to him. He had seen a few elves meet with his father in the past, but for the most part, it was all new and scary, and he could remember vividly the distrust that came with that feeling. *"I bother because I am trying to rectify the mistakes our people have made by being cut off from the rest of Orana, our ancestral home,"* he said, glancing over at Gin sadly. *"Nothing more than that."*

Annie smiled at him. "You *are an amazing male, Sathlir,"* she said, a purr behind her words. Sath smiled back. *"And if you'll forgive me, the wood elf? Ginny? She doesn't know how you feel, does she?"*

Sath stared at her, but could not bring himself to be angry. *"No, she doesn't, "*he admitted. *"Keep your voice down."*

*"As you wish,"* Anni said, smiling. There was still a chance after all.

"What do you think they are talking about over there, Tee? Your Qatunari is better than mine," Gin said. The dwarf frowned.

"I can't tell," Tee said, looking at the ground as though concentrating. "We're too far away. Sath will be back soon and we'll be on our way to rescue that other Cat."

"I have wanted to get into that Tower for ages," Elysiam said, rubbing her hands. "We cut our teeth on the stories about the sorceress who lived there, remember, Gin? Everything inside is enchanted."

Gin frowned at her druid companion. "Everything inside the Tower is dangerous, that was the last part of that story or have you forgotten? The sorceress at the top of the tower can bend the will of others to her own!"

"Bah, that's just a story and besides, you and I both have magic that will keep us safe from some moldy old sorceress," Elysiam retorted.

"To be fair," Teeand said, stepping between the two elves, "it's not a sorceress exactly. Our lore calls her an *enchantress*, and that means all sorts of awful magic. Makes me a bit twitchy, does that business." He shook all over, as though ridding himself of something unseen to the rest. "So we'll not be goin' up there unless our Sath has a proper good reason for it."

"I just wish they were closer," Gin muttered. "Can you hear them well enough to understand what they're saying? I tried earlier but that female has a different accent from Sath's and I was not understanding much. She used words I've never heard before."

"No, I didn't," Tee lied. He had a lot on his mind, and wished that the druids would settle down and leave him to it. For once, the gnome was the quiet one! Tee looked down to find Hack meditating with his giant axe gripped in his tiny hands. Fusing his will with his weapon, of course that was why he was so quiet. "Oi there, wee man, knock that off, we're not in battle yet."

"Shush, Tee!" Hack responded, his voice a hiss. "I want to be ready in case I have to take that Anni off my list."

Tee looked back toward his old friend and the new Qatu female, still hissing and spitting at each other. He knew he had heard the word Rajah from them, and that the female had called Sath something that translated to Your Highness. *"What are you playing at, Sath?"* he muttered in his native tongue.

"Did you say something, Tee?" Gin asked, laying one oaken-tinged hand on his green clad armored arm. "Can you hear them?"

"Just wondering what's going on over there. Clearly that female is someone our Sath knows, but I don't trust her. Not one bit of her is truthful, not one bit," Tee said, his brow furrowed. He would have to be more careful. The wood elves had near preternatural hearing, and he knew that Gin was almost fluent in Teeand's own language now, thanks to his excellent tutelage. Thankfully, the language lessons happened before they took up again with Hack and Elysiam so he could still keep SOME things to himself.

*"You would tell me if something was going on between them, right?"* Gin asked him in the language of the dwarves, moving around to look him in the eye. *"I mean, it's none of my business, but…"*

*"But I'd be a fool to miss how you two feel about each other, Flower,"* he responded. *"Now let's keep this talk to a minimum, shall we, or the other two will want to know what's up?"* Teeand patted Gin on the shoulder and she smiled at him. They had spent too much time at odds and in truth, Gin was like a daughter to him. Teeand renewed his silent promise that no harm would come to her…even if it meant squaring off against his best friend and that Qatu female.

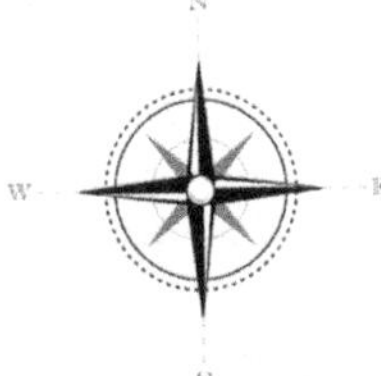

# Twenty-Seven

"Right, so what's the plan, Sath?" Hackort said, hopping up from his meditation with Elysiam hot on his heels. Teeand hadn't even noticed that Sath had returned, he'd been so lost in thought. Gin was standing behind Teeand, trying not to glare at Anni.

Sath looked around at the faces watching him expectantly. "This is not something that I ask of you lightly," he began, "and I will understand if you wish to stay behind. None of you know Kazhmere, the female that has gotten herself stuck in the Salynth's Tower, and I cannot ask you to risk your lives for someone important only to me." Gin's face fell but she quickly cast her eyes down, fiddling with an imaginary string on her tunic. Teeand reached back to her and squeezed her arm.

"You don't even have to ask," Hackort said, shouting a bit to make sure the extra tall Qatu could hear him. "That's what we do, Sath. A friend of yours is a friend of ours, and if she is in need of your help she will get OUR help." Noticing that no one was agreeing with him, Hack kicked Elysiam soundly in the boot. "Right?"

"Oh, you will SO pay for that, gnome!" she hissed. "Of course he's right, Sath. Name the time and you know we will be there to help your Kazhmere." She elbowed Teeand in the ribs, and he nodded his head vigorously. Gin alone remained silent.

"Gin?" Sath said, looking cautiously down at her, his teal eyes wide with worry.

"I go where you go," she said, her voice tight. "All of you, I go where all of you go." Sath smiled at her, but when she looked up at him, she noticed that the smile did not go all the way to his eyes. Gin returned her focus to her tunic.

"Right then!" Sath said, turning back to Anni who was beaming with relief and happiness. "We leave at first light. Tonight, or what's left of it, will be for planning and rest." He nodded to Anni. "You have provisions of your own, I presume?"

"Aye…Sath," she said, still smiling at him. Sath suppressed a shudder and led her back to the fire that was beginning to smolder.

"So what is the plan of attack?" Elysiam could hardly hide her enthusiasm. "How many were in your group?"

"There were fifteen of us including me and Kazhmere," Anni responded.

"Were?" Gin asked, fearing the answer.

"Aye," Anni said sadly. "While I am most sure that Kazhmere still lives, I watched the rest of the party die at the hands of the undead inhabitants of the tower." She shuddered violently and Sath instinctively put an arm around her, stilling Anni and infuriating Gin. "Thank you," Anni said as she gazed up at Sath. He shook his head and removed his arm, moving to sit on the other side of the fire from her.

"So we charge in, we kill anyone in our way, and we save Sath's friend Kazhmere, yea?" Teeand grumbled. "That sound like a good idea to anyone?" Before Hackort or Elysiam could answer, he held up one scarred and weathered hand. "Not you two. I'm asking anyone sensible."

"I think it's the only plan we've got, Tee," Sath said. "Besides, Gin's gotten loads of rest, she can keep us healed up and safe can't you, Gin?" He beamed a toothy grin at her and she merely stared back at him.

"Sure," she said, her voice pinched. "I'm sure that Lady Salynth will be no match for the six of us. She's only dragonkind, is all." She rolled her eyes.

"Ginny is right, Sath," Hackort said, stepping clear of the swat from Gin at the use of the nickname. "This will be easy. I'm taking her off my list right now."

Anni cleared her throat. "Have any of you been there before?" she asked carefully. All of them shook their heads save Sath and Teeand, who studied the ground. "Right, I was afraid of that. Let me tell you a bit about the tower. Do forgive my skill with the common tongue." She closed her eyes a moment, calling up gory memories of the recent failure in the icy Tower. "Something horrific happened there, and I'm willing to bet it was at the hands of Lady Salynth or her minions. Kazhmere had done some research with some of her contacts outside of Qatu'anari and had come up with a plan of attack that our new groupmates found to be a bit on the conservative side."

"Are all of you Qatu alike?" Elysiam exclaimed, chuckling. "That sounds just like Sath, taking the careful way in, when I'd just ride up and ROAST anything in my way."

"A druid after my own heart," Anni said, beaming a genuinely appreciative smile at Elysiam, who smiled back. "No, all of us are not so conservative but I understand Kazhmere's ways in battle. There is no Qatu I'd prefer to have at my side in a fight than her." Her eyes immediately flew to Sath's. "Apologies, I meant no disrespect, Sath."

"None taken, Anni, please continue," Sath said, his eyes clearly communicating a warning. Gin marveled at how they could communicate with each other via eye contact, and at how daft Sath must think she was if he thought she didn't see what was happening between the two Qatu before her.

"Right, so our group agreed to follow Kazhmere's lead and we met with no resistance on the ground level of the Tower. Some of the more skittish members of the group tried to jump ahead of us, but we found the door to the only upward-leading stairwell locked. Upon rummaging about in the belongings of the ghastly inhabitants," Anni said with a shudder, "we found a ring of keys in a drawer. We tried the keys and thankfully one of them opened the door."

"Where are those keys now, Annilanshi?" Tee asked, making sure to pronounce her name correctly. Her eyes widened a moment at him, but after a glance at Sath for support, she began digging through her haversack.

"I have them with me," she said, producing a heavy iron ring with six metal keys hanging from it. Each one engraved along the shaft with strange letters, one of them seemed to be glowing with a blue light. "I was the only one to escape, and used the keys to move back down through the floors of the tower. I think that the inhabitants no longer need the keys for they are all shades, they may pass through walls…and that it was locked as whomever caused their demise moved upward through the tower, to prevent anyone from coming to their aid."

"What was the makeup of the group you were with?" Hack asked after standing up to make sure Anni could see him. "I want to know if we need to recruit anyone with special skills. We seem to have almost two of everything now...well, two Qatu anyway."

"Too bad we don't know any wizards," Sath said. "That sort of fire power might come in handy." Gin's mind flitted briefly to Taeben, and then to that blank space in her memory that always followed her remembrance of his face. She frowned.

"Is there something wrong with mine and Elys's magic?" Gin asked, her tone acerbic.

"Of course not," Sath said, immediately wishing he could eat his words. "I just want to make sure you two can focus on healing magic if need be." Gin met his gaze and he knew he'd put his foot in it again. "Not that healing is all you're good for, mind you," he stammered. "Help me out, Tee?"

"Oh no, old friend, you're in this one up to your pointy ears," Teeand said, cracking a grin. "Tis much more fun to watch, I think. We'll be okay as long as we know what we're up against and," he pointed at Anni, "you listen to us and do as we say?

"Of course. I owe all of you a huge debt for helping my friend. I can certainly understand how Sath commands such loyalty and respect in his soldiers, though," Anni said. Elysiam blanched and Gin leapt to her feet. Teeand stared at her and Hackort started to laugh. "What?"

"Sath isn't our leader, Anni," Gin said. "We're all on equal terms here." Teeand shot a look at Sath that made the Qatu swallow hard. Teeand knew what he and Anni had been talking about, and it was going to be tough to keep him from making sure they all knew.

"Of course you are," Anni said quickly, not daring to look at Sath. "I'm sorry, that was a poor choice of words. My common tongue is clearly not as fluent as I thought." She held out a clawed hand to Gin. "I would really like to undo whatever I've done to wrong you, Gin," she said to Gin's clear surprise. "I feel we have gotten off on the wrong foot and I want to do whatever I can to make that up to you. I want you to be able to trust me."

Gin studied her a moment and then took Anni's large, furry hand in both of her tiny hands. "I want to be able to trust you," she said. "But I will defend my friends to my own death against you if you cause them harm. Understood?"

"Aye," Anni said, swallowing her revulsion at the love the wood elf clearly bore for the Prince. She looked at Sath who was grinning down at Gin like a fool. This did not bode well for a future Rajah. Not at all. "Now, my only other words of advice are that we need to stay together and hope for the best as far as Kazhmere's safety is concerned. Any questions?"

"None from me Flower," Teeand said, keeping his gaze firmly on Sath. "Sath? Anything else we should know about this Kazhmere?"

Sath squirmed under his old friend's gaze. "No, Tee, only that she is a young female like Anni and has only limited training to her credit. I don't imagine her pet has survived one floor of that cursed tower, and on her own without her companion she is defenseless." He swallowed hard before continuing. Despite his loathing for his father, Sath adored his younger sister. He regretted every moment that he had been unable to shower her with attention and training before he left Qatu'anari. "She…is very important to me, and I trust that's all you need to know."

Gin stood and busied herself in her haversack, pulling out her own bedroll and settling by the fire. "I assume we're returning to our watch rotation, then?" she called out over her shoulder.

"Aye, Gin," Sath said sadly. "Tis my turn still I believe? Anni, you will sit up with me and tell me more about your time with Kazhmere before you started out on this failed adventure?" Anni nodded but Teeand walked in between the two Qatu and sat down.

"I think I'll stay up as well," he said, glaring at Sath as he did. "I do love a good tale spun round a fire." Elysiam and Hack mumbled their agreement as they slipped into their bedrolls and drifted off to sleep filled with dreams of battle. Anni glared at Teeand but Sath just sighed loudly.

*"Out with it, Teeand,"* he said once he was sure that Gin's breathing had settled into the same rhythm of sleep as Hack's and Elysiam's.

*"What are you playing at, Sathlir?"* Tee hissed, careful to keep his voice low. *"You and this one here, you're not telling us everything and expecting us to just blindly follow you."* He opened his flask, ever at the ready around a fire, and took a deep swig of it. *"Out with it. I consider you my brother, Cat, but I'll not lead the rest of them to their deaths because you're too proud to tell us the truth."* He paused a moment, noticing that Anni was staring at him, slack-jawed. *"What's wrong with you, female?"*

*"Your Qatunari is very good, Teeand,"* she said, *"so good that I am amazed that our…Sathlir allows you to speak this way to him. Surely you know…"* Sath's staff swinging up from his side and nearly cracking into the side of her head cut off her words.

*"Bah, he doesn't **allow** anything,"* Teeand growled. *"I do as I please. Our Ginolwenye was right when she said none of us are better than any other,"* he said, leaning in close to glare at Sath, *"wasn't she Sath? On the other hand, should I call you Rajah? Your Highness,*

*perhaps?"*

Sath looked at Teeand sadly. *"I hope you never call me that, Teeand,"* he said. *"Annilanshi knows me from my former life, a life that I...happily left behind."* He looked earnestly at his old friend. *"I'm serious, Tee. I have left my royal family, title, and all of that behind me for good. I have no need for any of that pomp and circumstance nonsense. The only thing that worries me is...Kazhmere. Please trust me when I say that she is very important to me and that I can't tell you why."*

*"Oh aye, I trust you Sathlir. And I hope you'll trust me when I say that if at any time this fool's errand looks to cause harm to any of our rag-tag little family over there,"* Teeand replied, staring Sath right in the eye and gesturing in the direction of Gin, *"I'll take you out myself to save them. Do we understand each other?"*

*"Now, listen here, little man,"* Anni began but fell silent at a raised finger from Sath, who was looking at Teeand with a mixture of wonder and respect.

*"We understand each other Teeand. At least I hope we do."* Sath made a mental note to ask Teeand later why he was specifically pointing out Gin, and then stood. *"Off with you two, get some sleep. We have a lot of work ahead of us now, and none of it will be pleasant."*

Gin sat up alone, startled out of a dream filled with vengeful opponents back from the dead pursuing her and her companions. She took a few deep breaths to clear her head of the visions still hanging on to her subconscious mind, wrapping her arms around her torso and rubbing her elbows to warm them, and then pulling the bedroll back up around her. The sun was rising in the east, unfurling plumes of red, orange, and yellow into the sky and pushing the moon down below the horizon for another day. Soon it would be time to wake the others, and get going, but for the moment, Gin was enjoying the quiet.

"The Highlands are truly the best place to watch the sunrise," Sath said, making Gin jump. "I'm sorry; I didn't mean to frighten you."

"You didn't," Gin said as she continued to stare out across the now warming horizon. "The best place is from the checkpoint tower to the south, but this is beautiful." She turned around to look at Sath. "I need to ask you a question. You wouldn't lie to me, would you, Sath?"

The Qatu cocked his head to one side and studied her as his stomach flipped over with dread. "Why are you asking me that, Gin?"

"Answer me."

"Gin, you know me," he said, trying to ascertain the reason for the question before he answered it.

"Sath."

"No, no I wouldn't." Sath's heart sunk at the potential for untruth in that statement. "Tell me what's bothering you, Gin; I'll help if I can."

"Who is Kazhmere to you?"

Sath closed his eyes a moment and took a deep breath before answering her. "She is someone I grew up with," he said, thankful that so far he was not lying to her.

"Someone you loved?"

"Well, yes. I suppose I did, and still do," Sath said. An awful realization coupled with a tiny ray of hope crept in around the corners of his heart. "Gin, are you asking me if I'm involved with Kazhmere?" Just the thought repulsed him but saying it aloud nearly brought bile into the back of his throat.

"Are you?"

"**No.**" Sath nearly sank to the ground with relief, followed by the thought that she was asking him because she was interested in him. "The absolute truth, Gin, is that I am not in a relationship with Kazhmere, not a romantic one anyway."

"I see," Gin said, her countenance still stern though her heart sang. "So what's the plan then? We charge in and demand Kazhmere's release?" She grinned in spite of herself. "I'm sure you and Tee and Hack will find new and exciting ways to test my healing abilities."

"If it was up to me, Gin," Sath said, leaning over to whisper to her, "I would take Anni and Tee and leave now so that the rest of you are safe." He fought the urge to touch the scar on the side of her face. Gin giggled but her laughter soon faded as she realized that the look on his face was serious.

"I can't believe you're even thinking such a thing," she said, scowling. "It's not going to happen." Before he could stop her, she hopped up out of her bedroll and pounced on Hackort and Elysiam. "Get up! Sath's thinking of going without us!" she called out as Sath scrambled after her to silence her.

"What?" Hackort rolled over and rubbed his eyes with his tiny fists. "What's wrong, Ginny?" Elysiam had come up out of her bedroll just as before, scimitar in hand and swinging madly. "Really, Elys? Do you ever really sleep?" he muttered as she missed stepping on him by a narrow margin.

"What does Gin mean, Sath?" Elysiam growled, pointing her blade in the direction Sath had just vacated as he grabbed onto Gin, holding her fast with his hand around her mouth as she struggled. "What are you doing? Did that other cat charm you?"

"I did no such thing," Anni said as she slowly pushed herself up on her elbows. She was half in and half out of her bedroll. "What's going on?"

"Gin thought that YEEEOUCH!" Sath dropped Gin as if she was a hot stone when she sank her teeth into one of the fingers he had held to her mouth. He roared in frustration at her and his pet appeared at his side, looking befuddled at his master's current choice of targets for his ire. "Oh, take off, you silly cat," Sath barked, waving his magical companion away.

"What you said is that you'd rather just wake Tee and Anni and go to Salynth's Tower without us. What else was I supposed to think, especially after you'd just said you would never lie to me," Gin said, her tone accusatory and biting. Sath winced at her words.

"Because I don't want the other three of you in danger," he tried to explain but Elysiam wagging her blade close to his face cut him off.

"What makes Tee so special? It can't be his training because Hack is just as steady a warrior as the wee green man there," she said.

"Aww, thanks Elys," Hack said, blushing a bit as he pulled on his helmet.

"I also can't imagine why you would want to go into a place like that without me and Gin and our FIRE MAGIC, Sath. That's just suicide. I mean, how important can this Kazhmere be to you for you to…" Elysiam's mouth slammed shut. She looked back and forth from Gin to Sath. "Oh."

"We're all up now, let's just head on out and stick to the

original plan, yeah?" Teeand said from behind Sath. "No one is leaving anyone anywhere, least of all Sath's Kazhmere." The dwarf raised his hands as protests came from all sides. "Enough! My wee children back in the Mountain follow direction better than you lot!" He bent over and started rolling up his bedding to stuff in his haversack, and the rest of them, one by one, did the same. Finally, they were all packed and standing around the cold remains of their fire, all doing their very best to avoid eye contact with each other.

Gin whistled for Beau, her magic pony, who appeared next to her and whinnied as she swung up into his saddle. Elysiam was next into the saddle of her own horse, pulling Hack up into its saddle behind her. Sath's horse appeared third, a huge warhorse that suited his size, leaving only Teeand and Anni standing and watching. "Come on, wee man," Sath said, holding out a hand low to the dwarf.

"No," Gin said, her voice even and steady. She rode over to Teeand and put a hand down which he used to swing up behind her. "There's no way that Anni would fit on my horse. She needs to ride with you, Sath." Tee wrapped his arms around Gin and gave her a squeeze and she smiled.

*"You know I've got yer back, our Gin?"* he whispered to her in Dwarvish.

*"Aye, Petal, I do,"* she whispered back, her accent in Dwarvish making Tee laugh heartily. *"And I yours."* She raised her eyes to meet Sath's and frowned at the sadness she saw there. "Shall we go, Sath? Daylight's wasting and so is your Kazhmere." Urging Beau forward, she took the lead as they rode, up into the snowy Highlands and closer to freeing Kazhmere and defeating Lady Salynth.

Gin's pony whinnied loudly in protest each time his feet hit the increasingly icy ground. Gin stroked his neck and whispered to him, but his nostrils still flared with unease and suspicion. "We can just make our way on foot," Teeand suggested, "if our Beau isn't sure he wants to be here." Gin frowned, and then nodded her head.

"I'm sure the other horses don't like this weather either," she said, turning to Elysiam as she and her mount materialized by Gin's side. "Hang on, Tee," she said, whispering release to her magical steed who disappeared, leaving Gin and Teeand in a heap on the ground. Elysiam grinned at them as she too released her horse, but not before she pitched Hackort off into a snowdrift.

"Seriously, Elys, you're coming off my list. Right now," he said, sputtering and spitting snow everywhere. The others tried not to laugh out of respect for Hack, but failed. The laughter ceased, however, as Sath and Anni caught up to them on the back of Sath's huge red and white warhorse. The giant animal sniffed the air with its massive, blunt-nosed head, and snorted. Sath looked at the rest of them, all on foot with no mounts in sight, and quickly dispatched his own horse. He helped Anni back up out of the snow and then turned to face his compatriots.

"Tower is off to the west from here," he said. "I suggest we get going." Anni remained silent as she fell in step behind Sath, followed by Hackort and Elysiam. Gin stood still a moment, taking a deep breath, and then moved to follow Elysiam. Teeand stopped her by placing an armored hand on her arm.

"I meant what I said, lass," he said quietly. "I've got your back. Always." Gin turned quickly, threw her arms around Teeand's neck, and then released him, and ran to catch up with the others. Teeand plodded along behind, keeping an eye out as was his role in the group. "Always, Flower," he muttered.

The Tower cut an imposing figure on the bleak landscape of the finger islands where the Highlands met the Dark Sea. A tall, cylindrical building, it was surrounded on all sides by what resembled giant dragon talons rising up out of the snow. A snaky looking bit of frozen tundra wound its way around the outside of the Tower, but it seemed to lead nowhere. Almost out of sight was a small window on the western side of the Tower.

The imposing façade of the Tower was enough to turn back even the most fearless adventurer, but to further put off those who would enter and explore, the entrance was enchanted and moved about the base of the tower, back and forth between decoy "doors" that lead nowhere and deposited unwary travelers back out in the snow. When Lady Salynth first inhabited the Tower, it was said those nearby could hear her maniacal laughing echo across the tundra as explorer after explorer was unceremoniously dumped into the frozen landscape.

Lady Salynth was not a dragon per se, but was of dragon blood, an unhappy accident that occurred when the dragons burst forth from Orana so long ago. She was descended from humans that were unfortunately exploring the volcanic mountains in search of new land to colonize, and were caught in the flurry of magic, lava, and dragons that spewed forth onto the land from deep within Orana's core. Some were killed by the lava and rock but others were caught in the tide of unfettered magic that poured out of the chasm and then separated the edge of the Highlands that became the Qatu Islands and created their inhabitants, the Qatu. Those caught in the magical flow were transformed into hybrid creatures, both humanoid and dragon, called dragonkind and gifted with magic and the ability to fly on huge, leathery wings. Such a creature was Lady Salynth.

The group approached the Tower on foot; all moving slowly and carefully. "It's…tall," Gin murmured, staring up at the horrific edifice. "Are we sure this is a good idea?"

Elysiam laughed heartily. "Well of COURSE it isn't. When have we ever done anything that's a good idea?" She clapped Gin on the shoulder and Gin smiled at her fellow druid. "Now then, how do we know which door is the entrance? Anni?"

The Qatu female furrowed her brow. "They are enchanted and only one of them is the actual entrance. We just have to try them. The problem is that they spit you out onto the other side of the tower so it's hard to know which one you've tried."

Hackort ran up to them, having made a circuit of the perimeter while no one was looking. "There are six of them all together!" he exclaimed. "That means we all go to each one and if it spits you back out, you stay where you've been…spit." Elysiam made a face at him and he stuck his tongue out at her. "Then we know not to try that one again. We just move clockwise around the tower until we're all standing at a door."

"That is an excellent plan, tiny warrior," Anni said, "as I was thinking back on our first attempt to enter the Tower. My group had no invisibility spells available and just plunged into one doorway after another. It took us the better part of the first day just to find the true door." Hackort ran past the group before anyone could stop him and plunged headlong through the door.

"Aaaaaa that's not it!" he cried out from somewhere on the other side of the tower. The group moved clockwise around the tower and stopped in front of a door just before Elysiam threw herself through it. They soon heard a thud just to the left of them followed by a string of curses in common tongue and Elvish.

"Guess that wasn't it either," Sath said with a chuckle. Gin giggled in spite of herself. "I'll go next," the Qatu male said. The group moved to the left and stopped at the next door and Sath hurtled himself through it…landing with a crunch opposite the group on the other side of the Tower.

"Hey, Sath, you okay?" they heard Hackort ask.

"Yep, right as rain," Sath said, wincing. Gin heard the pained tightness in his voice and knew that he was not, but also that she could not go heal him. "Try another door," he called out.

The group moved to the left again and this time Gin volunteered to go. Her thinking was that if she came out on the other side of the Tower at least she could heal the others there. She jumped into the open doorway and gasped with surprise when her feet made contact with a stone floor. She could not feel the icy wind swirling under her cloak and howling in her ears any longer. Rising slowly, she turned around to look behind her and motion for the others to join her, but there was no door there, only a solid wall. She turned back around to look into the first floor of the Tower and stifled a gasp. She seemed to be in a foyer of sorts that led to a larger room but offered her a bit of cover from whatever might be waiting in that room.

She carefully scanned the entryway where she had landed but saw no one, friend or foe, so she turned back the way she had come. With anxious fingers, she inspected the wall that had only just moments before been a doorway, but she could find no crack or secret door or lever to make the wall open. Was she in the Tower after all? She had heard of rifts in their world where one could go to a completely different plane of existence and knew that to be how her own transportation magic worked. However, this was different. This was like a prison.

"Help?" she said softly. There was no response, neither from outside or inside, so she beat on the wall frantically. "HELP!" she screamed. Her hands ached from hitting the wall but she continued, hoping against hope that someone on the outside would hear her and know that she was inside.

"GIN!" bellowed Sath. "Answer me!" He stayed at his door where he'd been thrown back out of the Tower, but ran back and forth by the entrance, his keen hearing alert for anything that might tell him where she was. Nothing came. He could hear the other members of the party calling out for her, then some arguing, and then suddenly Anni was flying out at him through the mystic doorway. Sath had no time to move and Anni crashed into him, knocking both of them backwards into the snow.

Anni rolled onto her back and then pushed herself up on her elbows, only to run into Sath's rage-etched face. "Where…is…Gin?" he asked, clearly trying to contain his fury.

"She got in, Sath. I came over here to get you and the gnome. We know which door it is," Anni said, deciding to meet his gaze rather than shy away from it. She no longer feared him as a loyal Qatu should fear her Prince. Something was wrong with him, some enchantment or illness had befallen him, most likely at the tiny hands of that wood elf. When Gin had not come out the other side, Anni had been sorely tempted to run away from the tower and leave her there to the mercy of the inhabitants but she knew that was NOT the way to win over Sath and make sure that her oldest friend, his sister, was safe. *"If I may be permitted to return to my feet, Majesty?"* she said in whispered tones, speaking Qatunari so that the gnome would not understand.

Sath growled low in his throat as he pushed himself up and off Anni and then held out a clawed hand to help her up. She took it, relishing the feeling of his hand in hers, and then shook her fur clean of the swirling snow. *"Which door, Annilanshi?"* Sath growled. Anni understood the warning in his tone and headed back around to the other side of the Tower with Sath and Hackort hot on her tail.

Teeand was holding Elysiam by her arm, his boots dug

into the icy ground, when the other three appeared around the side of the Tower. "You'll wait for the others is what you'll do, lass!" he shouted at her as she struggled to free her trapped arm.

"Gin may need help!" the druid argued, her face red with frustration. "Also, you are leaving bruises on my arm with that armored glove Tee!" At that, Teeand released her and she jumped forward into the correct doorway.

"So much for having a plan first," Hackort muttered as he ran at the door and passed through as though it was made of water. The others followed in a clump of bodies and arms and weapons, and landed on the stone floor inside in much the same fashion.

"That was one of the best entrances I think I have ever seen," Gin said, laughing. She was standing in the entryway, watching the rest of them untangle and get to their feet. "Now, would you like to know what I've found out while you were all trying to use the door at the same time?" Gin stood, hands on her hips, with her lips pursed together in a thin line, waiting for an answer. Sath stood first, pulling Anni to her feet. Finally, they had all gotten off Teeand, who somehow was under the pileup. "Well?" she said, clearly a bit annoyed.

"Keep your hair on, Flower," Teeand grunted as he got to his feet and brushed himself off. "Now then, what's our plan?"

Gin made a face at Teeand that made him chuckle. "There are shades everywhere in here...Elys?" she asked, frowning when she noticed the bloodthirsty grin that split her sister druid's face. "Oh dear."

"Nothing wrong with sending a few of the undead on their way, now is there?" Elysiam asked, licking her lips as she wrapped her hands around the hilt of her scimitar. "We're doing them a service, Gin! Dispatching them to where Sephine intended and all that…"

"Elysiam!" Gin said a quiet prayer under her breath to the All-Mother, asking forgiveness for her daughter Elysiam's bloodlust. "Why can't we just make our way through until we find Kazhmere?" She frowned at Elysiam's evil grin.

"Even better, bring it. I'm ready," Elysiam said, gripping her scimitar tightly. Hack looked up at her and smiled.

"That's why I…we love you, Elys," he said. Elysiam looked down at him but he recognized the look in her eyes. The only thing that would get her attention now was a good fight. Hackort thought back to meeting Elysiam and the many long nights they had in the cells in the dungeons, plotting their escape from the dark elves that held them prisoner. She was there already when he arrived, and he found it tough to reconcile the Elysiam that was before him now with the wide-eyed, nearly feral wood elf druid he had met in the dingy, dripping dungeons. Even then, though, he had seen flickers of the warrior she had become.

She had surpassed her training with a fierceness that had almost been her undoing among her kin in Aynamaede. Only Gin had taken her as she was, and dared to journey out to explore Orana alongside Elysiam, in spite of what it meant for her reputation in the tree city that was their home. Gin probably did not have much to go home to now that she was a known associate of both Elysiam and Sathlir, the Bane of the Forest. Hackort's mouth pressed into a thin line as he fused his will with his axe in readiness to protect Elysiam…and the rest of the group.

Sath swiftly moved between Elysiam and her view of the first floor. "Listen, we are not going to get anywhere toward rescuing *Kahzi* without tipping off our Lady that we're here," he said.

"Who?" asked Gin, puzzled and trying to block out Sath's use of a Qatunari nickname for their target. She was certain there was more going on between them than he had told her, and was keeping up every hope that he had not broken his promise not to lie to her.

"Lady Salynth," Sath said, whispering the name, wishing he had not used Kazhmere's nickname.

"She's a right nasty one, a dragonkind who holds the lot of them undead here in her thrall." Teeand said, and then shuddered at the thought.

"Oh, right, the sorceress," Gin said, grimacing. "Are we still sure this is a good idea?" She looked up at Sath. "How do we know your Kazhmere is even still alive?"

"I would know if she wasn't," Sath barked at Gin, immediately wishing he had not. The sting of his words was evident in the look on her face. "Sorry. So, plan is we move up to the top floor slowly, yes?" All of them nodded at him. "Right then, everyone stand back, and I will…"

"Oh keep your stand back," Elysiam hissed, no longer able to wait before she struck. "That's my line!" The druid barreled past Sath, almost knocking him to the ground in surprise. "Well, hello, tall dark and smelly!" she called out to a shape in a shadow. "You look a lot like the wyverns back in Bellesea Keep…but I think they actually smell better." The wyvern gazed down at her, its dark eyes flickering with what appeared to be amusement. That sentiment soon faded as flames exploded from Elysiam's fingers and set its nearly translucent wings alight. The creature roared and swung at Elysiam who quickly and deftly dodged its blow. "Hey that was…whoa!" The icy floors were the druid's downfall, quite literally. She lost her footing and slid on her backside right up to the feet of the monster, whose mouth watered as it gazed down at her. "I can still roast you!" she screamed, as the beast tried to get a grip on her to pick her up. "You just set me on my feet and I will ROAST you!"

"No you won't!" Hackort shouted. He had dashed in behind her and jumped over her head so that he was between her and the monster…only now he was sliding toward its feet as well. "Curse this icy floor! Elysiam, why don't you do something USEFUL and roast the floor to melt this ice?"

From the doorway where she still stood, Gin summoned up healing magic and hurled it in Elysiam's direction. Spell after spell landed on the druid and the warrior, and finally Gin felt that they were out of mortal danger long enough to summon up another spell that would levitate them above the floor on cushions of air. Elysiam laughed as her feet left the floor and she floated right toward the monster's nose.

"That's the stuff, Gin!" she called out, aiming her scimitar for the monster's head. Before she could execute the blow, however, the monster swatted her away like an insect, focusing its attention on the tiny warrior now floating at the level of its kneecaps. Hackort rained blows down on the monster's legs as Teeand rushed up to and behind the monster and began his own assault only slightly higher than Hack's. Sath hung back from the fray near Gin who was pumping healing magic toward the two warriors and the other druid who had floated up to the level of the monster's head and was unleashing swarms of magical insects toward its eyes and ears. The monster howled and swatted at the phantom bees as Hackort and Teeand made quick work of him from below. Soon the three of them, plus some well-placed spells from Sath, killed the wyvern and it crumpled to the floor in a heap.

"Right!" Elysiam shouted, wiping some of the black blood spatter from the beast off her right cheek and tunic. "Next!" Sath swooped in and grabbed Elysiam, pulling her to his chest and holding her tightly.

"Easy, druid!" he said, chuckling, but his smile did not spread all the way to his eyes. "We will never get anywhere if we have to stop each one of these in that kind of fight. Only Anni, Teeand, and I have any idea of the hordes of undead that are just waiting on the upper floors for a chance to take us down. And all of them won't hesitate to run to their mistress and let her know we are here, if they haven't already."

"Right, so LET ME GO so we can get started!" Elysiam begged as she struggled against Sath's strength.

"Normally I would agree with you, Elys," Hackort said as he floated over to her, grinning, as he looked her in the eye for a change, "but not this time. We need to sneak by some of them so that we will be ready for the bigger ones upstairs." Elysiam slumped in Sath's arms, defeated.

"Fine. Not that I saw anyone but Hackort and Teeand in there helping me this time, though," she muttered. Gin inhaled sharply, glaring at Elysiam. "Well, of course, you too, Gin," she said, frowning. "I'd be dead a thousand times over if you weren't around." She beamed a smile at her sister druid, who returned it with a scowl. "I was thinking, though, that the two felines were awfully quiet over there?"

"I was helping," Sath snapped. "Your bees weren't the only insects that beast was fighting off." Anni looked at the floor. "You can't hold Anni responsible either; she's only just a young bard." At Sath's comment Anni raised her eyes to meet his, hers burning with indignant anger.

*"Young bard indeed…be glad you're on my side, Highness,"* she hissed. Sath frowned, and then released Elysiam.

"We need to keep moving," he said, ignoring Anni's outburst. "Gin? If you and Elys don't mind, another bit of cloaking magic would be good right about now." Gin bit her lip and made eye contact with Elysiam, and then both began the chant at the same time to ward off the undead. Soon the entire group was ready to go and even floated in front of a few skeletons to make sure that they wouldn't be seen.

"Great, we're invisible, now what do we do?" Elysiam snapped. "Has anyone but me noted the serious lack of staircases or anything?" She looked around, clearly annoyed. "Nothing here," she said, dashing around a corner, the group hot on her heels, "but another stupid door that is locked, I think. Wait..." She dashed at the door before Sath or Tee could stop her and bounced off it, landing in a heap on the floor. They quickly took their places at the entrance to the small corridor while Gin and Hackort rushed to Elysiam's side. Gin held her tiny hands over her sister druid, whispering words of healing that cancelled out her invisibility magic. She could only focus her energy on one type of magic at a time, it seemed.

"Hurry, Gin, there are a few skeletons about to poke their bony noses down here that will see you," Sath said.

"I'm working on it, Sath, but she's still out and I'm a bit worn out from the invisibility spell," Gin hissed back.

"Perhaps I can be of help," Anni whispered. She pulled out a small lute from her rucksack and started playing a soft tune. As much as she hated to admit it, Gin felt better and better as the song went on. Anni changed the tune and suddenly she was working in another line of beautiful harmony. Gin felt the music was surrounding her, strengthening her and her magic as she worked on Elysiam. She felt safe, warm, and almost sleepy as she worked, and even found herself smiling up at Anni in thanks. Her gaze landed on Sath, who was watching her over his shoulder as Teeand kept an eye on the skeletons. He shot a toothy grin her way, and Gin smiled back, causing his breath to catch in his throat.

The music ended suddenly and Gin looked up at Anni, surprised. The bard was glaring at her. "What happened?" Gin asked, getting to her feet and then helping Elysiam join her.

"That was for you, Gin," Anni hissed. "That song was meant to replenish your spirit and allow you to help Elysiam there to heal, nothing more."

"Isn't that what happened?" Gin said, confused. "I don't understand why you're so upset, Anni?" She rested a hand on Anni's arm, but the Qatu female yanked her arm free of Gin's grasp.

*"That was not to help you to try to charm our Sathlir,"* Anni said under her breath in Qatunari. Gin stared at her, trying to make the words make sense as Anni stalked away, stowing her lute in her haversack.

*"What about our Sathlir?"* Gin called after her in halting Qatunari. Sath's gaze flew to hers and then to Anni, his eyes narrowing. Anni ignored Gin, and kept hunting around in her bag for something. She did not see Sath approaching until he was nearly on top of her.

*"What was that about, Annilanshi?"* he whispered, his tone menacing and almost…royal. Anni's heart dropped into her stomach. *"Answer me."*

*"It was nothing your…Sath. I merely misunderstood the druid's intent was all,"* she said, fighting the urge to fall to the floor.

*"It needs to STOP, do you understand me?"* Sath said, his teal

gaze burning into Anni's eyes.

*"Yes."* Anni finally found the strength to look away. It was no wonder his mother, the First Wife Savra, had left all that she knew when she had become pregnant with Sath. Anni could only imagine how the Rajah was when he was angry if Sath's behavior was any indication. Yet Anni could not seem to tear herself away from him. There was something between them, she just knew it, and he had to see that she was a more suitable mate than that wood elf. Imagine! A wood elf, First Wife to the Rajah of Qatu? Anni shuddered in spite of herself, catching Sath's attention.

The son of the Rajah shook off his princely demeanor and frowned. *"Anni, I'm sorry,"* he said, placing a finger under her chin and lifting her face until she again looked him in the eye. *"I don't mean to…I mean, I'm afraid that I…The last thing I want to do is be anything like my father. Just now, in your eyes, I saw the same fear that I saw from many citizens back home when they faced him, and I do not ever want to see that from you. Can we make a deal?"* he said, his eyes soft. Anni felt faint.

*"Of course we can, Sath,"* she said, musing for a moment that this was the first time she did not have to work to remember to call him Sath rather than Your Highness or even Sathlir. *"Whatever you ask."*

*"**No**."* Sath pulled his hand back from her face, disgust creeping into his expression. *"That is not what I want. I want a friend, Anni. I have not seen another of our kind in ages, not since I left Qatu'anari, and I need that. You're the closest thing I have right now to a sister, and I don't want you to ever feel afraid of me."*

Anni's face fell. A sister? *"Sath, I only meant that I will try to remember that at least for now, for here, you and I are on equal footing. Is that what you meant?"* she asked, fearing the answer.

Sath's face split into a grin and a purr could be heard behind his words.

*"That is exactly what I meant,"* he said, still grinning. Anni thought her heart would burst through her chest at the sight. *"But part of the deal is that you…you need to leave the situation between me and Gin alone. It is complicated. She has more reason to hate me than to even like me, let alone love me. Somehow, when she looks up at me with those wide blue eyes and forgives me all my sins, all my time hunting and killing her kind…something in me wakes up. Does that make sense?"*

Anni swallowed a wave of nausea. *"Of course it does, Sath. I have felt that way for others in the past. For now, though, we need to keep moving up through the tower. My team got to the fourth floor before everything went wrong so I can get us through this door at least. Let's keep moving."* She pushed past him, wiping angry tears from her eyes as she approached the magical doorway. A plan was coalescing in her mind; she only had to separate the wood elf from the others and then move as quickly as she could to the top. How could Lady Salynth resist a trade like that?

Anni approached the door as she had done with her first team. Her heart constricted as she could imagine Kazhmere next to her, leaning in close, excitement written all over her face. "Now," she said, "Everyone get close and grab onto each other and me. When I pass through the doorway, the magic will permit you to follow me. If you are left I cannot come back for you." A strange look passed between Teeand and Sath, but Anni ignored it and placed a hand on the door as she slid the key into the lock. As she had expected, her hand disappeared through the no-longer solid door as the enchantment took hold. "Quickly! Grab hold of me and each other!" she cried out as she moved through the doorway, the other five hanging onto her for dear life.

Again, there was a pile up on the floor on the other side of the doorway, and this time they found themselves in what appeared to be a library. Shelves of books seemed to go back into the huge room as far as they could see, and shades of people reading books and checking the shelves floated here and there. A male shade, dragonkind in size and body but Elvish features, sat at a table to one side of the room, and seemed to be pouring over a book himself.

"You see, this is what breaks the old heart," Teeand said. "There is no escape for these poor souls. They are still doing exactly what they were doing when they met their end, and will continue to do so for eternity."

"I thought you meant it was sad that they had to read," Hackort whispered. "I don't like reading as much as I like killing, so having to spend eternity doing it wouldn't just be sad, it would be awful. That's why the only thing I read is my list." Elysiam elbowed him in the ear. "What? It would be," he said, stomping on her foot in mock frustration. Elysiam grimaced, but did not cry out.

"What's the plan for this floor," Gin asked, holding up a finger as Anni started to answer her, "Sath?" Anni glared at her but quickly looked away. "You've explored here before, haven't you?"

"Aye, we both have, haven't we Tee?" Sath said, grinning as he clapped Teeand on the shoulder. Tee was gripping his axe anxiously. "You'll have to forgive my old friend, Anni, he doesn't really care much for magic and this place is loaded with it."

"I can't believe I'm about to say this, Sath, but perhaps we should try to sneak through this one," Elysiam whispered. Five sets of eyes trained on her in disbelief. "I know! I should feel the overwhelming NEED to dispatch them, but all I feel is…sorry for them." Hack looked up at her and grinned and she pinched him.

"I agree with our battle druid," Teeand said, smiling affectionately at Elysiam as he would at one of his many children. Unwittingly, Teeand had taken on the role of father to the band of adventurers, and he had never been more proud of Elysiam than he was just then. "You're learning compassion, little hot-head," he said, pinching her cheek. His hand fell away as her scimitar came up under his chin.

"You attached to that beard, wee man?" she said, barely able to contain a giggle.

"Honestly, do you lot ever just do anything or do you stand around and crack jokes all night?" Anni said, exhaling a loud and exasperated sounding sigh as she spoke. "If we're going to sneak through, we'd best re-cast that invisibility spell. I fear that passing through the magical doorways can cancel magical enchantments." Her mind flew back to her team's entrance to a higher floor, her ears filling with the screams of her companions as Salynth's minions advanced on them and killed them one by one. She was still not sure how she escaped, but felt sure it had something to do with the ragged looking Elvish male that the dragonkind sorceress pulled along by a chain. He had been mouthing something as the ranks of undead advanced; a spell perhaps, as his eyes bored into her. The next thing she knew, she was in the snow at the bottom of the Tower. She shook off that memory quickly. It was probably just another in her legions of undead minions.

"Shall we move on then?" Gin said sharply, and the others nodded as Anni led the way to the next doorway, past the lost souls that were still engrossed in transparent books.

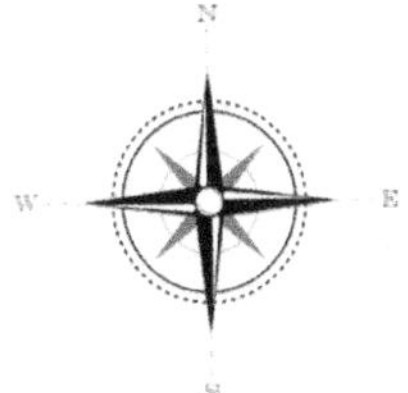

# TWENTY-EIGHT

Lady Salynth had been in the Tower for so long that she could not remember being anywhere else. Nor could anyone else that was unlucky enough to find the right door and make it all the way up to the top where she resided. It had not always been that way, however. When the dragons emerged from Orana's core and their magic created the dragonkind like Salynth from those too close to be able to escape, those new beings that survived the transformation were taken as slaves of the dragons who thought themselves to be the true children of Orana herself. For centuries, the dragonkind served their beastly masters until, in the midst of the Forest War, there were enough of them to revolt and break free of their enslavement. The dragons, who considered war and battles to be utterly pedestrian anyway, had already set their sights on the ruin of the rest of the races of Orana and seemed to forget about most of the dragonkind who attacked them. Lady Salynth was not so lucky.

The dragon master that owned her ancestors was the sole frost dragon. He had left the birth land in the Volcanic Mountains and moved southward to the Highlands to find his own empire. In time, he was the only dragon that could command ice and snow, and it was said that he had built the tower by merely breathing its icy walls into existence. Salynth had caught his eye, as happened often between the dragon masters and their dragonkind slaves, and in order to keep her for himself had locked her away in the tower. While she had killed all of the inhabitants that made the tower their home as well as any unlucky adventurers and trapped their souls there, she was just as trapped there as they were. Her dragon master, Lord Kalinth, had woven a spell around her that would instantly end her if she ever set foot outside the tower again. It was no wonder that she took out her frustration on the denizens of her personal prison.

Her latest pet came in the form of a wizard who unfortunately thought that he could take her on all by himself. He had come in with a hunting party but soon struck out on his own, hiding as the rest of his companions died. Once he saw her in action, however, he tried to make a deal with her similar to the one he had made with a previous dragon foe, but he had soon found Salynth to be a different sort all together from Taanyth, and not because Taanyth was full-blooded dragon and Salynth was only dragonkind. Salynth, made bitter and cruel in her imprisonment in the tower, showed the wizard that he had only scratched the surface of her sadism and had yet to find the key to coming to an agreement with her of any kind. He had sought her as a teacher but she only wanted a slave.

"Now, what have we learned, Pet?" Salynth said with a cackle. Taeben sat on the floor in a heap, a spell book open on the floor in front of him. She had the heavy chain that attached to the metal collar around his neck twined into her fingers, and she held it as though it was weightless. Now and then, she gave the chain a yank, nearly pulling Taeben over onto his face. He exhaled sharply, his eyes narrowed in anger.

"That you are a heartless…" Taeben cried out as he doubled over in pain. Mysterious symbols floated on the edge of his vision, red and angry, as they seemed to sear into his mind.

"A heartless what? Oh, I think we both already knew that," Salynth said, clucking her tongue. "Now then, you've had a taste of my power, so I will ask you again…what have you learned?"

"Mesmerizing an opponent is the first step to charming," Taeben replied, quoting the spell book. "First you must confuse your victim, then enchant. Then, in my case, burn," he finished, a small smile dancing across his face as it followed the image of Salynth alight through his mind's eye. She clapped her hands and laughed with glee.

"Yes! Oh, I can't wait to see that in action," she said.

"Me either," Taeben muttered. "Will I have a chance to practice, Mistress?"

Salynth drummed her spindly translucent fingers on her chin. "I think so, yes," she said, her face splitting into a terrifying grin. "I think I know just the subject: That cat in your room, Kazhmere. She will make a wonderful minion for you."

Something deep inside of Taeben stirred, then fell silent. Was that…pity? He suddenly found that he could not rid himself of images of Kazhmere's face, the happy smile that spread warmly into his bones as she healed the scars on his wrists, and those inquisitive eyes that drank in his every word as he told her about his time in Bellesea Keep.

She was just a young one... The window to the part of his

soul that housed pity slammed shut. She was a young one and therefore would be an easy mark for practice. "Agreed, Mistress," he said, and in that moment made a silent vow that he would never be in such a subservient role again. Kazhmere would see to that. Taeben beamed a complacent smile up at Salynth, who in turn giggled with glee.

"I do love a good cat fight," she said, her voice trembling with maniacal pleasure. "Let's go see what you can do, my Pet." She yanked the chain around Taeben's neck, pulling him to his feet roughly and positively skipped out the door and down the hall to the room where Kazhmere was.

"Mistress…" One of the shades that patrolled the halls of that floor, appearing as an empty suit of armor, blocked her path. To Taeben, those horrible creatures seemed to enjoy lying in wait with the other armor that was hanging from the wall and then jumping out at him as he passed, but they had never done that to Salynth. Something must be wrong.

"Not now, my Pet, I have matters to which I must attend," she barked at the shade, attempting to push past it and continue down the hall.

"You may not pass, Mistress. There are invaders in the tower, on the lower floors," the shade said, its voice barely an icy whisper.

Taeben felt the hair stand up on the back of his neck. More invaders? Salynth had forced him to practice his wizard magic on the last group and he had not yet been able to shake the image of the Qatu female he had removed from the tower with a transportation spell. Her eyes had locked on his, and the fear he saw there…the window of pity opened just a crack for a moment, and then slammed down shut again. "Fear is weakness. Weakness is death," he whispered to himself.

"Then handle it," Salynth said, her voice filling with rage. "Is this not why I keep you here? Is this not why I spared you from the cold and dark embrace of the Void?" The shade nodded its head and turned to float back the way it came. Salynth's face changed as an idea occurred to her. "A moment, my Pet?" The shade halted and turned around.

Something in its manner of movement unsettled Taeben. It was as though an invisible puppet master that pulled and jerked the strings to cause it to move was controlling the suit of armor. However, this was no puppet master, invisible or not. This was the dark magic that Salynth possessed; the magic that she fed into the Tower as though it was a living being. The shade, the magic doorways, even down to the very stones that made up the walls, all of it was an extension of Salynth's magical prowess. Taeben looked at her in wonder. Could he be that powerful one day?

"Yes, Mistress?" the shade said, again bowing its armored yet invisible head.

"Describe the invaders. Tell me; is there a Qatu with them?"

"Aye, Mistress, in fact there are two, a male and a female. The female was here before, just recently, until your pet wizard threw her back out into the snow." Taeben's vision began to turn red around the edges as he stared at the shade.

Salynth chuckled. "Pet wizard indeed! You'd be well served to show my Pet some respect, minion," she hissed at the shade through a fangy grin. "I could let his magic loose and then where would you be?" Taeben thought he could just detect a mild shiver run through the suit of armor that hung in the air before him. Good, the shade feared him. "Is the male Qatu…the Rajah?"

"No, Mistress. It is called 'Sath' by its companions. There are two wood elf druids and two warriors, one dwarf and one gnome, in the party as well as the other Qatu," the shade said.

"Ah, Sath, I do believe I know that name. Is the dwarf warrior called Teeand by any chance?" she said, eyeing the suit of armor.

"Aye, Mistress. The tiny one in green armor is Teeand, who did come here with Sathlir in the past and defeat…"

"Enough!" Salynth's sudden outburst accompanied a bright shock of lightning that flew from her fingertips and absolutely incinerated the shade, armor and all. It barely had time to cry out, as it seemed to burn out of existence. She turned to Taeben who was staring at her with a combination of amazement, horror, and utter respect in his gaze. Salynth beamed a fangy grin at him. "Liked that, did you Pet?" she said, moving closer to Taeben as she yanked him close by his collar. He tried to fight back revulsion as her cold fingers caressed the side of his face. "I can teach you to do that, and so much more," she whispered. "There is great untapped power in you, I can feel it." Taeben nodded, swallowing hard. "Power to rule, to dominate, and to destroy. Is that your wish, my Pet?"

Taeben looked up at her, knowing that this moment would seal his fate. He clicked the lock on the metaphorical window that looked in onto his capacity for pity, compassion and love; and then faced the horrible red gaze of his destiny. "Aye Mistress, as you command," he said. "I wish only to learn." Images of Salynth begging for her life, alight with wizard's fire, and then torn into thousands of pieces floated randomly across his mind as she dragged him on down the hall by his collar. "I wish only to learn."

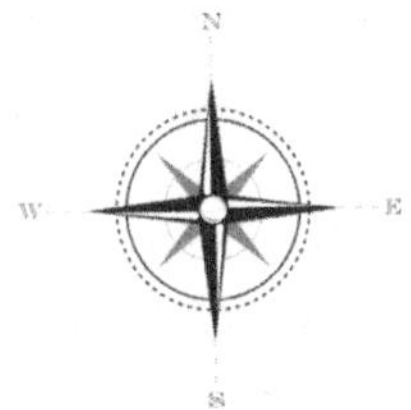

# Twenty-Nine

Passing through the enchanted doors was a strange experience for a magic user, but for the two warriors it was downright torture. Hack clung to Elysiam's leg as she sprinted along behind Sath, and Teeand held Gin's arm in his hand as she crossed through the doorway, his eyes squeezed shut. "I hate magic!" the dwarf exclaimed as they landed, again in a heap, on the stone floor. They had made it to the fourth floor, which seemed to be a crypt.

Dark colored tiles that seemed to ooze and drip with a foul brownish substance covered the walls, floor, and ceiling. Here and there were sarcophagi, some open and empty, some sealed, and some broken apart as though the inhabitant had second thoughts about being entombed. ,Gin shivered a bit and unwittingly moved closer to Sath making him smile down at her and Anni growl low in her throat.

"We gonna cloak up to hide or suit up to fight?" Elysiam

said, her annoyance clear. She had grumbled softly across floors two and three at their clandestine advance and was itching for a good brawl with the inhabitants of the fourth floor, but it seemed that someone had already put them to their final rest.

"I don't see anything here to fight," Anni said. "Though I do remember a particularly nasty witch down the other end by the next doorway." She shivered a bit and tried stepping closer to Sath, who patted her on the head in a most sibling-like manner and then shifted his attention back to Gin.

"Aye, that witch is a nasty one, that's the truth! She's got some dark magic in her and can pull up a whirlwind that will flatten you into these hard stone walls." Teeand said as he glanced over at Sath, a wry smile peeking out from under his beard. "Remember, Cat?" he said, and Sath nodded gravely.

"A little less nostalgia, a little more action, please?" Elysiam said as she flipped her weapon up into her hand. "Fighting or hiding? Someone make the call before I take you lot on myself."

"I guess it can't hurt to fight our way through this floor can it?" Gin said, hoping against all hope that someone would disagree, and then they could just sneak past whatever horrible thing was resting in each of those stone coffins that littered the floor.

"We'll be fine," Anni said. Everyone turned to look at her. "I said the witch was nasty, but she doesn't always come out to strike out against strangers in her den. My group was unlucky enough to witness her ire but we got past her and through the doorway at the other end." Anni grinned. "The witch doesn't have the magic she needs to get through the doorway to the other side." Her gaze fell on Gin, ever the sycophant, who was staring worriedly at Anni's Prince. This might be her chance to run on ahead with the druid! She had no doubt that Sath and Teeand and the others could defeat the witch, and she was certain that they had already passed through all the doorways in the past and were just letting her take the lead. Such an honorable soul was Sath. It only made Anni love him more.

Teeand folded his arms over his chest with some difficulty due to the heavy breastplate he wore. "Now I'm not saying that I want to run away from a fight, you understand, but do we really want to leave Kazhmere a moment longer than we must? If we can slip past this floor and the next one I think we will be getting close to where that demon dragonkind keeps her prisoners."

Hack shook his head and tapped Teeand on the elbow. "I think we need to let Elys fight her way through here or she is going to flip out on us, Tee." He deftly dodged a kick from the wood elf as she scowled at him.

"Oh, aye, Hack, I'm afraid you're right," Teeand said, looking at Elysiam's scowl and wincing. "Right, let's get this over with then, shall we?" The dwarf raised his axe and ran down the first corridor they found, shouting insults as he went, and then stopped for a moment to listen. The group gathered around him, eyes peeled in the semi darkness and ears pricked for any sounds.

"What is that?" Gin whispered. Sath looked down at her and smiled his best confident smile, but it did not go to his eyes. A low moan had started up in the dimly lit corridor ahead, past the open room with the stone coffins in all manners of opened states. A second otherworldly voice joined the first, followed by a third, all of them magnifying the off-pitch howl that was rising and bouncing off the tiled walls and ceiling.

"Healing magic at the ready, Gin?" he whispered and she nodded.. "Good girl. You are on that solo, I think, because Elys seems to have other plans."

At the sound of her name, Elysiam turned to face them. Gin recognized the bloodlust in her sister druid's eyes and frowned. "I think you're right, Sath," she said. *"May you have nothing but luck,"* she whispered in Qatunari, and he smiled at her pronunciation.

"That's getting better, Gin," he whispered back, clearly proud of her. Anni rolled her eyes at both of them.

*"The phrase is 'may fortune perpetually shine on you,' Sath,"* she muttered. Teeand looked over his shoulder and glared at her, so Anni gave him a "Who, me?" look and readied her instrument.

"You going to play them to death," Teeand said gruffly, "or are you just planning to alert all the other floors above us to our presence?"

"You've never fought with a bard before," Anni replied in curt tones. She strummed her lute and started in on a song with sharp, staccato notes. As she wound into that severe melody a softer, earthier tone, Gin started to feel a bit fuzzy headed. She shook off the sensation and concentrated her focus on Teeand and Hackort, as she knew they would be the first ones into the battle, but soon she was feeling almost sleepy. She moved away from Anni and into a corner, her normal spot so that nothing could sneak up on her, and went back to her spell work.

Sath summoned his magical pet immediately and sent the beast over to guard Gin while she healed the group. Elysiam, barely able to contain herself, was inches behind Hackort and Teeand as they advanced into the dimly lit corridor. "Move up to me!" Teeand called out, and the other three obeyed. Gin again found herself a comfortable little corner and readied herself to keep her friends alive, Sath's pet positioned between her and the group for safety. Anni moved up next to Sath and intensified the earthier of the two melodies that now wound their way from her lute like snakes and wrapped themselves around Sath. The staccato melody stretched its influence over the two warriors, winding them up in a red cloud of bloodlust and the desire to fight, while it seemed to tickle at the back of Elysiam's neck, causing the hair there to stand on end. There were almost no staccato notes left for Sath, which was Anni's plan.

As she continued to weave the two melodies together into a healing harmony that drove listeners to battle, she added a third strain as her guild master had taught her to do. The third lulled the enemy and slowed them down, charming them into an enchanted sleep. Elysiam, Hackort and Teeand were positively chewing through the shades and phantoms that came from all directions as though they were made of paper, and Sath's pet, who had moved up to his master, was keeping him from harm's way, so Anni focused the third melody on Gin, still in her corner.

She watched out of the corner of her eye, as Gin rubbed her eyes and then focused on her healing. If she glanced Anni's way, the bard would pull back on the strength of the melody. All she needed was for Gin to figure out what she was doing and alert the Prince. Anni concentrated again on the first two melodies, reigniting the fire in Elysiam's attack and pushing Hackort and Teeand to bellow with new fury, pulling ghostly bodies out of their coffins with their words and force of will.

"Who dares disturb our peaceful rest?" bellowed a scratchy female voice that seemed to have a dozen or more deep voices echoing behind and through it.

"It's the witch," Sath whispered, anxiety clear in his voice. "She's awake."

"Awake and here," said the same cackling voice from just behind Sathlir. She was a small woman with green skin the same shade as the walls around her. Her chin jutted out, causing her face to wear a permanent hideous grin. Sath braced himself as he turned, but the whirlwind hit him in mid-turn and he flew across the open room, bouncing off one of the walls and coming to rest half in and half out of one of the open stone coffins. Gin started toward him but his pet stepped into her path, snarling at the witch and bearing his teeth. Again, the wind rose up and the pet disappeared into a cloud of dust, reforming across the room. It shook itself hard and again lunged for the witch, giving Gin a clear path to get to the male Qatu whose breath grew shallower by the moment.

"SATH!" She screamed as she reached him. There was no answer. Gin did not wait, but put her hands on his chest and frantically spoke words of healing. "ELYS!" She looked frantically for Elysiam who was hurtling all sorts of fire magic at the witch, keeping it stunned, and made no move to help Gin. "Oh, no, please, come on, Cat!" Gin cried out as she continued pumping the healing magic into Sath's body.

"Just…promise you won't…singe my fur?" Sath murmured, groaning as he lifted one giant clawed hand and rested it on Gin's head. She cried out and threw her arms around his neck. "Ow, careful you, don't make me put you in my pocket."

"The Mistress will not be pleased," hissed the witch. "Not. Pleased." She waved her arms and disappeared in a cloud of vile smelling green smoke.

"What did she mean, the Mistress?" Elysiam said, breathing heavy as she got up from the floor and dusted herself off. "Salynth?"

Teeand nodded. "Most likely. She's popped upstairs to tip that hag off that we are here." He frowned and stroked his beard. "This is not good, mates. Not good at all."

"No, it isn't," Anni said, but she was hardly talking about the situation with the sorceress. She could have driven Gin through the magical doorway and left her there, but then who would have healed Sath? Disgusted, she admitted to herself that that she needed the druid for the time being at least. The other one was no help when it came to healing, a fact that was abundantly clear. Her own healing songs were getting stronger but she was not skilled enough yet to keep Sath alive and safe and that, aside from rescuing Kazhmere, was the only thing that mattered.

"MISTRESS!" The witch ran through the corridors on the top floor of the Tower, its foul stench following her like a cloud. "MISTRESS!" It skidded to a halt as Salynth coalesced in front of it in the hallway.

"There had better be an extremely important reason why you have summoned me this way," she hissed at the witch, who immediately bowed in front of its mistress.

"They are here, Mistress, and they are formidable," the witch said, its voice a crackly whisper. "All of my minions, my brothers and sisters in death, they are all gone," it wailed. Salynth reached down and lifted the witch's chin in her fingers until the pitiful creature was looking her in the eyes.

"You left them to die so that you could come tell me what I would have found out anyway, did you?" The witch's eyes opened wide for a moment, and then the preternatural light that cast an amber glow on Salynth's hand snuffed out. "Pitiful really," she said as she dropped the witch's body. The witch had been kept alive for so long by Salynth's magic that without it, its body shriveled and rotted before it had even hit the floor.

"We have to keep moving, but no more fighting, Elys," Teeand said. "We need to be ready for when we meet Salynth, and I need both of you on your toes this time." Elysiam opened her mouth to protest but he held up a hand. "No arguments lass. Gin might have gotten our Sath back into the fight faster if she'd had a bit of help back there." Elysiam scowled but nodded her compliance. "And as for you," he said, turning to Anni, "keep that calming spell up and playing, yeah? I don't know if it will work on the dragonkind but it might keep her minions from noticing us."

Anni stared at him, saucer-eyed. "What are you talking about, Teeand?" she said, feigning innocence.

*"I'm talking about whatever you were doing that made our Ginolwenye miss a healing spell on Sathlir. I have seen you mooning over him. The only way to keep him safe is to stay away from our Ginolwenye. Do you understand me?"* Tee hissed at her in Qatunari. She nodded. "Good. Now, let's move on through to the next floor. Gin? Elys? We'll need a new invisibility spell once we land, quick as you ladies can, yes?"

"Thanks, Tee," Sath said. "I'll be back to 100% soon, and…"

"Save it, Cat," Teeand said, grinning. "Let's go get your Kazhmere and get out of here. I'm about ready for some warm and sand and sun once we're finished here."

"And maybe a few fire dancers from Qatu'anari?" Sath said, grinning back at his old friend. Teeand laughed heartily and nodded at Sath, then moved to the enchanted doorway.

"Let's get this over with," Hackort said as he joined Tee. "I hate this magic stuff. It makes me itchy." Elysiam strode over and wrapped a protective arm around Hack's helmet. He grinned up at her and then held a small hand out to Gin. "Come on,

Ginny!" he called out. Grimacing at the nickname, the druid joined the group along with Anni and Sath brought up the rear. Anni stepped through the doorway and then reached back through. Gin grabbed her arm and Anni suddenly yanked her through the doorway before Sath had a chance to take her hand.

"What the…?" Elysiam ran at the door that had swung shut, intent on following her sister druid through to the next floor, but bounced off the wood and back into Teeand's waiting arms.

"NO." Sath ran at the doorway and because he had been there before he started passing through it. "Tee, wait, if I'm not back in…well, you know…"

"Aye, Sath," Teeand said, his voice breaking a bit. "You go get your Kazhmere and our Gin." Sath passed on through the doorway, but not before he heard Elysiam cursing Teeand. The dwarf was not going to have an easy time of it.

"This is wrong!" she screamed at Teeand. "We have to get Gin out of there!"

"Just be still a moment, lass!" Tee screamed back. Hack was beating the doorway with his axe, and Tee had to haul him back by his neck. "And you, wee man, you'll break the doorway and then where will we be?" He flopped down on the floor, his breath heaving. "Now, listen, here's the plan. I can get through the doorways too. We just need to give Sath time to make Anni think she's got the upper hand."

"Seriously?" Elysiam asked. "You expect us to believe that you got all of that from a look?"

"He and Sath have been together even longer than we have, Elys," Hack said, his voice quiet and cautious, "and I sometimes know exactly where you need me to be in a fight just from a look." Elysiam looked down at Hack, and the blazing fury in her eyes faded.

"I know, I know all of that," she said, clearly defeated. "But I just wanted to…I mean I think we need to…" She paused, biting her lip and trying to get herself together before she burst into tears. "I want that Anni, Tee," she whispered. "She's been lying to us the whole time, and now we've given her what she wants. SATH." Fury began to ignite in her eyes again. "There probably isn't even a Kazhmere! I bet that bard made it all up, so that she could get Sath alone and now…now she is…now Gin is… Oh, Ikara's TEETH she's got them where she wants them and we can't help because YOU WON'T ACTIVATE THE DOORWAY!"

Teeand took a deep breath before speaking. He had learned through raising his many children that greeting anger with anger will never help anything. Elysiam was standing over him, waiting for an answer, and Hack had risen to his feet and was tugging on her tunic, trying to rein her back in to calm. The dwarf looked up at the wood elf. "Elysiam, sit down," he said in his most authoritative voice. She just stared at him. "SIT." Elysiam plopped down on the ground in a huff and Hack scooted over close to her, putting a hand on her knee that she promptly shook off. "Now, Hack was right when he said that I don't always need to talk to Sath to know what's going on with him or what his next move will be. But this is not one of those times." Elysiam started to hop back up but Hackort held her down.

"You're mighty brave for such a tiny wee man, Hackort," she snarled at him.

"Elys, please…" Hackort and Elysiam shared a look for a moment, and then she relented. "Now, go on, Tee," the gnome said.

"I'm guessing that Sath is going to let Anni think she has the upper hand and then take her down, because she's just a young bard and shouldn't be any trouble for him, really," Tee said. "But that won't work if all of us go charging in after him." The dwarf laid a fatherly hand on Elysiam's arm, but she yanked it away. "None of us want to see Gin get hurt, Elys, lass. None of us. Nevertheless, you know our Sath will not let that happen. He will send for us when he needs us, or when I feel it has been too long we will go on through the doorway and go find them. However, for now, our Elys, you need to remain calm. Please?"

Elysiam snorted. "Me. Calm. Sure, no problem," she said, rising to her feet and beginning to pace back and forth in front of the doorway. "No problem."

"That's not going to last very long, Tee," Hack said, leaning over to whisper to the dwarf. "She isn't going to be reasonable for long. Gin is the only druid from Aynamaede that will have anything to do with Elys any more, you know that. When she calls Gin her sister-druid, she means it." He rubbed his face with his tiny hands. "What can we do to help Gin and Sath?"

"Give them a few more minutes," Teeand said. "But I'm getting a bit uneasy myself, if I'm honest. Young bard or not, that Anni has some natural skill and talent and I fear that Sath is underestimating her because he's the…because he is who he is," he continued, hoping that he had covered for his slip well enough. It would do no good to out Sath at this point. Besides, Elysiam was not likely to believe him anyway.

"Okay but only a few. If I have to stun you and carry you through that doorway, little green man, you know that I will do it," Elysiam barked. Teeand glared back at her for as long as he could, but his face soon split into a wide grin and he laughed heartily. Hackort joined in the laughter and finally Elysiam grinned. "Well, I would certainly try," she said.

"Aye, of course you would, Elys," Teeand said, getting to

his feet. "Gin and Sath are family, and you don't abandon family, regardless of how hard-headed they are." He winked at Elysiam as she grinned back. "Oh, fine, we've given them enough time. What is it our Gin says? Doorway ahoy, everyone hug the dwarf!" Hackort laughed and grabbed onto one of Teeand's arms as Elysiam grimaced and grabbed the other one. The three of them walked toward the doorway and passed through as though it was made of water. "Elys? Invisibility magic now, please?"

"Anni, what are you doing? Why are you doing this?" Gin whispered as Anni dragged her down the corridors of the uppermost floor of the Tower. "Please, I will help if I can, please just…"

"Do you never, ever shut up?" Anni exclaimed, turning to face Gin as she skidded to a stop. "Seriously, you talk more than the other four put together except maybe that other wood elf. It must be in your genes or something." She resumed her frantic pace as she zoomed up and down hallways, her nose in the air. Gin struggled against her but Anni's grip was so strong that she could not pry the Qatu's strong hand off her arm.

"Okay, I didn't want to do this, but…" Gin summoned up a fiery magic that set the fur on Anni's arm alight. The Qatu howled in pain as she released Gin and beat at the flames to put them out. Gin saw her opening and ran, trying to remember the path they had just come but failing. All the hallways looked the same to her.

"GIN!" At the sound of Sath's voice, Gin's heart leaped up into her throat. "ANNI?" He was livid; Gin could tell that from his tone, and with each call, it sounded as though he was getting closer. She pressed on; following what she thought was a Qatu shadow moving away from her, always one turn ahead of her.

Finally, she was close enough and leaped forward, grabbing at a tail that was disappearing from view.

"What the?" Anni looked down and beamed a toothy grin at Gin, who was clinging to her tail. "WRONG cat, druid," she said as she snatched Gin up from the floor. "Well, wrong for you anyway. Now, we have to find Kazhmere, come on." Gin shrieked but this time Anni was ready and she wasted no time wrapping one of her clawed hands around Gin's face to stop her from making any more noise.

"*Annilanshi*!" Sath roared as he followed the weak trail of her scent. *"If one hair on the wood elf's head is harmed, just one hair, I will forget who I am and take it out of your hide!"*

"Forget who you are?" Salynth said as she appeared in the hallway Sath had just run through. "I won't forget who you are, Cat, now that I have your little sister in my thrall." Sath skidded to a halt and spun around to glare at the dragonkind sorceress. "Oh, my you are a handsome one, aren't you?" she said, licking her lips. "Pet, what shall we do with this one? Would you like another kitty to keep you company?"

A puff of smoke blinded Sath for a moment and he pawed at it, trying to speed it to disperse. Next to Salynth, he saw a young elf in a tattered cobalt robe wearing a heavy-looking metal collar around his neck. Salynth tapped her foot impatiently and then gave the chain a violent yank. "Pet?"

"Aye, Mistress, if you think I should have more than one cat. My will is yours," the elf said. Sath could clearly see the disgust on the Elvish features. His red hair, streaked with white, was tied back by a piece of leather but was escaping in wisps around his sharply featured face. His wrists bore scars from previous heavy chains, probably not unlike the one currently around his neck. There was something familiar about him, but

Sath could not afford the time required to search his memory.

"Another…Cat?" Sath asked, daring to hope. "Enough games, witch, show me where my sister Kazhmere is at once!" He puffed up his chest as he had seen his father do hundreds of times, in an effort to look bigger than he was and intimidate the sorceress. She laughed in his face.

"Your sister, the Princess, is here in my Tower. On that point you are exactly right," she hissed, a maniacal smile spreading across her dark features. "But to show you where would take away the fun, don't you think? People don't want to work for things anymore," she said, wringing her hands. "I think we should have a scavenger hunt, what do you think, Pet?"

"You don't have to help her," Sath said to the elf. "We can help you, me and my friends. We will get you and my sister safely out of here."

"What makes you think he wants to leave?" Salynth roared. She flung some brightly colored magical butterflies at the elf's face, and he smiled as he watched them flit about. "Do you want to leave me, my Pet?"

"Of course not, Mistress," he said, his voice soft and childlike.

Anni heard voices around the next corner. Sath? Had he found the witch? Tightening her grip on the druid, she ran forward and came upon the other three standing in the corridor. Salynth laughed heartily and clapped her hands when she saw Anni.

"What have you brought me, Kitty Cat?" she asked. "A wood elf? Hmm…what can I do with her, and from the look of her a druid as well! I already have a wizard but a druid might be a nice addition to my collection." She drifted over toward Anni only after speaking ancient words that called roots up out of the ground that wound around Sath's feet, holding the now hissing and spitting Qatu in his place. "She's pretty too, much prettier than any of those cats, don't you think my Pet?"

Still enchanted by the magical insects, the elf nodded his head. "As you say, Mistress," he mumbled, though she was completely blocking his view of Gin and hers of him. Salynth held her arms out to Anni.

"Give me the present you've brought me, Annilanshi," she said as Sath roared his objection in the background. Anni hesitated as Gin fought against her and finally bit down hard on the sensitive skin on the inside of Anni's hand.

"OW!" Anni screeched, dropping Gin as she did. The druid wasted no time dashing away from Anni and toward Sath, even though that put her closer to Salynth and the other elf…who looked strangely familiar to Gin. She skidded to a stop and looked him full in the face, her eyes widening as she recognized him.

"Taeben?" Gin whispered, moving closer to him though Sath grabbed an arm and tried to hold her back. "Ben? Is that you? Do you remember me?" Something gnawed at the back of her mind, something to do with the forest and Gaelin, but it was gone as soon as it surfaced.

The wizard, still enthralled by the butterflies, looked down at Gin at the sound of his name. "Ginny?" he whispered, as though he was seeing a ghost. "Ginny, what are you doing here?"

"Oh, this is too much!" Salynth exclaimed, clapping her hands with glee. "They know each other! It is like a storybook!"

"Ben, what are YOU doing here?" Gin said, moving close enough to touch his hand. Taeben jerked away from her. "What's happened to you? I left you…I mean I saw you…I mean…" She looked sadly at him, inwardly frustrated at the memory that would not coalesce.

"Gin, you need to get back behind me," Sath warned. *"Anni, I don't know what you're playing at here but if you know what's good for you, you will take Gin back to the others and keep her safe."* Once again, he tried to emulate his father in tone and stature, and it seemed to have the desired effect on the other Qatu.

*"Aye, majesty, I will do as you ask,"* Anni said, begrudgingly. She scooted past him and grabbed Gin up as she moved, carrying the screaming wood elf back to a point behind Sath.

"Bah, we're not ready yet anyway," Salynth said, moving close to Taeben who had not taken his eyes off Gin yet. "Soon, Sathlir Clawsharp of Qatu'anari. Soon. For now, Pet, if you will?" She wrapped a bony arm around Taeben who sadly spoke ancient words of transport magic, his eyes still following the path Anni had taken with Gin. A yellow ring of fire appeared around them and they seemed to wink out of existence as he mouthed the word *Tower*.

"NO!" Sath screamed, lunging at them just as they disappeared. "Tell me where my sister is you witch!" He hit the floor with a thud and just stayed there a moment, pounding his fist into the stone beneath him.

"Sath, did you say your…sister?" Gin whispered, her voice barely audible to even his keen feline hearing.

"Shut it, druid," Anni snapped. "You may have just ended our Kazhmere's life. Now go find your friends and I will tend to Sath." Gin stepped back from her, eyes like saucers. "GO!" Gin took one last long look at Sath and then scampered away, back down the corridor using her tracking abilities to find her way back to the doorway. She was watching her feet and ran headlong into Teeand, who was charging ahead watching his own green armored boots.

"Ow!" Gin yelped as she fell backward. Teeand scrambled to help her up off the floor and then grabbed her up in a bear hug. "Tee, I can't breathe, please?" she whimpered as he held her tightly. He released her, with an embarrassed chuckle, and looked her over from head to toe.

"You're all right then, our lass?" he said. Gin nodded. "Where's Sath? You leave him behind to deal with Anni?"

"Tee, did you know that Kazhmere is his sister?" Gin asked, looking the dwarf in the eye. Tee looked away but she moved around to make eye contact with him again. "Tee? Don't lie to me, please."

"She is Sath's sister?" Elysiam had run up to join them, and she stared at Gin. "He didn't think that was important enough to tell us?" She poked Teeand in the side. "Did you know that?"

"Aye, I did know that. Remember when we sat up telling stories?" Tee said, avoiding Gin's gaze.

"Yes, you were over there purring and growling and keeping us awake," Elysiam snapped. "Is that why you were speaking Qatunari? Because we can't understand it?"

Teeand looked away from all of them. "Yes," he said. "There is more, more that you don't need to know right now, but that I swear to all of you I will hold that Cat's feet to the fire until he tells you all of it. Once his sister is safe we will be done with all the secrets between us. Deal?"

Elysiam walked over and squatted down in front of Teeand so that she could look him in the eye. "We will talk about it afterward. There will be no more secrets. If I can't trust you I won't fight beside you. I will walk away; do you understand me? I will WALK AWAY." She stomped back toward the doorway, muttering angrily. Hackort smiled apologetically up at Teeand and then ran after Elysiam. Teeand looked at Gin, who was still staring at him.

"You knew. What else do you know, Tee?" she said, her gaze accusatory.

"Afterward,"" he said.

"No, now." Gin stood her ground. "What else do you know?"

"He...cares about you, all right? That's all I can say, but Gin, please, you know I adore you, but I...You and I both know what he can be if he loses his...focus. Don't make him lose focus," Teeand said, his words coming out in a rush. "Blimey, I'm terrible with words, I just...just be careful, our Gin, please?"

Gin smiled at him, but her smile didn't go all the way to her eyes. "I won't, Tee. Now, let's get his sister back." Teeand halfheartedly smiled at her and they joined Hackort and Elysiam.

"Let me tell you how we can beat that hag," Teeand said.

"WHAT DID YOU DO??" Sath bellowed at Anni. He had risen from the spot on the floor where he had tried to catch Salynth and Taeben before she disappeared and was bearing down on Anni, his eyes blazing with raw fury.

Anni fell to her knees, pressing her face to the floor. *"Forgive me, Majesty, I only thought of your sister, the Princess, and her safety. I thought that because the sorceress seems to appreciate magic users...well, I thought that she would trade..."*

*"You thought WHAT??"* Sath yanked Anni to her feet by the scruff of her neck and held her there. *"You were going to trade Gin's life for Kazhmere's?"*

*"Yes, Majesty,"* Anni said, sniffling. *"I was only thinking of Kahzi!"* Tears rolled down her cheeks and when Sath brought her face close to his he could smell the fear rolling off her in waves. He dropped her suddenly and backed away, holding his hands out to her.

*"I'm sorry…Anni, dear spirits, I'm sorry."* He would not permit himself to become his father even though his sister was…Kazhmere…an image of her playing in the nursery danced through his mind and took his breath for a moment. His need to protect his younger sister was all-consuming. In that moment, something snapped in Sath. He felt the bloodlust coming over him, as it had back before he met Gin in the tunnels…as it had when he was still hiding in the woodlands, waiting for a wayward druid or ranger to stumble into his path. He felt like he did the first night after he left Qatu'anari, the last time he had spoken to his father.

*"How can I help?"* Anni whispered. Sath ignored her and stalked back toward the way that he had come, where the other Fabled Ones were waiting. *"Sath? Your highness?"*

*"You can help by getting out of my sight,"* Sath growled. *"NOW."* Anni stared at him for a second and then slowly got up from the floor where he had dropped her. She looked at him one last time, and then walked toward the doorway that would take her to the uppermost floor without looking over her shoulder.

Gin and Elysiam were tracking Sath through the corridors when they ran into him, sitting on the floor in the same room where Salynth had vanished with Taeben moments before. Gin ran over to him and knelt, wincing as he growled at her when she tentatively put a hand on his arm. "Sath, where is Anni?" she asked, steeling her voice though her insides were churning.

"Leave that be, Gin," he said, not looking up at her. He glanced up at Teeand. "I thought you were going to take the others to safety, Tee?" he said, frowning.

"Not the plan, Sath," Teeand said, moving closer and resting a hand on Sath's shoulder. "You know that. I don't leave friends behind."

"Where is the bard?" Elysiam said. "And don't try growling to change the subject, Sath…that may work on Gin but not me."

"I don't care where Anni is," Sath replied. "All I care about is finding my…Kazhmere."

"Your sister," Gin said, smiling sadly at Sath as his gaze flew to meet hers. "I know, I overheard you and Anni and my Qatunari is better than you think."

Sath locked eyes with Teeand, wondering that if she knew who Kazhmere was, did she also know who he was? An almost imperceptible shake of the dwarf's head told him that she did not, and he exhaled loudly. "You are all willing to help me?" he asked, making eye contact with each in turn, his gaze finally coming to rest on Elysiam. "Elys?"

"After we rescue your sister, Sathlir, we will have a long talk, you and I. Deal?" Elysiam said, her voice cold and business like. Sath nodded his head. "Fair enough. Now, after hearing from Tee about the Tower, I think we have a plan if you'd care to hear it?" Sath nodded again. "But first I think we need to know if Anni is still on our side or if we're going to be taking her off Hack's list."

"Annilanshi is inconsequential," Sath said, his tone icy. Gin looked over at him, her brow furrowed in concern. "What is the plan?"

"Fine, moving on, Tee told us about what we may encounter on the uppermost of the floors. Our plan is that we go as far as we can under an invisibility spell and then fight only when we have to fight. But first we need to have a rest here, since this area seems uninhabited." Elysiam paused for a moment, looking around at the others. "Eat and drink and rest, because Tee thinks that will make the upcoming fight easier. Then, when we are rested, Gin and I will work to ward off evil magic and grant us invisibility, and we move out."

"Yep, sounds like a Tee plan," Sath said, his face a blank slate. "Let's do it." He straightened up, sitting in the position that Gin had seen him take many times when he was meditating before engaging an enemy. She tilted her head to one side, trying to remember the last time she had seen him do that. He closed his eyes and fell silent.

"I don't need to rest," Hackort whined. Elysiam pushed him down on to the floor and then plopped down next to him. "I don't like resting. It isn't fun. Fighting is fun. Killing is fun. Rescuing Sath's sister is fun."

"Shutting you up will be fun," Elysiam hissed at him.

Gin moved closer to Sath and reached out for his arm. Just before her fingers brushed his fur, he pulled his arm away. "Sath, I…"

"Don't. Not now, Gin," he hissed.

Teeand moved over and patted her on the shoulder. She leaned over onto the dwarf like a tired child, her eyes closed, and he hugged her to him for a moment before releasing her. Sath looked at him and Teeand held his gaze. His look warned Sath against hurting the druid, and Sath's clandestine nod told the dwarf that he understood the caution.

"Let's go," Sath said. "I've waited long enough."

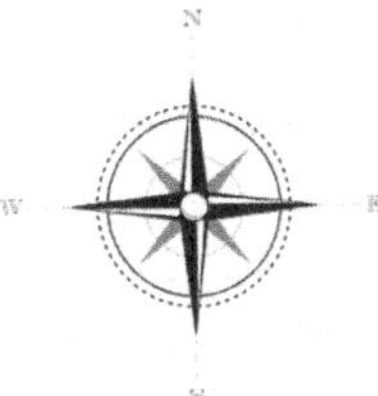

# THIRTY

Taeben hated using magic to teleport with another person. It normally felt like being inside out, but was especially bad when you did not know it was coming. Salynth had left him back in the room where he was being held, and once the fog in his mind cleared, he could see the Qatu female in the corner. She was wearing her chains again, and he feared that meant she had tried to come after him when Salynth took him before.

"Stupid Cat," he murmured as he crept toward her. She seemed to be asleep and he loathed to wake her. "There is no reason for you to make her hurt you over me," he whispered. "I am certainly not worth that."

"Yes you are," Kazhmere said, opening her eyes slowly. "You're just as worthy as I am, as anyone is." She made eye contact with him and he looked away.

"Are you hurt?" he said, his voice soft. "I don't have

healing magic like you do so I can't help, really."

"No, I'm all right," she said. "Where did she take you?"

"That's really none of your concern, Princess," Taeben said, hoping that she would be so outraged that he had referred to her by her title, she would shut him out to keep her secret.

"Really, you can call me Kahzi," she said. "No need to stand on ceremony here, Taeben." He frowned. "What did Salynth mean when she said she was taking you for your lessons?"

"None of your concern," he barked at her. Why did she care so much about what he did? It would make it harder for him to practice his new skills on her if he thought of her as a friend.

"Why do you have to be so difficult?" Kazhmere asked under her breath. "Are all elves as difficult as you?" She tried to curl up as much as she could but the chains kept her from any more than a seated position on the floor. She leaned her furry head back against the stone and closed her eyes.

"I will ask you again, are you hurt?" Taeben asked tentatively after a long pause. Kazhmere ignored him. "I might be able to conjure you some food and water if that would help." He cursed himself inwardly for extending kindness to her but found himself to be unable to stop. "Kahzi?"

"Princess will do, thank you wizard," she snapped. Taeben narrowed his eyes and returned to the opposite corner of the room to meditate. "If formality is what you wish, then that is what you shall have from me."

"Fine," he muttered. As soon as he settled into the proper meditative position and cleared his mind, images of the earlier scene in the corridor with Salynth began interrupting his calm.

Taeben scanned the image now burned into his mind and again settled on the wood elf he had seen. Ginolwenye! That was too much of a coincidence to have been random, that she would be here with his Mistress's enemy. "Must have been an illusion," he murmured and again cleared his mind to focus on that scene. He knew that Salynth would want to rehash it as she did all interactions with outsiders in her Tower, and he wanted to be able to answer her questions on the first try. Much less painful that way, he had found.

The image appeared in his mind again. The Qatu that she called Prince standing before her, the other Qatu female clinging to him and looking up at him with some sort of hero worship written all over her. Taeben shuddered. That sort of devotion was akin to worse weakness than that brought on by fear. *Familiarity breeds softness and softness is weakness*. He had seen the male before, in Bellesea Keep. Those memories, though still muddled due to his Mistress's magic, were becoming clearer.

In his mind's eye, Taeben looked beyond the two Qatu to the group that ran in at the last moment, before his Mistress commanded him to magically teleport the two of them away. "The Prince and his concubine, a dwarf, a gnome, and two wood elves," he murmured, studying the group. Had the rest of them been in the Keep? He could not be sure, so he focused on the Qatu male and Gin specifically.

Kazhmere's attention rocketed to Taeben, but she kept quiet to keep from rousing him from his meditation. The Prince he spoke of had to be Sathlir. Stupid proud brother of hers! Kazhmere bit her lip to keep from crying out. Why had Anni brought Sath here? And who was the 'concubine' that the wizard mentioned? She stilled her mind that roared like a hive of bees for answers and listened for more clues from the wizard.

Taeben was focusing on the two wood elves. "Both druids, interesting," he murmured. He didn't recognize the blonde right away, but the other one was most certainly the Ginolwenye that he had known as a child. He moved the memory forward in his mind to the point that he had spoken the long-forgotten nickname he'd had for her... "Ginny," he whispered, and the memory-Gin looked up at him with a mixture of wonder and horror. "Ginny, what are you doing here?"

The memory-image of Gin stared back at him. "Ben, what are YOU doing here?" she said, and he echoed her with his own voice. Kazhmere watched in wonder. "What have they done to you?" Taeben found his memory wandering backward even further, back to his childhood, and he let it go there. His mind filled with images of Alynatalos, the gleaming elven city of gold on the southern edge of the forest. Tears pricked the backs of his eyelids as his mind's eye visited his parents, and then flew along to schoolrooms where Taeben saw his younger self, pouring over spell books and ignoring the calls from his friends to come outside and play. "Lazy idiots," he mouthed as the memory-Taeben called back to them.

He gasped as the scene shifted and a red-headed teenage female elf's face appeared before his. "Tairn..." he murmured. The memory-Tairneanach was joined by a tiny wood elf with a bobbing auburn ponytail. The little wood elf looked up at him and he heard her voice trying to pronounce his name. "Oh, just call me Ben, you've butchered my name enough, Ginny," he joined memory-Taeben in chastising her. He found himself frowning as she burst into sobs, and was amazed at how the sight of her tears caused such a pain to shoot through his heart even now. Taeben squeezed his eyes shut as tightly as he could to try ridding himself of the vision.

"Who is Gin?" Kazhmere said, unable to contain her curiosity any longer. Taeben's eyes flew open. "And the Prince, Ben, the one you mentioned; that was my brother Sathlir was it not?"

"Do they not teach you in Qatu'anari to mind your own bloody business?" Taeben thundered, enraged that his meditation was interrupted, and still fueled by emotions brought on by the visions of his past. "My name is Taeben to you, Cat," he hissed at her. "You may ask my Mistress who she currently entertains in her Tower for I am sure it is not my place to tell you." He closed his eyes again before he caught sight of the sadness in her face at his outburst, only to see memory-image Gin's bright blue eyes, etched with concern for him, floating in his mind.

"They teach me to be honest and fair, Taeben," Kazhmere whispered, "and above all, to harm none if at all possible." Holding her head in her hands, she started her own meditation in the hopes that her connection to her brother was intact, and that she could warn him to leave the Tower and forget her before he was hurt. Her heart and her fear betrayed her, and all she could visualize was begging her brother to save her as he had done so many times when they were younger cubs. Her shoulders shook as she cried silent tears, wincing and gasping as the manacles cut into the flesh under the fur at her wrists.

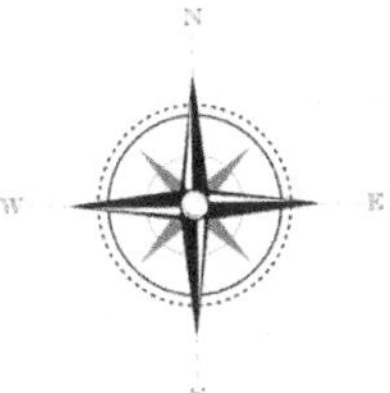

# THIRTY-ONE

Under the cloak of invisibility magic, the five moved through the fifth and sixth floors of the Tower, unnoticed by the ghostly inhabitants. Elysiam had cast the spell with Gin's help, making sure that they could see each other. The warriors did not like magic, and Hack would only agree to it as long as he could see everyone. The gnome took the lead with Elysiam right behind him, ready to club him on the head if he made a move to attack anything. She looked down at him from time to time, amazed that he still had her back just as he had done when they first met so many years ago. Her mind wandered back for a moment, and she shuddered.

"You okay, Elys?" Hack whispered, stopping to look up at her and causing everyone behind him to crash into each other.

"Aye little man, you just keep on your way," she hissed at him, smiling inwardly as he turned back to the task at hand and kept moving. Again she was reminded of times long past, when he had first asked her that same question. They had escaped together from the dungeons in Calder's Port, and were about to embark on what had become one of the most important relationships in her life. *Fair enough, tiny man!* Elysiam smiled as she remembered what she had said to him that day so long ago. *I can at least stay with you until I have paid off my debt to you for saving my life…which, we will never mention again, deal?*

"What did you say, Elys? What about a deal?" Hack said, looking up at her and shaking her hand off his helmet, bringing her back from her musing.

"Nothing. I hate having to move like this, it's so cramped!" she retorted, trying to shake off the memory.

Hackort patted her hand. "You just want to kill things. I understand, Elys. We'll get to kill things soon enough," he said.

"What are you, my mother?" she snapped, yanking her hand away from him. He shook his head, having come to expect these fits of temper when she was not getting her way. "Sorry." Hackort smiled under his helm. Elysiam was one of a kind.

"Would you two zip it, please?" Sath hissed from his place in the lead. "It's hard to sneak when you sound like a gossipy herd of elephants!" Gin muttered something under her breath about falling like a cat that made Sath chuckle and lightened his mood. "We're almost to the doorway and then we can…"

"Can what? Save my friend? Concentrate on the mission?" said Anni, appearing from behind a pillar in the room they had just entered. Sath stood straight up, focusing on her and calling his magical pet to his side. "Oh, now there's no need for that, Sath," she said, glancing around the room. Sath followed her gaze and gasped when he saw all of the ghostly inhabitants of that floor standing at attention and watching Anni. "Oh, well, maybe there is." With a flick of her wrist and a new tune from her lute, the reanimated began a slow walk toward Sath and the others, arms outstretched, voices joining into one bone-chilling moan.

"I guess they can see us?" Teeand asked, tightening his grip on his poleaxe.

"Um, yes, yes they can," Sath answered. "Anni, stop this, we're both here for the same reason. You don't have to do this."

Anni looked at him strangely, her head cocked to one side. "Are we here for the same reason, Sathlir? Did you not just give up your sister's life in favor of a wood elf who doesn't even know how you…" Sath cut her off with an enraged roar. "Right. Sorry, didn't meant to let that cat out of the bag," she said, waggling her eyebrows and taking a step backward. The shades formed ranks around her, their dead eyes all glaring at Sath and the others. "Now, I am going to save my friend Kahzi, with or without your help. I would have preferred to have you on my side, Sathlir, but that is your choice." She changed the tune on her lute and all the shades seemed to fall into a trance. With a final look over her shoulder, she moved to the nearest doorway with preternatural speed and disappeared through it.

"We've got about a minute before…" The sound of that unearthly moan interrupted Teeand. "Now!" He charged into the middle of them, bellowing curses directed at their mothers and anything else vile and malicious he could think to shout. Hackort was hot on his heels, following suit. Elysiam and Gin moved to opposite sides of the room, watching each other carefully as they did, and Sath stayed where they had come into the floor. He held back his magical pet tiger for a few moments, allowing all of the creatures in the room to focus their ire on the two warriors first, then released the cat to join the melee while casting his own magic spells intended to slow down the progress of the mob.

"Quake incoming!" Elysiam shouted to Gin across the

growing din of magical weapons clashing with mundane steel. The druid ran to the middle of the room, dodging grabs from specters and jumping over slowly dissolving undead corpses as she went. Once she was sure she was in the middle, she motioned to Gin who did the same, only having to stop one time to shake off an undead grip on her boot as she leaped over a fading body. The two wood elves stood back to back and simultaneously lifted their arms, calling in unison on Kildir to deliver a shocking blow to the ground beneath them and swallow up the ghosts that threatened them and their companions. Seemingly, on demand, the room shook and pitched and most of the ghosts fell to the stone floor and disappeared into the cracks.

"Show offs," Teeand spat. "Hack and I had them right where we wanted them."

"Yeah! Druids are kill stealers!" Hackort agreed, scowling.

"Right where you wanted them, right," Elysiam said, chuckling darkly. "If you wanted them to be on your heads then yes, you did." She wiped her brow on the back of her hand, plastering her fringe up against her helmet. "Ginny, pleasure as always," she said, clapping her sister druid on the back. Gin beamed a grin back at her.

"Aye, Elys, we make a pretty good team," Gin said, scratching the ears of Sath's tiger who had wandered over and begun rubbing his head on her hip. "You too, sweetie. Now, where's your master?" She scanned the room for Sath, her anxiety level rising as she failed to locate him. Taking a deep breath to steel herself against what she was afraid of most, she turned her eyes downward to look for him among the dead, but again did not see him. "Hey, guys…where's the cat?" she asked, her voice filled with fear. The tiger winked out of existence under her hand.

Tee spun around in a circle and then swore in Dwarvish.

"Sorry Gin," he said as her face blanched at his words. "Forgot you could understand that, Flower. That mangy cat must have used the fight as a distraction to go on ahead without us." In what seemed to be one fluid motion, Tee swung his poleaxe around and placed it in its holster on his back, replacing it with his twin short swords. "He won't get far," the dwarf rumbled as he charged through the fading carnage toward the doorway. Hackort and Elysiam followed him, but Gin hung back a moment.

"Trade the life of your sister for a wood elf who doesn't know…doesn't know what?" she wondered aloud to herself. "More secrets and lies, Sath?" she said sadly, as she ran to catch up with the others. They all knew that the ranks of undead they had just killed were not defeated, but instead were dispersed and would soon be gathering their strength together in order to exact revenge. She caught up just as they were heading through the doorway and into the hall that lead to Salynth's chambers at the very top of the Tower.

The door to the cell swung open and Salynth marched in, a cold and howling wind seeming to follow her like a train hanging off her cape. Her dark eyes settled first on Kazhmere, who had drifted off to sleep while meditating, and then moved to lock with Taeben's own as he stared up at her from his own meditation pose on the floor.

"Well? Have you been practicing, my Pet?" she asked him as she drew closer to him. As always, in her presence Taeben felt his skin grow icy as the ocean outside.

"No, Mistress, I am sorry but I have not," he replied, bracing himself for her chastisement. It did not come. "I fear that our transport earlier did take a lot of out of me, and so I have been in meditation to regain my strength so that I can do as you ask."

His words were like bile on his tongue. Nothing made Taeben angrier than being subservient to another, especially one he deemed as low as Salynth. However, knowing already her magical prowess, he had decided that he would live longer if he played the part of the obedient student.

"So you have regained your stamina. Begin," she said, pointing one clawed finger at Kazhmere. "Claim her will for your own." Taeben took a deep breath and got to his feet, holding out his manacled wrists to Salynth.

"Ah yes, my Pet, my apologies. Let me remove those awful things. Come closer." Taeben did as told, grimacing as Salynth ran one finger down the side of his face. "You would make the most beautiful dragonkind," she said softly, her voice husky.

"As you wish, Mistress," he said, his stomach doing flips at the prospect of her touching him in that way again. He would kill her or die trying if she were to try that, he decided. The ancient dragonkind sorceress ran her hands slowly down Taeben's neck and onto his shoulders, then trailed her knife-sharp fingernails down his arms to the heavy chains around his wrists. "I do like seeing you trussed up like this, my Pet," she said softly, "but it will not get us where we need to be today, will it?" She moved her hands in the shape of a long forgotten rune and the chains fell away from his wrists. Taeben swallowed back the bile building in his throat. "Now then, on to your homework?"

Taeben nodded solemnly and then turned to Kazhmere to find her awake and staring at him. Her teal eyes searched his, her furry blonde face wrought with curiosity but no fear. *She does not fear me,* Taeben thought, frowning. *She will.* He felt Salynth's eyes burning into his back so he moved closer to Kazhmere, kneeling down to her level and taking her furry chin in his hand. With all of the magic he possessed, he forced his will into her mind, burning his gaze into hers. The Qatu Princess thrashed for a moment, squeezing her eyes shut. Taeben panicked and with his other hand grabbed the side of her face, trying to pry her eyes open.

"Oh, dearie that's the hard way!" Salynth hissed from behind him. "Move." Unseen hands shoved Taeben to the floor as Salynth glided across the room and knelt in front of Kazhmere, who still held her eyes shut tightly and her head high and proud. "Now, sweetie, there's no need for all that," Salynth said, stroking the side of Kazhmere's cheek gently. After a moment, Kazhmere's eyes fluttered open. "Oh yes, that's so much better," Salynth cooed at Kazhmere, who smiled cautiously up at her. The sorceress deepened her gaze at Kazhmere and the Qatu's chains melted away as though made of butter. "See, Pet? There's no need to be rough, is there, my Princess?" Kazhmere's eyes drooped and soon she seemed to be asleep again. "I say, there is no need to be rough, you will do as I ask will you not?"

"Yes, Mistress," Kazhmere murmured, her face turning upward toward Salynth like a flower opening to the sun. "Anything you ask, Mistress."

*"That wizard over there troubles me, Kahzi,"* Salynth purred at her in Qatunari. *"Be a lamb and get rid of him for me, would you?"* Kazhmere was on her feet immediately, stalking toward Taeben who skittered toward a corner away from her.

"What did you tell her to do?" he cried out to Salynth. "What did say to her?" Salynth laughed maniacally as Kazhmere picked up Taeben by the front of his robes and hoisted him into the air. He fought her off but she was much stronger than he was and fueled by Salynth's magic to boot. "PUT ME DOWN!" he screamed.

"This wizard, Mistress?" Kazhmere asked, her focus solely

on Salynth.

"Aye, my Pretty Pet, but I think he has learned his lesson. You may drop him now." Kazhmere did as told and as she released him, Taeben crashed down to the stone floor. He leaped to his feet, swearing in Elvish and calling up the most damaging spells he could to direct at Salynth. He hurled lightning bolts, fire, and ice at her, but all of his magic faded to nothing as it bounced off the magical arcane shield she had thrown around herself. "Tsk Tsk, Pet. That was naughty. Are you not thankful that I called my new Pet off before she hurt you?"

"He is…trying to…hurt my Mistress, may I kill him please, Mistress?" Kazhmere asked, her eyes glazed over with Qatu bloodlust.

"Not this time Pet, in fact, I think you've done enough," Salynth replied, turning her magical focus on Kazhmere. Translucent butterflies shot from her gnarled and clawed fingertips and surrounded the Qatu Princess, who laughed happily and then sighed in contentment, watching and swatting at them. "And then a bit of amnesia, I think?" Salynth said, speaking ancient words while focusing her will on Kazhmere, who blinked a few times and then shook her head, looking around as though lost.

"What happened?" she asked as she backed away from Salynth. "What have you done to Ben to make him attack me like that?"

"Oh, it's Ben is it?" Salynth's voice oozed with jealousy. "That's awfully familiar. Well, perhaps I shouldn't have left you two alone up here."

"Don't be…ridiculous," Taeben said, his breathing still labored from the rough meeting of his ribcage and the floor when Kazhmere dropped him moments before. "I would like another turn, please?" He stood cautiously and then approached Salynth, kneeling before her and keeping his gaze on the floor to hide his contempt. "Please, Mistress, allow me another practice?"

"Just this once," she said, a fangy grin splitting her face, "since you asked so sweetly, my Pet." Taeben smiled up at her, but his smile did not reach his eyes. He rose and turned on Kazhmere, moving toward her quickly.

"Are you all right?" he asked her as he drew near, reaching out for her. She flinched away from him.

"What are you playing at, Ben?" she asked, her voice a whisper.

"Just play along and I will make sure she doesn't hurt you again, Kahzi," he whispered back. He reached for her again and this time she did not move away. "There, yes, just play along," he cooed at her, stroking the spotted fur on her arms and hands as he pulled her closer to him. As he stared into her eyes once again, he pushed his will into her mind, and found to his great surprise that she let him.

"I trust you not to hurt me, Ben," she murmured, and then blinked a few times. "Command me, Master?" she said, staring up at him. Her once inquisitive and bright teal eyes had gone dull and lifeless, and they stared up at him anxiously, awaiting his instruction. Taeben felt his stomach flip over but he took a deep breath and focused on the task at hand. *Weakness is death.*

"Kahzi, I know that you know my will already, do you not?" He pushed images of Salynth dead at his feet into her mind and she smiled wickedly, those dead eyes locked on his.

"Aye Master I do. Will you let me serve you?" she asked, purring behind her words. Taeben smiled. *One step closer.*

"Not yet, my Princess, not yet," he said, his voice oozing over her like syrup. Kazhmere pouted. "Sit," he commanded, and she immediately flopped down on the floor at his feet. He turned back to Salynth, whose eyes were glowing with an ethereal light.

"Yes, my Pet, that is how it is done," she purred. "You are a natural. You will be the first of your race to wield this magical power and you and I will rule Orana." She moved over to him and stroked the side of his face until a growl from Kazhmere stopped her. "Ah, it is loyal as well, you have outdone yourself," the sorceress said, her voice heavy with pride and admiration. "Enjoy your new pet, dearie. You will move on to more challenging game very soon." She snapped her clawed fingers and seemed to wink out of existence.

Taeben's shoulders sank in relief as he turned his attention back to Kazhmere. "Enjoy my new pet?" he mused aloud. "I think not. There are others more suited to my tastes." An image of an upturned wood elf face and sparkling ice blue eyes passed through his mind. "Much better suited indeed."

"May I find her for you, Master?" Kazhmere said, clearly growing impatient with nothing to do for him. Taeben turned his attention back to her, realizing that he did not possess the magic needed to release her from her enchantment. Cursing under his breath, he tried the simple mesmerization spells that Salynth had taught him but only managed one or two butterflies.

"Drat. Well, I'm sorry, *dearie*," he said, imitating Salynth's dragonkind accent on the common language as he said the word dearie, "but this may sting a bit." He focused his will and spoke words that called up magical lightning from the ground and sky, making them meet with Kazhmere at the dead center of their path. She wailed and collapsed, knocked unconscious by the force of the electricity in the bolts. "Next step," Taeben said as he turned his back on the smoking pile of fur that was Kazhmere, "is to learn the stronger mesmerization and amnesia spells. Then it will be on to you, my Mistress," he said, spitting the word as his words filled with anger, "and then I will be free." The image floated before his eyes again, complete with a memory that he sank into like a comfortable bed. "Okay, Ben it is then. I'm Ginolwenye but you can call me Gin," the memory-image said, a smile spreading across its translucent freckled face. Taeben could almost smell the sunflowers.

Sath had tried shaking off the after effects of passing through the enchanted doorways, but it seemed with every successive floor, the icy cold that clung to his fur got worse and worse. He could only imagine how bad it felt for the non-magic-using warriors. He rubbed his arms vigorously through his armor, but to no avail. Sath sniffed the air, searching for the telltale scent of another of his kind and soon found two distinctive scents. There was one, but it was not his own family… must be Anni. The next one caused tears to prick behind his eyes. *"Kahzi,"* he purred deep in his throat as he took another deep breath to get his bearings and looked into the giant room he had entered off the hallway.

He seemed to be on a platform in the middle of a body of water, but that was not possible inside a tower, was it? More enchantments. Sath moved forward cautiously, very aware that the invisibility magic Gin and Elysiam had cast on him was long gone. There was a walkway ahead of him and he followed it, careful not to slip off the sides into what seemed to be icy water. Soon, before him was a large empty room save a few drakes flying about at the ceiling and the largest creature he had ever seen in his life.

It was male, and appeared to be a full-grown dragon like

those he had heard tell of in the past when he was on the hunt. They were the creatures of legend on Qatu'anari, and young Qatu were taught to fear the flying reptiles. That fact alone should have been enough to set his blood boiling. Sath hated dragons for their terrorizing of his homeland. But this one gave him pause as it turned slowly and set its frozen gaze right on him.

"Sathlir Clawsharp of Qatu'anari?" the dragon asked. Sath didn't take his eyes off the creature and nodded his head. "Ah, excellent, my Lady Salynth will be well pleased. She's been waiting for you, your Highness."

"I'm no one's highness," Sath barked back. "I'm just Sathlir, plain and simple. Who are you?" He thought that if he could keep the dragon talking, he might just be able to slip past it and avoid a fight…though the thought of another dragon kill was very tempting, especially here.

"Oh, but you are, Prince! You are the next Rajah of Qatu'anari are you not?" The giant dragon chuckled. "I am Lord Kalinth," it said, its voice booming. "You'll forgive me if I don't bow, your Majesty, but I feel we are on equal footing."

"I am no Prince!" Sath bellowed back. "My father disowned me, you see, so I am no more Majesty than you are, my Lord Kalinth." He took a few tentative steps to the side, pleased when he saw that the dragon seemed to take no notice of him whatsoever.

"Shall I go tell my Lady that you are so close?" the dragon asked, shaking its head and snorting icy blasts of snow into the air. "She will be so happy! Our plan is coming together. The throne of Qatu'anari is within reach. The Prince and Princess are in place!" Before Sath could attack or even speak, Lord Kalinth winked out of existence.

"Ikara's TEETH!" Sath swore, racing back through the

room to the doorway and plunging through. He barely felt the icy grip of the magic this time, and hit the ground running. He could hear the cackling laughter of both of the dragons, and the sound chilled him to the bone. Sath skidded to a stop. Ahead of him was nothing but a series of rooms off one main corridor, and the stone walls and floor made it impossible to trace sounds. He took a deep breath to scent the air, and his heart tightened. Both Qatu females were there. The connection he had always had with his sister was strong now that they were back in close physical proximity, and a sudden searing pain that ricocheted through him told him she was in mortal danger. He had to make a decision, and fast.

Taeben sat on the cold floor, making notes in the tiny leather-bound book that Salynth had not taken from him when he was brought to the Tower. It was the only way that he had any idea of how much time had passed. The book and the robes he wore were the only things she had allowed him to keep. Taeben wrote in the journal every night, even the nights after lessons when it hurt him to even hold his head up, let alone to make notes with the quill. He made a practice of not re-reading the notes, even when he couldn't remember things that he knew he would have to know in order to keep from angering Salynth. Looking back too soon would be his undoing.

Kazhmere sat up suddenly from the heap she had been lying in ever since Taeben shocked her to release her from the mesmerization magic. "Sath," she whispered, feeling their connection rekindle. He must be close by! She focused on him, trying again to warn him but instead her soul screamed out to his to save her. Taeben's gaze leveled on her.

"Did you say something, Kazhmere?" he asked, his voice low and even. Kazhmere's skin began to crawl under her fur.

"No," she lied.

"I told you before that I don't like liars," Taeben said, rising and moving closer to her. Kazhmere tried to back up but did not have the strength. "You are up to something. You said the name "Sath", is that the Qatu male that my Mistress was so happy to see in the hallway?"

"I don't want to talk to you," Kazhmere responded, looking away from him toward the doorway. *Do not come up here, Sath!* Her thoughts were edged with panic that was so strong Taeben could feel it rolling off her in waves.

"He is special to you, is he not?" Taeben stared at her, trying again to push his will into her mind but failing as she pushed back against him. "A childhood friend? A lover, perhaps?"

Without warning Kazhmere lunged forward and shoved Taeben away from her. He fell over backward in surprise, scrambling to get to his feet. "Shut your mouth!" she roared at him.

"You will regret that," Taeben said as he swept back to her and positioned his face directly in front of hers. He spoke quick magical words that drew roots inexplicably from the stone floor to hold her fast, and then took her face in his hands, shoving his will forward and into her mind. Kazhmere's consciousness fought against him like a moth beating its wings against the sides of a glass, but he was rested now and easily forced her mind to still and acquiesce. She blinked a few times, and then looked up at him with those awful dead eyes.

"Master?"

"Who is Sath?" Taeben asked roughly.

"My brother," she answered, her voice innocent and childlike. Something in Taeben's mind screamed out for attention, another childlike and innocent voice from his past. Sathlir was the Qatu in Bellesea Keep with Gin. Gin…He shoved that memory away and focused on the Qatu female in front of him.

"You are the Princess Royal of Qatu'anari, yes?"

"Yes, Master."

Taeben licked his lips. "That makes your brother the Prince, next in line for the throne of Qatu'anari, does it not?" Kazhmere's face clouded over. "What?" He took a slightly calmer approach. "What troubles you, Pet?"

"He is not in line for the throne at all, Master," she said, tears forming in her large, sightless eyes. "My father disowned him. He told the kingdom that I was stillborn because I was female and therefore not worthy of the throne. There is no heir at this time unless he forced my mother to bear him another cub."

"The throne is ripe for the picking," Taeben murmured. "Thank you, Pet, you have been most informative," he said to Kazhmere, stroking her cheek and drawing a deep purr from her. "That is all I need from you. I command you to go to sleep." She nodded and curled up as best she could while still encumbered with the magical roots. Once he was sure that she was asleep, he moved back to the other side of the room, grinning from ear to ear. He had done it! He had gotten into her mind without resorting to the coddling, sugary-sweet methods to which his Mistress had been forced to use. That meant he was ahead of her in terms of skill. An evil grin spread across his face. "She is correct on one point, I clearly AM unique," he whispered, rubbing his hands together. "The power that I could possess is limitless. Not bad for one you thought would never amount to anything, is it my old Master?" Visions of the face of his old guild master in the mage's enclave in the high citadel swam before his vision and he narrowed his eyes as he made a plan to stop in for a visit once he was free of the tower.

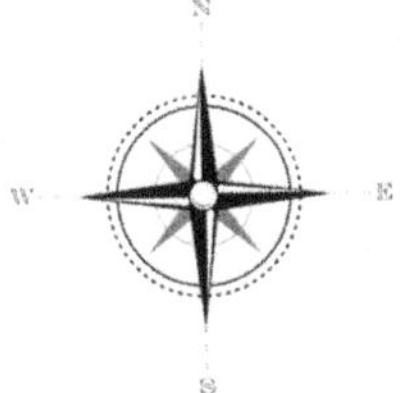


# Thirty-Two

"All right, listen. We've gotta play this smart, you understand?" Teeand said, looking at each of them in turn as they huddled up right next to the doorway they'd just come through. "She's a master enchanter. She can turn us against each other. She may already have Sath." Gin's breath caught in her throat. "I'm pretty sure that's why she's holding Kazhmere, to get to Sath." He stopped a moment, remembering his promise not to reveal Sath's identity. "We came here once before, Sath and I, with a team. We made it all the way to the top floor and met up with that crazy bird, Salynth. We weren't able to defeat her and she escaped as we were forcibly removed from the Tower."

"Forcibly removed?" Hackort asked, raising an eyebrow.

"Aye, Hack, as in thrown from a window on the top floor. Had it not been for the druid in our group and a well-placed spell that let us rise up like birds on the wing before we crashed into the icy ground below, we would have been finished. Rayhnee was her name, I think," Tee said, smiling sadly at the memory. "Don't know what happened to that little halfling."

"So you made her mad and she threw you out and now she wants revenge? That doesn't make a lot of sense, Tee," Gin said, scratching her head. "I mean, if you had beaten her or taken something from her I might understand. But how would she have even remembered who Sath is, let alone set up this elaborate plan to capture his sister? I mean who even knew that Sath had a sister?"

"I see what he means now," Teeand muttered. "You, lass, have been hanging around with that gnome too much, you're starting to sound like him."

"I was just thinking that," Elysiam said, smiling. The smile didn't go all the way to her eyes. "But all that aside, Gin has a point. There has to be another reason why Salynth wants Sath and unless we know what that is, I don't think we are going to be successful just charging in there."

"And you, Elys, have been influenced by our resident pacifist druid I think!" Teeand exclaimed, clearly amazed at the fact that she did not just advise that they charge on ahead, killing as they went. "I don't know what she wants with him, but clearly there is something there. When she found out who Kazhmere was, she saw her chance to get Sath here to rescue his sister."

"There's more," Gin said. "She has another prisoner, a wizard that I think I know. I remember him from when I was a child. I last saw him in Bellesea Keep, and helped to free him when I stayed…well, anyway, I have no idea how he ended up here." Elysiam turned on Gin, eyes warning her to leave that in the past. "You may remember him too, Elys, he was from Alynatalos. Name's Taeben."

"Of course I remember him." Elysiam snarled. "Prancing around, thinking he was better than us because he was from the high citadel." She spat onto the floor. "He was the one to rat me out for my warrior training, if I remember correctly? I was working under a paladin called Nelenie, remember her? I think she was the older sister of your friend Tairneanach?"

"Yes! I did know about that, Elys," Gin said, looking sad. "Nel…she was like an older sister to me as well. I don't know what happened to her."

"I do. She was banished," Elysiam said, frowning. "Her Paladin guild leader couldn't accept that she was training me because I was a wood elf. Banished her from the guild and then her family turned their backs on her. Last I heard she was living rough, working as a mercenary. She had amazing skills." Elysiam wiped a tear from her eyes. "Taeben was the cause of all of her pain. I think you just gave me renewed reason to fight, Gin."

"Great, that makes me feel so much better," Hackort said, rolling his eyes. "No, really, actually it does make me feel better because now I want to fight things." The gnome was practically vibrating. "Let's go!"

"We need a plan first," Teeand said, putting a hand on Hack's arm. The dwarf breathed a sigh of relief that they seemed to have forgotten about Sath's identity. "Now we have a dragonkind sorceress and her pet wizard to deal with on top of all the undead minions. Why don't we throw in a few sand giants and a wyvern or two and make it a fair fight?" He sighed and pulled on his beard as he did when he was deep in thought.

"I think we need to have one druid on each of you for healing magic," Elysiam said, "much as I hate to even think that because it means all I'm doing is healing."

"I disagree," Teeand said. "Hack and I can hold our own. We will need you two to be pouring as much magical unpleasantness onto them as you can. That's the only way we're going to get out of here alive and with Sath and his sister."

"What about that other Cat?" Elysiam said, her eyes narrowing. "How did you get away from her, Gin?" She turned on her sister druid and stared at her, head cocked to one side, but Gin stared right back.

"I don't know. She was taking me to trade me for Sath's sister but he…interrupted her. Then Salynth appeared and that's when I saw Taeben with her." She looked from face to face. "I don't think he is there of his own free will. He didn't look…right. He looked like he was in a daze."

"He was most likely charmed," Teeand said. "That's how she does it, how she keeps all these shades at her beck and call, and I imagine how she got Anni to come get Sath for her."

"I don't think Anni is working with Salynth," Gin said, frowning.

"But why else would she try to…" Elysiam started to ask, but Teeand held up a hand.

"It doesn't matter," he said. "Gin, I'm sorry, but I think we have to count that Anni is not on our side and I fear that Sath may be charmed against us too."

"I don't believe for a minute that he would hurt us," Gin said.

"Then you're a fool," Teeand said. They glared at each other for a long minute. "But fool or not, I've got your back, Flower." He grinned at her and she grinned back. "So we need a plan."

"How about this," Elysiam suggested, her tone positively effervescent. "You two take the lead. Bellow, scream, insult, whatever you need to do. Gin and I will call up our magic to nibble at their heels. Then, when they aren't paying attention, we run in and pull down a quake on her head. Easy peasy. Take Sath and Kazhmere and get out of this creepy Tower."

"It's not that easy, Elys," Teeand exclaimed, his face reddening. "You can't just run in against an sorceress."

"I say there's only one way to find out," Elysiam said as she darted away from the group and into the tunnel that Sath had run through only a short time before. The others followed her and soon all of them were in the cavernous room normally occupied by Lord Kalinth. "Holy…this is a huge room! The Tower's not this big on the outside, is it?" she whispered. "Looks clear."

Teeand swore under his breath and followed her into the large room with Hack and Gin right behind him. Gin scanned the room, her tracking abilities keen. "Sath's been here. Not long ago, either. We need to move on through here though, I sense something else lives here and I doubt that it's friendly."

"Clever druid!" Lord Kalinth's voice boomed through the cavernous area. "Why, I'm having all kinds of visitors tonight! What fun!" The dragon circled the ceiling, barely able to spread his wings, and then came to rest in back of them, blocking their exit.

"What's your name?" Gin asked, motioning for the others to keep moving toward the doorway.

"Oh, no, I'm not falling for that again," Lord Kalinth said, chuckling. "The Prince tried that one before, tried to distract me with names, but I didn't fall for it then and I won't now."

Teeand's face tightened at the mention of 'The Prince.' He turned to Gin and whispered, "Keep him occupied." Using hand signals, he directed the other two to take the opposite corners, and then he went to a corner directly across from Hackort. Gin waited until she got a nod from Tee and then walked out in front of the giant dragon who peered down at her, icy blasts shooting from its nostrils.

"My name is Gin," she said as loudly as she could. "Will you let my friends and me pass? We have business with the Lady Salynth." She heard a gasp and looked over at Elysiam who was staring at her as though she had three heads.

"You know my Lady, do you?" Lord Kalinth asked as he lowered his head to peer more closely at Gin.

"Aye," Gin said, hoping against hope that her knees did not buckle in fear. Thanks to Sath's hatred of them, they had fought dragons and dragonkind plenty of times, but Gin had never been this close to one of this size and considerable age before. "Now, will you let us pass?"

"I am afraid I cannot, little one," the dragon rumbled, chuckling. "You see I know who it is that my Mistress has business with today and it is not you. For your bravery, however, I will give you a head start to leave the Tower I have made for her before I have to dispatch you myself." Lord Kalinth moved his massive head down very close to Gin and looked her in the eye. She shuddered at the large icy eyes that stared into hers. "Do not make me regret my generosity, Ginolwenye of the Forest," he whispered. Icy shivers rolled down Gin's spine. "Now, GO!"

"Yes, GO!" Gin shouted as her companions slipped back through the doorway as she headed for it, running as fast as she could. Lord Kalinth chased her over to the door, wings flapping madly and laughing heartily. Gin ran up to the doorway and jumped into the air, thinking she would pass through it, but she only bounced off the closed door.

"Oh dear, did I forget to tell you that the magic in these doorways only goes one way if you are new to my Tower? How else would I keep my Lady safe here?" the enormous dragon giggled. "Now what shall we do, my little druid?"

Gin sat on the ground in front of the door with the mammoth dragon hovering just above her head. She closed her eyes, thinking the end was near for her and was thankful that the others had gotten through the doorway to save Sath and his sister. "Just make it quick," she whispered, thinking that every moment Lord Kalinth was occupied with her was one more moment that the others could gain ground above.

"Now that is no fun at all," the dragon grumbled. To Gin's amazement, he drifted backward a few paces from where she had landed. "I hope the others in your group are more…HEY!" He turned his back to her, scanning the room for the others. "WHERE ARE THEY?"

"Heading off to destroy your Mistress, I would imagine!" Gin shouted as she scrambled to her feet. She dashed between the legs of the dragon and then turned back to make another attempt at passing through the doorway.

"Oh, no no no, you will not…You cannot evade me, Gin!" the dragon roared. Gin found herself flying through the air backward toward the dragon and she screamed in frustration just before she hit the floor at his feet. Using adrenaline she didn't know she had, she hopped to her feet and cast a spell that would cause roots to grow around the dragon's tree trunk sized legs, slowing him down as he pounded toward her. He paused to complain and tug at the roots, giving her time to turn back to him and hurtle a spell full of stinging insects to keep him further distracted. He batted the swarm away with one clawed hand, pulled his feet free, and thundered after her.

Gin reached the doorway and tried again to run through it but remembered that she didn't have the magic key just before she slammed into the wooden door and was thrown backward. "I cannot catch a break!" she hissed in frustration, then fell silent as one of the dragon's giant clawed feet stopped inches from her.

"Naughty, naughty druid," Lord Kalinth rumbled. "How shall I present you to my Lady? Dead is no fun." He squatted down to peer at her, effectively blocking all of her chances to run past him. "Inside out? I haven't seen a wood elf inside out in a long time. Should I start from the bottom or the top?" Gin scooted back until her backside hit the cold wall next to the door as she stared at him in horror. "Maybe tied in a bow? No, her little arms and legs are too short for a proper bow. Hmmm...."

"Seriously?" Anni's voice came from the other side of the doorway. "You could have killed her several times by now." A furry arm moved through the wooden door as though it was water and hooked around Gin's head, pulling her backward and into the doorway. Gin grabbed Anni's elbow to keep from being strangled and to make sure that she was not dropped in the middle. She could hear Lord Kalinth screaming and pounding on the other side of the door.

"What did you do that for?" Gin wheezed as Anni released her on the other side of the doorway. "You going to...try to trade me again?"

"No." Emerald eyes shone out of grayish fur as Anni stared down at the druid. "Sathlir needs your help...I need your help to help him."

"What has happened? Where are the others?" Gin said, her heart jumping up into her throat.

"They are on their way to engage Salynth and her pet wizard," Anni said, scowling. "The wizard is the deal breaker. Your friends will not be able to manage Salynth and the wizard together," she said. "But he knows you; I heard that he recognized you."

"Aye," Gin said sadly. "I knew him when we were children and…yes, I know him."

"Then you must use that to your advantage," Anni whispered to her. "He will hesitate to hurt you if he knows you, and that's when the others will strike."

"But he is a prisoner too, just like Sath's sister, is he not?" Gin asked. "Why must we strike him? Can we not rescue him as well?"

"Eyes on the target, druid. That wizard is collateral damage," Anni hissed. Gin frowned at her. "Our goal is to rescue Sathlir and Kahzi. I would have thought that you of all people would put Sathlir's wellbeing first?

Gin cocked her head to one side. "What do you mean by that, Anni?"

"Gin, only a fool would not see how you feel about him. We all love Sathlir and must work to make sure he is safe, yes?" Anni said, her emerald gaze holding Gin fast.

"We…we do all love Sath, yes," the druid said quietly. "What is your plan, Anni?"

"Simple," Anni replied. "Sathlir has charged on ahead to engage Lady Salynth. Your friends are on their way to…help." She choked out the last word, almost unable to keep back her disgust for them. "We need to hang back a bit and let them become embroiled in the melee before we offer help. That way we can use the element of surprise to our advantage and hopefully they will have taken care of all of her minions so we can concentrate on ending her." Anni's gaze remained fixed on Gin's face as she began drumming her fingers almost imperceptibly on the skin of the drum she wore on her belt. *"Do you understand me, Ginolwenye?"* she purred in Qatunari as the drum's rhythm began to drill into the druid's awareness. The beat began to synchronize with Gin's heartbeat, and Anni smiled as Gin blinked, and then turned her face up to look at Anni, her eyes blank and staring.

"Yes, I understand Mistress," she said. "How many I serve you?"

"Follow me," Anni said. She crept away from the door leading to the enchanted cavern and toward the hall, where a loud melee was erupting. Gin followed her closely, grabbing onto the large feline's tail periodically. "Cut that out," Anni hissed.

"Apologies, Mistress, it is a habit developed while running with Sathlir. He often has me hanging onto his tail so that I do not become lost," Gin said, her eyes wide and void of the emotion usually there when she spoke of Sath. Anni spat.

"Well stop it," Anni said, increasing the frequency of the drumbeat. Gin's eyes shut for a moment and then opened again, nothing but a void present in their depths as she released Anni's tail. "Much better." She sprinted down the hall again with Gin following closely but not touching Anni's tail until she reached the spot where the fighting had broken out. "And you will never do that to…oh, dear spirits, never mind!"

Teeand and Hackort were up to their eyes in shades and ghosts when Gin and Anni arrived. Elysiam was off to the side with fire shooting from her fingertips. With every blast, the flames grew weaker and Elysiam grew angrier. "Stop the torching and shoot us some healing magic, would you please?" Teeand shouted over his shoulder. Elysiam scowled at him but did as he asked. He and Hackort felt the wave of magic sweep over them and immediately increased their attack rate and accuracy. "Thanks Elys…Elys?" He had glanced back over his shoulder and she was nowhere nearby. Hackort spun around then and let out an anguished cry followed by a bellow of pure rage. He ran toward the shade that stood on Elysiam's body, now prone on the floor, passed out cold. With a shriek that woke the rest of the dead in the room, Hackort cut the ghost's head from its transparent shoulders. He grabbed Elysiam by one of her arms and dragged her to the side before jumping back in to dispatch more of the minions.

"Gin! Thank goodness!" Teeand shouted as he removed yet another ghostly head. The room fell silent, as he had just dispatched the last of that wave of undead. He turned to face her, and stopped in his tracks when he saw her eyes. "Gin? Flower? What has…?" Anni appeared next to Gin, stepping out from behind the cloak of invisibility that her magical music was providing. Teeand's eyes narrowed. "What have you done to our Gin?"

"Oh, stop it," Anni said, her voice only wavering a bit as she struggled to keep her fear in check. "I've got her a bit sedated to keep her from running after Sath like she is prone to do and making things worse than they already are." She bit her lip hoping that Teeand would accept her answer.

"Aye, she is known for that," he said, pulling at his beard as he did when he felt conflicted. He leveled his gaze at Anni. "And as we sit here talking, he gets further away from us and closer to harm's way while these minions are reborn undead. Shall we go?"

"Yes!" Hackort jumped to his feet.

"Hold on a minute," Elysiam said, grabbing Hackort's foot as she pulled herself up to a sitting position.

"Oh, no," Hackort sighed as he sat back down.

"I won't fight alongside her," Elysiam said, pointing at Anni. "Wizard or no, I will not do it."

"Don't be ridiculous," Anni said. "I don't care whose side you're on once we are finished here, but without me there is no hope that you will defeat Salynth."

"Awfully sure of yourself, aren't you?" Elysiam got to her feet slowly, leaning on Hack as she did. He looked up at her and smiled, and she winked back at him.

"I should have eaten you when I had the chance," Anni said. She stormed toward Elysiam, ceasing her drumming. Gin blinked and then looked around. Just in time, she jumped in between the Qatu and her sister-druid.

"Enough!" Gin hissed. "We have a mission and we are going to finish it! We will bring Sath and Kahzi home and then I am done with the lot of this fighting!" She stomped her foot in frustration as all of them stared at her. "NOW then, Sath is down this hall. We do not know where Kahzi is or if Taeben is with his Mistress. Tee, how do we proceed?"

"Why does Tee always get to make the decisions?" Hackort whined, hushing immediately as Gin shot him a silencing look. "Sorry, Ginny."

"We don't have a plan, Flower," Teeand said sadly. "All I know to do is keep going as we have been until we find Sath. We need to move on down the corridor though, before these shades gather their energy and return for round two."

The rest of them nodded and picked up their weapons and bags. They did not make it more than a few feet before Sath came into view, further down the corridor, fighting in one of the doorways. Gin wanted to run to him but remembered Anni's words and hung back, sending him healing magic instead.

Sath felt the wave of light and health wash over him, recognizing it immediately as Gin's. He pushed forward, removing heads from transparent shoulders and not looking back. He knew that the others would join him soon, and a wave of buoyant joy filled his fighting arm. He swung faster, his blows more lethal, as he pressed through the crowd of shades surrounding him. Again, he felt the light touch of Gin's healing magic but this time the shades noticed it too and changed their course.

"Fall back, Gin!" Teeand cried out as the horde descended on them. He and Hack jumped in front of the teeming undead mass, trying to draw their ire away from Gin as she moved to a new corner of the hallway. The diversion worked, and soon the ghostly figures converged on Hackort and Teeand, before dissipating one after another in gruesome fashion. Elysiam was even able to get in a few shots at the enemy, though she was still weak from her earlier hit.

"Sathlir, how nice of you to stick around," Salynth said as she and Taeben appeared in the room Sath had been working to enter.

"Wouldn't miss it, hag," Sath spit back. "Where is my sister?"

"Manners! Gracious! *That is no way for a Prince to speak, now is it?"* she said, switching to Qatunari halfway through her sentence. Sath's attention riveted to her as she spoke. *"Yes, yes, your precious secret, don't you worry, Your Highness, your secret is safe with me."*

"WHERE IS MY SISTER?" Sath bellowed as he ran at the dragonkind sorceress. She held up her hand and he bounced off an invisible wall that formed around her and Taeben.

"Now, Pet. Take him, take his mind," Salynth barked at

Taeben as she gave the chain around his neck a yank. "NOW."

Taeben stumbled forward and lunged for Sath, pushing his will out as he searched for Sath's mind. Sath turned to look at him, blinking.

"Nice try, wizard," Sath snarled. "Defense against magic already deployed." A bolt of icy lightning rocketed down from the ceiling and pinned Taeben to the floor, shivering in pain.

"Oh, naughty cat," Salynth whispered, a sadistic smile oozing across her face. "He is still learning, my poor Pet. You are not as easy as your sister was, clearly." At the mention of Kazhmere, Sath leaped into the air, heading for Salynth, claws outstretched. The sorceress answered with her own hands outstretched as ancient symbols flew from her fingertips and surrounded Sath. The Qatu roared and fell to his knees as pain assailed him from every angle. *"Now, let's see, how can you make it up to me, Your Highness?"* Salynth purred. Sath's eyes widened as his body moved without his consent, standing and moving in between Salynth and the doorway. "Call your friends, Cat, let's have everyone in on our party shall we?" Sath shook his head.

"You can make me stand, hag, but you can't control my mind," he spat at her. "Call them yourself."

"Fine," Salynth said, leveling her gaze at him. She spoke ancient words and Sath watched in horror from the prison of his own immobile body as her skin split and bubbled and fur sprouted all over her body. It was as though he was looking in a mirror. "Down here!" she called out in his voice. Sath tried to yell but found that he had no voice. She turned back to him; and then shook herself and the illusion fell away as though she had stepped through a waterfall.

"On our way, Sath!" Sath heard Teeand's call back from the hallway. Sath seethed inwardly, trying to force his body to move with no luck. He roared with frustration.

Out in the hallway, Teeand turned to face the others. "Hack and Gin, you two are with me. Anni and Elys, you find Kazhmere and free her." Elysiam started to protest but a look from Teeand stopped her. "I need Gin on heals, Elys," he said, placing a hand on her cheek. "You're not 100% yet and I need that 100%, you know I do. You go with the cat here and make sure all is on the up and up, yeah?" Elysiam scowled as she nodded.

"I will do no such thing," said Anni. "I will help my…Sathlir."

"Over my dead body," Gin said under her breath.

"Just go, Anni," Teeand said, switching over to Qatunari, *"or I'll tell what you know about our Sathlir, got it? How happy do you think that would make him?"*

"More Qatunari, Tee?" Elysiam said, glaring over her shoulder at the dwarf who just winked at her. Anni was staring at him as though she wanted to gut him, but she recovered herself and stalked off toward the rooms down past the room where Sath was, Elysiam hot on her heels.

"Now then, let's go help our boy Sath," Hackort said, grinning up at Teeand. "Or maybe you just want me to go in on my own?"

"Don't make me get your leash, Hack," Gin said, smiling bravely at the gnome. Her heart was sinking as she followed the two warriors toward the room. They turned the corner and entered the room slowly. At the far corner was Salynth, holding onto a heavy chain attached at one end to a thick metal collar around Taeben's neck. Tearing her gaze away from that sight, Gin scanned the walls for other opponents but found none of the shades there. Only the horrific tableau that was in front of them:

Sath in front of them in a defensive stance, his eyes as wide as saucers.

"You seem to be missing a druid," Salynth said, chuckling. "How careless of you." Tee took a step toward her but she held up a hand. "Now, now, dwarf, steady, let's not be hasty. I'd hate to have to sic my new pet on you." She drifted forward a foot and put a hand on the side of Sath's face. His disgust was evident on his face but Sath couldn't make a move if he tried. Gin gasped loudly, gaining the sorceress's attention. "Ah, it's the wood elf again, come to save your Cat have you?"

Taeben's eyes widened. "Ginny," he whispered, garnering a sharp tug on his collar from his Mistress.

"Maybe she's come for you, my Pet?" Salynth said. "Perhaps she wants to leave the cat for me?" Sath managed a strangled roar, catching her attention. "Oh, no, bad kitty," she said, again stroking the side of his face.

"Take your hands off him!" Gin cried out.

"Rude, that was. I do not like rude. Kill her," Salynth said, clasping her hands in front of her gleefully as Sath started walking toward Gin with slow, agonized steps. "Well? Get on with it!" Taeben let out a strangled cry but was silenced by an overzealous jerk on the chain held by the dragonkind sorceress.

"Gin…get…out of…here," Sath said, each word a monumental effort. "I'm…serious…TEE, get Gin OUT OF HERE!"

"I won't leave you here!" Gin cried out in response. Teeand tried to grab her as she bolted past him toward Sath who had raised his clawed weapon as he advanced on her. "You won't hurt me, I trust…" Her voice cut off as Sath backhanded her, sending her flying across the room and into one of the bookshelves with a sickening crack. An avalanche of ancient tomes rained down on her as she lay in a heap. Sath's voice thundered in anguish as Salynth, like a puppeteer, guided his body back to stand in front of her, guarding her from Hackort and Teeand.

"Well, that was fun! Who's next, then?" the sorceress cackled. "Who's next?"

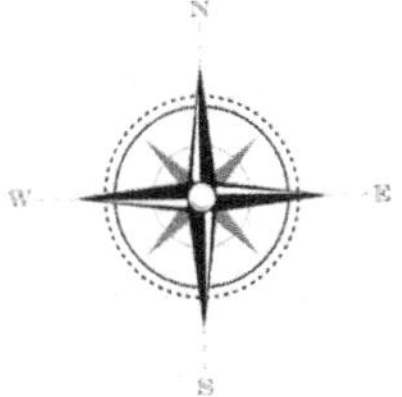


# THIRTY-THREE

"Do you know where she is being held?" Elysiam barked at Anni as they ran down the corridor. "Or are you leading me to my death?"

"I can smell my own kind," Anni hissed back. "I'm surprised you don't know already, I thought you elves were supposed to be masters at tracking your prey."

"I'd happily show you the skills I've mastered, but it wouldn't help us find Sath's sister for me to singe that already charcoal-colored fur of yours," Elysiam retorted. "Wait!" A mewling cry had caught her attention from one of the rooms. "I think she's here!"

Anni spun around and charged through the door at which Elysiam was pointing. Inside the dimly lit room was a heap of rags under a tiny slit of a window. "She's not here," Anni said, turning back to face the door.

"Anni?"

Anni froze. "Kahzi?" she said, turning back around slowly. A teal pair of eyes stared out at her from the heap of fur and rags. "Dear spirits, Kahzi!" Anni exclaimed, running to Kazhmere's side. "Kahzi?"

*"You...brought...Sathlir here,"* Kazhmere said, her eyes saucer-like.

"Are you hurt? We need to get you out of here, can you stand?" Anni put an arm around Kazhmere to help her up, but the Princess hissed and struck out at Anni. Kazhmere stood on her own and then flattened herself against the wall.

*"You risked the entire future of Qatu'anari, you stupid, stupid fool!"* Kazhmere shouted at Anni, who was cowering in front of her.

"What are you two saying?" Elysiam demanded. "Stop that growly rumbly talking! I'm trying to help you here, but I can't if I don't know what you are saying.."

*"Kahzi, let us help you out of here and I will do whatever I can to make this right, you know I will!"* Anni whined. Kazhmere stood stock-still against the wall, a feral look in her eyes. *"Let us get you out of here."*

*"I know that you THINK that you were doing the right thing, my friend,"* Kazhmere said, spitting the words more than saying them. *"In my darker moments I admit that I wanted*

*nothing more than my brother to rescue me. Even so, I had to think of the grander picture, of our home and our people, and by bringing Sathlir here to die alongside me you have ruined us all. If she takes Qatu'anari it will all be over, you foolish, foolish female!"* Kazhmere roared in frustration as Anni hissed and backed away from her.

"Okay, listen, before this turns into a right bag of wet cats, how are we going to get out of here? Does my transport magic even work in here?" Elysiam said. Both the Qatu females looked at her as though she was a genius. "What?"

"It does, tiny elf," Kazhmere said in the common tongue, beaming a fangy grin at Elysiam who glared back at her. "You do your race credit! Taeben transported the Mistress all over the Tower."

*"The Mistress?"* Anni regarded Kazhmere with suspicion. *"She hasn't…I mean, she didn't…"*

*"No, of course not,"* Kazhmere said. *"Taeben is her pet, not me."* She looked away, her eyes meeting Elysiam's for a moment. "Where is my brother?" she asked, slowly and carefully in the common tongue.

"He is with Salynth," Anni said. "They sent us to rescue you."

"WHAT?" Kazhmere staggered away from the wall. *"That is suicide!"* She tried to get to the door but stumbled and fell. Anni rushed to her side to help her off but Kazhmere shook her off. *"Don't touch me."*

Elysiam put an arm out to Kazhmere. "Even I

understood that! You really are Sath's sister, aren't you? Just as stubborn. Now stand up before you get singed fur to match your brother's as well!" Kazhmere fought back a smile, but failed. She took Elysiam's offered hand and stood, as Elysiam channeled the energy of Orana herself through her hands and into Kazhmere, healing and strengthening her.

"I could have done that," Anni muttered.

"You could have done a lot of things but thankfully we were here to stop you," Elysiam snapped. "Now then, Kazhmere, my name is Elys, not Tiny Elf, if you don't mind?" Kazhmere beamed a fangy grin at the druid. "Wow, thank the dear spirits I've been running with Sath all these months or that grin would have me beating a retreat!" she said, laughing along with Kazhmere. Anni glowered and moved to the corner, resuming her drumbeat.

"You can knock that RIGHT off, Annilanshi," Kazhmere said. "None of us need a nap at the moment, thank you very much." She smiled sadly at her old friend and Anni smiled back at her, although reluctantly. "Now then, what is the plan to help my brother and free that poor elf from Salynth?"

"Poor elf?" Elysiam scoffed. "He's no poor elf; he's a monster in training, Kazhmere."

"Call me Kahzi, please," Kazhmere said, her countenance clouding with concern. "Why do you say that, um, Eh..lees?" Elysiam looked at Kazhmere, clearly amazed.

"That's good! It took Sath a long time even to speak

to me, let alone call me by my full name and you've pronounced my nickname almost right on the first try," Elysiam said. "I don't think this one," she said, indicating a scowling Anni, "has even tried. She thought I was food at first."

"You will have to forgive us, Elys," Kazhmere replied. "We are not taught much about the other races; the only ones native to our home, the island of Qatu'anari, are the Qatu. We are not accustomed to being *companions*…uh…friends with any other than our own." She smiled at Elysiam, happy that she had found the correct word.

"Makes sense. But trust me on this one: Taeben is not worth saving. He has ruined many lives in his short time walking Orana and there are many that would see him remain here forever, myself included. As for your brother, he has turned out to be an ally after all. You see, there was the problem of Sath being the Bane of the Forest before he met Gin but she straightened him out," Elysiam said. Anni's ears pricked. "There are not many of my kind that trust your kind, thanks to your brother's shenanigans." Kazhmere looked puzzled for a moment until Anni translated the word shenanigans into Qatunari. Kazhmere's face fell.

"What did he do, exactly? I have not seen nor heard from my brother since our father…well, since Sathlir left Qatu'anari so many seasons ago," Kazhmere said, sadness creeping into the corners of her eyes.

"Do you know the word Bane?" Elysiam asked, fury

dancing around the edge of her words. Kazhmere again looked at Anni who shrugged her shoulders. "Bane means…someone you fear or hate above all others, I suppose." Kazhmere nodded, her eyebrows furrowed. "With Sath it was definitely more fear than hate. He hid in our forest home, hunted us, and caused the deaths of many of my kind." The color slowly drained from the druid's face as she spoke. "I can remember being a young one and having a curfew…and hearing bedtime stories about how the Bane of the Forest would eat little druids and rangers if we were out of our beds at night. As far as I know, Sath didn't **eat** any of the druids or rangers that were unlucky enough to cross his path, but he certainly did kill them for their money and food." She looked away a moment to regain her composure. "I'm sure it was because he was living rough at the time and had to do something to survive." A faraway look came over Elysiam, and her voice sounded wistful and sad. "I can certainly understand that."

"But you say that this Gin straightened him out?" Kazhmere asked, trying to move away from the image of her brother as a bloodthirsty killer. "What is a Gin, if I may ask? How did she…straighten out…my brother?"

Elysiam laughed. "She is a wood elf and a druid, like me. She is probably the only one of our kind that has no fear of Sath. Never has, as far as I know." Her face darkened a moment. "Well, doesn't now anyway. I have heard the story of how they met, and I am sure that she was terrified of him once she learned who he was."

"Terrified of my brother? Impossible," Kazhmere said, shaking her head vehemently. "I will have to discuss with both her and Sathlir this Bahn of…"

"Bane," Elysiam corrected her, grinning.

Kazhmere smiled. "Yes, Bane of… of the wood elves. Now, I am feeling much better. Can we please go help my brother the bane and save Taeben from that awful dragonkind sorceress?" Elysiam's eyes narrowed. "Whatever he has done to you and your kind, Elys, he has more than made up for here. Salynth's treatment of him has been worse than if he had been a dog at her feet. He and I have shared this cell on occasion as of late, and the condition in which she leaves him…well, it is shameful to say the least. But throughout it he has kept his dignity, something I only wish I could say for myself." The Princess's eyes darkened. "I would take it as a personal favor if you and your friends would help rescue him from Salynth. What he does after that is on his own head."

"We'll be lucky if Gin will let us leave him behind," Elysiam said, scowling. "Seems she knew him when they were children and she has a heart as big as all of Orana. She can forgive anyone anything. That must be why she's so in love with…" The druid stopped short, pursing her lips together. "That's why she is such a good member of our team; she's devoted to all of us like we're family."

Kazhmere looked over at Anni who was growling softly in the corner, and leaned in closer to Elysiam. "When this is all over you will tell me more of this elf that so adores my brother. Sathlir needs a good female to keep him straight." She winked conspiratorially at Elysiam, who grinned back, ignoring the increasing volume of Anni's complaints from the corner.

"I have had just about enough of this," Teeand snarled as he advanced on Salynth. "I'm not afraid to hurt Sath; he knows why I am doing what I'm doing."

*"Oh, you do not pick your friends well, Rajah,"* Salynth hissed at Sath, a fangy grin spread wide across her face.

*"And your Qatunari is almost as bad as Gin's,"* Tee said. The sorceress spun to face the dwarf as Hackort snuck up behind her and Sath. Sath's eyes darted down to Hackort, who placed a tiny finger over his lips and winked at Sath. Unfortunately, Taeben saw the gnome as well and stood up to defend his mistress. Hackort focused his will into his weapon and charged at the wizard, bonking him soundly on the head. He jumped back before the wizard's unconscious body pinned him to the floor and then kept on his path toward Salynth.

"A dwarf that speaks Qatunari!" Salynth clapped her hands with glee again. "What's next? A wood elf that speaks dwarfish?" She pointed a clawed finger toward Gin's lifeless body. "Oh, no, not that one I suppose, she's a bit…indisposed…" She dissolved into cackles as Teeand advanced on her. Ancient symbols shot from her fingertips and surrounded Teeand as he froze in his tracks, howling in pain.

"That's it! I don't like you!" Hackort shouted as he threw his axe and embedded it in Salynth's leg. She roared in pain as she pulled the axe from her thigh. She looked up in time to see the tiny warrior advancing on her. He leaped into the air and swung at her head with his sword. She batted him away but he shook it off and was back on his feet and after her in no time.

"You will pay for that, tiny man!" she shrieked. "Sathlir! Save me from this pest!"

"Ikara's TEETH!" Sath roared as his body turned and advanced on Hack, clawed weapons raised. "Don't make me do it, Wee Man! Go help Gin! I can't stop myself!"

"I don't want to hurt you, Sath, but I will," Hackort said, standing his ground. Salynth limped away from him. She could do a great many things with magic, but heal herself was not one of them. Her dragon heritage brought accelerated healing abilities with it, but Hackort's well-placed strike left a chance she would still bleed out before she healed.

"That's it, Hack!" Teeand struggled to get to his feet after the spell forced him to his knees. "Attack Sath. Just trust me and do it."

"Do it, Hack!" Sath shouted through gritted teeth.

"I don't know, Tee, if Ginny wakes up and sees me hurting Sath…"

"Fine. I'll do it," Teeand said. He ran over to Sath and, looking up at Sath silently and begging his old friend to forgive him, sunk his poleaxe into the unprotected space between Sath's greaves on his left leg. Sath howled in pain and just as Teeand had hoped, the Qatu's magical pet tiger appeared and charged at Teeand.

"Kill them!" Salynth bellowed at Sath once she found Taeben to be out of commission. The supernatural tiger shifted its gaze to the sorceress and lunged for her, pinning her to the ground and effectively dissolving the hold of the charm spell she had cast on Sath. He fell forward onto his now bleeding leg but soon recovered and lunged for Salynth.

"You're mine," he roared as his pet winked out of existence. Seeing her chance, she hurled defensive magic at him as she crawled backward but still he came after her, his clawed weapon glinting in the candlelight that provided the only illumination in the room. In one fluid motion, he grabbed the sorceress by her throat and pulled her close to his face. "Where…Is…My…Sister?" he snarled at her. Her face split into a grin.

"She's here…somewhere," Salynth said. "Now, if you will excuse me and my Pet…" She snapped her fingers and Taeben was on his feet. "We are due elsewhere. Pet?" Taeben spoke some words in Elder Elvish that Sath didn't understand and a ring of fire formed around him. Salynth looked Sath in the eye and blew him a kiss before disappearing out of his fingers.

"NO!" Sath bellowed, driving his now-empty fist into the floor. "NOT AGAIN!" The smoke cleared from the fire ring and Sath felt another pair of eyes on him. He spun back around to see Taeben standing there with his hands in the air.

"Before you say anything, I know where your sister is," Taeben said. Sath growled loudly and Taeben took a wobbly step backward. "I could have left with her and left you to find her on your own, but I didn't and that has to be worth something right?"

"Where is Kahzi?" Sath asked through clenched teeth. He balled up his fist and cracked his knuckles loudly.

"I'll take you to her," Taeben said, silently thanking whatever deity might be listening for the wisdom to know when to throw himself on Sathlir's mercy. Perhaps this way he could get into the cat's good graces and be able to leave with him and Ginny…she had stirred something in Taeben that would not let him go, and he needed to find her again to find out what it was. He glanced over as the dwarf headed for Gin's unconscious form, and shuddered.

"Go, Sath, I'll look after Gin," Teeand called out over his shoulder. He was already removing books from Gin's head and gently picking her up like one of his own children. Sath nodded and turned to the wizard.

"Lead on. Any false moves and I will end you, wizard, understand?" he hissed.

"Of course," Taeben said.

"So I don't get to kill ANYONE?" Hackort pouted. "Worst day EVER."

"Can you walk, Kahzi?" Anni asked, moving close to her friend. Kazhmere considered her for a moment, realizing that she could not remain angry. Anni had done what she thought was best, and Sath was the best fighter among the males she knew from home. Sath. Kazhmere's eyes lit up suddenly. He was very close; she could feel their bond growing stronger.

"Sath is here," she murmured, stumbling away from them toward the door of the room where she and Taeben were kept. "He's close!" She broke into an ungainly lope toward the open door and ran face first into Taeben as he rounded the corner, Sath hot on his heels. Both of them lost their balance and Taeben instinctively threw his arms around Kazhmere to keep her from hitting the stone floor. She landed on him with a grunt, and then quickly freed herself from his arms and rolled off him. "Tae…Ben!" she exclaimed. "Are you hurt?" She scanned his face, smoothing his red and silver hair off his forehead gently, avoiding accidentally scratching him with one of her claws.

*"He does not matter,"* Sath spat as he flew to his sister's side and pulled her up from the floor. *"Kahzi, my sister, my heart,"* he murmured in their native language as he held her to him. Kazhmere forgot the elf at her feet for a moment and clung to her brother, tears finally flowing down her furry face. *"Are you all right? Has that witch hurt you? I'll kill her myself if she's harmed one hair on your…"*

*"Ssh, Sath,"* Kazhmere said. *"I'm okay, none the worse for wear."*

*"Where is your tiger?"* Sath said, looking around the room. "Oops, sorry about the Qatunari, Elys." She was glaring at him.

"Salynth took him soon after I got here. She charmed him to defend her against me, but I would not take up arms against him. She dismissed him and I have not called him back since, for both of our safety," Kazhmere said. "Sath, she will not rest long before she comes back. If we are to leave this tower…we need to leave now. There is a druid here; she can use her transportation magic to get us to safety, yes?" She looked at Elysiam. "If you have your strength back, that is?"

"I could port us out of here," Taeben offered, and suddenly Kazhmere remembered that he was on the floor at her feet.

"OH! Ben, dear, are you all right?" she asked, squatting down to study him. She reached for his face again but he flinched away from her. "What's wrong? Are you hurt?"

"No," he said, overwhelmed with the notion that she did not remember what he had done to her…or if she did, she had forgiven him. "Kahzi, do you…I mean, while we were here together, I…" He stopped with a pointed look from Sath. "I hope that you are indeed unscathed from your time here in the Tower. I would like to be of service, if you will allow it." He got to his feet and took several steps back as Sath glared at him, growling.

"Your help would be appreciated, Taeben," Kazhmere said, rolling her eyes at Sath. "Ignore him, sometimes he is the protective older brother a bit too much." Taeben smiled at her, but it was not a convincing smile. "Anni? Be sure to get close or the magic will not reach you and you will be left behind."

"Wait, what about Hackort and Teeand and GIN,

Sath?" Elysiam asked, looking pointedly at the Qatu male. "I suppose she will port them out? Are they all right? Why are they not with you?"

"Tee stayed behind to…make sure that the way was still clear and everyone was all right. I am not sure she can port them, though." Sath frowned, visions of his own hands sending the tiny druid flying into the bookshelves. "Elys, if you can port us out, the wizard can stay and bring Tee and Hack and Gin." Kazhmere started to say something but a look from her brother silenced her. "No arguments. *Annilanshi*, come over here by me or I will leave you." She looked up at him, and then moved close to him, her eyes on the floor. Sath put the tip of one of his claws under her chin and raised her face to look at him. *"You and I will settle things when we are away from here."*

*"Yes, Your Highness,"* she responded, her emerald eyes shining with tears. Sath scoffed and removed his hand, leaving Anni to look back at the stone floor as Elysiam began reciting the spell that would magically transport them to the Outpost and safety. As the spell cast, Anni's face split into a wide grin. *"As you wish, Sathlir,"* she murmured.

Gin's eyes fluttered and Teeand's breath caught in his throat. "Thanks be," he whispered. "Gin, Flower, can you hear me?"

"Of course I can, Tee…you're about an inch from my ear," the druid said, her voice raspy. "What happened?" In an instant, her last memories flooded back. "Sath! Where is Sath?"

"Ginny's awake!" Hackort shouted with glee as he ran over to where Teeand was still cradling Gin in his arms. "Good! Now we can go find Sath's sister and lose the wizard. I don't trust him and I want to take him off my list, right now."

"Taeben is a prisoner just like Sath's sister is, Hack," Gin whispered. "He didn't want to help Salynth, she forced him."

"He hurt Elys," Hackort said darkly. "I think he's off my list."

"Come on, let's get you on your feet. Can you stand? I'd not like us to be in here if that hag returns," Teeand said as he gently put Gin on her feet. She wobbled a bit, but then stood on her own. "Need to do a spot of healing, I think?"

"Aye. Everything is so fuzzy, Tee, all I remember is Sath telling you to get me out of here, and then nothing. What did I hit?" She blushed, her oaken-tinged skin turning a peachy color. "I didn't hit one of you with my magic, did I?"

"What you have to remember, Ginny, is that it wasn't Sath's fault. He was charmed, you see, and so when I cut him with my axe…" Hackort stopped talking as all the color, so recently flushed, drained from Gin's face. Teeand glared at the gnome from behind Gin's head.

"You what?" she whispered, gaping at Hackort.

"Now, Gin, take it easy. What the gnome says is true. That hag charmed our Sath. He didn't know what he was doing," Teeand said, patting Gin gently on the arm.

"Sath…did this to me?" she said, her voice tight and pinched.

"Aye, Flower, but in all fairness he did warn you. I'm just sorry that I couldn't catch you." Teeand hung his head. "You're a lot faster than you look."

"Where is Sath now?" Gin said, scanning the room. "Is he…did he…?"

"No, Ginny, he's okay. He took the wizard and has gone to find his sister," Hack said. "I just wish we'd killed that sorceress. She was all kinds of awful and she hurt my friends." The gnome pouted. "What kind of adventure is this anyway? I haven't gotten to kill anything that wasn't already dead!"

"If that wizard steps out of line I feel like you'll have your chance," Teeand grumbled. "Or that bard…anyone know where she and Elys are?"

"Oh dear spirits, Anni…" Gin leaped to her feet and dashed on wobbly legs to the door and out into the hall. Cursing, Teeand and Hackort hopped up to follow her. From everywhere and nowhere, it seemed, a keening cry was rising throughout the Tower. Gin seemed not to hear it as she ran toward where her tracking ability told her Sath was, but Hackort and Teeand looked at each other and then stepped up the pace to follow her. Salynth knew that her prey was escaping and she was not happy about it.

Taeben pressed himself against one of the walls to avoid touching the magic that flowed from the druid's fingers and still he felt a tug on the edges of his consciousness. How dare that Qatu order him around as though he was already the Rajah? Taeben smiled wickedly. Sathlir Clawsharp would never be Rajah if he had anything to say about it. His eyes had locked with Kazhmere's just before the spell went off and he had almost lost his resolve. How could one so kind be related to vermin such as Sath?

He was startled from his musing by another familiar voice and opened his eyes. "Ben?" Gin stood in front of him, peering up at him as she had when they were but children. "Ben, are you all right?"

"Get behind me, Gin, Ikara's TEETH you are a stubborn one!" Teeand exclaimed as he ran through the doorway and grabbed Gin by the arm. She tried to shake him off but he managed to pull her around behind him. Taeben glared down at the dwarf.

"Is that really the way your kind treat women?" he said, immediately wishing he hadn't as both Teeand and Hackort drew weapons and pointed them at Taeben's midsection. "Apologies, good warriors, I fear I am still not quite myself." He held up his alabaster skinned fingers in a gesture of peace and the warriors re-sheathed their weapons. "Ginny, is that really you?" Taeben gazed at her in wonder. "I have not seen you since…well…we were in the Keep."

"Since you helped to drive Nelenie from her home?" Gin said, scowling. "Since you turned Elys in for studying and training with Nel?" She pushed Tee out of the way and got as close to Taeben's face as she could. "I felt sorry for you back in the Keep, I really did, but…" She rubbed her temple as a memory threatened to resurface but instead slipped into the murky depths of her mind. "Do you have any idea the pain you have caused?"

"Collateral damage," he said coolly. "I do what I must to survive, Ginny."

"Ben, for the Mother's sake, call me Gin, please?" She allowed a tiny smile to curve the corners of her mouth, and Taeben found himself driven to distraction by her lips. "There are only a few that are allowed to call me Ginny."

"I call her Ginny because I can't say her full name either," Hackort announced. Gin patted him on the helmet and he smiled, but the smile faded quickly. The gnome frantically looked around the room. "Ginny, where is Elys?"

"Good question. Why are you the only one here, Ben?" Gin said, her hands on her hips as she stared him down. All traces of her smile were gone.

"The other druid ported them to safety," Taeben said. "The Qatu male was concerned that you might not be strong enough to port the rest of us out, so he left me here to help if needed."

"You mean let the rest of us leave so that you can run back to your Mistress and tell her where we have gone?" Teeand asked, narrowing his eyes as he looked at Taeben.

"Hardly. I am a prisoner here, just as Kahzi was. Now if you want my help, please draw in close so that I can make sure we all go together. Ginny, if you are strong enough, may I please ask that I be included in the transport so that I can be a back-up to make sure we get out of here?"

"Of course, Ben," she said, eyeing him warily and deciding not to chastise him this time for the use of the nickname. "I am strong enough, thank you, all thanks to YOU, Tee." She smiled at the dwarf affectionately and Taeben felt his stomach flip over. What had gone so wrong with her that she was that close to a dwarf, a gnome, and a Qatu? A fleeting thought of her being close with the Prince crossed his mind and he felt for a moment as though he might wretch. "Ben, are you all right?"

"Aye, Ginny, I'm fine," he said. A tug on his robe got his attention and he looked down to see the gnome staring up at him angrily.

"You're on my list for now, wizard. But only I call her Ginny, got it?" Hackort said. Taeben beamed a gracious and facetious smile at the warrior.

"Of course, my apologies," he said, the wave of nausea rising. The Gin he remembered was too good for this lot. Something needed doing about this, and soon, but for now it would do no good to tip his hand.

"Now then, hug the druid!" Gin said, grinning. Teeand and Hackort grinned back at her, sharing in the inside joke, and each grabbed her arms. Taeben looked down at her and placed a hand on the side of her face, causing her to blush under his fingers. He smiled as she started reciting the spell.

"Will that do?" he asked, enjoying the feel of her oaken-tinged skin under his fingers. The smell of sunflowers filled his nose. Gin nodded, looking up at him with her ice blue eyes, and he felt warmth in his chest he had not felt in a long time. He would get her away from this group and especially from that Qatu if it was the last thing he did.

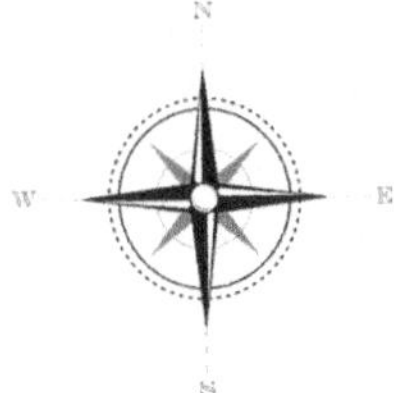

# THIRTY-FOUR

"I see your landing skills haven't improved, Elys," Sath grumbled as he untangled himself from his sister and Anni and stood up, brushing off the eternally green and fragrant grass from the spot in the Outpost where they magically appeared moments before. The grand hall of the Fabled Ones stood just beyond where they had landed, and they all were positively aching for a soak in the magical waters inside.

"Gin's aren't any better," the druid retorted. "I would think you'd be used to that by now, Cat." She stuck her tongue out at him causing Sath to roar with laughter.

*"You travel with this Gin a lot, Brother?"* Kazhmere said, looking at him quizzically.

*"Aye, Kahzi, and I want to tell you all about it, but we will have to catch up later. Right now I have business with Anni."* He glared at the bard who shrank away from him. "Anni? Great hall, if you

don't mind?" He held out his hand to her but she got to her feet on her own, nodding and heading up the ramp into the Guild lobby. Kazhmere stood as well, but Sath turned to her, one hand held up. *"Please, I must settle things with Anni alone, Kahzi. When Gin arrives, tell her… well…just tell her where I have gone. I have much to settle with her as well."*

The pain in his eyes at the mention of the name Gin coupled with, what looked to the Qatu Princess, to be strong and deep bonds of love. Kazhmere nodded sadly at her brother and stepped back, only to have Elysiam in her face. "What are they saying? It is so RUDE to speak that growly language in front of people that don't understand it," she said, pouting. Kazhmere laughed softly.

"Sathlir has to settle things with Anni, Elys," she said. "He is very angry with her, as was I, truth be told, but he will understand that she only did what she did to try to help me. Her methods are not always the best, but she has a good heart."

"That good heart was going to hand our Gin over to Lady Salynth in trade for you, did you know that?" Elysiam said. "I bet you…oof!" Her words cut short as Gin, Teeand, Hackort, and Taeben materialized and landed on top of her, knocking her to the ground.

"Elys!" Hackort squealed happily. His tiny hands roamed her face and hair as his eyes, shining with tears, took her in. "Are you all right? I know that nasty minion hurt you but you were able to heal, right? Anni didn't do anything to you did she? Where is she anyway? Where is Sath?"

"That seems to be the question of the day," Taeben said. He got to his feet and reached down to help Gin stand up. She took his hand, blushing a bit, and got to her feet. He held her hand a moment longer than necessary, memorizing the feel of her tiny fingers in his. "A slippery one, that Sathlir," he said, pushing into Gin's mind but finding no purchase there. She looked up at him, confused, and pulled her hand from his grasp. Seeing nothing but resistance from the faces turned his way, Taeben nodded his head reverently toward Gin and turned on his heel, headed for the tavern just past the grand hall, doubled back once he was out of sight and headed for the grand hall instead. He had seen in Kazhmere's mind an image of Sath and Anni entering just before he had arrived, and he was curious as to why. Gin turned her attention back to Kazhmere.

"Where did you say Sath was? I…need to speak to him about…some things," she said shyly.

"He has taken Anni to the grand hall of the Fabled Ones to straighten things out with her," Kazhmere replied. "So you are Gin? I have heard a great deal about you. I am Kazhmere, but you can call me Kahzi," she said, holding out a clawed and furry hand to Gin. Gin took it in both of her tiny hands, smiling broadly.

*"I am very pleased for your friendship,"* she said in broken Qatunari.

"Ah, my brother has fallen down on his duties as a tutor, clearly," Kazhmere said, chuckling softly. *"I am very pleased to meet someone my brother thinks so highly of that he would share our language with her."* Gin thought for a moment and then smiled. "You understood me! Excellent."

*"My lady Kazhmere, I am at your service,"* Teeand said, bowing politely. "I am Teeand and have been friends with your brother for a long time."

"Teeand, oh, you are Tee, are you not? Elys spoke of you. That must make you Hack?" she said, looking down at the gnome who grinned, then looked at Elys.

"What did Elys say about me?" he demanded.

"Nothing, you egomaniac," Elysiam said, kicking him with a studded boot. He yelped and then grinned up at her, making the druid roll her eyes. "What say we hit the tavern for a few pints while we wait on Sath to tell off that bard, hey?" She headed down the hill toward the tavern before anyone could disagree with her, Hackort hot on her heels.

"I never turn down a pint when a druid is buying," Teeand said, grinning and tugging at his beard as he headed off after Elysiam and Hackort. "Gin, you coming?" he called over his shoulder.

"In a bit, Tee. I'd like to get to know Sath's sister a bit better," she said. Teeand waved in response and Gin turned back to Kazhmere. "We might be more comfortable in the grand hall," she said. *"Perhaps Sath and Anni are finished with their talking?"*

Kazhmere took Gin's hands in her own and knelt so that she was at eye level with the wood elf. "You must make my brother continue to teach you our language, for you have an excellent ear for it I think. But, I fear I must be off for home now, Gin," she said. "I am quite positive that my mother is worried sick, and…I just need to sleep in my own bed, if that makes sense?" Gin smiled at her.

"Of course it does. Would you like me to accompany you to make sure you get there safely?" Gin asked.

"Tis no need," Kazhmere said. She spoke familiar words in the language of her ancestors, and a magical tiger appeared at her side, rubbing his massive head against the palm of her hand. "It has been too long, old friend," she said, squatting down and throwing her arms around the tiger's neck as she buried her face in his fur. The supernatural beast purred and licked her face. "As you can see, I will be well protected."

"Indeed," Gin said. She had heard those same words spoken by Sath so many times. She almost reached out to stroke the tiger's head but remembered that this was not Sath's and would not recognize her, so she thought better of it. "Kahzi, do promise me that you will visit? I would be honored to hunt with you."

Kazhmere grinned. "Every chance I get, Gin…only let's go somewhere a bit warmer next time?"

"Agreed," Gin said, returning Kazhmere's grin. I've had quite enough cold and ice for now I think." Kazhmere nodded her head, spoke something in that same ancient language to the tiger, and the two of them loped off toward the north, on the path that would take them to the Dark Sea, just this side of their island home of Qatu'anari. Gin watched them go, still grinning, and didn't notice that Taeben had returned to her side until she turned to enter the grand hall front lobby and ran headlong into his chest. She tumbled backward, landing in the grass on her backside.

"Oh! I'm so sorry, let me help you up," he said, offering her his hand and smiling down at her. Gin looked up at him, her expression wary.

"I thought you'd gone, Ben," she said as she took his hand, and then quickly released it when she was back on her feet.

"I didn't want to disturb Sathlir and Annilanshi," he said. "I don't speak Qatunari very well, but it sounds like a right cat fight is going on in your Fabled Ones' grand hall."

"Oh no…" Gin dashed past Taeben, heading for the grand hall and he ran to catch up with her. She yanked her arm away when he grabbed for her elbow just after she pushed through the door, but slowed to turn and look at him, expectantly.

"Wait! It might be dangerous in there," he cautioned her,

racking his brain to think of a reason why she should not go inside. Gin paid him no mind whatsoever and ran through the ornate lobby, bypassing the throng of merchants and others always gathered in the middle of the giant entryway to dart around the side corridors toward the Fabled Ones' grand hall entrance.

Taeben let his mind wander through the souls sharing the lobby a moment as he followed Gin, searching for a host that would let him enter and take over a mind. There was no way to catch her without reinforcements in his current state. He was shocked for a moment when it worked, but surprised mostly at whose mind and that he found not it only willing, but with an ulterior motive that complimented his own. A wicked smile oozed across his features. This had not turned out to be such a bad day after all.

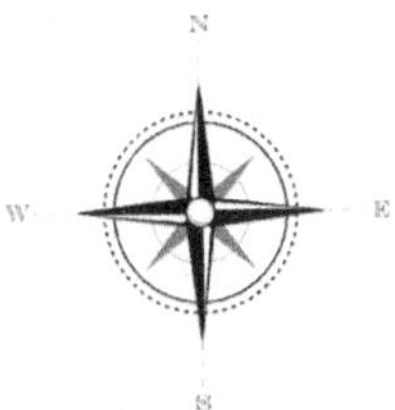

# Thirty-Five

*"Your Highness, if you will just let me explain..."* Anni said as she stumbled through the great hall doors and lost her footing, ending up sprawled across the floor. Sath slammed the doors behind them and stalked around in front of her, remaining silent. Anni pressed her forehead to the floor, as she should in the presence of a member of the royal family of Qatu'anari.

*"You must think that I am an utter fool,"* Sath said, his voice a menacing whisper. *"Who sent you with my sister? Who do you work for, Annilanshi?"*

Anni frowned into the marble floors of the grand hall. *"Work for, Highness? I am afraid I do not understand the question."*

*"Let me make it plain for you then,"* the Qatu Prince said, his voice deepening with barely controlled rage. *"Did my father send you with my sister to make sure that she never returned to Qatu'anari?"* Before she thought about what she was doing, Anni sat up,

looking at Sath in shock at his question. He charged over to her and yanked her up off the floor by the scruff of her neck, bringing her face dangerously close to his. *"You will answer my question, Annilanshi! Does my father wish to make sure my sister is exiled from Qatu'anari, as I was, or worse?"*

Anni stared at him in horror. That thought had never crossed her mind. It was true that the Rajah had not publicly acknowledged Kazhmere's birth, saying instead that the cub was stillborn, because she was not the son he had hoped for, but as far as she knew he bore his daughter no ill will. It was unthinkable. The First Wife would never have allowed the Rajah to do anything to harm either of her children. Anni came back from her musing at a rough shake from Sath who was still holding her fast by the fur at the back of her neck.

*"Well?"* he roared, his fangs inches from her nose.

*"No…no Highness of course not! Kahzi and I set out on an adventure on our own! Your father knew nothing of our plans, nor did he have any hand in them, I swear to you!"* she stammered, her words falling out of her mouth faster than she could even think. *"If you will permit me, your mother, our First Wife would never ever have allowed anything like that. She loves both of you so…"* Sath roared again and Anni managed to keep her feet and stood, staring at him, her face a mingled mess of fear and shame at her boldness.

*"You know NOTHING of my relationship with my mother. NOTHING,"* he said, glaring at her, his teal eyes ablaze with fury. Anni hit her knees, forehead again pressed to the floor in supplication. *"Do not EVER presume to know anything about my family, do you understand me?"* Anni whimpered in agreement and Sath paced about the floor, seething as he cracked each of his large knuckles in turn. Anni jumped with each popping sound, her heart in her throat. *"So you and my sister just walked out of the city one afternoon, made your way to the mainland, found that blasted tower*

*on the coast of the Forbidden Sea, and fell afoul of one of the most powerful and dangerous sorceresses of our age AND her ancient dragon captor?"* he asked, growling deep in his chest as he spoke. *"A sorceress, by the way, who just happened to have connections in the empire that would love a shot at the throne of Qatu'anari?"*

The hope that he would forgive her sank to the bottom of Anni's stomach like a stone. She had no idea what he was raving about; she only knew that she and Kazhmere had landed in a hornet's nest when they arrived at that cursed Tower. Putting aside ideas of telling the Prince that it was his sister who insisted on the destination and his sister who met up with the group that eventually led to her own capture, Anni swallowed her pride. *"I knew nothing of any of that, Highness. All I can tell you is the truth, and that is that I am ever devoted to and in the service of your sister, the Princess Kazhmere."* Sath growled loudly in warning but Anni kept talking. *"I would follow Kahzi to the ends of the Void, for she is like a sister to me, a sister I never had by birth. And, since she is your blood kin, that devotion and service extends also to you, my Prince."*

She closed her eyes and knelt, forehead pressed into the floor, expecting to feel his claws slice into her back at any moment. Anni had seen Sath's father, the Rajah, deal with all manner of traitors and other undesirables when she and Kahzi would sneak out of the royal nursery, and she had been present the night that Sath had defied his father and was exiled from Qatu'anari. She knew the tone in Sath's voice, knew what would come next, and tried to steel herself against the blow. But none came. After a very long few minutes, Anni lifted her forehead until she could see Sath sitting across from her on the floor, his head in his hands.

*"Highness?"* she said quietly, not daring to rise from the floor.

*"Recover yourself, Annilanshi,"* he said, his voice barely a

whisper. *"Do not ever, EVER prostrate yourself before me like that again, do you understand me?"* Anni sat up slowly, noticing with no small degree of surprise that Sath had not raised his head to look at her as he spoke. *"I am no Prince. No one of that station would ever frighten another living soul as I have just frightened you."* Anni opened her mouth to protest but he stopped her with a look as he slowly raised his head. *"I can smell it rolling off you in waves, and I am utterly dismayed that I am the cause of that fear."*

Anni's heart skipped a beat. She got up from the floor and moved over to Sath, kneeling down in front of him but not bowing as she had before. *"I do not fear you, Highness,"* she lied, looking him in the eye. There was no time to get out her lute, even though her training as a bard had made her very convincing. Sath did not answer her, but instead stood and walked into a room off the grand hall where there was kept a pool of magical healing water. Anni remained a moment, unsure what to do, when she felt a strange sensation in her head. She rubbed her temples with her fingers but the sensation lingered.

"Let me in," said a male voice. Anni looked around the grand hall in a panic. Who else was there? "Let me in, Anni." The voice was familiar but she could not place it, and it sounded for the entire world as though it was coming from inside her own head. "I know that you love Sathlir and I may be able to help rid you of a roadblock to happiness with him."

"Who are you?" Anni whispered.

"No need to talk out loud to me, Anni," the voice said. It seemed to resonate inside her head. "I can hear you if you merely think your response."

"How can you help me with Sath?" she thought, still looking around for the source of the voice.

"I can help you make sure he is rid of the wood elf," the

voice said in her mind. Anni's face lit up in understanding.

"Taeben?"

"Aye. Now listen to me, this is what you must do. If you follow my instructions, you will have a happy life with the Prince and I will have the druid all to myself. Sound like a fair trade to you?"

*"Oh, aye,"* she thought. *"Indeed. Just tell me what I need to do."*

"First, do you have your lute with you?"

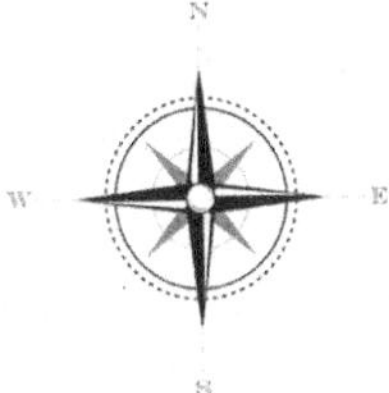

# THIRTY-SIX

Gin pounded on the heavy doors of the grand hall, the carvings there cutting and bruising her skin. "SATH! Let me in!" she cried. Why had he locked the door? Finally, she remembered the system of locks on the door that she and Sath had created to keep non-members out and she ran her fingers across the length and breadth of the door, touching all of the secret locks in turn. The heavy doors swung inward and Gin stood in the doorway a moment, just listening. Taeben cursed inwardly that she had moved too fast for him to memorize the sequence.

"It seems to have gone quiet," she whispered to Taeben who was hovering just outside the doorway. "I hope they're okay." Taeben smiled to himself. He hoped so as well. "Hello?"

"Gin?" Sath called from inside the Great hall. He was sitting directly opposite the door, his back up against the wall. Anni sat next to him, her back against his side, gently strumming her lute. "Come on in, we're all right in here, no need for all that yelling."

The wood elf entered and stopped short when she saw the scene that greeted her. Sath had thrown his arm lazily over Anni's shoulders, and he absently stroked the fur on her arm as the soft music continued. "What…are you doing, Sath?" Gin asked, her brow furrowed in confusion. "Have you and…Anni…settled your differences?"

"Aye, we have," Sath said, a purr resonating in his words. "Anni is an amazing female. I had no idea…" He stopped, a low and threatening growl replacing the soothing purr, as his teal gaze settled on Taeben. "Brought your wizard with you I see?" he said icily.

"My what? Oh, Ben?" Gin said, looking over her shoulder. "Yes, I suppose he followed me in here. He said that the hall sounded like a cat fight so I came as soon as I…you two worked out what you were fighting over?" Gin stammered. Anni looked at bit too comfortable next to Sath. She was almost in his lap! The tune she was playing changed slightly as the bard focused her attention on Gin. "He's not me…I mean my wizard, he's not that, Sath, what's happening here?"

"What do you mean, Gin?" Sath said. Gin's gaze locked on his for a moment and he blinked, seeming puzzled. The tune started over just then, though, and his gaze again softened as he looked toward Gin and Taeben. "Nothing's going on here. Anni and I have been talking about old times, and she's catching me up on life back home." Gin sucked in a breath as Sath ran his claws down Anni's back and she arched in response, purring loudly. "We have a lot more in common than I thought, it seems."

Gin took a step backward. "But you and I…I mean, with the others…are we going to keep traveling together?" She shook her head, trying to clear it.

"Oh, aye, eventually," Sath said. "Once we've all

recovered from our ordeal and you've rid yourself of…unpleasant and unwelcome company," he said, staring pointedly at Taeben. The music grew a bit louder, and Gin could almost make out Anni whispering something to Sath. He laughed loudly and smiled back at her. A hot, steely pain resonated through Gin's heart as she recognized the smile as one he had reserved for her in the recent past.

"Not possible," she muttered to herself. "It's not possible. This is NOT possible." She backed out of the main room of the grand hall, almost running over Taeben in her regress. "He hated her. She tried to…do I mean nothing to…" Gin gripped the wall as she stood in the foyer. Taeben reached out to steady her but stopped, his hand hanging in midair just behind her shoulder. She turned to face him and he removed his hand quickly. "It's like…like she's charmed him or something?"

"I'm not sure what you mean, Ginny," Taeben said, hoping the use of the childhood nickname would snap her out of the lull that Anni had put her in with the music from her lute. He carefully touched her arm, and smiled inwardly when she did not flinch away from him. "Why don't we leave them here for now and go join your friends for that pint at the tavern, hmm? Perhaps the crisp evening air will clear your head, tis a bit stuffy with incense in here I must say." Again, he tried to push into her mind but found that same barrier as before. Make her come with me, he silently commanded Anni, smiling wickedly as the song changed and intensified. Gin blinked twice, and then turned her face up to Taeben's.

"Maybe that would help," she said. "Let's go. I just…" She looked over her shoulder at Sath and Anni just as Sath took Anni's face in his paw and brought her close to him, sniffing deeply. Gin's shoulders sagged as she turned back to Taeben. "Yes, let's go." The wizard wound his slender arm around her and led her to the hall door, watching more carefully this time as she opened all the locks and then the door.

*Have the Cat change those once we are gone,* he silently commanded Anni.

*Yes… What should I call you?*

*Sir will be just fine, Anni,* Taeben thought, grinning.

*Yes, Sir.*

Taeben tightened his grip on Gin's shoulders and led her out into the lobby as Anni slithered closer to Sath, nuzzling her head into his neck and purring loudly. The wizard inhaled deeply, reveling in the smell of sunflowers.

Teeand looked up when the tavern door opened and scowled. Elysiam had her back to the door, so she did not see what made the dwarf's face contort. "What is it, Tee?" she asked.

"It's Gin, and that wizard," he said, his voice barely a whisper. "I had hoped I'd never see that charlatan alive again."

"All of us hoped that," Hackort added. The gnome wiggled around in his seat and stared at the door as Gin stood there, looking forlorn and lost, with Taeben's arm around her shoulder. As soon as the wizard made eye contact with the three of them, his arm slipped off Gin and his face contorted into a frown. Hackort hopped off his seat and scampered over to Gin, his face split wide in a grin. "Ginny!" he exclaimed as he threw his arms around her knees. She absently patted him on the head.

*"Ginolwenye, what's the matter?"* Teeand said in his language, jumping to his feet and running to her side. He wrapped his arm around her and guided her to their table. *"Did the wizard do something to you, Flower?"* he whispered as he helped

her to her seat.

"No," she said, her words as hollow and quiet as her stare.

"Gin, where's Sath?" Elysiam asked, her eyes narrowing as she locked her gaze on Taeben, who glared back at her.

"Sath is with Anni," Gin whispered. Tears welled up in her eyes but did not escape. She wiped her eyes on her leather bracer and then held her face in her hands a moment to get herself together. "They have a lot in common and he seems…he seems…" She stopped a moment before she started sobbing again.

"He what?" Teeand exclaimed. "That's impossible, he…that's impossible!"

Taeben moved to stand behind Gin's chair. "We saw it with our own eyes, didn't we Ginny?" he said, putting his hands protectively on her shoulders. Teeand's eyes narrowed as he noticed that Gin did not shrug Taeben's hands off.

"I am the only one that calls her that," Hackort said, balling up his fists. "Not you, wizard."

"His name is Ben… Taeben," Gin said. "He is a childhood friend of mine and I think we could use his firepower when we're hunting, especially if Sath is…well, he said that he would be hunting with us again eventually, but…"

"Right, I'm off. Be right back," Teeand said, stomping out of the tavern. Hackort returned to his seat and finished the rest of his pint of ale as Elysiam glared at Taeben across the top of her mug.

"Here, have a seat Ben," Gin said, patting the empty chair that Teeand vacated. "And call me Gin, Hack isn't kidding that he's the only one that calls me that." Taeben inclined his head to her, put on his best smile, and sat down.

"Sathlir Clawsharp!" Tee bellowed as he made quick work of the locks on the grand hall door and shoved it open. "SATH! Where are you?"

"What's got your beard on fire, Tee?" Sath asked as he came around the corner from the stairway that lead to the upstairs rooms. Anni trailed behind him, stopping cold in her tracks in the doorway as soon as she saw Teeand standing there.

"NOT in front of her," Tee said. "I need to speak to you. Alone."

Sath's eyes narrowed. "Anything you need to say to me you can say in front of Anni, Tee. Since when do we not trust each other?"

"YOU, I trust," Tee said. "HER? Not so much." He folded his arms across his chest. "But if that's the way you want to play it, fine." He walked over to Sath who knelt so that he was eye to eye with the dwarf. *"Tell me that you are with Anni of your own free will and I will leave it alone,"* he said in his own language, knowing that Sath was as fluent in it as he was in Qatunari. Many nights in many different dungeons across Orana had left them with plenty of time for language learning. Sath's eyes were like slits in his furry face as he stared at Teeand. In the next room, Anni held her breath. There was no time to start up the lute again, so she hummed the tune as quietly as she could.

*"Of course I am, Tee, don't be ridiculous,"* Sath said, his language as fluent as ever. *"I'm trying not to be offended at the question."* Anni, who could not understand them, let out a relieved sigh at his tone, but kept humming the tune as she did so. She came through the doorway into the main room, and then

moved closer to them.

"How is Gin?" she asked, looking as concerned as she could manage. She had no idea what they were saying in the funny, grunty-sounding language that she could only assume was that of the Dwarves. "She left so quickly, I was concerned that something was wrong."

"Nothing is wrong with her. And I'll be going now, if you don't mind. I know when I'm being a third wheel," Teeand said scowling.

"What's going on, Tee?" Sath said, looking concerned.

*"Nothing at all, Your Highness,"* Tee said in flawless Qatunari. "You know where to find us if you want to hunt again." The dwarf turned on his heel, rage burning in his eyes as he stalked out of the grand hall.

Anni moved closer to Sath and put her hand on his forearm. He covered it with his own and squeezed slightly. *"That was about me, wasn't it?"* she purred as she buried her face in his fur. He turned to face her, lifting her chin until she looked him in the eyes.

*"It doesn't matter,"* Sath said. *"All that matters now is how happy you've made me. I cannot believe I didn't see it before. I had forgotten the beauty of our language, having spent time only with those who either cannot speak it at all or at the least not well. And as for you…All this time we've known each other,"* he murmured as he ran a claw down the side of her face, *"and I never noticed how lovely you are."*

*"You flatter me, Highness,"* she said, blushing.

*"Anni,"* Sath said, his eyes dancing. *"Please, call me Sath? I find that I like it very much when you say my name."*

*"Sath,"* she said, barely getting the name off her lips before he pulled her to him in a rough kiss. Anni melted into him, her heart soaring. *You were right, Sir,* she thought.

*Just keep him there,* came Taeben's silent command.

*Forever, Sir. Forever. This I swear.* Anni forgot all about wizards and magical tunes and gave herself over to Sathlir, her spirit leaping with joy when, without her tune, he continued the kiss. He was hers, finally, and he would forget about that wretched little wood elf and his life here among these commoners. They would rule Qatu'anari.

Sath did not think about what he was doing, only that he had to do it. Why not? Anni was utterly devoted to him. She was his kind. They had grown up together. She understood him, she spoke his language. He pulled her closer to him, drinking in her scent as he did, feeling her claws rake down his back. A memory nagged at him, one that he could not quiet form in his mind. It was like looking at something through a dirty window. And why on earth was the lingering scent of sunflowers in his nose, or the feeling of tiny fingers, not Qatu claws but human-like fingers winding their way into his fur…why were those thoughts poking at him from somewhere way back in his mind?

*"Are you all right?"* Anni asked him, and he looked down at her, puzzled. Her eyes engulfed him and he felt like he was lit with emerald fire that sizzled the length and breadth of his body and his mind. It was a good feeling; a safe, warm, and happy feeling and he sighed, content.

*"I am,"* he murmured. *"As long as you are with me. Please, Anni, promise me you will not ever leave me, as my mother left my father? Can you promise me that?"*

*"Oh, aye Sathlir. I will never leave you,"* she said, tears shining in her eyes. *"Never."*

"Well?" Hackort asked, in a voice thick with the drowsiness that always accompanied a night at the tavern. Elysiam was already asleep on the table; her head was nestled on her folded arms. Hackort rubbed her arm from time to time and she would murmur something to him about waking her up that involved a weapon or threat of a magical swarm. He would wait until she was almost unconscious again and then rub her arm, grinning wickedly. "What did you find out from Sath? When is he joining us to hunt?"

"He isn't," Teeand said brusquely as he flopped down in a chair. "I suppose I'm too late for last call, am I?" One of the tavern girls heard him and, winking at him, shook her head as she headed off behind the bar to pull him a pint.

"What do you mean he isn't?" Gin said, rousing from her half sleep. She was leaning against Taeben who met Teeand's disapproving look with a glare. Sitting up in her chair, she leaned across the table and took Teeand's weathered hand in both of hers. "He told me himself that he would join us…oh…once I had…" She looked back at Taeben apologetically but he waved her off.

"No worries, Ginny," he said, his slender fingered hands raised in a gesture of finality. "I know that none of your companions know me and they are certainly right not to trust me after the circumstances that recently forced us into each other's lives." Elysiam looked up from the table and said something untoward at Taeben in Gnomish before putting her head back down, leaving Hackort to blush madly. He stood and started collecting his things, and then took Gin's hand in his. "I only hope that you will continue in safety and success, my old friend, and that if you and yours ever have need of me you will not hesitate to ask. I am forever in your debt for rescuing me from the clutches of that hag in the Tower."

"Wait, wizard," Teeand said, not breaking eye contact with Gin. "If our Gin thinks enough of you that she'll welcome you into our little family then I'll not be the one t'say no." He took the mug from the barmaid and took a long drink, and then put it down on the table. "Another, my dearie, and one for our skinny friend here. In fact, you might bring us all some stew, and him a double portion, he looks like it wouldn't take much to blow him over." The girl giggled and scampered off to the back to order the stew and then to the bar to pull another round of pints for them all.

"Thank you, Tee," Gin said, smiling at Taeben who felt like his heart and mind might just burst right out of his body. "You'll see, it will be good having Ben around, he's always said himself that he was one of the brightest wizards of our age." She grinned at him, poking him in the ribs playfully as he sat back down. "Truthfully, though, he's made some bad decisions but who among us hasn't? I think that he has more than done his time for his past while being held by that awful woman in the Tower and by Lord Taanyth in the Keep."

"I suppose," Hackort said slowly, "that I can put your name back on my list for now. After all, you need us to keep you safe from the dragons and dragonkind, it seems. But I'll be watching you, wizard, you understand?"

"I do, thank you good sir gnome, Hackort was it?" Taeben said, trying to keep the grin he felt from exploding across his face. "And your lady there, I won't wake her." Hackort erupted with laughter, waking Elysiam as he scrambled not to tip over his mug of ale.

"My what?" he said, overcome with giggles. Gin wiped the tears from her eyes as she laughed along, and even Tee chuckled a bit. Elysiam looked from face to face, fury spreading across her face like a wildfire through a forest.

"What is so funny?" she demanded, looking at each in turn and then settling on Taeben. "What is HE doing here and where is Sath?"

"Taeben is going to join us hunting," Teeand said, holding up a finger as Elysiam opened her mouth to protest, "on our Gin's recommendation." Elysiam looked at Gin for confirmation, and then studied a loose thread on her tunic after Gin nodded; she was clearly hurt by the trust Gin was placing in Taeben. "Sathlir has taken another path for now, with those of his own kind." He swallowed hard, pushing both anger and sadness back down into manageable forms in his chest as he did. "We wish him well. In fact," he said as the girl returned with their pints, "to Sathlir and his Anni, may he find whatever it is he's after."

Hackort and Taeben raised their mugs and joined the toast. Elysiam raised her mug and remained silent, and Gin pushed her chair back from the table. She locked eyes with Teeand for a long moment, and then left the table and headed out the door of the tavern. Taeben stood as if to follow her, but Teeand grabbed the elf's arm.

"Let her have this one, Taeben," he cautioned. "There are strong feelings there that she needs to work through. She will be back though. Our Gin is a loyal one. She knows who her family is." Taeben nodded and took his seat again, deciding that he would have to ingratiate himself to this crowd if he was ever going to get Gin away from them.

Outside the tavern, Gin ran toward a small hill just behind the stone building that housed a variety of traders for explorers who had been lucky on their travels and wished to trade. She skidded to a stop and flopped down into the grass, breathing in the scent of the tiny flowers that grew there and finally releasing the tidal wave of sobs that had threatened to overcome her.

How many times had she sat just there, just in the few weeks prior, her spell book open, trying to memorize her magic while Sath sat opposite, training his magical tiger? How many times had he yanked the spell book from under her nose, knowing there was no way she could reach it, just to get her to relax and laugh for a bit? She looked back toward the Great Hall. It was there, in the grand marble building, that their former leader had introduced them, and had asked Sath to keep an eye on Gin. "Make her feel at home here, Sathlir," he had said, "for I fear our little druid has had a rough start of it, and doesn't know quite where she fits in our world."

"I've found my place now, Cat," she whispered as she dried her eyes on her tunic. "Seems like you have as well." Memories of Sath holding Anni in his arms surrounded her, threatening to smother her with their vividness. "Good luck to you, Sathlir Clawsharp, and to your Anni, that neither of you ever cross my path again." Gin held her head in her hands and sat very still, meditating and trying to forget how Sath's voice sounded or his fur felt. "Good riddance," she said in a whisper. "Good riddance."

Sath and Anni left the grand hall and lobby, heading for the path to the north that his sister had taken earlier that evening. Anni reached out and took hold of his tail as she followed along behind him, and for a moment, a memory surfaced and Sath turned back, expecting to see Gin's tiny fingers holding on to his tail as she had done in the past so that she would not get lost. However, all he saw was Anni, and because he could not really remember why he was expecting anything any different, he returned her smile and turned back to the path. As they followed the cobblestone road that lead out of the Outpost, Sath thought about what it would mean to return home to Qatu'anari, to do as Anni had suggested and present himself to the royal court. He could return to his life as the Crown Prince of Qatu'anari. He would not have time for hunting and adventuring. Somehow, that struck a sour note with him, and just before they left the Outpost, he stopped in his tracks.

*"I don't want to go back there,"* he said. Anni spun around to face him, lightly tapping her drum as she did so. *"I feel like you want me to want to, but I don't yet."* He took her in his arms, pulling her close and making it impossible to reach her drum. She frowned. *"I want to go somewhere that feels more like home, Anni, somewhere that you and I can…get to know each other better. What do you say?"*

*"You want me with you?"* Without her magic compelling him? *"Of course, Sathlir, you have only to ask and we will go."*

*"Let's stay here for now,"* he said, turning her back toward the center of the Outpost. *"I know a guy, a halfing, actually, who might rent us a room above…"*

*"Not here,"* Anni said, humming the tune under her purr. *"Anywhere but here."*

Sath blinked a few times and then looked down at her. Anni found that the vacant look in his eyes began to pain her. *"Where would you suggest then?"*

*"Not the palace, but the coast of Qatu'anari, our home. What do you think? We make our own dwelling. We hunt our own food. We are just us. Yes?"* she said, humming a bit louder.

*"Excellent idea,"* Sath said. *"I don't know why I hesitated at all."* Taking her hand in his, he led her out the gate and out of the

Outpost, without a single look backward toward the grand hall or the tavern…or his life with the Fabled Ones.

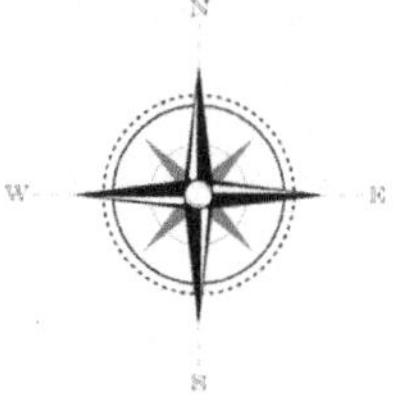

# ABOUT THE AUTHOR

Nancy E. Dunne is the alter-ego of Ginolwenye, and is an avid gamer, adventurer, reader, language nerd and all around geek girl. The Nature Walker Trilogy is a love letter of sorts to the various worlds in which she has found herself immersed over the years, and the lifelong friends and memories that have come along with them. When not writing, Nancy is an American Sign Language/English interpreter and spends her free time drawing inspiration from her dogs and her husband as well as dreaming of visiting her second home, the United Kingdom.

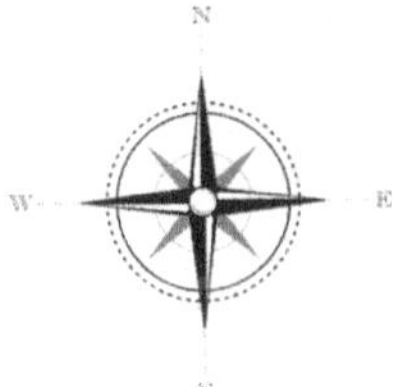

## BOOKS IN THE NATURE WALKER TRILOGY

*Wanderer: Origin of the Nature Walker*
*Tempest: Fall of the Nature Walker*
*Guardian: Rise of the Nature Walker*

Made in the USA
Columbia, SC
05 August 2022